"This hilarious romantic comedy is unputdownable. The characters have instant chemistry, and their well-written dialogue is peppered with witty banter. Readers will be riveted through all of the twists and turns as the protagonists race across Europe with the bad guys hot on their heels. Those who grew up reading Carter's Gallagher Girls teen series will tear through her adult romance debut and clamor for more."

—LIBRARY JOURNAL

"I am a Gallagher Girls fan, and *The Blonde Identity* satisfied ALL of my GG cravings! Carter has that magic formula of the perfect amount of brilliance, fun, and sizzling banter down pat!"

—JESSE Q. SUTANTO, bestselling author of *Dial A for Aunties* and
Vera Wong's Unsolicited Advice for Murderers

"I absolutely adored *The Blonde Identity*! I loved the humor, Zoe and Sawyer were perfection, and the chemistry. . . . I couldn't put it down."

—LORRAINE HEATH, *New York Times* bestselling author

"Completely captivating—funny, fresh, and deliciously swoon-worthy, *The Blonde Identity* had me smiling over every action-packed page. I loved it."

—ANNABEL MONAGHAN, author of
Nora Goes Off Script and *Same Time Next Summer*

"*The Blonde Identity* is explosively funny and jam-packed with chemistry! I couldn't have loved this hilarious rom-com more. The story is full of humor, action, romance, and emotions that tug on your heartstrings. Ally is a rom-com genius!"

—SARAH ADAMS, author of *The Cheat Sheet*

"Fun and pulse-pounding, *The Blonde Identity* will keep readers turning pages."

—PARADE

THE BLONDE WHO CAME IN FROM THE COLD

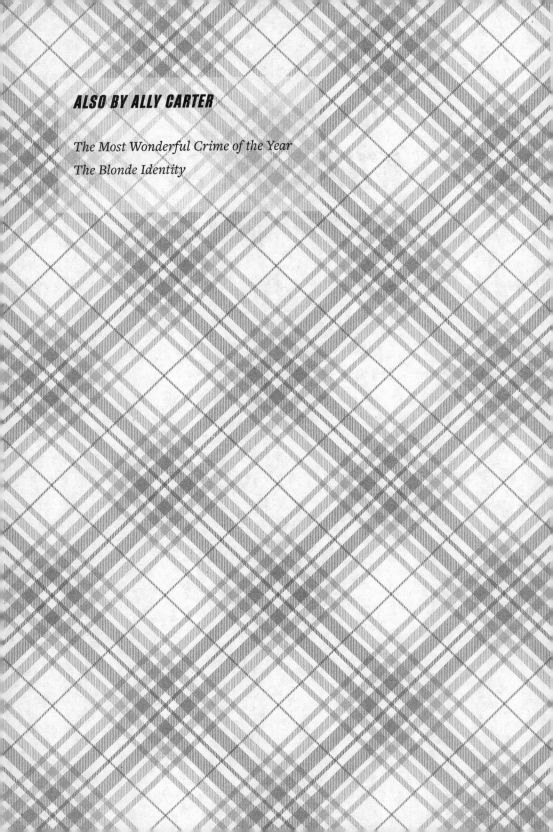

ALSO BY ALLY CARTER

The Most Wonderful Crime of the Year
The Blonde Identity

THE BLONDE WHO CAME IN FROM THE COLD

a novel

Ally Carter

AVON

An Imprint of HarperCollins*Publishers*

This is a work of fiction. Names, characters, places, and incidents are products of the author's imagination or are used fictitiously and are not to be construed as real. Any resemblance to actual events, locales, organizations, or persons, living or dead, is entirely coincidental.

HarperCollins books may be purchased for educational, business, or sales promotional use. For information, please email the Special Markets Department at SPsales@harpercollins.com.

hc.com

FIRST EDITION

Based on the design by Alison Bloomer

Plaid illustration © Anya D/Shutterstock

Library of Congress Cataloging-in-Publication Data has been applied for.

ISBN 978-0-06-338697-6
ISBN 978-0-06-344928-2 (international edition)

25 26 27 28 29 LBC 5 4 3 2 1

To all the little girls who wanted
to be spies when they grew up.
Who's to say you're not already?

*I thought our story was epic, you know, you
and me. . . . Spanning years and continents.
Lives ruined, bloodshed. EPIC.*
—Logan Echolls, Veronica Mars Season 2,
Episode 20: "Look Who's Stalking"

chapter one

Ten Years Ago
Washington, DC

As luck would have it, the first time Alexandra Sterling really wanted to kill a man happened to be the night before she started spy school.

Of course, technically, the program was called the Clandestine Operative Training and Assessment Course, but technically, COTAC didn't even exist, so Alex was going to call it whatever she wanted. In fact, until she got on the bus at six a.m., she was also going to eat whatever she wanted. (Chicken fingers.) And wear whatever she wanted. (Her stretchiest pants and a ratty old T-shirt from a German band she told everyone was her favorite. Her actual favorite was Taylor Swift.)

Alex was going to spend her last night as a regular person taking the world's hottest bath and watching the world's trashiest TV before starting on the world's most covert adventure.

But she couldn't do any of that until her chicken fingers got there, and that's what brought Alex to the bar of the airport Ramada and the guy who had been staring at her for the better part of twenty minutes.

The problem wasn't so much that The Guy was staring—it was how. Usually, Alex could read people in three seconds flat from fifty paces. She could always pick out the women who hated her because she smiled too much and the men who hated her because she didn't smile enough; the boys who looked at her strangely when they found out she'd set the curve on every test she took at MIT—as if they didn't know whether that should make her hotter or more frigid. (They always settled on frigid.)

Alex had been interpreting looks from nurses and doctors for as long as she could remember, all of them wondering how such a little girl could have caused her sister so much trouble.

It was as if the whole world had decided that Alex was just too bold, too sassy, and too selfishly strong for her own good—and they did it all without ever saying a word.

She had grown up speaking English, French, German, Russian, and a little Italian. But, most of all, Alex was fluent in people. Still, as she studied The Guy at the end of the bar . . . Alex didn't know what to make of him.

He was white and midtwenties. Maybe a little older because his eyes looked tired in a way that had nothing to do with jet lag. He kept an elbow on the bar and a beer in his hand—sipping slowly—like all his problems were waiting at the bottom and he wasn't in a hurry to reach them.

His white dress shirt was open at the collar, and he had the kind of haircut you could find on half the male population, but his dark hair had turned wavy and mussed from the snow. It should have made him look worse, but it actually made him look better, and Alex started to wonder if she'd remembered to pack a hairbrush and also when was the last time she'd used it?

At first glance, there was nothing special about The Guy at all. A man made to fill the background, a nonplayer character in the game of life. But that didn't change the fact that Alex *had* noticed him. And now she couldn't *un*notice him.

The TV over the bar showed a football game. On the screen, a giant in shoulder pads was spiking a ball and dancing in the end zone, but the man at the bar didn't even glance in its direction. He didn't officially glance in Alex's direction, either, but she'd felt his eyes on her from the moment she sat down. Silent and assessing and . . . unimpressed.

She should have brushed her hair.

She should have put on a bra.

She should have forgotten about the chicken fingers and gone to bed hungry because Alex felt awkward for the first time in her twenty-two years. Uncomfortable. Second-guessing everything from her T-shirt to her food choices to the fact that she was probably making a mistake with her career and her whole, entire life. She was second-guessing everything that had brought her to that moment even though Alex didn't do second guesses. Or second chances. Or second place. Alex didn't do seconds of any kind. Or, at least, she didn't use to.

But, in a year, she'd probably have a different name. She'd be living in a different country and speaking a different language. She'd be a different person. And then she'd have a second life. But at the moment, she was just a woman who was tired and scared and wishing that her chicken fingers would get there already.

The restaurant was loud and busy. It was January, and sharp little *pings* sounded as sleet hit the slanting windows that had turned into a frosty blur with the storm. The airport must have started canceling flights because the place was filling up with flight crews and business travelers and a dozen twentysomething blondes in T-shirts that read BRIDE SQUAD and another blonde whose shirt read BRIDE.

The Bride Squad must have ordered a bottle of tequila because they were doing shots and eyeing The Guy, but The Guy stayed at the other end of the bar, eyeing Alex.

So Alex did the only thing she could do and eyed him back.

"I'll go check on those chicken wings." A distracted bartender topped off Alex's club soda and headed to the back before Alex could shout "Chicken *fingers*!"

The wind was roaring now. It made a haunting sound, and the glass had frosted over—little beads of condensation running down, revealing strips of blurry lights and blowing snow while a dozen more people crowded into the bar, looking for tables.

"Really coming down out there," a voice said from nearby, and Alex turned to see a *different* guy sliding onto the empty stool beside her. His watch was worth more than most cars, and he was going to order the most expensive scotch in the place and then slam it before offering to get one for Alex. "It's packed in here," the new guy said.

Alex nodded, distracted and a little numb. "Yeah."

"I was lucky they still had a suite. Macallan. Neat. And leave the bottle," Bromeo told the bartender before shifting his gaze onto Alex. "And I think we'll take another glass." The grin he gave her was supposed to be smooth, but it was closer to leering, and it was all Alex could do not to sigh in relief because, finally, a guy she could read! A guy who made sense! Everything from his fancy watch to his slicked-back hair told a story of mediocre grades at top-tier schools, of nasty divorces and bad credit and jobs he got from friends of his father.

On the other side of the room, there were a dozen bridesmaids who should have been getting drunk en route to some all-inclusive in Jamaica—women a little bitter that their friend had made them pay for new highlights and an expensive trip, and now they were probably stuck sleeping four to a room until the weather cleared.

Go tell them about your suite, she wanted to say, but Bromeo was looking at her lips and asking, "So what's your name?" Alex told herself she should lie—make something up. She should flirt and kiss and pretend she was the kind of woman who could be attracted to that kind of man. She had one last night of freedom—one last night of life as she knew it. And he wasn't entirely asymmetrical. Maybe . . .

"Her name is Mrs. Masterson," someone said, and Alex turned to see The Guy standing behind her, a proprietary gleam in his eye. "I'm Mr. Masterson. Thanks for keeping my seat warm."

The Guy didn't shove, but his words—or maybe just his presence—pushed the stranger away so smoothly that it was like the stool had iced over.

"Hi, gorgeous," The Guy whispered near Alex's ear, so close it probably looked like a kiss. "Sorry I'm late."

Then he took the empty stool and angled his body toward hers, and Alex tried her hardest not to gape.

"Ladies! Can I join you?" Bromeo picked up his bottle and headed toward the Bride Squad, but The Guy acted like he hadn't heard a word.

Alex glowered at him. "Was that necessary?"

"No." The Guy finally took a gulp of the beer he'd been sipping. His lips quirked around the rim of the glass. "But it was fun."

He looked up at the TV like he was superinvested in the game and hadn't spent the last half hour on the other end of the bar, looking down his nose at Alex. Something about the cool, casual way he watched the screen made Alex's skin prickle and her blood boil.

"That could have been the love of my life."

"He wasn't."

"You can't possibly know—"

The Guy turned toward her—just slightly. "He took his wedding ring off when he came in, did you see that?"

Alex hadn't seen, but she wasn't surprised. "He was just talking to me—"

"He was hitting on you."

She didn't even try not to grin. "No shit."

"You've got a mouth on you."

"Is this the part where you say I should put it on you?"

"No." The Guy looked slightly offended. "I would come up with something significantly more original than that."

"Screw it." No one needed chicken fingers that badly.

She pushed away and was starting to leave when he said, "You're welcome."

Alex spun back. "I didn't need your help. I didn't even *want* your help."

"You didn't want *him*."

"Oh yeah?" That time, Alex had to laugh. "What makes you so sure?"

When he turned on his stool, they were the same height for just a moment, inches away, and Alex felt herself breathing hard even though she'd barely moved in twenty minutes.

"Because you want me."

He didn't . . . He didn't just . . . *say that*? No one just *says* that. Alex had never heard such audacity. Such certainty. Such . . . confidence. But the worst thing was that, deep down, a tiny part of her knew that it was true. So Alex laughed louder.

"Nice try, Cowboy. But you don't know anything about me."

"Sure, I do." His grin was dark and slow. "I know you're drinking something caffeine-free because you have to be up early and something boozeless because you have to be sharp. You asked for extra ice because you've been out of the country for a while—my guess is Europe—so now you're jet-lagged, but you're also hungry. You don't eat fried food often, but this is a special occasion. And you're nervous, which is why you're not already asleep, but you know you should be. How am I doing?"

He was doing way too well, but Alex didn't dare to say so.

"You're indulging tonight . . ." The Guy went on, gaze dipping for one millisecond. "And there's a reason you've been watching me for twenty minutes."

Now, Alex was angry. "You've been watching *me*."

From the corner of her eye, Alex saw the kitchen door swing open. "Put them on my tab," The Guy said when the bartender slid a box full of chicken fingers in their direction, but he never took his gaze off of Alex, and all she could do was stand there, staring. Thinking.

Wavering.

She hated everything about that feeling and that moment and that man. But mostly she hated how right he was.

She looked him up and down, from his plain white shirt to his dark blue jeans—the jaw that was a little more rugged up close, and not just because it was covered with stubble. But it was the hands she lingered on—long, strong fingers that screamed of quiet, practiced competence. Maybe he was a concert pianist or a surgeon? They were the hands of a man made of patience and precision. They were hands that didn't dabble. They performed. And a part of Alex itched to see what kind of performance they might coax out of her.

"Come on." He slid off the barstool and reached for her to-go container. "You'll want these later."

"Later?" The word jerked Alex back. "I want them now. I wanted them twenty minutes ago when I ordered them but—"

"Tell me you're ready to get out of here." He was suddenly so close that she could feel the rise and fall of his chest. Close enough to make out the little ring of green around the blue of his eyes. Close enough to feel . . . and forget. Close enough that when she swayed, she found herself pressed against him and unable to sway back.

"Are you asking if I want to see your room?"

"No. I'm asking if you want to see stars."

Alex didn't exactly *decide* to follow him out of the bar. Her hand just sort of slipped into his, which was silly. It made her feel young and weak, like someone had to guide her through the Bride Squads of the world. Like she couldn't make it alone. Which she could—she would. She was going to. Just as soon as she got on that bus at six the following morning. But until then . . .

The Guy was right about one thing—she was having one last night of indulgences, and maybe . . .

When they reached the bank of elevators, The Guy stopped and pressed her against the wall and whispered, "Tell me your name."

They were alone. No more laughing or touchdowns or little pieces of falling ice pinging off the frosty windows, cold and sharp enough to sting.

"I . . . I'm . . ." Alex's brain stopped working as lips brushed the underside of her jaw. "Tell me yours."

"Call me Cowboy." The words startled a giggle out of Alex.

"So now you're into it?"

"It's growing on me." He pressed against her, strong and sure. "Tell me your name," he asked again, and she felt warm breath on the side of her neck and those competent fingers at the curve of her waist, brushing against the smooth skin beneath her shirt.

He wedged a knee between her legs, and Alex gave up any pretense of not wanting him and this and now. She sounded almost breathless when she said, "Alex. My name is Alex." She went up on her toes to kiss him properly, arms around his neck and—

Suddenly, he stilled. His body slumped against hers, like a marionette who had just lost a string, but the grip on her waist went tighter. When he whispered in her ear that time, the voice sounded like midnight feels.

"Never give anyone your real name, Ms. Sterling." Alex froze. "Never invite a stranger into your room. And never go to theirs." He pulled back but didn't look at her, like in spite of everything he felt almost guilty.

"Who are you?" she asked, but he didn't face her. "Who—"

"I'm the guy telling you to go home. Lead a good life. Be happy."

"*Who are you?*" She reached for his arm, ready to force an answer out of him, but it was like he read her mind—like he'd leapt forward in time to get there a split second before she did, and, suddenly, he had her wrist pinned against the wall over her head and his chest was pressing against hers. He was too tall and too strong and too much. It was the first time Alex had ever felt like she wasn't enough because all she could do was stare up at him as he leaned down and whispered, "I'm the Ghost of Christmas Future, and I'm telling you, you're gonna want to miss that bus tomorrow morning."

The bus. Spy school.

"I don't know what you're talking about."

She hated the way he looked at her. Like her attempt at the lie was funny. Like she was so bad, it was laughable. Like she wasn't worth the effort, and so he pushed away. "Goodbye, Alexandra. I trust we'll never see each other again."

"As long as I miss the bus."

"Precisely." Then he turned and pushed open a door and disappeared into the storm.

At six a.m. the following morning, Alexandra Sterling was the first person to board the bus to COTAC.

One guess who was the second.

chapter two

Present Day
Location Unknown

It wasn't the first time Alexandra Sterling had woken up tied to a chair in the dark, but it was the first time she couldn't remember exactly how she got there.

Her head hurt, and her throat burned, and she didn't even know if it was day or night, winter or summer. If she was dead or alive.

She shifted on the cold metal seat, and a sharp, searing pain streaked down her spine.

Alive, she decided. *Definitely alive.*

When she heard the clang of handcuffs hitting a metal chair, Alex had to wonder how much longer she could stay that way. But Alex didn't panic, thank you very much. She was too well-trained for that and far too jaded. Panic was for the very naive, the supremely unprepared, and the extraordinarily stupid, and no one survives ten years in her business by being any of the three, so Alex tried to focus on what she *was*: Confused. And concerned. And, most of all, *caught*.

Alex had been caught, and no matter how hard she tried to think—how desperately she needed to remember—she couldn't put her finger on how.

So that brought her back to the hard chair and the dark room and the pain in her neck that told her she'd been sitting there for way too long.

She had to get free, and that was one of very few things she knew for certain.

THINGS THAT I KNOW
A List by Alexandra Sterling

- My name is Alex Sterling.
- I'm in a dark room that smells like dust and mold and other people's feet.
- I'm handcuffed.
- My head hurts.
- My neck hurts.
- My stomach hurts.
- I don't know who brought me here or when or how or why.

But the most important thing was simple:

- My name is Alexandra Sterling. And I used to be a spy.

It was the past tense that mattered. For a moment, in the darkness, with nothing but the beating of her heart to mark the time, Alex had to wonder if the last year had been a dream. Maybe she was still undercover with Kozlov? Maybe she was waking up at the Farm? Maybe she was still a little girl and she was going to look over and see Zoe sleeping in a twin bed on the other side of the room . . . But no.

Her head hurt and the handcuffs rattled, and Alex couldn't help but remember icy falls and hard landings and then walking—no, *running*—away from her job and her world and her life. She remembered hiding and worrying that someone might find her. She remembered wondering if that would be better or worse than waking up one day and realizing that no one had bothered to look.

Of course, someone *had* come looking, it turned out, but she didn't have a clue who. Or why. And Alex couldn't make it all make sense.

For a time, every intelligence service in the world had been trying to track her down, but that was more than a year ago, and Kozlov was dead now. Alex hadn't officially resigned from the CIA, but disappearing without a trace for a year was the same thing, wasn't it?

And, besides, Alex had been a very good girl since she jumped off that mountain in Italy—literally flew into the sunset and disappeared.

But maybe that was her first mistake. People liked Alex more when she was bad.

Her Agency-assigned therapist had told her once that most of her issues stemmed from childhood trauma and survivor's guilt and the need to act out first—cause trouble and drive people away because, on some level, Alex felt like she didn't deserve them. It wasn't her fault she'd gotten the good heart and the good veins and the good nutrients—sucked them right up in the womb.

She hadn't actively *tried* to kill her sister, but Alex had been a greedy little embryo, and she doubted ten years in the field had made it any better. So maybe it was just a matter of time until she ended up tied to (yet another) chair in (yet another) room waiting for (yet another) bad guy to come try to boss her around.

It didn't matter that her wrists were still cuffed and the room was still dark and she wanted to sneeze—just a little. It was a room that felt like it had never been clean and never would be. Just four walls she couldn't even see, but she could tell the floor was concrete and the chair was metal. It made a scraping sound when she moved, and Alex had to bite back a grin. That fact was going to prove handy.

And speaking of hands, she gave hers a jerk in the darkness. They didn't make a rattle or a clang, so she wasn't handcuffed to the chair itself, and whatever was on the other side of those cuffs had a little give. If she could get it to break . . .

She pulled harder.

And then she heard it—a groan in the darkness—a low, aching sound that meant one thing: she wasn't alone.

Alex went still. The pain faded and her senses sharpened and, suddenly, she could smell everything, hear everything—feel everything about the room around her.

There was a sound, like a foot dragging across concrete. And a voice saying—

"Hello, Alexandra."

And just that quickly, Alex knew who she was going to kill first.

chapter three

Ten Years Ago
Camp Peary, Virginia

No one knows anything about the Farm. Officially, it doesn't even exist. Baby Alex had first heard the term on one of the two dozen spy movies she used to watch under the covers in hospitals, ready to shout *Wrong sister!* to anyone who might want to try to cut her open.

The spies in the movies were tough. They were fearless. They knew how to stab with pencils and strangle with string, and they never, ever cried because their twin sister was about to have her heart pulled out of her chest and then sewn back together—again.

They wore fancy dresses and drove fancier cars, and they didn't need the person in the twin bed on the far side of the room because they weren't half—they were whole. And they learned it all on some farm in Virginia.

It didn't matter how many stalls she had to muck or tractors she had to drive, nine-year-old Alex had sworn that she was going to learn to do those things too.

It wasn't until much, much later that Alex learned it wasn't *that* kind of farm. What the CIA grew at Camp Peary, it turned out, were secrets. But that was okay. Alex had a knack for those too.

So it didn't seem quite real, that January morning, as Alex gazed out the tinted windows when the bus stopped at the gates. German shepherds circled, sniffing at the wheels. Guards scanned for bombs, but Alex was more concerned with the man who was staring holes in the back of her head from the row behind her.

She turned and whispered, "Oh my gosh, was *this* the bus I wasn't supposed to get on?" She gave a gasp. Then a giggle. "This is so embarrassing."

"You seem pleased with yourself."

"Me?" She turned in her seat and watched the gates swing open. "Absolutely."

When they climbed off the bus ten minutes later, the sky was the color of gunmetal and the parking lot was rimmed with piles of dirty snow. Alex's breath turned to fog in the chilly air, but she could have stood there for an hour—a day—taking in the sights and sounds of that place that had loomed so large in her imagination. In reality, it was just a collection of neat, government-issue buildings surrounded by dense forest. On the drive, she'd spied (*Ha!*) shooting ranges and an airstrip and fractured glimpses of glistening water through breaks in the trees. It was all perfectly . . . ordinary.

"So this is it?" a voice asked from behind her, and Alex turned to take in a shadow that was the wrong shape—a voice that was the wrong tenor. The sky was just dull enough that she would have looked stupid in sunglasses, but she still had to squint against a glare as she looked up at a guy who was definitely not *The Guy*. Alex tried not to think about why she felt so disappointed. "I'm Tyler."

He held out his hand and Alex took it because she was going to play nice, she'd decided. Make friends. She was a new person here, and she was going to learn how to be a million more people. No one knew about Zoe or the hospitals. If anything, her history might have been an asset. Not a lot of people could almost kill someone in the womb. At spy school, that might make her a badass.

So Alex looked up at the new guy and told herself to smile. He looked . . . nice. The human equivalent of a photograph that had been put through so many filters that it couldn't help but look appealing, lines blurring together until there were no shadows anymore. He was attractive and easygoing and probably just not-threatening enough to make people feel like they could tell him their secrets. If so, he was in the right place.

So she asked, "Is that allowed?"

He exhaled about a third of a laugh. "Excuse me?"

"Names," she went on as he held open a door and they followed the group inside. "Or is Tyler a code name?" He gave her a look that said he didn't know if she was teasing or serious. "Because if you're going with Tyler, I guess I could be *Falcon*. Or *Dragon Rider*. Or *Gemini*."

"I don't know much about astrology." He sounded leery, like the CIA might have just invited a crazy person into their inner sanctum. What Tyler the Kind of Boring didn't know was that Alex's sarcasm was the most ordinary thing about her.

"I guess I'll just be Alex, then."

Tyler smiled down at her. "Alex, it's my pleasure." And the thing was, he even sounded like he meant it and not in an overly creepy way.

They'd reached a large sort of multipurpose room. There were tables and chairs. A few people helped themselves to coffee, but no one touched the donuts. She could feel the tension in the room—like the air before a storm. Charged and a little dangerous.

There were twenty-four recruits in the class—plus faculty and staff—and it made for an interesting mix of people. Big and small. Dark and fair. There was no pattern or mold. This wasn't a casting call for a spy movie; this was a training ground for people who were supposed to blow like dust to the four corners of the earth and disappear.

The rest of the class was talking and mingling, shaking hands and slapping backs. A little friendly ribbing in languages Alex recognized but didn't know. There was a quiet competition going on, but The Guy was on the far side of the room, leaning against a beam in the world's most average jeans and the world's most average shirt, trying not to be seen at all.

His shirtsleeves were rolled up, though, and his forearms were lean and corded with muscle, a hint of a tan line around one wrist—like he'd been lying on a beach somewhere a few days ago, like he belonged in the sun and not an Army base in Virginia on a cold, gray January morning.

The room smelled like burnt coffee and flop-sweating geniuses. The new recruits were trying to be cool, sure, but acting cool and being cool were two totally different things. And yet The Guy just stood there, looking . . . indifferent. Like he'd seen the movie, read the book. He knew the twists and nothing could surprise him. He was bored. And maybe that's why he didn't look around or study the people. Instead, he stayed on the far side of the room, studying Alex.

He was like a nature biographer—the Jane Goodall of covert operations—and if he stood still enough and stayed quiet long enough, then two dozen keenly observant people might fail to notice his existence.

Except . . . forearms. And a stare that was probably going to turn Alex into ash.

"Is that . . ." Tyler trailed off, following her gaze, and Alex felt the words rising up in her throat *No, that guy isn't bothering me!* "Michael Kingsley?" Wonder filled Tyler's voice. He let out a laugh. "It is! No way!" he called out with a grin. The Guy shifted his gaze off Alex, and the room suddenly felt cold without the heat of it. "I don't know if you remember—"

"Tyler." The Guy held out a hand. "Of course I remember you."

"Of course." Tyler gave a self-deprecating grin. "I forgot." He tapped his brain in a gesture that made Alex want to ask a million questions, but Tyler was already pulling The Guy into a backslapping hug. "I thought you were dead." It was a joke—or it was supposed to be, but Alex watched Tyler remember a moment too late that it wasn't funny. "I'm sorry. I—"

"Yeah, we kind of fell out of touch, didn't we? How have you been?" It was a graceful cover, an easy exit, and Tyler took it.

"I've been good. Just . . ." Tyler must have followed The Guy's gaze, which had, of course, gone back to Alex. "Oh, I'm sorry. This is Alex. Alex, meet Michael Kingsley. Mike and I . . ." He trailed off, like he really didn't know what to say. "Our parents . . ."

"We were neighbors," The Guy filled in. "For a while."

Tyler gulped. "Yeah. A while." An awkward silence descended, and Tyler looked down at the floor, a little sheepish. "I heard about . . . I'm sorry . . ."

Heard about what?

Sorry about what?

Alex was brimming with questions because she was, at her core, a nosy bitch (and hence: *spy school*). But she was also smart enough not to push it.

"I'm gonna grab a coffee before we get started." Tyler gestured to the table. She was aware, faintly, of him walking away, but Alex didn't follow. It was like she couldn't move, couldn't speak, couldn't do anything but stand there, overflowing with questions she couldn't ask.

Like had The Guy—Michael Kingsley—been following her at the hotel last night? Waiting for her? How did he know her name? And why did he look like a dark cloud was hovering over his head all of a sudden? But the question she most wanted to ask was *Why her?* Was she so unqualified that he'd had to track her down at an airport Ramada and steal her chicken fingers?

Suddenly, Alex was too hot. Her face was flushing, and her fingers were shaking, and it was all she could do to unzip her heavy coat, but then The Guy's gaze just shifted to her chest—though not for the reasons men usually looked at Alex's chest.

"Is that . . ."

She glanced down at her T-shirt. "I lie for a living." She pointed to the words as she read them.

"Very . . . covert."

"It's called irony, Cowboy."

"If you're not going to take this seriously—"

"I left my *Future Spy* hoodie at home."

Alex had never seen someone stumble while standing still. "Tell me you're not serious."

"Of course I'm not serious." He gave a sigh of relief. "If you think I'm coming to the Farm *without* my *Future Spy* hoodie, you don't know me at all. Except—oh wait. You *don't* know me." Alex wasn't hot anymore. If anything, she was freezing when she lowered her voice and whispered, "At all."

"I knew this was going to be a disaster."

"Take it easy, Cowboy." Alex wanted to roll her eyes. "You know who no one thinks is a spy? The chick wearing the hoodie that says 'future spy.'"

"This isn't a game, Ms. Sterling."

Alex reached for a donut. She took a big bite and felt the glossy sugar glaze break against her tongue—sweet and a little bit spiky. "Then why does it feel like I'm winning?"

The look on his face told her he felt it too. She should have been scared and trembling and cowering in his presence. Alex didn't know who he was or how he knew so much about her, but he was good at this. She could just tell—from the stillness to those ridiculously competent fingers to the way he'd inferred half her life story just by watching her order takeout.

"I got it at the International Spy Museum." She glanced down at her T-shirt, then licked donut off her fingers. "I bet they could find something in your size if you wanted."

"No. Thank you." The words were clipped and brisk—like little pieces of sleet that had been chasing them for twelve long hours.

"So . . ." Alex took a long, slow look around the place. Part of her kept waiting for a wall to slide aside, revealing a plexiglass elevator or, at the very least, a hidden cache of weapons, but what she got was a room that was so chilly she kept her coat on and another scowl from The Guy.

"Do I get to pick my own code name?" She asked him. "Can I be—"

"No."

"Do you think any of those chairs are actually ejector seats?"

"No."

"Trapdoors?"

"No."

"Are martinis the official drink, and if I want mine stirred instead of shaken, what—"

He pushed off from the beam and stood upright—leaned closer—but Alex had to bite back a grin.

"Is this a joke to you?" It was the loudest she'd ever heard him. A pair of trainees talking not far away trailed off and glanced in their direction. They were causing a scene, which Alex was pretty sure was a super spy no-no, but it didn't feel like a failure. She'd flustered Mr. Unflusterable, and Alex thought someone might rappel down out of the rafters and give her a medal.

"At the very least"—she dropped her gaze and her voice—"can I wear a switchblade in a garter belt? Please? Please?"

He was opening his mouth to chastise her—or maybe just gape— when a voice said, "You can borrow mine."

Alex didn't know who the woman was, but one thing was certain: Alex wanted to be her. Immediately.

She didn't so much walk to the front of the room as float, a vision of white hair and a white suit. She gave a white smile, and for a brief moment Alex wondered if she was an angel. Or a ghost.

"My name is Margaret Merritt," the woman began. "I am seventy-one years old and still alive, which makes me an *old spy*. We are rare and we are precious. I have been doing this job since 1965. I've seen presidents come and go, regimes fall and rise. I worked both sides of the wall, back when Berlin had one, and I knocked more than a few holes in it along the way. Both literally and figuratively," she added as an aside. "In short, I have seen things and done things, and the Agency has asked me to teach you how to not die. With a little luck, it might even work."

Alex tried not to gulp as Merritt took a step, her gaze sweeping across the group.

"Who knows how many applications the Agency gets every year?" she asked, but the room stayed silent, and Alex cut her eyes up at The Guy because he knew. She *knew* he knew.

"Michael?" Merritt asked.

The Guy recrossed his arms. "Fifty thousand."

"Correct." Merritt nodded. "But I want you all to remember a different number: twenty-four. That's how many are in your class. You're here because you passed the right tests and impressed the right people. You have the right skills and exhibit the right . . ." Merritt cocked her head, considering. ". . . *characteristics*." She smiled, as if pleased that she'd gotten it right. But then, just that quickly, her eyes turned to granite. "And the vast majority of you should go home."

Heat began to swell in Alex's chest and sweep up her neck. Even before she turned, she knew what she was feeling: eyes. A stare like a laser.

"I'm *not* going to teach you how to blend in; I'm going to teach you how to *cease to exist*," Merritt went on, but Alex couldn't look away from Michael Kingsley. "You aren't walking away from another job. You're walking away from your other *life*. The person you were this morning died the moment you set foot on that bus. From this point forward, anyone you ever loved will believe a lie. Everyone you meet will be introduced to a mirage. Everything you do will be life or death. Make no mistake, even if this job doesn't kill you, the person you used to be is already dead."

The first time Alex ever thought about death, she was four years old. Zoe was going to go away for a little while, her parents had told her. It was a place called a hospital. And there was a chance she wouldn't come back. It wasn't Alex's fault . . . exactly. And maybe they'd get lucky. Maybe Zoe wouldn't die.

Alex couldn't help but wonder if her luck might have just run out.

"But if you want to stay"—Merritt looked at them all in turn—"know this: you don't have friends anymore. You don't have siblings or parents or sweethearts. There are only three types of people in the world going forward: targets, assets, and threats. If that doesn't sound like how you want to live—or even if you just want to Not Die . . . A bus back to DC will leave in fifteen minutes. If you know what's good for you, you'll get on it."

No one moved or spoke or even breathed, and Merritt gave a slow, sad smile. "No one ever does."

chapter four

Present Day
The Shack

KING

"King?"

When King heard the voice in the darkness, he didn't know whether to feel relieved or downright angry. He'd been sitting there for at least twenty minutes, listening to the unconscious figure behind him breathe and groan and stir. It had sounded like her, but he hadn't been sure. Not until—

"Kingsley?" It was more curse than question, and that's how he knew for certain.

His head hurt. And his arms hurt. He couldn't even feel his hands, they'd gone so numb in the too-tight handcuffs. The dusty air made him feel like he was going to sneeze, which would have added a new layer of insult to his injury, but King couldn't help himself. He went boneless, one thought echoing over and over again in his mind.

She's alive.

She's alive.

She's—

"King?" Her voice cracked, and he thought of a million things that she might say. *I'm back. I'm here. I'm sorry.* But what came out was "What did you do?"

King couldn't help himself: he laughed. Nothing was funny, and yet . . . "What did *I* do? You're the one who's been out in the cold for a year, Sterling. What did *you* do?"

"Let me go." She pulled at the handcuffs again, trying to break free from whatever was holding her back. She clearly hadn't realized that the thing she was handcuffed to was *him*.

"Ow." His voice was flat, and she went still.

"You've got to be kidding me!" She jerked her arms again—which hurt. But not as much as his pride. "Of all the idiots in all the abandoned shacks in all the world, I had to get tied up with you."

"Actually, you're tied *to* me," King corrected, and Alex gave an exaggerated gasp.

"You're *actuallying* me? Now? At this moment?" Then she jerked her arms again, just to spite him. Because, after all this time, she was still the girl in the *Future Spy* hoodie, and he was still . . .

"Kingsley!"

"What?" he asked.

"Tell me what you see." The room was pitch-black, nothing but a few traces of faint light drifting through cracks in the walls. It wasn't a house. Maybe a barn or shed. It was dusty and dry and had the smell of disuse and desperation.

"Not much on this side. How about on yours?"

"Nothing," she conceded. "What can you hear?"

"Nothing."

"You have to hear something. You've been awake for longer than I have and—"

"I stand corrected. I hear nothing but the sound of you yapping—"

"Yapping?" The handcuffs jerked as she tried to spin. "Little dogs in expensive purses yap. I do not yap."

"Clearly."

"They're going to try to torture me, but they're too late." She drew a dramatic breath. "Because *this* is torture. *This.* Waking up, restrained in the dark, with you should have been outlawed by the Geneva convention."

He felt a tug on his hands, like she was making sure he was still with her, and then Alex went silent in the darkness. It was his turn to lash out, but King was too busy thinking . . . and remembering . . . and smiling.

"Come on, Sterling. It's not like it's the first time."

chapter five

Ten Years Ago
Somewhere in Virginia

KING

The first thing King noticed was the darkness. Then the smell. Then the feel of sweat sliding across his skin even though it was the middle of winter.

It was hard to get his bearings because something was over his head. His hands were zip-tied behind his back, and his legs were bound at the ankles, and even though the space was small, it felt like he might be adrift out in space, too far away to see the stars. Or else he was lying in a grave somewhere, too stupid to know he was already dead.

But that wasn't it either.

King . . . remembered. Everything. Always. It simply wasn't in his DNA to forget, so that might have been the weirdest thing about coming awake in the dark with no clue where he was or how he'd gotten there. But then he shifted slightly—a dull ache shot through his arm, and he flashed back to the Agency doctors lining them up for a routine shot after dinner.

"B-twelve, my ass," he said to the darkness. He didn't actually think the darkness would talk back.

"So it turns out"—the voice was wry and more than a little condescending—"*spies lie.*"

When he was five, King's grandfather had bought him his first bicycle without training wheels. They were living in Vienna at the time, and as it turned out, bikes and centuries-old cobblestones don't mix, so King had fallen and scraped his elbow. No matter how many times his mother washed the wound, he could always feel a little piece of grit under his skin. They said it was in his head, but King knew better. It was a part of him now, and he'd either have to cut it out or learn to live with it.

That was how it felt when he met Alex Sterling.

He'd known she was trouble from the moment she clocked him in the hotel bar. The place had been crowded, and he'd been alone in the dimmest corner, damn near a part of the wall. She shouldn't have seen him—but she did. And he'd hated her for it then. He hated her more now for how pleased she looked when she pulled the bag off his head and smiled down. "Did you miss me?"

King didn't even bother with an answer, because no. How could he miss her when she was always there? Everywhere. All the time. For the last month, she'd been behind him on the ropes course and ahead of him in the cafeteria and beside him at the shooting range, drilling bull's-eyes and giggling in a way that made her part prodigy, part psychopath.

She was oxygen and he was too stubborn to breathe, so it was fitting, he supposed, that she would be the person he'd be locked inside a small, enclosed space with, sucking up all the available air.

Time was ticking away and there was no chance they weren't being monitored, so King twisted and turned and tried to get his bearings.

There was hard metal above him, a scratchy fabric underneath. "I think we're in the trunk of a car," King said for no reason other than to make his mind start working.

A light flickered on, faint and golden. After the bag and the darkness, it was like staring at the sun. "No." She sounded smug as she finished twisting two wires together. "We're in the trunk of a 2012 BMW 5 Series."

"That's what I said."

"No. It's not."

No, it wasn't. Though he wasn't going to say so, not with her lying smushed against him. The two of them were far too close, and the trunk was far too tight, and her hair looked far too golden in the light, and . . . Wait. *How was the light on?* Not that it mattered. King had to get to work. He tried to turn so that he could reach the emergency latch with his bound hands, but when he tugged, it didn't do anything because the Central Intelligence Agency wasn't about to make things easy.

"Yeah. They disabled the emergency release, but that's not a problem." She was tearing at the upholstery.

"Why aren't *your* hands behind your back?" He felt cheated.

"They were." Sterling didn't look at him; she was too busy feeling along the walls of the trunk. "I shimmied my legs through."

"You shimmied?" He sounded like a snob, but what he really *was* was jealous. Why couldn't he shimmy?

"The model matters, you see," she went on as if he hadn't spoken. "Because everyone knows the 5 Series had a design flaw that . . ." She slipped her still-bound hands into the hole she'd made and, as if by magic, the trunk popped open.

"How did you . . ."

"I'm a mechanical prodigy."

"No." He wasn't in the mood for sarcasm. "Really. How—"

"Who do you think told them about the design flaw?" She turned and swung her bound legs out of the trunk and . . . yeah . . . shimmied out. "That's how I ended up working on a Formula One pit crew."

He studied her voice—her eyes. "Those drugs must have really knocked me for a loop because I honestly can't tell if you're lying."

"Of course I'm lying!" She laughed like he was the punchline of her favorite joke. "I wasn't on a Formula One pit crew." *Of course not.* "I was in the engineering department."

He stopped and studied her in the moonlight. Hair blowing around her. Dark clothes blending with the night. He could just make out a smudge of dirt or maybe grease on her cheek. He didn't know why, but it looked right on her. Like it belonged—like *she* belonged.

They had nothing in common. She was brash and bold, the center of attention and the life of the party. There wasn't a covert bone in Alex Sterling's body, and yet he couldn't shake the feeling that this was King's world—his birthright—but she was the one who was alive there.

The clock in his mind ticked louder. Her hands were still zip-tied, and he told her, "Here. Hold your hands like—"

But before he'd even finished, she put the end of the zip tie in her teeth and pulled it tighter; then she raised her hands over her head and brought them down quickly, snapping the tie in two. "Like that, O Special One?"

"Yes," King had to concede. "Like that." He mimicked the gesture while she found a small stick and used it to pry open the ties around her legs, and he realized that, of all the infuriating things about Alexandra Sterling—from her too-big eyes to her too-blonde hair—she was her most annoying when she was good. And, as badly as King hated to admit it, it happened a lot.

"So this is a test, right?" It was cold, and her breath was an icy cloud that surrounded them like a fog. King blew out a tired sigh, and in the stillness, even that low sound seemed to echo.

"Yes, Sterling. Everything is a test. We have to get out of here and then run the gauntlet of whatever they have waiting for us"—he motioned to the dark terrain that surrounded them—"out there." They were on the edge of the woods. Maybe they were still at Camp Peary? Maybe they weren't? There was only one way to find out.

"Cool." She grinned. "Come on, if we're being timed, I want to win."

"And if we're not?" It was a ridiculous question. Of course they were being timed. And videoed. And graded in a hundred different ways, and yet he had to hear her say—

"I always want to win."

Because King was wrong about one thing. He and Alex Sterling had something in common after all.

chapter six

Present Day
The Shack

ALEX

"I'll handle this," King said when they heard the doorknob start to rattle.

"Yes, because, historically, that has never gone badly."

"Well, what's your bright idea?"

"Rip Van Winkle?" Alex suggested.

"No."

"Elle Woods."

"No."

"Dead Man's Bluff?" she tried just as the largest figure she'd ever seen filled the doorway, backlit by moonlight. "Finally!" she shouted at the man who stepped forward, slowly. "Get in here! Now!"

The man hesitated on the threshold, as if kidnappees weren't supposed to give orders to kidnappers and maybe he'd missed a memo.

So Alex yelled louder. "Oh my gosh! Oh my gosh! Oh my—"

"You are awake." The giant had the kind of vague European accent that bad guys in movies always had and something about that made Alex want to smile. But first—

"You have to untie me! Now! Please!" She was breathing too hard. Her voice was breaking and—

The man hit her. Hard. Her head snapped to the right and Alex thought that she might bruise. All told, it wasn't the worst part, but it wasn't good either.

"Whew." She let out a breath. "Thank you. Yes. I feel calmer now. But . . ." Her lip trembled. "I'm still handcuffed *to a dead body*!"

The figure was more shadow than man then, and she watched him turn and call over his shoulder.

"Prishlo vremya!"

Alex hadn't heard the Russian language in a year, and just the sound of it made her blood turn cold.

Kozlov was dead. *He was*, she reminded herself. *She'd killed him.* But Kozlov had friends. And enemies. And Alex wasn't on good terms with either, so . . .

"Untie me," she begged as the goon flicked a switch. Instantly, a dim, dusty bulb sliced a circle of light out of the shadows. "Please? Please? Pl—" Then another figure filled the doorway, even larger than the first. *Great.* Had these guys fallen in a vat of radioactive waste? Maybe they were the product of a KGB experiment program?

The first guy had glasses, and the second had a goatee, but neither of those features went with either of their bodies, Alex thought as they huddled together for a moment, close and whispering. Whatever they'd been expecting to find, it wasn't this, and they didn't know what to do. *Good.*

Alex felt a tug on her arm that told her King was getting impatient. She slapped at his hand. He slapped back.

"He's dead!" she cried again, and the goons looked back at her. "I don't know what you idiots did, but you killed him!"

Glasses walked around the chairs and leaned close, reaching for King's limp head, feeling for a pulse—

And that's when it happened.

King pulled back and headbutted him—hard. Alex heard the glasses crack as the goon yelled, then fell to the ground, still conscious but groggy and unmoving and bleeding around the eye. And then King was up, practically dragging Alex out of her chair. Which was when Alex realized that they were in a classic good news/bad news situation.

The good news was they were temporarily down to one extremely large (and probably Russian) bad guy. The bad news was that they were still handcuffed together, back to back. Her right wrist bound to his left. His left to her right. And the other (extremely large, extremely ticked off) Russian was rushing toward them with a grunt.

"Not exactly ideal positioning." King dodged like a bullfighter, and Goatee went wide.

"Thank you, Captain Obvious."

Goatee lunged again, but Alex kicked her chair and sent it sliding across the concrete floor and the goon stumbled over it in the shadows.

They had no weapons, no backup, and no choice. These guys were going to kill them—eventually. It was just a matter of how much torture they had to endure first. But Alex wasn't afraid, and that should have terrified her. She didn't know where they were or how they got there, but this was familiar territory somehow. She'd spent nine of the last ten years fighting with Michael Kingsley—in one way or another. It was the first time in a long time that she'd actually felt at home.

"Bend over," Alex said, and King didn't argue. He just did it. Because hesitation is a death sentence, and if a seasoned operative says "duck," you duck. If they say "bend," you bend.

If Michael Kingsley III tells you not to come back . . .

Goatee was coming toward them, and Alex hurled herself backward, kicking out and catching Goatee under his chin as she flipped over King like they were contestants in the world's deadliest dance-off. It might have been funny, if not for the deadly part. It might have been fun if she hadn't found herself suddenly inches away from the face of someone she used to know but who, suddenly, felt like a stranger.

"You grew a beard."

It was a stupid thing to say—a stupid thing to think—but for a moment she just stood there, frozen in that pale circle of light, trying to reconcile the man with the thick beard and too-long hair against the clean-cut, all-American guy who had once told her she didn't belong at spy school. Even his eyes looked haunted, and Alex couldn't shake the feeling that she'd been gone for a year, but he was the one who hadn't stopped running.

It wasn't like him. Something was wrong. But it wasn't the moment to ask questions, not with the two of them standing there, hand in hand, like they were about to promise to love and cherish for the rest of their lives. Or make London Bridge come falling down.

There was movement on the ground, and Alex saw Glasses draw a gun, and then she dove, dragging King with her as—*BAM BAM BAM*—Glasses shot up from his place on the floor, leaving holes that looked like stars in the darkness of the metal roof. He was shooting half-blind, glass and blood in his eyes.

"Move!" King shouted, taking off to his right.

Which was unfortunate because Alex took off to his left, and they both came to a shattering halt at the same time, shoulders nearly jerking out of sockets, handcuffs biting into skin. Their arms were strung between them—taunt and vibrating like a string—and King looked like he was seriously considering letting the goons have her when Glasses raised his gun to shoot again, and the bullet zoomed between them, striking Goatee right between the eyes. He dropped like a rock.

Well, that was lucky.

Glasses swore and shot again, but this time the bullet connected with one of the handcuffs, and Alex stumbled a little when her right hand was no longer anchored to King's left.

Well, that was convenient, Alex thought as her gaze found King's. They were still standing there, tied together, when Glasses gave a roar and King gave a shrug that said, *Why not?* Then they turned and ran for Glasses, clotheslining him and knocking him to the ground. The gun went flying, but the man was agile and angry, and in the next moment he had a knife.

Alex didn't think—she dove. And then the gun was in her hand and she was pulling the trigger, over and over until—

The man stopped.

The knife fell.

And then the only person left who wanted to kill her was the one on the other side of those handcuffs.

For a moment, she and King just stood there, breathing hard. She wanted to say something—she really should *say something*—but her heart was pounding too fast, and her mouth was too dry, and the last fifteen minutes were too surreal to be anything but a dream. The only thing that rang true was the look on his face when he turned to her.

"Good job, Alex. Perfect. Now we have two bodies and zero answers."

"You can't possibly blame me for this."

He looked offended. Like she'd underestimated him. "I can always blame you."

"Fine." She aimed the gun at their remaining handcuff.

"Wait!"

She pulled the trigger and then . . . *nothing*.

They were all out of bullets. And maybe options. And probably time. So Alex hurled the empty weapon at the wall. She couldn't read his mind, but King looked like a cloud before it rained—dark and ready to storm. "What?"

He shook his head slowly. "Some things never change."

"What's that supposed to mean?"

"It means"—he threw open the door—"you never did know when to stop fighting."

chapter seven

Ten Years Ago
The Farm

ALEX

"Tell me about Zoe."

Alex took a deep breath and reminded herself that, at the Farm, therapy wasn't optional. At the Farm, therapy was good. At the Farm, people were taught how to plant bugs and make bombs, so it was important to ensure that trainees weren't absolutely insane. Of course, if the last six weeks had taught Alex anything, it was that no one would willingly do this if they weren't a little bit crazy. She didn't know what it meant that it was the happiest she'd ever been in her life.

"Are you and Zoe close?" Dr. Abrams asked over the top of her cat-eye glasses, vintage and a little too funky for someone employed by the CIA. Her skin was very pale, and her hair was very dark, and she looked like she might be about to offer Alex an apple. There wasn't a doubt in Alex's mind that it was poisoned.

"Zoe doesn't have anything to do with this."

The woman gave a subtle shrug. "Tell me about her anyway."

So Alex started with the obvious. "She's my sister."

Dr. Abrams was a pro, so she stayed silent, waiting for Alex to get uncomfortable and start jabbering to fill the void because most people hate silence and they hate awkward. But Alex wasn't most people. Alex would've sat there until she starved to death before she said another word.

"Did you like being an identical twin?" the woman asked

eventually, and Alex gave herself a mental high five for not being the one who cracked first.

"I don't know." Alex looked down at her hands. She still had paint under her nails from camouflage class and bruises on her wrists from the zip ties. "That's like asking me if I like being right-handed. It's all I've ever known."

"Did you ever think about what it would be like if Zoe died?"

Once upon a time, Alex had thought of almost nothing else, but that didn't matter anymore, because—"She's okay now. She's fine. Her heart's as good as new." *But it might not stay that way.*

"Did you talk to her? About your decision to come here?"

"Of course not." Alex didn't talk to Zoe because Alex didn't talk to *anyone*. Not about this—that would have violated more rules and laws than she could count. But she didn't tell her sister about anything else, either, Alex realized. She and Zoe were identical in ways that went beyond DNA. The same nature. The same nurture. And yet they were totally different because one of them had been born healthy and whole and the other one had paid the price.

"How does that make you feel, knowing that Zoe will never know the truth about you?"

Alex didn't say what she was thinking: that no one ever had.

When Alex left the office fifteen minutes later, she should've felt a million pounds lighter. Her checkup was done. Her head was shrunk, and she wouldn't have to do it again for six whole days. She was finally free to focus on other stuff, real stuff—*spy stuff.*

"My door is always open, Alex," Dr. Abrams called from the doorway and Alex forced a smile. "If you ever want to talk about Zoe . . ."

It was the kind of offer that felt like a threat, and Alex darted down the hall and around the corner, finally coming to rest with her back against one of the glass-fronted display cases that lined the long, wide hall.

Usually, Alex loved those exhibits. There were tubes of lipstick that were actually cameras and cameras that were actually guns. Loafers with knives in the soles and a ring where the ruby was actually cyanide. It was the only part of spy school that was actually like the movies, and Alex felt at home among those things that were so much more than they appeared. They were like her, she told herself, but at the moment, she just felt achy and out of place, like something was wrong.

She'd forgotten a test, a paper—her pants. She was stuck in that dream where you're back in high school and standing in a crowded cafeteria, totally naked. Except Alex was wide-awake and all alone. Still, something was missing, and Alex had to find it. Right then. Before it was too late. She had to call home. Then she remembered she no longer had one.

So she leaned against the glass and closed her eyes.

She tried to focus on her breathing.

She told herself that no one would be in the gym at this hour; she could sneak in and hit as many things as she wanted for as long as she wanted and—

"The kid *is* impressive."

Two men were walking through the lobby. Alex couldn't see them, but she could hear their footsteps, easily make out their words.

"He should be, given his pedigree." The second man gave a low, dry laugh. Then he stopped. Alex could practically hear him turn. "Did you know he has a photographic memory?"

"Like the old man?" The first guy sounded torn between being surprised and impressed.

"Exactly."

The second man gave a low, slow whistle, and Alex knew exactly who they were talking about. She could tell from the hushed and reverent tones.

It might have been easy to call Michael Kingsley a kiss ass, but he wasn't. If anything, it was like the instructors wanted to impress *him*.

"Michael, my boy!" the deputy director of the CIA had said after a guest lecture in their second week. "How's the old man?"

"Mr. Kingsley." Their demolition and explosives lecturer had slapped him on the back two weeks ago. "Give your father my regards."

Just that afternoon, their shooting instructor had taken one look at King's targets and proclaimed, "You could have given your grandfather a run for his money."

Needless to say, Alex hated him.

She had always been the top of her class because she was the person who tried the hardest. And now he was top of the class, even though, as far as Alex could tell, he didn't try at all.

In the lobby, the footsteps grew louder—closer—as the men headed toward the main front doors.

"You'll probably hear from his father eventually," one of the men said.

"He called me last week."

"No shit." The footsteps stopped. "Let me guess, he wanted to know when you'll be covering Nikolai?" The man's voice was flat, but there was something in the inflection that made the hair on Alex's arms stand up. "What'd you tell him?"

"That we'll get to it just as soon as we finish our unit on the Easter bunny." The second guy laughed like they were so funny. But, to Alex, they just sounded mean. "Of course, we'll have to save some time for Santa Claus." Their chuckles turned to cackles as they pushed through the double doors, and Alex stood there for a long time, until the laughter disappeared on the wind.

She didn't know what she'd just heard, but she felt guilty. For eavesdropping. For wondering. That conversation wasn't even classified, but somehow, it felt like the most top secret thing she'd ever heard.

"Ask me."

Alex turned at the sound of the voice, hating herself because she hadn't heard him—hadn't felt him. Maybe she really didn't belong at spy school, she wondered, but she'd rather die than admit as much, so she looked him up and down instead, as if she were already bored.

"I'm sorry. Were you speaking to me?"

"You know I was. So ask me."

"Do you really have a photographic memory?"

It surprised him, she could tell. That wasn't the part that'd had him worried. "The technical term is eidetic."

"Do you?"

"It's not photographic, per se. There's no such thing, technically, and—"

"Do you?"

"Yes." He didn't move. He barely breathed. He just stood there, staring at her as the night got later and the world got darker and the whole universe seemed to narrow down to the three feet between them. "*Ask me.*"

"About . . ." But that was when she saw it. Maybe she followed his gaze. Or maybe it was the work of her subconscious and six weeks of training on how to notice reflections and catch details. It was like an echo—a hall of mirrors. A trick of the light.

Because Michael Kingsley was there—looking at her. And he was also *there*—hanging on the wall, a photo in black and white.

Slowly, Alex stepped closer to the photograph—of him.

Only *not* him. Not exactly. The suit was gray and the tie was thin and the glasses were dark-rimmed, but more than anything, there was a look in the man's eyes that said he'd done things he was proud of (and a few more that he wasn't).

The plaque beneath it read "The Michael Kingsley School of Cold War Studies."

She glanced from King to the photograph. "Are you a vampire?"

Alex wasn't prepared for the quirk of his lip, like he was amused—with her. Like maybe he actually knew how to smile. Which . . . oh . . . there it went, turning into a scowl. It was a look that said the CIA had made a clerical error—a drastic mistake. Like at any moment a black ops team was going to breach the perimeter and come take her away, and he was only standing there because he wanted to be close enough to see her sweat.

"So that's *no* to vampire, then?" Alex asked, then reconsidered. "Time traveler? Shapeshifter?"

"Are you finished?"

"Ooh!" She thought of one more. "Evil clone!"

He gave her a look like *Go ahead and get them all out of your system*, but Alex just shrugged as if to say she was finished.

"Grandson." He turned to face the image in the frame. "I'm his grandson."

No wonder he was able to carry himself like he belonged. Like he was bored. Like he'd already learned all of this in the cradle and why were they making him go back to kindergarten when he should have been working on his PhD?

"So that's why everyone treats you like a baby duke." Alex thought it made perfect sense. It was the first thing since she'd met him that did.

"Notice how I'm not asking you what that means."

There was a kind of chill that radiated off him, like nothing in his vicinity was allowed to be cooler than he was. Alex felt it as she gestured toward the plaque.

"I thought no one was ever supposed to know our names?" It felt, to Alex, like an excellent point, but King just looked at the photograph.

"He was the Berlin station chief in sixty-two." His voice was soft and reverent. "Everyone knows his name." Then he seemed to remember who he thought he was speaking to—like she of all people wouldn't get the reference. "That was the Golden Age of—"

"Tradecraft," she cut him off. "I know."

"They were going to make a movie about him."

"Really?" Alex couldn't hide her excitement. "Why didn't they?"

"I'd tell you, but then . . ." No man had ever looked more smug than he did in that moment. "Sterling?"

"What?"

"There'll be another bus tomorrow morning. Get on it."

But she just turned and walked away.

chapter eight

KING

King watched her go. More angry than embarrassed.

Legacies are fickle things. Sometimes they're buoys and sometimes they're weights, and King knew that as long as he lived in the shadows of all the Michael Kingsleys who had gone before him, he'd have to deal with unfair expectations—both the good and the bad.

Maybe that's why he stood there, almost envious of the girl who got to be the only Alex Sterling.

He watched her turn right, toward the barn, instead of left, toward the barracks. It was full dark and the base was sleeping. They were scheduled for a run at five a.m.

"Where are you going?" he couldn't help but call after her.

She stopped and spun. "Where do you think?"

"It's late."

"I'm busy."

"Busy with what?"

"You know . . . places to be. Things to hit . . ."

He watched her push into the big building that served as the Agency gym. It was the oldest building on the base—a barn that was part of the original homestead. It should have been locked at that hour, but that didn't seem to matter to Alex Sterling.

He should leave her alone, he told himself. Let her get caught and kicked out. Let her get hurt and kicked out. Let her be so tired she couldn't function the next day . . . as long as she . . . yeah . . . got kicked out. He absolutely had no reason to follow her. And yet . . .

She was working the heavy bag, leg arching gracefully through the air before making contact and spinning smoothly in the other direction, when he got there. She had to have heard him, but she didn't fidget—didn't turn.

Not until he asked, "Who's Zoe?"

She stopped and found his gaze in one of the mirrors that lined the wall. "Who's Nikolai?"

She didn't know. He didn't know why, but the thought was almost soothing.

"I'll tell you mine if you tell me yours." King was relieved when his face didn't betray a thing. Maybe because he actually was good at this—highly trained and exceptionally intuitive. A natural. Or maybe it was just a wound that was so scabbed over that he couldn't even feel it anymore. "You shouldn't be in here by yourself."

She wiped the sweat away from her face. "And why's that, exactly?"

"It's not safe."

She gave the bag a roundhouse kick, probably because it was closer than his head. Then she pointed to her surroundings and said, "Spy school."

"It's not called—"

Alex kicked the bag again, and this time it almost swung free of the hook. "Do you think I don't know that?" She didn't even try to keep her voice down. "Of course you do. You think I'm too stupid to be here. You think I'm too stupid to live."

She pulled back and hit a speed bag as hard as she could. It bounced back because that was its job and she dodged it expertly, because that was hers, but King lunged forward and grabbed it—as if that was his. But it wasn't.

"You're going to get hurt."

She was up on her toes and leaning close. "Too. Late." She was covered in bruises—they all were. But that wasn't what she meant and he knew it. Some people choose this life because they're running *to* and some because they're running *from*, but for most . . . it was both. Suddenly, he wanted to know what thing had hurt Alex Sterling; he wanted to hurt it back.

"Come on." She stepped back and bounced on the balls of her

feet a few times, keeping her blood pumping and her energy up. "Let's see what you've got."

After six weeks, King was fairly certain she knew exactly what he had, but before he could say so, Alex went for his teeth. It served him right for smiling.

"What's the matter? Afraid of getting beaten up by a girl?"

She flicked him on the end of his nose, and he blew out a breath of frustration.

"I'm not going to get hurt by you, Sterling."

"Yes, you are. Because I'm going to punch you in your perfect face."

"You're not—"

"On the count of three."

"We have an early workout in the morning—"

"One."

"I'm trying to help you. This isn't a place where you can ignore rules and—"

"Two."

"Will you listen to me? I get that this is a game to you, but it's not to me! This is life." *His life.* "And death . . ." Did his voice crack? King didn't know—didn't necessarily care. He just knew that—"If you can't appreciate that fact—"

"Just to be clear"—Alex stopped bouncing—"I'm not going to *say* three and then punch you in the face. I'm just going to hit you as hard as I can and—spoiler alert—I can hit pretty hard. For a girl."

Maybe King could hog-tie her and put her on the bus? She'd be cold overnight, and she might need a bathroom eventually, but it was for her own good because she simply couldn't understand what she was signing up for. She had no idea what she was about to give up.

"You appear to be under the misperception that a life in the clandestine service is some kind of movie. Fast cars and tuxedos and ball gowns, but—"

Then she punched him. He actually staggered back a half step, momentarily stunned. "I got my first black belt when I was twelve. Or didn't you read that in whatever file you pilfered?"

He touched his lip and his finger came away bloody. Alex looked like she was wondering if she should feel bad—maybe apologize. They were on the same side, technically. Officially. But she also had the look of a woman who had been fighting her own, personal demons since she was old enough to know what the words meant. She looked relieved to finally have one who could hit back.

So she hit him again. "You want to fight, let's fight."

"Sterling—"

She pulled back to hit him again, but that time, he blocked it, and Alex gave him a look that said, *It's on.*

The night was dark and still. There was nothing but one lone bulb and the filtered rays of moonlight shining down like spotlights as they danced across the dusty floor. It was a ballet of punches and parries, kicks and thrusts. She was warmed up and dressed for a workout, and he was fighting cold and in street shoes, but that didn't matter.

"I never said you weren't good enough," King said after she landed a blow to his stomach and he stumbled back, unsteady.

"Pretty sure you did." Alex charged, trying to take advantage of the moment, but he shifted his weight and pushed, sending her wide and making her angry.

"I said this is the real world. People get hurt, Sterling." He was breathing hard, even though he'd hardly moved. "They die."

"There are stars on the wall at Langley. I know."

"You don't know!" She lunged for him, but she telegraphed the move and he caught her, forearm tight against her throat, as he leaned close and whispered, "You'll never know until you've lived it. And by the time you've lived it, it's too late." He felt her go still in his arms. "Say mercy," he whispered in her ear, and Alex choked out a snicker.

Then she kicked him in the shin and slipped his hold. "Never."

"You fight dirty," he told her, hobbling slightly.

"I fight to win." She charged at him again in a flurry of punches, but he blocked every one, blow after vicious blow until she stopped—momentarily stunned and suddenly furious. It was like she'd finally realized—

"Hit me back."

"I am."

"You're pulling your punches. Stop it."

"*Never.*" It was fun, using her own words against her, and something about it snapped something inside of her. She charged, but he dodged her, and that made her even angrier, which made King feel even more certain.

"See? This!" He batted away her kicks and felt her form get sloppy. "You're emotional, and you take everything personally. That makes you volatile and—"

"Call me a hysterical woman." Alex was breathing hard, but the look in her eye was even harder. "I dare you."

He caught her arm, pulled her tight, and whispered, "Say mercy."

So she flipped him.

All the air whooshed out of his lungs when King landed—too hard—on the mat, but the most painful thing was the way she stood over him, looking down and mouthing *oops* as he frowned up.

Her hair was dark with sweat, and her eyes were bright with rage. She looked like some kind of avenging angel—mythical and revered—and he wanted to tell her that she was the one who was wrong to doubt her place there. She was smart enough. She was strong enough. She was scrappy and resourceful and—

She was going to get them all killed.

"You don't scare me, Mr. *My Grandfather Founded the CIA.*"

"Well, that's not accurate at—"

"I'm not scared of you! Or Merritt. Or anyone here. And I'm not afraid of anything *out there.*"

"And that's the problem!" He rolled and swept a leg, knocking hers out from under her, and she crashed to the mat beside him. "Nothing scares you, and you should be terrified." She moved fast but he moved faster, and he caught her fist before it landed. "I know this world, Sterling. People die. The people you love die. I'm telling you, it's not like the movies. At least not the kind with happy endings."

Alex was flat on her back and King was on top of her, a hand on each of her wrists, pinning her down. He could feel the rise and fall of her chest, see the green of her eyes. Her cheeks were pink and she looked like how sunshine feels, and all he wanted in the world was to never lay eyes on her again.

"Say"—he banged her hands against the mat—"mercy."

If she'd had any sense, she would have done it. If he'd had any sense, he wouldn't have cared.

"I'd rather die first," she ground out, and King felt the fight leave his body—a subtle snap and then the tension ebbed away as he told himself he didn't have to save her.

He just had to not care.

"Good." He pushed away and collapsed on the mat beside her. "Because that's exactly what's going to happen."

He watched her struggle to sit upright. He heard her draw a ragged breath. "Why do you hate me so much?" Her breath came hard, and she blinked like she knew there might be tears there. "Is it because my family isn't important enough? Fairies didn't visit me in the cradle and bless me with divine arrogance or—"

"Because you're too beautiful." He hadn't meant to say it, but the words were out now and floating around the room. He wanted to shoot them out of the air, break all the windows and let them fly away on the wind. But he couldn't, so he ran a hand through his hair, frustrated and angry with himself—with her.

"What . . ."

"Spies disappear, Alexandra." Those weren't King's words. They were his father's. And his grandfather's. Those words had been handed down for centuries, and he was just the messenger. There was probably a tablet someplace in Langley. Somewhere, they were carved into stone. "Spies blend. They fade into the background and slip through cracks, and believe it or not, that's not easy to do when you're the most beautiful woman I've ever laid eyes on."

"But . . ."

"You stand out. And you're reckless and dangerous and arrogant as hell, and you're going to get someone killed someday. I just hope I'm far away when it happens."

They were still too close. Her eyes were too big and her breath was too warm, but he couldn't help but press against her—nothing but sweaty skin and stares like lasers and two pounding hearts in the shadows when he whispered, "Say mercy."

But she didn't.

Not for a long, long time.

chapter nine

Present Day
The Desert

ALEX

The door was standing open, and outside, the night was quiet and still. After the darkness of the shack, it felt like broad daylight, the way the full moon shone overhead. They were surrounded by at least a billion stars, but absolutely nothing else. No trees. No buildings. Just a chilly wind and dry air and miles of rocks and sand and—

"Desert," King grumbled. "Of course we're in the middle of the desert."

But that was hardly their only problem because Alex was looking around, and realizing—

"There's no car? Seriously? Tweedledee and Tweedledee-er—"

"That's not how that goes—"

"Couldn't have left a vehicle conveniently parked outside?"

"Someone must have dropped them off."

"Ya think?" She spun on him, but he went on, colder than before. Still put together. Almost unmussed and certainly unfussed, as if he had been pulled from a very important meeting and was eager to get back to the office.

"Of course, we would have known that if it hadn't been for the yapping—"

Alex couldn't help herself. She jerked her arm and felt the handcuff bite into her skin. It was worth it when he growled, "Ow."

"Oops," she said. Then she looked around. "I would say we should split up and vow to never see each other again, except . . ."

She shook their joined hands, rattling their handcuffs and making her point. "Which is a shame. That's the one thing we can usually agree on." But something in his gaze made Alex look away when she asked, "How many times would that make? Cartagena? The Amalfi Coast? Scotland—"

"I didn't say it in Scotland."

It was the first time she'd ever heard him sound defensive, and it should have felt like victory. Instead, she just felt cold.

The moon was high overhead, and they had no way of knowing what was east or west. North or south. Safe or incredibly dangerous. The only thing that was certain was that they couldn't stay there.

"I'm going that way." She didn't know why she pointed to her right. It might have been instinct, or maybe her subconscious had made some calculation that was so minute she didn't know she'd even done it. But it didn't matter, because—

"I was going to go that way," King admitted.

"Then I guess I'll let you come with me," she said.

"You're too kind."

But what they really were was handcuffed together in the middle of the desert, possibly the only people for a thousand miles in any direction they could trust.

They must have walked for hours—a fact made worse by the fact that Alex was wearing a sundress and a pair of flimsy sandals. Her skin had gone sweaty during the fight and was now covered in goose bumps and sand.

King was in jeans and a sports jacket (no tie) and she tried not to shiver.

"Here."

"What?" She sounded almost afraid, but he was slipping off his coat then turning it inside out as he dragged the sleeve over his still-cuffed hand and then onto hers.

She wanted to shove it down his throat, but it wasn't just a Tom Ford blazer. It was an olive branch, and part of Alex knew she'd be a fool not to take it.

"Thank you."

The fabric was soft on her skin and warm from his body. It smelled like the happiest days of her life, and Alex wanted to close her eyes and sink into a memory. She also wanted to cut out that part of her brain and set it on fire. She couldn't do either, unfortunately, so she just kept walking.

There was light on the horizon, like the sun was coming up even though the moon was still too high.

"Guesses?" he asked.

"Syria," Alex said on instinct.

"Too cold," he told her.

"Afghanistan," she tried again.

"Not mountainous enough."

"Well, what's your big idea?"

He looked around. "Iran?" He gave a shrug.

"Maybe."

They crossed a rutted trail and scrambled over an outcropping of rocks, eyes and ears tuned to any sound of approaching vehicles or voices carrying on the wind.

He looked at her. "What's the last thing you remember?" It should have been a simple question, but it felt like a test because everything felt like a test when it came from Michael Kingsley.

They were ten years out of the Farm, but she was still the girl in the hoodie she bought at the International Spy Museum, and he was still the Golden Boy. He was still unflappable and Alex was still unworthy. She was still covering up her fear with her bravado and he was still looking at her like he had no idea how they ever ended up in the same career.

"You tell me first."

He blew out a breath and hung his head, and Alex could feel the frustration coming off him in waves. "Not everything is a fight, Sterling. Sometimes a question is just a question."

They started to climb a rocky hill. Her feet slid in the sand and small stones, but she wasn't about to take the hand that was bound to hers.

"Sterling—"

"I was home," she admitted, and then she felt him stop. Turn. Stare. Looks can't kill, Alex knew that for a fact. But they could wound sometimes, and she wanted to hide against the gaze that pierced her.

"Which was *where*, exactly?" He sounded like the guy from the Farm again, like the virtual stranger who had hated her on sight and on instinct. He was cold and hard and . . . wounded. A brittle shell that wasn't quite enough protection.

"What about you?" Her throat burned. She'd been breathing too much dust, and the air was too dry. It wasn't because a part of her felt like crying. Not even a little. "What do *you* remember?"

"I don't"—the words were a whisper—"*remember*. I can't." He sounded mad enough to rip their cuffs in two. He hung his head as if trying to shake it off. "The last thing I remember is being home. In Scotland." The words were crisp and clean, like a break. "Now it's your turn, Sterling. Where exactly have you been calling home for the past—"

"We don't know how long we were out," she said.

"I know exactly how long you were missing."

"I wasn't *missing*."

"No. Of course you weren't missing." His voice turned harder—colder. An icicle sharp enough to kill. "You were just straight-up *gone*."

She looked away and kept climbing while the sky grew brighter on the horizon. There was something over that ridge, and Alex only hoped it was a pair of bolt cutters. "We need to find cover. Lie low. Get some water and a clean phone to call it in."

"Sterling—"

"Let's just focus on getting out of Pakistan or Syria or wherever the . . ."

But Alex trailed off as they crested the ridge. She had to. Because she didn't know what to say. She didn't even know how to feel as she looked down on the sea of light that stretched out beneath them. Neon blinking and burning and turning night to day as they stared down on the city of Las Vegas.

"Well, it could be worse," King said. "It could be Cartagena."

chapter ten

Nine Years Ago
Cartegena, Colombia

ALEX

"Hello. Checking in. Reservation for Shriver." Alex made herself smile—but not too big. She gave details—but not too many. She made eye contact—but not for too long. Most of all, she studied her surroundings—but not too overtly. In short, Alex tried to remember every single thing she'd learned at the Farm—and in the six months after. But mostly, she tried not to throw up, because it's one thing for a girl to dream about her first solo mission, it's another to stand in the lobby of a luxury hotel in Cartagena and say, "Molly Shriver? I'm—"

"Yes, Mrs. Shriver." The man was young and trim and almost painfully efficient as he typed away at a keyboard. "Welcome to Cartagena!"

Alex didn't try to speak to the young man in Spanish because Molly Shriver, aspiring *jewelry designer–slash–influencer–slash–spender of other people's money*, didn't speak Spanish. Alex had spent weeks working on that cover, and it wouldn't do to ruin it within the first five minutes.

So she looked around. "The hotel is so pretty." An ornate crystal installation was suspended from the towering ceiling, catching the light and filling the lobby with tiny rainbows that twisted and swirled and seemed to float across the shiny white floors and sleek modern interior. "Ooh. Would it be possible to, like, sit on that dangly thing and get some videos?"

"No!" Judging by the panic in the guy's eyes, Molly Shriver wasn't the first person to have that idea. She was guessing one or two had even tried it.

"Darn. Had to ask!" Alex gave a giggle and then she slumped against the counter and tried not to look nervous. It would have been better not to *be* nervous, but the op details had been need-to-know and, evidently, Alex hadn't *needed* by the time she left Virginia. She was supposed to check into this hotel and wait for further instructions. She had her cover and her legend and her mind—those were the only things a good operative really needed. Everything else would be waiting for her here. A weapon. A villain. A—

"—husband."

Wait. What?

"I'm sorry?" Alex leaned closer to the guy who looked up from the screen and flashed a smile. Loud, techno music boomed out of hidden speakers, filling the air and echoing off all that chrome and glass. She'd misunderstood him. There was simply no way he meant—

"Your husband has already checked in."

It was ninety degrees outside with eighty percent humidity, but it was suddenly freezing—what with the air conditioner on her skin and Alex's blood turning to ice.

This was supposed to be a solo mission. This was supposed to be *her* solo mission. But maybe there had been a change of plans? Maybe she was meeting Tyler? She liked Tyler. Didn't she? He was fine. She could work with Tyler. Or someone else. Some stranger. Maybe an older operative who was experienced and knew his way around the Colombian coast? Yes. That was it. She was going to go upstairs and meet some seasoned operative and not—

"Hello, sweetheart." There was a hand on her back and a solid presence at her side—a pair of warm lips brushing against her cheek as a familiar voice said, "How was your flight?"

It had been six months since she'd seen him. Hardly enough time for a massive change, so Alex didn't know why she stood there, staring at Michael Kingsley. His hair was a little longer and she wondered if it was as soft as it looked—if maybe Mrs. Shriver was the kind of person who would run her fingers through those silky strands. And then pull them until he cried like a baby.

"Did you miss me?" His voice sounded like hot tea with too much sugar.

"Yes. But I can reload and try again."

He gave a dark chuckle, then leaned down and brushed a kiss across the top of her shoulder. One of those ridiculously competent hands started rubbing circles on the small of her back—against the bare skin left exposed by her dress and, in that moment, Alex wanted to kill the inventor of the halter top.

She had goose bumps, and she hoped he couldn't feel them—see them. It was the air-conditioning. It was. But the guy behind the counter was looking at them with hearts in his eyes. Like Alex had entered the hot-guy lottery and King was the winning ticket.

"We'll just take that key now," King prompted, and the guy blinked.

"Of course. Penthouse elevators to the right. It's a wonderful room. For newlyweds."

"Oh. Yay." Alex looked up at King. "I'm so excited, I could scream. But that's for later, isn't it, sugar lips?" The look on his face almost made it worth it. *Almost.* Then she gave the clerk a wink and didn't protest too loudly when King started dragging her across the shiny lobby and into the even shinier elevator.

He swiped the card and the doors slid closed, and the next thing she knew, King was pressing her against the mirrored interior. Leaning close as he whispered, "Not. A. Word."

"I know." She wanted to bite his lip off—and not in the sexy way.

He was looking down into her eyes. Fingers running through her hair, a whisper-soft brush against her neck. "There are no doubt cameras everywhere. Possibly audio."

"Not. A. Moron." She echoed his earlier cadence and pushed against him, but he didn't budge. It was highly annoying. *He* was annoying, with his stupid shoulders and stupid hands. Stupid stubble covering that stupid jaw.

"Did you forget your razor?" Alex asked him.

"Did you forget the other half of your dress?"

Alex didn't want to smile, so she pinched one of his nipples instead.

"Ow." But he didn't move and didn't wince, and his gaze didn't even start to waver. "What are you doing here . . . sweetheart?"

She was going for the nipple again when he grabbed her hand and interlaced their fingers, pushed her arms over her head and pressed her against the wall more fully—all of him pressed against all of her. From the camera in the corner, they either looked madly in love or insanely hot for each other. Or both. Probably both. They were as indecent as you can be with your clothes on, and Alex didn't like that one bit.

"Me?" She tried to reverse their positions, but he dropped his hands to her waist and lifted. And then Alex had no choice but to wrap her legs around him. And squeeze. Like a snake. "What are *you* doing here? This is supposed to be my . . ." *Cameras. Audio.* "Vacation. I worked hard for this vacation."

"No. It's *my* vacation, so I'm going to ask one more time—"

The elevator stopped. The doors opened. And Margaret Merritt said, "Well, it's about time."

chapter eleven

ALEX

Alex didn't move. Not a muscle. She couldn't even think as she looked at Merritt—the quirk of her lip. The tilt of her eyebrow. She'd always seemed omniscient and all-knowing—more angel than agent—and, not for the first time, Alex got the feeling that this might just be some elaborate game—a silly lark. Like the fates were toying with Alex and making her dance.

With *him*.

"Now, before you tell me how much you hate each other, you may want to straighten your clothes and . . . disengage . . . before we get kicked out of this hotel for indecent behavior."

Alex dropped to the floor and stepped out of the elevator like she and Michael Kingsley had never even met.

Merritt opened a pair of double doors, and Alex followed her into a room that felt like a slightly smaller version of the lobby below. White and glossy. The furniture was modern, and the finishes were chrome, and the whole thing felt like it was made of ice even though the sun was almost scorching as it burned through the wall of windows. Alex told herself that that was why her face was red and little beads of sweat were sliding down her skin.

But King looked like a man who had never been embarrassed in his life. If anything, he just looked angry.

"Is it clean?" he asked under his breath. The penthouse felt as sterile as an operating room, but that wasn't what he was asking and they all knew it.

"It is," Merritt told him.

"Good." King took off his linen jacket and tossed it over the back of the long white couch. Then he started rolling up his shirtsleeves. Slowly. "So there's no reason why you can't explain why my first solo mission is not as solo as I was led to believe?"

For the first time, Alex was grateful King was there, asking questions so she didn't have to. She didn't know how a senior intelligence officer with the CIA would take to being challenged, but she definitely wasn't expecting Merritt to pull something from her pocket and toss it in King's direction. He caught it in a flash.

It was a pouch, small and black and velvet. There was an intricate *L* embroidered on the side in pale gold thread, Alex noticed, while King tossed it gently, testing its weight.

"Go on," Merritt told him, so he loosened the strings and tipped the pouch over, sending dozens of small green stones tumbling out onto the palm of his hand.

"Are those . . ." Alex inched closer.

"Uncut emeralds?" Merritt filled in. "Yes. Approximately ten million dollars' worth."

King cut his eyes at Alex.

"I'm not going to steal them." Alex pouted back.

"Go right ahead and try, Alexandra," Merritt told her. "You won't get far. Because those are equipped with trackers." Of course, to Alex, that just made them cooler.

King put the stones back in the bag. "I'm still not sure what *we're* doing here?"

It was the *we* that mattered, because King didn't like her, didn't need her, and didn't want her. She was cramping his style and trying his patience.

"I thought you knew?" Merritt gave them a wide-eyed innocent look. "You have a mission."

"*I* have a mission." King gave an annoyed glance at Alex. "And I suppose it's possible that *she* has a mission. But *we* do not have—"

"You have whatever I say you have, and I'm saying you have a mission." Merritt's gaze swept between the two of them like a searchlight. After a prison break. "This is a team sport, and like it or not, the two of you have to learn to play. Together."

As much as Alex wanted to kill King, she wanted to impress Merritt more. "What's the op?"

Merritt nodded as if to say, *Finally, someone is asking the right questions*. "I'm sure I don't have to tell the two of you that uncut gems are the currency of choice for very bad people. Your mission—"

"Should we choose to accept it?" Alex couldn't help herself. She'd been waiting her whole life to hear those words, and if they made King sulk and roll his eyes, all the better.

"Should you accept it," Merritt echoed, and Alex couldn't help but smirk in King's direction, "is to swap our stones for theirs and then *get out*. We have people in place who can track the stones and see where they go."

"Who's the target?" Alex asked.

"Unclear," Merritt admitted. "We overheard chatter that a local jeweler was contracted to procure ten million dollars' worth of uncut emeralds and, naturally, we got interested. But we don't know who the buyer is or why he needs them."

"Hence the trackers." King sounded resigned.

"Hence the trackers," Merritt agreed. "There are some new players entering the field. That's why it's so important that we see where these end up."

King clasped one tiny stone between two fingers, holding it up to the light. "I can do it alone."

"King is very shy," Alex said. "Performance issues, you know. I make him nervous."

King chose to ignore her. "This is too important to leave to chance."

"Precisely." The word was clipped and left no room for debate. "Which is why I personally requested the two of you."

"To do what? Exactly?" King asked, because there was obviously more to the story.

"Easy, Michael. You're going to buy a very large emerald." She smiled at Alex. "For your wife."

chapter twelve

Present Day
Las Vegas, Nevada

ALEX

The sun was almost up by the time they made it into Vegas. Or maybe it just felt that way, among the neon lights of the Strip with the traffic streaming by—sidewalks full of people venturing home or venturing out. Tired cocktail waitresses changing shifts as the city turned over but never slept.

Alex's feet were blistered and her wrist was sore, but the thing that hurt the most was her pride.

She was a seasoned operative—a trained professional. She should have been beyond making mistakes by that point, but evidently, she'd made a big one. Otherwise, Alex never would have ended up limping down the Las Vegas Strip—

With him.

Caught with no plan and no intel and no resources.

Except him.

Utterly exposed and completely without backup.

Unless you counted him.

"Just act naturally," King had the audacity to say.

"Yes." Alex rattled their connected hands. "So natural."

Her wrist hurt. The cuff was too tight, and the constant pulling and tugging had left her skin red and bleeding. He looked down at it and stumbled slightly.

"Fine. Here." He sounded like he'd just agreed to cosign a loan when he interlaced their fingers. It took the pressure off her wrist, but other parts of her felt a different kind of ache, and Alex didn't know which was more painful.

"We need to get off the street and find a phone," she said.

"We *need*"—he emphasized the word—"to keep our heads down and keep walking."

"Yes. Excellent." She gathered his inside-out jacket around her and held it more tightly. "Great plan! It's not like there are *surveillance cameras*. In Las Vegas."

"I'm trying to help here, Sterling."

"I'm capable of helping myself, King."

"Clearly." He stopped walking. "So help yourself, then. Go on. Be my guest."

"I'd love to. Except." She held up their cuffed hands as if seeing them for the first time. "Where did those come from?"

"Put those down." His voice was so low, it was almost a growl.

"What? You want me to hide our handcuffs?" she shot back, a tad louder than necessary. A group of college guys was walking by—bleary-eyed and smelling like smoke and bad decisions—but they perked up at the words, and Alex couldn't help herself. "We wouldn't want anyone to know that I woke up in Vegas!" she exclaimed, even louder. "Handcuffed to you!"

The college guys gave a chorus of "right ons" and "way to gos," so Alex threw her free hand out as if to say, *I rest my case.* They were out of earshot when she added, "It's Vegas." She huddled into the warmth of his jacket. "Waking up after a night you can't remember is practically a rite of passage. They literally make movies about it."

The silence was dark and heavy as they put their heads down and kept walking.

"What?" he asked.

"I didn't say anything."

"I know. That's what has me worried."

"Ooh! I've got an idea. Maybe we can use the stick up your butt to pick the locks!"

"It's too big, Sterling. You know that."

She stopped, and for a moment, she just stood there, staring.

"Was that . . . a joke?"

"I'm not sure." He actually looked sheepish. "I've never made one before."

It wasn't true, of course. Most people never knew that Michael Kingsley III could be funny. He could be kind. He could make soup and mend wounds and clothes and people. He was more than his family and his memory, but Alex was the last person who would ever say so, so she just whispered, "Don't do it again."

"Very well."

"We need to find some way to open these."

He looked around. "Shouldn't be hard. We just need a clothes hanger or paper clip or—"

"Sex shop," Alex filled in. "What? *It's Vegas*. They'd have hand-cuffs. And keys."

"Yes. True." He swallowed hard and, to Alex, it felt like victory. He was looking around. "I suppose . . ." But as he trailed off, every-thing changed. His posture and his tone and even the way the air crackled and buzzed around him.

"What?" she asked, but she already knew. She didn't actually need him to say—

"We have company."

chapter thirteen

ALEX

It wasn't hard to spot the tail. The people after them weren't exactly subtle, but then again, neither were King and Alex as they fell into step together, wishing for heavier foot traffic. For the cover of darkness. For some kind of distraction or disaster. Anything that would help them disappear.

"I have two at two o'clock," Alex said.

"It might be nothing," King said, even though it *wasn't* nothing.

He kept trying to put his arm around her, but the cuffs got in the way, so he squeezed her hand a little tighter and dragged her across the street, against the light.

It was still early, but there were always people on the street in Vegas, so King and Alex slipped into their midst, heads low, steps unhurried.

"How are we doing?" He pressed a kiss against her hairline as she rested her head on his shoulder. Because that was the cover. Only people in love would be out all night, dressed as they were and holding hands.

Casually, she checked their tail in the reflection of a window. They might have been clear. They were almost okay, but King stopped—frozen—as he looked at her. He brought his free hand up to cup her face. His thumb brushed against her lip—it was cracked and almost as tender as his voice when he said, "You're hurt."

"Yes. That happens on occasion." The words were dry like the desert and just as dangerous. "Come on." She dragged him over an arching walkway that crossed the Strip. There was no shouting. No running. It honestly felt like they were in the clear, but then, down below them, tires screeched. SUVs swarmed. People stormed out and started searching. It didn't take a genius to know for what. Or whom. A pair of men headed in their direction.

"I'm getting quite annoyed," King said.

"With them or with me?"

"Toss-up," he admitted as they took off running down the Strip as if their lives depended on it. Probably because they did.

So they ran faster, dodging in and out of tour groups and leaping over luggage. Three huge motor coaches were parked in front of a sweeping drive. Sleepy tourists were waiting to board, and King dragged Alex through the crowd, shouting, "In here," as he pushed her toward the towering entrance of the casino.

"Great. Yes. Let's go into a place with even more cameras."

The lobby was bustling with people hurrying to catch early flights, stumbling out in dark glasses while hovering on the line between *still drunk* and *hungover*. But King didn't even slow down. He just kept dragging Alex across the marble floor.

"Don't mind us!" Alex called to the slack-jawed security guard. "What happens in Vegas, am I right?"

She winked and—

"Did you just do finger guns?" King whispered.

"When in Vegas?" she replied, but he was already pulling her onto the casino's floor.

It was a maze of blinking lights and ringing bells. People went in but they were never supposed to get out, and Alex wondered if that was in their favor or against them.

Music and laughter and the constant ringing of slot machines filled the air, and for a person who was trained to see everything, hear everything—*notice everything*—it was torture. There were too many sounds and lights and people. Every part of her was overwhelmed by every part of it, and Alex was grateful for the man holding her hand. King was an anchor in that moment. He was the only thing she needed to focus on as they ran down the aisles that seemed to sprawl and spread, and she had to admit he was right about one thing: a person could get lost in here. Maybe *they* could get lost in here.

But there was no way to disappear—not really. Every square inch would be under surveillance. "If these guys can get access to the casino's system—"

"They can't." He sounded so sure—so certain. So . . . King.

"But if they—"

"They're going to think they lost us in here." He pulled her down the darkest part of the casino floor. There was a wall to their left and a row of dollar slots to their right.

"But how—"

He stopped and looked at her like the answer was the most obvious thing in the world. "Because they're *going* to lose us in here."

"But how—"

"Because of this." There was an emergency exit in the corner—a lever labeled DO NOT PUSH. ALARM WILL SOUND.

And then he pushed it.

Instantly, alarms began to wail. Lights began to swirl. King pushed Alex between a gap in the slots and into the next aisle while security guards shouted and headed toward the open door. A moment later, King was leading her down a dim and narrow hallway marked EMPLOYEES ONLY.

"Just out of curiosity, what is your plan? Exactly?"

"My plan is to keep us alive, Sterling."

"And you're doing a phenomenal job. What with us being handcuffed and hiding in a place where it is literally impossible to hide."

"This is a blind spot."

"Oh, is it? You psychically divined that, did you?"

"There's nothing to steal here. Nothing to protect."

But all she did was cock an eyebrow. "So what's your big plan now?" He stopped in front of a service elevator and started punching numbers into the keypad. "Seriously? That's never going to . . ." But Alex trailed off when the doors slid open.

King just took her hand and said, "Come on."

chapter fourteen

Nine Years Ago
Cartagena, Colombia

KING

King didn't complain because it wouldn't have mattered. If Merritt had wanted this to be a solo mission, it would have been. If she had thought him ready to be on his own, he would be. And, most of all, if this job hadn't required a certain kind of female operative, he wouldn't have been walking down the stone streets of the walled city at that moment, holding the hand of Alex Sterling.

All spies are chess players, but Merritt was a grand master. King knew she was a dozen moves ahead and well aware of the endgame and she wasn't going to share. But, in the meantime, King had other problems. Specifically, he had three:

There was the mission.

There was the woman.

And there was the hat.

"I can't believe you wore that."

"Wore what?" Alex tilted her head up to look at him, and the wide brim of the big white hat tipped back, exposing the long line of her throat to the sun.

"Could you have found a bigger hat? Perhaps one that doubles as a hang glider or maritime vessel?"

"Someone sounds jealous."

"Someone is on a mission," he growled in her ear, but Sterling, being Sterling, simply smiled as if he were the love of her life and not the bane of her existence.

Her dress was white with a long skirt that flowed around her in the breeze. The air was hot and stifling—the high was expected to be in the nineties, but with the heat of the Colombian sun it felt like triple digits and King thought his skin might actually catch fire. Sterling, on the other hand, looked like a cone of soft serve ice cream—cool and smooth and swirling.

"What's wrong with my hat?" She sounded almost petulant—like for all their slings and arrows, *that* was the thing that had finally hurt her.

"You know the objective is to blend in?"

"And see, here I thought the objective was to not get caught."

She was swinging their hands between them as they walked among the crowds of tourists. People rushed around them, selling cool bottles of water and little bags of coffee, paper fans and fake emeralds. He would have been tempted to buy a hat for himself, but he wasn't about to give her the satisfaction.

"You're drawing too much attention to yourself." Because of course she was. She was the only cool thing for a hundred miles. She was brighter than the sun and more refreshing than the breeze, and every person who laid eyes on her spent a moment wondering who she was or how King got lucky enough to be the man holding her hand. And it was unacceptable. Every bit of it.

"Oh, darling. I can't help drawing attention to myself. I'm adorable."

"I know." King had always prided himself on his excellent poker face, but the look on hers . . . "I mean, I know that you can't help it."

"Oh well . . ." They stopped in the shade of a church spire, and she reached for his white linen shirt—toying with the buttons. She raised her head slightly, eyes hidden from the world behind the brim of that ridiculous hat, but he could see her. He could *always* see her. There wasn't an ounce of teasing in the voice that said, "I don't say mercy, remember?"

"I remember everything."

King regretted the words as soon as they were out, but Sterling just smirked up at him.

"Because I'm special?" The tease was back in her voice.

"Because I'm cursed."

That, at last, surprised her. "What do you—"

"Okay, you two, this is a work trip, or do you need the reminder?" Merritt's voice was in his ear then. Because Merritt's voice was *always* in his head. "The shop is the one on the corner with the vines arching over the doorway." They knew this already, but Merritt wasn't in the mood to take chances. "Our man is Señor Lozano. His buyers are coming to town tomorrow morning. You need to get him to open the safe so we can see if our stones are in there. Then, if you get a chance, make the switch. If you don't, we'll send a black bag team in to do it tonight. For right now, we just have to get eyes on those stones."

"We know," King said, feeling frustrated. "We're"—he couldn't help but look down at the woman beside him—"ready."

But the strangest part was when he realized it was true.

chapter fifteen

ALEX

"Baby, come look at this one." Alex beckoned to King from across the jewelry store. "What do you think?"

She pointed through the glass to an emerald that was deep green and perfectly clear and the color of the little rings that circled the blue of King's eyes. Alex hated it instantly. She also wanted it desperately.

"Not big enough." It was the size of a postage stamp and easily worth six figures, but Michael Kingsley III managed to look at it like it was a pebble in his shoe.

"But, sir . . ." the clerk started.

"Have you seen her?" King pointed at Alex. He let his hand linger on her back, then dip to the curve of her butt and tug her closer. He was still staring when he said, "Something bigger."

"This is our largest stone on the floor at the moment, señor."

"So it's not the largest stone you have in the store?" King challenged, and the man blanched. He was young, and his suit was cheap and he had the nervous eyes of a dog that's been kicked—hard and often.

"Well, we do have one larger stone in our office safe, but I'm afraid . . ."

"We'll take it," King said.

"But you have not seen—"

"Then show it to us." King sounded impatient—maybe it was the role. Or maybe it was just him.

"It is not insured for the floor, señor. If you can come back in a few days . . ."

"Oh no!" Alex put a little extra whine in her voice. "We're leaving tomorrow. Can't we go to the office and look at it there?"

The door to the back opened and an older man emerged. Dark suit. Dark eyes. Slicked-back hair and perfect posture. Lozano. The salesman bristled just enough to show exactly who had been doing the kicking as Lozano headed their way.

"I'm afraid it's now or never, my man," King said. "Take us to the office if you have to, but if you can't find a stone worthy of us, we'll have to look elsewhere." When King looked at Alex that time, there was something like hunger in his eyes. "My wife does not wear baubles."

Maybe it was sound of hearing his inventory labeled as baubles—or maybe it was good old-fashioned greed—but Miguel Lozano stopped halfway to the door and asked, "Is there a problem?"

Sometimes covers were shelters, and sometimes covers were keys. Used properly, they could get you in anywhere (even the most exclusive jewelry store in South America). They could unlock anything (even that store's state-of-the-art safe). But, most of all, covers were reality—at least for a little while—so Alex couldn't help but feel grateful that King's cover was "American Asshole" and they didn't have to work too hard to make it stick.

"I told my wife she could pick out a present, but none of these are worthy of her."

"I've been a very good girl," Alex said, and King coughed but Lozano was looking at her, almost leering.

"Is that so?" The man's gaze traveled the length of Alex's body and she leaned a little closer to King.

She didn't need Merritt's dossier to know this man liked his women like he liked his cars—fast and sleek and meant for far younger men with better reflexes. Alex could tell from the way he watched her. King was unnecessary then. Just a prop—a crutch. She wasn't afraid of Lozano, but she was glad not to be alone in his presence. Because her cover wouldn't want that.

Her cover wanted Michael Kingsley.

So Alex let herself gaze up at him. His hand was warm through the thin fabric of her dress. It felt good against the chill of the air conditioner. She rested her hand on the linen of his shirt. Toyed with the buttons.

"What kind of stone would the lady prefer?" Lozano asked, but Alex didn't face him. There was a loose thread on King's shirt and it was, suddenly, the most fascinating thing in the world.

"Tell him." King's voice was raw and low and so close, she could feel his breath on her cheek.

"Oh. Well, I want a big stone on a long chain. But not too long. Just long enough to dangle . . ." She blushed and looked away, too embarrassed to say it.

"Tell him." King wasn't coughing anymore. His eyes were dark and his lips were parted and it was like this whole moment was a punishment—or a dare. She'd made her bed, his look said. He was going to make her lie in it.

"Here." Alex brought her fingertip to the neckline of her sundress and brushed against her cleavage. She watched King's gaze go dark.

"Here?" King's finger dipped in beside hers, rubbed against her soft skin, and so help her, it was all she could do not to whimper. The air was getting sucked out of the room, and for a moment, their eyes locked. Alex felt herself sway. She was actually grateful for the way his arm wrapped around her, anchoring her and keeping her close.

"Like I said . . ." King never took his eye off Alex and his finger stayed tucked inside her neckline, but it was the look that had them entangled. "We're going to need that bigger stone." One more brush of his finger. Deeper. Slower. "She's been a *very* good girl."

Alex was going to kill him for that. Later. But right then his gaze was like a tether and she couldn't bring herself to break it.

Because of the cover. And the mission. And the lie that even Alex was tempted to believe.

"I see." Lozano spoke to his employee in rapid Spanish, something about a call from a customer and a timeline being moved up. Lozano needed to lock up the store because whoever was coming was in a hurry and they didn't like company.

She could see on King's face that he'd heard it too. That he knew what it meant. And a silent conversation took place between the two of them.

Our buyer is on the way, isn't he?

Yes.

We're not going to have the option of breaking in tonight, are we?

No.

We have to do something now, don't we?

You are going to do nothing. I will do something.

I could do something.

Do not—

"Tell me what you're interested in, señor." Lozano was talking to King because King was The Man, and The Man had the money and the power. And, besides, King's finger was still tucked into the front of Alex's dress, which meant no one was paying attention to Alex's eyes—which was exactly how Alex liked it.

King was talking about carats and cut and clarity, but Alex was aware of the puppy clerk going to flip the sign to CLOSED. She could see the sky getting dark outside, but, mostly, she was aware of the way Lozano kept glancing at the door, nervous and distracted, even if he didn't want to show it. He was subtly shifting side to side, and his left hand kept brushing over his jacket pocket, as if to make sure something was still in there.

Something the size of a small pouch.

Something heavy.

Something he might have already taken out of the safe.

When Alex pushed away from King, he flinched, like he hadn't realized he was still holding her. Like he'd forgotten she was there. But she was. She was there and she was just as good as King. Just as covert and twice as sneaky, and in the next moment Alex was teetering, swaying . . .

"I don't feel so . . ." She slumped in Lozano's direction. Instantly, the man's arms went around her, and Alex didn't even try to move away. "I'm so sorry. The room's spinning . . ."

"What's wrong?" There was fire in King's eyes.

"I need . . ." She was practically clinging to Lozano. "I don't know. The room just sort of . . ." She swayed again for good measure, but King was already pulling her away from Lozano and sweeping her up into his arms.

"What's wrong?" His eyes were soft, but his voice was hard.

"It's nothing." She cupped his face. "I just got a little light-headed." She glanced at Lozano. "It happens sometimes now. Because of the baby."

chapter sixteen

KING

The air outside was hot and thick. It was going to rain. Vendors were packing up their stalls, and tourists were making their way back to hotels and cruise ships, so the streets were emptier than they had been as King carried Alex down the cobblestones.

They should get a cab. Call for backup or extraction. Maybe a straitjacket or a zookeeper.

"What was that?" King looked down at the woman in his arms.

"What was what?" She had the nerve to cock an eyebrow, like she'd just pulled ahead in a race he hadn't even realized they were running, which was partially true. King hadn't had a clue what was happening when she went limp, literally falling into Lozano's arms. King had felt his heart stop beating. It didn't start back until he said—

"*Baby*, Sterling? Baby?"

No operative had ever looked prouder. "I thought that was an excellent touch."

They were a block away from Lozano's shop, so King stopped and tipped Alex out of his arms, then pressed her against the side of a building, hand on her cheek, like he was still worried. Like he cared and wasn't contemplating murder.

A dark SUV pulled to a stop in the shade of the vines that arched over Lozano's doors. Some hired muscle got out and opened the back door for a man who was far older than King had been expecting. Dark hair. Dark suit. Dark glasses. The man stopped and scanned the street, and King swore he would remember that face—he had to. They didn't have a name, but this was better than nothing.

"Are you feeling better, sweetheart?" he asked with exaggerated sweetness. "Proud of yourself?"

"So proud," she said.

Lozano opened the doors and the buyer went into the shop, leaving his goons by the door. "Well, I hope you're happy because there goes our chance of getting into the back room."

"We don't need to get into the back room." She was walking her fingers up his chest like his heart was the real safe and she was going to crack it.

"Of course we—" King pulled back. He didn't like the look in her eye, the cocky gleam and knowing smirk. "What . . ."

And then he felt her hand slip into his pocket. Something heavy but soft landed there. Something with a familiar size and weight and . . . no. "Is that . . ."

"The ten million dollars' worth of emeralds that Lozano had in his pocket?" she asked with mock surprise. "Oh my gosh, I think it is! How did those get in there?" He actually thought it was an excellent question, but Alex just rolled her eyes. "Come on . . . sweetheart. You had your finger down my dress; where did you think Lozano was looking? It's a *very* nice dress."

"Yeah." King couldn't help but huff. "I'm sure the *dress* was what had his attention."

It was the first time he'd ever seen her blush.

"He was never going to take us to the back, but then I saw a bulge in his pocket—"

"I'm not going to say what I'm thinking right now." King pinched the bridge of his nose.

"You're just jealous." She sounded smug. "I saw. I swooned. I swapped. I didn't learn that at the Farm—"

"Clearly."

"I improvised—"

He stepped closer, crowding against her. "That wasn't improvisation. That was playing games you can't win."

"I already won."

"Did we?" He honestly wasn't sure anymore. Maybe it was the

coming storm or the eerily quiet streets, but something made the hairs on King's arms stand up. He glanced back to the store and the SUV and the guards. "Because from where I'm standing, the buyer's muscle is extremely interested in us right now. And interested—in case you didn't know—is bad."

"That's okay." She sidled closer, gazing up at him with wide-eyed . . . lust. Yes. That was the only word that described it. "We have Lozano's stones. And Lozano has ours—"

"Which is the last thing we want them to know!" King felt like he might snap in half with the words.

"We left because you were very concerned about your wife. Because you love me. And you cherish me. And you want me."

His jaw ticked. "Well, how do you propose we—"

King didn't want to kiss Alex Sterling. He'd never thought about it or considered it or woken up dreaming of such a terrible, heinous thing.

And yet it felt inevitable when he leaned down and pressed his lips to hers. When her hands gripped him tighter as the sky opened up and the thunder struck and the world disappeared behind a curtain of hard, hot rain.

An engine revved. Headlights burst on, cutting through the storm like a spotlight on the raindrops. But when Alex tried to pull away, King had no choice but to cup the back of her head with one hand—fingers in her hair, eyes on her lips.

"Kiss me," he ordered. "And don't stop. Don't you dare stop."

So that's exactly what she did.

It didn't have to change anything—mean anything. It was just another cover, another lie. And after this . . . Well, it was a big world full of dark corners. If he was smart and careful and good, chances were he'd never lay eyes on Alexandra Sterling again.

chapter seventeen

Present Day
Las Vegas, Nevada

ALEX

The elevator was scuffed from decades of laundry carts and room service trays. It felt like they were a million miles away from the swirling lights and ringing bells of the casino floor, so Alex wasn't quite prepared a minute later when the doors slid open to silence. There was thick carpet and a long hall and, out the window, a view that seemed to stretch forever. They were on one of the guest floors, evidently. The *top* floor. And somehow Alex wasn't even surprised when King let them into the biggest hotel suite she'd seen since Cartagena.

"Oh yes. Very covert. I'm sure no one is monitoring this place." She looked at him. "That was sarcasm, by the way. In case it was too subtle."

"Trust me, Sterling, 'subtle' has never been a word I associate with you."

She batted her eyelashes at him. "Oh, you charmer."

The glance he shot her was lethal, and Alex had to bite back a laugh as she looked around the opulent room. Floor-to-ceiling windows overlooked the Strip. There was a balcony and plunge pool, a sunken living room and bar. Judging by the number of doors, there had to be at least two bedrooms. She watched King walk to a galley kitchen and tap a switch. The lights came on and the windows went dim. It was like he controlled the sun.

"We'll be safe here," he said simply.

"And you know this because . . ."

She had never seen Michael Kingsley look guilty—not until he glanced away and muttered, "Because I own it."

It actually took a moment for the words to land. "You *what*?"

She'd honestly forgotten about the handcuffs until she tried to spin away and got tugged back too quickly. He started throwing open drawers with his free hand, finally finding a small leather-wrapped kit and unzipping it with his teeth.

"Stay still," he ordered, but the angle was weird, and he wasn't as dexterous with his left hand. Alex could have stood there for a week, watching him struggle. It was literally the most fun she could remember having in days.

"Do you need some help?"

"I do not." The words were crisp and brittle.

"Because it *looks like* . . ."

"Here." They must have been in worse shape than she thought for him to hand over the tools that quickly.

Two seconds later, Alex's cuff was popping open and she was wriggling her fingers. It took all her self-control not to say *ta-da*, but King just grunted and held out his own hand. A moment later, his cuff sprang open. They were separate. They were . . . free.

On instinct, Alex looked at the door, like maybe she should turn around and walk away. Like maybe she was safer on the street than she was with him. She'd spent the last year telling herself she'd gotten good at hiding. But she was wrong, evidently. The red ring around her wrist was proof that someone had found her. Someone who wasn't King. But that might have been because he hadn't even bothered to look.

"Go ahead. Run if you want to." The voice was darker than the windows. "Goodness knows I couldn't stop you if I tried."

He sounded bitter and cold, and Alex didn't want to argue. She didn't want to fight, and she absolutely refused to explain. They were both better as free agents. That was true a year ago and it was true now.

"King—"

"You can go take a shower if you want to. I'll scrounge up something for you to wear."

He went into one of the bedrooms and Alex wandered toward the darkened windows. It was the middle of the day, but it looked like the middle of the night. And that just made Alex remember—

She didn't know what time it was. She didn't even know what day it was.

"King?"

"Yeah?" he called from a bedroom.

"What day is it?" Alex couldn't imagine a more embarrassing question, but (for once) the man in the other room didn't mock or scold. He just came out and tossed a heavy robe in her direction, then picked up a remote control, and the TV flickered to life.

"Thursday. January sixteenth," he read from the hotel information page. "Eight forty-five a.m."

There were dark spots on the edge of Alex's memory, looming like a total eclipse that stretched across her mind. She remembered waking in her little cottage, groggy because she'd stayed up too late, *one-more-chaptering* herself until she finished a book at four a.m. She remembered making a grocery list and being out of coffee. She remembered . . . home. And solitude. And silence.

And missing . . .

"So?" King sounded impatient.

"Okay." She had to get her act together. "It's Thursday. I remember . . . Wednesday? No. Tuesday. I remember two days ago." She turned and looked out the window. "I lost two days," she whispered, but the reflection in the glass just stared back, indifferent and uncaring. She wished he'd go back to hating her. It was so much better than this.

"Okay."

"See, now it's your turn. What's the last thing *you* remember?"

He turned off the TV. "Yeah. Sure. Two days sounds about right."

"But what do you remember?"

"I don't remember anything!" He was mad at himself for shout-ing, Alex could tell. Not because he'd hurt her feelings but because he'd showed his cards. "I don't remember."

"I know—"

"No. You don't." He went to the kitchen and poured a glass of water. "You don't have any idea what this feels like." He drank the water down in three whole gulps.

"You were in . . . Scotland?" At least she didn't choke on the word.

"I think so. That's the last place I remember, but I come here a lot," King told her. "Just because I don't remember being in Vegas doesn't mean I wasn't here when they grabbed me."

"Oh. Okay. That makes sense." But it didn't. Not really. Alex had never heard King talk about Vegas. He didn't even like Monte Carlo. He didn't gamble because he couldn't keep himself from counting cards, and Michael Kingsley was far too noble to cheat. He barely drank, and he wasn't a fan of crowds, and there was literally no rea-son for the man she knew to have an apartment here. But that just meant one thing: she didn't know him anymore. "What aren't you telling me?"

King was a brilliant strategist and a focused operative, but he wasn't a great liar—not when he was talking to her.

"Like I said, no one knows I own this place. Technically, I *don't* own this place. And it's sitting on top of a fortress. I'm not an easy target here. But, more than that . . . someone tracked *you* down, and so help me"—he let out a laugh that was more like a growl—"I'd like to know how. So whoever they were and however they did it, we know one thing . . ."

"They're good," Alex filled in.

King looked at her, long and hard. "They're very, very good." The moment felt charged and ready to blow. "Guest room's through there." He pointed to the closed door on the far side of the room. "Go clean up."

"We have to call it in."

"Do we?" A chuckle shot out of him. Michael Kingsley—a man who had probably memorized the Moscow Rules when he was five—

actually laughed at the idea of following standard operating procedure, and Alex didn't know what was happening. Up was down. Black was white. "Do we have to call it in? Because I'm out. Remember?" He ran a hand through his hair. "The only question is, aren't you out, too?"

And that was the problem. The elephant wasn't just in the room, it was standing on Alex's chest and making it hard to breathe. "I . . ."

"A *year*, Alex." She was Alex again—not Sterling—and something about that made her close her eyes, but when she did, images danced on the back of her eyelids, black and white and far too quick—like an old movie in fast forward. Too fast to read their lips. "I just lost forty-eight hours," he said, "but you've been missing for a year."

"I wasn't missing." Her voice was lighter than she felt. "I knew exactly where I—"

A crashing sound cut her off, and when Alex turned, she saw the glass King was drinking from lying shattered on the floor. The wall was wet. And he wasn't looking at her anymore.

"There are people in this world who care about you, Sterling. They were worried."

"People like Merritt?" She wasn't sure what made her ask it, but as soon as the words were out, she wanted to beg him not to answer. So why did it hurt so much when he didn't?

"Shower through there." He pointed to the guest room again. "Use it. Don't use it. Jump out the window for all I care. Just ask yourself this: Do you really want to make that call and explain where you've been for the past year and why you ran and what the hell you've gotten yourself into now?"

"Why does this have to be about me?"

"Because trouble usually is." He didn't even turn around before he slammed the door.

The robe was soft and warm, and Alex was finally clean and dry, but, more than anything, it was a relief to have finally stopped shaking.

She didn't ask for advice. She didn't need his permission. Alex knew what she was *supposed* to do, and her gut was telling her what she *had* to do, but it was still harder than it should be to drop down on the bed and reach for the phone.

Because King was right.

(Oh, how she hated that sentence.)

King had *walked away*, but Alex had *run away*, and she'd never been more aware of the difference.

The Agency might not know where she was yet. There might be a chance she could take the stairs to the lobby and disappear onto the Strip and into the desert and lose another year of her life. But it wasn't the last year that bothered her. It was the last forty-eight hours. It was the dark shed and the handcuffs and the man on the other side of the wall.

So Alex picked up the phone and dialed the number she'd hoped she'd never have to use again.

"Secure line," she said to the silence that answered. "Nine one seven alpha six." Her heart pounded and her mouth went dry. "It's me. I . . . I think I need help."

chapter eighteen

KING

Spies live and die by their senses. It was something King had known for as long as he'd known what to call them. He knew to trust only what he could see and smell and taste and feel, but right then, he was more concerned about his hearing. He was standing, too still, in the penthouse, listening to the sound of running water, not knowing if he wanted it to stop or run forever.

She was there. In his apartment. Showering on the other side of the wall, and King stayed frozen, lulled into a kind of trance by the sound.

When the water turned off, he went to the kitchen and opened the refrigerator. When he'd called down for the clothes, he'd asked the concierge to send up the usual provisions, and now they had milk and bread. Fresh eggs and cheese and some veggies, so he pulled out an omelet pan and went to work because King had to stay busy. Besides, he wanted to break something and the eggs were nice and handy.

"Thank you. For the clothes."

He stilled at the sound of the voice and felt his eyes cinch tight. He didn't dare turn around. He just said, "Oh. You're still here? I thought you'd run off while my back was turned." He tossed the words over his shoulder. Like a grenade.

"I wanted to say goodbye." Alex gestured down to the clothes he'd laid on the bed. It was nothing fancy. Some jeans. A shirt. Some shoes. Lingerie. (But King tried very hard not to think about the lingerie.) "So do you have a girlfriend who's going to wonder where her outfit went?"

Any other woman might have sounded like she was fishing for information, but Alex probably just wanted to know who she might have to kill.

He slid a pat of butter into the pan and watched it slide. "I know your size, Alex." The pan sizzled, and it was all King could do not to let his insides melt. "The building has a concierge. I made a phone call." He glanced at her. "I'll add it to your bill."

"Well, thank you."

"Be careful out there." He gave the eggs a quick whisk, then started slicing a ripe, red tomato. "I'd ask if you're hungry, but I'm assuming you've got to run."

"King—"

"I'd appreciate it if you wouldn't tell anyone about this place—at least until I can find alternate accommodations—"

"Michael," she snapped, and he froze.

How dare she call him that? How dare she stand there, bruised and blistered and beautiful? How dare she.

"So this is it?" She threw her arms out wide, and something about the gesture was too much for him. He should have put down the knife.

"I'd ask you to stay, but we both know how that turned out the last time."

"Last time we hadn't both been *kidnapped*."

"What do you want me to say, Sterling?" He gestured with the knife, but she didn't even flinch because she didn't need a weapon to take him. She could kill him with a look, slice him to ribbons with a word.

"You could say—" she started hard, but the rest didn't come. It was like the words were lodged in her throat, trapped in her mind. It was like they were a record that was skipping and something wouldn't let her move forward.

"Say . . ." he prompted when a shadow passed beyond the darkened window. Too big to be a bird. Too close to be a plane. And coming way too fast to do anything other than shout, "Look out!"

In the next moment, glass was raining down and a hot dry wind was blowing through the place where the windows used to be.

"Not again!" Alex shouted, because there were two guys soaring through the hole in the glass. Rappelling harnesses and cords and semiautomatics blasting up the room.

Alex dove behind the counter as King stood up and hurled the knife into the leg of the first man, who dropped just as King leapt over the counter and kicked him in the face.

The other man started for Alex in the kitchen and she reached for the hot pan. Butter ran down the side and streaked across the floor as she swung it. There was a sickening sizzle as hot pan met face, and the man screamed and fell to the floor, unmoving.

"I'd like to point out, I'm not killing anyone!" she said, a little snide.

"I appreciate the restraint."

King kicked the gun away from the man with the knife in his leg. He took off the man's own belt and made a tourniquet except . . . there was already too much blood and the man was already gone.

"Shit. Must have hit the femoral."

"That one's on you." She looked like she was almost enjoying this, and maybe that's why she didn't feel the movement behind her, didn't sense the threat—but King did.

In a flash, he pulled the knife from the dead man's leg and hurled it across the room, right at the chest of the man with the burned face who was up and lunging for Alex. The man staggered forward—one step. Two. Then he dropped on the spot. Dead.

"Oh." Alex sounded almost disappointed, but all King could do was roll his eyes as he looked at the two dead bodies and the gaping hole where the window used to be.

Curtains blew wildly. Alex's hair waved in the breeze. There was glass everywhere and his best omelet pan was ruined, but all King could think was—

"How the hell did they find us?" He wanted to tear the building down brick by brick, sift through the desert, grain of sand by grain of sand. He wanted answers. No, King *needed* answers because he never did well without them. "It's not like you called . . ." He had to trail off at the look on her face. "You called it in?"

"Maybe they found us because you brought us to *your* apartment? That *you* own."

"One, I don't own it. Technically. And two, we didn't exactly have other options."

"That is a matter of opinion."

"It's math!"

"That's not what math is!"

King went to the second body and kicked it over. Alex was already leaning over, rummaging through the pockets and she pulled out a phone.

"I don't suppose you have a Faraday pouch handy?" she asked, and King pulled one from a drawer.

"I've never been more insulted in my life," he said as she dropped the dead man's cell phone inside, where no signal could get in or out. And, together, they kept searching his pockets, but there was nothing else. No papers. No IDs. No credit cards or cash or handy *If found, please return to . . .* stickers.

"He's clean." Alex kicked the body for good measure, and King pinched the bridge of his nose. "What? He can't feel it. And it was just a little—" She did it again. "Who knows you own this place?" she asked.

"I don't own it—"

"So you keep saying, and yet . . ." She gestured toward the two dead bodies as if that made her point. And, in her defense, it kind of did.

"Two, maybe three, people know I have sole access. All high-level associates of mine. All people I can trust."

"*Can* you trust them?" She gave a *Can you really?* head tilt.

"Yes." King was a little insulted. Mostly that she had a point. "What about you? Who did you call?"

"Who do you think?" The words were sharper than usual. She wasn't in a teasing mood when the tables turned.

"You called Merritt?"

"Of course I called Merritt."

"Well, she would have told the Agency . . ."

The facts were simple and the truth was clear, but that didn't mean King had to like it.

"We can't trust my people, and we can't trust . . ." He gave her a caustic look.

"Are you asking if I have *people*?"

"I don't know who you have, Sterling. I don't know you."

"But you're stuck with me." She gave the smirk that had been haunting his dreams for the better part of a decade. "Because"—she hesitated. It was hard to admit—"you're right."

"Can I get you to say that again? Slower and for the record?"

"We can't trust the Agency. So I guess we have no choice but to trust . . ."

She searched his eyes and King searched his soul. It was like a whole other person who whispered, "Each other."

Only Alex could make it sound like an adventure when she said, "We have no safe house, no money, no allies, and no clues."

But that was when King saw it—a tiny image on the dead man's skin. He dropped to a crouch and pulled back the sleeve to reveal the tattoo—a triangle made out of three sharp daggers.

"Oh, I wouldn't say nothing." King couldn't help but smile when he said, "Look familiar?"

chapter nineteen

Eight Years Ago
An Airstrip the CIA Doesn't Admit Exists

Technically, the little airstrip on the outskirts of Lisbon didn't exist, but then again, neither did the woman who was standing on the tarmac, waiting for King when he arrived.

White hair blew wildly around her face, and her lips were painted the same shade of red she'd worn since he was a child. For all he knew, that was their natural color. She looked like a woman out of time, with her long trench coat belted tightly at her waist and billowing around her legs in the wind. She looked like she might have a derringer in a thigh holster. Like there was a German scientist she had to get over the wall, right then. She was even wearing a hat.

So King wanted to smile when he saw her. He wanted to tease her, but then he'd have to become someone who knew how to tease and that sounded like a lot of unnecessary effort, so he just said, "Hello, Margaret."

"Michael!" she exclaimed like she hadn't been expecting him—like *what a small world* and *fancy meeting you here*. As if she hadn't sent for him, specifically, and told him to meet her at this very time and place. "Come give an old woman a hug."

He hated when she said things like that. She wasn't old—except she was. It was a quantifiable, objective thing. She was in good health, yes. Youthful, even, for her age. Which was . . . old. And King hated the reminder. When he bent and wrapped his arms around her, she seemed smaller than she had last year, and he hated that most of all.

"Why do I get the feeling this is a trap?" He looked around the airstrip that was little more than a bumpy stretch of asphalt. "And why am I standing here instead of being up to my eyelids in code back in London?"

"Computers." She scoffed and waved a hand as if to say, *That's kids' stuff.* "Oh, Michael, you wound me. I wouldn't need to trap you. Now, do you have everything you need?"

"Everything I need *for what*?"

"Oh, never mind." She waved the worry away. "I thought of everything, and your suitcase is already on board." She motioned to the small private jet that was idling on the far end of the tarmac.

"On board going where?" King wasn't just skeptical. He was downright leery.

"Paradise."

He didn't believe her. "Why me?"

"You remember our emeralds?" It was a rhetorical question, of course. King remembered everything, and Merritt knew that better than most. "They've been popping up all over the map, but most have ended up in the hands of this man." She pulled a blurry photograph from an interior coat pocket.

"A hard copy?" He gave her a chastising look. "You know, we have digital things now."

"No one ever hacked my pocket," she said, then pointed down at the picture. It was grainy in a way that suggested someone had blown the image up from a much wider shot, so either the photographer was very bad—or the target was very good. King highly suspected it was the latter. "Do you recognize him?"

The photo was so blurry, it was hard to tell much besides the fact that he was a generic-looking white guy between twenty-five and forty-five. But King could be certain of one thing. "He doesn't look familiar. Should he?"

"Unlikely." She slipped the picture back in her pocket, then looped her arm through his and started leading him toward the waiting jet. "He just popped up about a year ago, making deals."

"What kind of deals?"

"Arms. Technology. Muscle-for-hire. A veritable one-stop shop for covert goods and services. We don't know much about him—just that he is very private. Very careful. He's not just brawn, Michael. This one has brains. We want to know what he's selling and to whom."

"And what, exactly, am I going to do when I get to . . ." He almost choked on the word. "Paradise?"

"Very little." It was an instruction and a warning. "You're going to get in. Drop a bug or two. And get out. That's it. We don't want to spook him. This is an old-school *SigInt* operation. Period. Which means—"

"Signal Intelligence, yes. I'm fairly certain those were some of my first words. Right after *Momma* and *ball* and—"

"No." Merritt's smile was almost wistful. "Your first word was *no*."

Of course it was. It would probably be his last word too. He should say it now, in fact—

"If all you need is a bug, you could send anyone. So I will ask again, Merritt my dear, why am *I* here?"

If he hadn't known her so well, he might have missed the sheepish look in her eye. Like she'd been hoping he wouldn't stop and ask about the fine print, but he wasn't getting on that plane until she read every word aloud.

"It doesn't matter—"

"Anything that has you biting your lip like that matters a lot, so—"

"There's been chatter." The wind was cold and the clouds were dark and threatening rain, but that wasn't why she shivered. "Our man has been doing business with someone."

"Sounds like he's been doing business with a lot of someones, so why—"

"Someone named Nikolai." Blue eyes looked into his. Piercing and icy calm. In moments like this, no one could ever mistake Margaret Merritt for an old woman. She was more deity than flesh and blood.

"Are you sure?"

"Positive."

"Have you told—"

"No." She shook her head. "Your father doesn't know. And he won't hear it from me. But he still has friends at the Agency. Allies— and enemies. And even if he didn't . . ."

King knew what she was going to say, but he didn't want to hear it. "Nikolai doesn't exist, Merritt, you know that."

"I *don't* know that. And neither do you."

"Grandfather always said—"

"Your grandfather is dead, Michael. And he wasn't all-knowing."

"If Nikolai were real—which he isn't—he'd be . . ." King trailed off and tried not to blush scarlet, but Merritt only cocked an eyebrow.

"As old as me?" She laughed. "Oh, dear boy. The thing you need to know about old spies . . ." She inched closer and dropped her voice, but it was the look in her eyes that stopped him. "We have absolutely nothing to lose."

She was right, of course, but King didn't want to admit it, so he just shook his head. "Someone has a sick sense of humor."

King waited for his heart to stop pounding, but Merritt merely answered with a sigh.

"Or a good sense of history?" She tucked her hands in her pockets. "In any case, we need ears in that house, and I thought you might like to be the one to put them there."

This job was never like the movies. It wasn't car chases or black-tie galas. Just well-placed bugs and scandalous secrets that weaved across the decades like a fuse. King had spent his whole life waiting for the *boom*, but something in his eyes must have given him away because Merritt pulled back.

"Of course, I know this might be hard for you, and if you'd rather—"

"I'll do it." He had to do it.

"I tried to spare you, you know," she admitted. "But the man owns a private compound. On an *island*."

"The Agency has divers. Submarines. Probably a mermaid or two."

"It's a fortress, Michael." Now she sounded like a very tired mother who just wished the little boy would run along and play and stop asking so many questions. "We have satellite surveillance. We've sent up a few drones. But, for the most part, we would be sending a team in blind, so we need to get boots on that island. There's only one weakness that we've found—one potential access point. He only owns *half* the island. The other half was undeveloped until recently, but a new business just opened its doors on the far side."

Suddenly, King got it. Or at least part of it.

"That's my way in?"

She nodded, a little too slowly.

"Merritt . . ." The word was a warning. "Why do I get the feeling you're *still* hiding something?"

She gave the smirk of a woman who is *always* hiding something. "It's a high-end retreat. For wealthy couples whose marriages are in trouble."

King couldn't help himself—he snorted. "Are you saying I'm going to be your boy-toy?" He looked down at the woman who was like a grandmother to him—waited for her to laugh or tease.

But all she did was turn when the jet door slowly opened and a familiar blonde head peeked out from the top of the stairs and shouted, "Hi, honey. I'm home."

chapter twenty

Present Day
Somewhere Over Nevada

ALEX

"This was a mistake," Alex said for the fourth time in ninety minutes.

"You are more than welcome to walk to the island . . . except . . . wait. *It's an island.*" At some point during the past six years, King had become someone who looked at home on a private jet on its way to a private island, and Alex didn't know what to make of it. "So if you have a better plan, my dear . . ."

"I'm not your dear." Instantly, Alex wanted to pull the words back. It was the kind of thing she used to say . . . before they dropped their guards. Before everything changed. Before Scotland.

"You said we were the only people we can trust," she insisted.

"And here I am . . . *trusting you.*" On anyone else it might have sounded smug, but on him it was just normal.

She ran a hand over a leather cushion. It was probably made from the skin of some endangered animal. It was almost disgustingly, criminally soft. "Well, the last I checked, your penthouse apartment was being shot up by a bunch of armed commandos."

"There were only two commandos." He sounded unimpressed.

"So, tell me . . . Exactly how is *this*"—she motioned at the glossy interior of the even glossier jet—"any different than a penthouse in the sky? A very crashable, explodeable, vulnerable-to-surface-to-air-missiles . . . penthouse?"

"Are you finished?"

Alex had to think. "Hijackable penthouse!" She was a little too proud of that last one, but King just looked tired and annoyed.

"This *penthouse*"—he made quote marks with his hands—"is not mine."

"Neither was the last one." Alex thought that was a very good point, but then she spotted a basket of snacks and decided that if she had to die at thirty thousand feet, at least she could go out with a belly full of Pringles.

"The plane isn't mine either, and no one will know you and I are on it."

"See, the problem is"—she plopped a chip whole into her mouth, cherishing the crisp salty taste and the scowl on his face as he waited for her to chew—"we are back to *you*"—she pointed for effect—"and *me*. Not being able to trust *anyone*."

He looked annoyed, mainly because she'd made something of a point. Which Alex took as something of a win. "The owner owes me a favor. This individual is very private."

Another chip. Another question. "Who?"

King snatched the Pringles from her hands and took a handful, as if to say, *These are mine now. You have lost your Pringles privileges.*

"They. Are. Very. Private."

Alex took a deep breath, suddenly bored, and stole her chips back. Only the crumbs were left, but the joke was on him because the crumbs were the best part. She tipped the canister up and drank them down. "Must be some favor."

King turned to the airplane's window. "It is."

"I'm going to go count the parachutes . . ." Alex got up and gestured to the back of the jet.

"You do that."

"For when we get shot out of the sky."

"I assumed."

"Because this is a *bad idea*."

"Suit yourself." He wasn't even paying attention and she almost missed the man who used to look at her like she was nothing but a mistake. Because that guy, she understood. That guy was calm, cool contempt, but this guy was indifference. Alex wanted to throw him off that airplane just to make him scream.

"I'm going to get some sleep." He started lowering his chair to a flat position, then touched a button and the cabin lights went dim. Alex should have felt more at home there, in the darkness and the shadows. It's what her life had been for years, neither black nor white, good nor evil. Her whole world was gray, but the man in the other chair was gunmetal. Darker and harder and even in the darkness, she had to look away.

She couldn't face him when she said, "Do we need to compare notes?"

"What notes?" The words were like ice. She hoped he broke a tooth.

"It's called a cover, King. They taught us about them. At spy school."

"Don't call it . . ." She watched the shadow shake its head. "We have our cover."

She flicked on the reading light over his seat and Alex watched him squint against the glare. "We *had* a cover. Nine years ago. It's not like it's fresh on our—"

"Eight," he corrected.

"What?"

King looked her dead in the eye and she wished she could turn the light off. Grab a parachute and jump. She wanted to turn the hourglass over and make time run the other way, because his eyes were as dark as the voice that said, "It was eight years, four months, and five days ago. And I remember every word."

The plane hit a patch of rough air and dipped suddenly. Or maybe Alex's stomach did that all on its own, but that didn't change the fact that she had to steady herself as she dropped onto the armrest of the seat across the aisle.

"Yay. Congratulations. I'm sure if they test us on the timeline, we'll be set."

"Indeed." He opened a compartment and pulled out a blanket, opened it with a flick of his wrist.

"Do we have kids?"

"What?" Oh, that got his attention.

"They're going to ask. About that. And about a million more things and—"

"Oh, I stand corrected, it's going to be incredibly difficult to convince people that ours is a marriage in trouble."

But he still didn't get it. Michael Kingsley was, without a doubt, the most brilliant person she had ever known. He was also the dumbest, and it was all Alex could do not to roll her eyes.

"The problem isn't that eight years, four months, and five days have passed and we still hate each other, Kingsley." She stood and started down the narrow aisle. "The problem will be getting anyone to believe we made it this long."

She heard him roll over, call out, "They believed us just fine the last time."

But Alex had to stop. And remember.

"That was before."

He pushed up on an elbow and looked at her. "Before what?"

He knew. He knew, but he was going to make her say it.

Alex turned off the light. "Before Scotland."

chapter twenty-one

Eight Years Ago
Somewhere off the Coast of Portugal

ALEX

"I'm going to kill her."

Alex shouldn't have gotten so much pleasure out of another person's suffering, but she'd spent the last two years having the CIA burn away all of her compassion, so she thought she might as well kick back and relish the way King twisted and squirmed.

He'd already banged his head on the low ceiling of the jet, and his long legs didn't exactly fit under the table that sat between them. The plane was lavish but small, just a (CIA-issued) pilot in the cockpit and four club chairs in middle—facing each other two by two. A sofa stretched across the back, but Alex sat by the window, legs crossed, manicured fingers drumming on the table in front of her, watching King shift, trying to get comfortable.

The island was a ninety-minute flight from the Portuguese shore, and, like it or not, she and the grouchy bear across the aisle had work to do, but he was still twisting and cursing and mumbling, "Going to kill her," under his breath.

"Why, Michael Kingsley! You mean there's someone you hate more than *me*?" She almost sounded offended, but then he glared in her direction.

"You're *why* I'm going to kill her."

He looked like a two-year-old who really wanted to have a temper tantrum, but it sounded like *so much work*. Alex didn't want to laugh at him. And she *really* didn't want to smile, so she reached for the materials Merritt had handed her that morning.

"Come on. We have work to do."

King grabbed the briefing packet and scanned through the things that Alex already knew.

"Is this right?" He sounded . . . concerned.

"You tell me, you're the genius."

"This isn't funny, Sterling."

"I'm not laughing, Kingsley."

She reached for a large manila envelope and spilled the contents out onto the table.

"This says we are tasked with infiltrating a literal fortress." He scanned down through the fact sheet, voice so low she wasn't even sure if the words were meant for her. "Portuguese fort . . . Volcanic rock . . . Shallow harbor . . . Decommissioned . . . You've got to be kidding me." Now Alex knew he was talking to her. "This." He tossed a glossy photograph onto the top of the pile. "This is the best picture we have of the place?"

It was nothing but a rooftop poking through a layer of fog and surrounded by mountains. "The peaks are tall enough that cloud cover makes satellite imaging an issue."

"You think?" Now he sounded angry.

"I don't control the clouds, Kingsley."

But his attention was already back on the materials.

"Yay. There are volcanic tunnels. And . . . excellent. It was once a stronghold for pirates." She was almost certain that was his sarcastic voice, but she didn't want to ask him.

"I hope they packed me a bikini. I've been doing a lot of crunches. I think—"

"Sterling!"

"What?"

"Have you looked at this?" He sounded . . . scared. Or at the very least concerned.

"I have!" Alex sounded excited. "I've always wanted to see a black sand beach. Do you think they thought of sunscreen? I hope they thought of—"

"This isn't an all-inclusive beach vacation."

"Oh, I'm pretty sure they'll feed us."

"This is a mission!"

"I know." Now Alex wasn't teasing anymore. "And I've already read all about it. I know how high the peaks are. And that we're the fifth team the Agency has tried to send in. I know that there's one airstrip that services both sides of the island, but that's the extent of the crossover because there's a literal mountain in the middle. I know one side is black sand beaches and waterfalls and hot springs while the other is nothing but volcanic rock and a real steep climb, sheer cliff faces, and an old fort with literal cannons. I know what we're facing, Kingsley. And I also know . . ." But Alex couldn't bring herself to finish.

"What?" He wasn't going to let her off that plane until she'd said it.

"They wouldn't be sending us if we couldn't do it."

"*Can* we do it?" It was like he really wanted to know—like their roles had been reversed, and for the first time, he was the outsider and she was the badass, so Alex didn't even blink when she leaned forward.

"You're smart and I'm fearless. Of course we can do it."

Instantly, Alex wanted to pull the words back, but King just looked out the window, like the answers were somewhere among the clouds. When he spoke again, the words were so soft, she almost missed them. "You're not *not smart*, you know."

She did know, but the fact that he'd said it . . .

It was all she could do not to smile.

She thought about the look on his face as he talked to Merritt on the tarmac, the guy in the shadows of the Farm. He was a man—close to thirty. But she'd seen him look like a child exactly twice. And both times—

"Who's Nikolai?"

He blinked—too fast—and spun on her. "How . . ."

"They teach lip reading at spy school." Alex felt almost guilty for a split second, but then she watched his features change and harden.

"Who's Zoe?" It wasn't a question—it was a dare.

"I asked first."

"It's need-to-know and you don't."

"We're on our way to a private island to take on an arms dealer. If that's not a need—"

"If you needed to know, then Merritt would have told you. But she didn't. So you don't." He wasn't just indignant; he was angry. And he was scared. "It doesn't matter."

"But—"

"Forget it, Sterling." Alex had seen a lot of Michael Kingsleys in the past two years. Bored and overly earnest and so stoic, she could scream. But she'd never seen him vulnerable before. And she was pretty sure she didn't like it. "Please. Please, just . . . It's not my secret to tell."

The contents of the envelope were still strewn all over the table, so Alex picked up a familiar blue booklet and looked inside. It was a good photo, and she had to bite back a smile as she slid the passport toward him. "Okay, Mr. Dixon. Let's get you ready to spend the next week with your loving wife of—"

Alex examined her own cover sheet. "Six blissful years. No way! Six? What was I? A child bride?"

She sorted through the scraps of a life that wasn't really hers. Officially, it was called pocket litter. Someone back at Langley had probably spent a week figuring out everything from the kind of gum Mr. and Mrs. Dixon would chew to the places stamped on their passports. The newest iPhone opened at Alex's touch—full of photographs and text messages and emails—receipts for clothes she didn't purchase. Lunch plans with friends she didn't have. There was an entire life spread out on that table, but none of it was real, and Alex didn't know why she felt so jealous of a woman she'd never meet but had to be.

"So . . ."

"So?" he asked.

"How were you?"

King blew out a tired breath. "I was doing a joint task force with MI6. The details are classified, I'm afraid."

"I didn't ask who you were working with or what you were doing. I asked *how* you were." The look on his face said everything, as if that was the most foreign of notions—that someone might ask. That someone might care. "You know what, never mind."

Alex started putting fake credit cards in her fake wallet and then slipped it into her fake purse. She stopped trying to talk to her fake husband.

"How were you?" a soft voice asked, and Alex froze. She didn't want to think about the answer—

A little homesick. Kind of afraid. And so lonely sometimes, it hurt. "I infiltrated the stronghold of a dictator who shall remain nameless with nothing but a push-up bra and a stiletto in my heels."

"That's not what I asked," he whispered, but his tone just said *touché*, so Alex leaned across the table and let her voice pitch low.

"I was very far away from you." Then she grinned like that was answer enough.

"Very funny, Sterling."

"Oh, now, Mr. Dixon. Is that any way to talk to your loving wife?"

Suddenly, the light in the cabin changed. A shadow crossed his face and she felt the jet dip as they broke through the clouds, but Alex couldn't look away—not until something out the window caught King's attention.

"If you were too loving, we wouldn't be going there."

It wasn't a large island. According to their intel, just a little over twenty square miles, but the peaks seemed to rise forever, rocky and jagged like a knife sticking out of the Atlantic and trying to stab the sky.

Alex couldn't help herself: she whistled. Then she reached for a button on the armrest. "Liz, can you get us a good look at this before you take us down?"

A woman's voice came through the speaker. "I can try."

The jet banked and took a slow circuit around the tiny island. They saw waterfalls and lush green foliage. Even the places that were hard and gray were also lush and green, and Alex couldn't make those two facts make sense, but there they were, right in front of her eyes.

"There." King pointed to a building near the top of the highest peak. There was a lone road zigzagging up the jagged rocks, and the whole thing looked like it had been carved into the mountain ages ago and had spent the last few centuries trying to fight the sky.

"Well, doesn't that look lovely."

"Not the word I would use," King said dryly.

"It's called sarcasm, darling."

She studied his profile in the bright, clear light that filtered through the airplane's window. There was a spark in his eye when he said, "If you say so, sweetheart."

"I do. *Dear*." Alex dropped the word like a hand grenade.

"By all means, love bucket."

Which was a step too far and Alex cringed. "Love bucket?" King looked . . . confused. Like this was a game and she'd changed the rules. "Love bucket?" Alex snapped again. "That sounds like something they'd have in a Victorian brothel. Love—"

But the plane banked again, harder and sharper, and Alex felt herself tipping and falling—right into Michael Kingsley. His hand felt impossibly large on her waist, and Alex thought it might burn a hole right through her dress—through her skin.

"Easy there, Sterling."

Alex didn't like it. Not the little dip she felt in her stomach as the plane started its rapid descent. Not the look in his eyes when the pilot said, "Hold on back there. This is gonna be quick." Not the way he gripped her tighter and tugged her down onto the plush leather seat when the plane dropped sharply over the edge of a rocky cliff and down into the lush green valley that stretched between the mountain and the sea.

Alex didn't reach for the seat belt. She didn't reach for anything. She was too busy trying to find her balance and her dignity.

On the other side of the window, the sand was black and the water was sapphire, but all Alex could think as the plane touched down and bounced along the too-short runway was *It's fake*.

Because of course it was. That was what she'd signed up for: fake names and fake loves and fake lives. They'd just landed on the island of one of the most dangerous arms dealers in the world, but somehow she felt safer there, as Mrs. Donna Dixon, than she'd ever been as herself.

The plane slowed, then stopped, but Alex didn't move off of King's lap. She didn't stand or scurry or pull on her sunglasses or her cover or her dignity. She just . . . sat there. Waiting until—

"Are you ready?" King suddenly looked like he wasn't at all sure of the answer.

"No." She didn't know where the word came from. It just popped out.

"Oh. Of course." King pulled back, and Alex waited for some insult or jab, but he just started looking around like they'd forgotten something, then he picked up a small velvet box. "I guess you'll be needing this."

And then the most infuriating man that Alex had ever known presented her with a four-carat Harry Winston. "For the cover."

Fake. Every last thing.

"And here I thought it was because of our undying love."

"Do you want it or—"

"Hey. A girl only gets Fake Married once." Which wasn't true. She'd already been fake married to him once before, but this time felt . . . "You're supposed to get down on one knee, you know? Ask my father's permission. Maybe spell out *Will you fake marry me?* in rose petals."

He closed his eyes as if to silently remind himself that Merritt was an old woman and a living legend and it would be a great mistake to kill her.

"Alexandra Sterling," he ground out, "will you be my fake wife?"

When he slipped it on her finger a moment later, Alex absolutely loathed how much she was smiling.

chapter twenty-two

Eight Years Ago
The Island

King should have stayed on the airplane.

On the mainland.

In bed.

He never should have answered Merritt's call or, for that matter, followed in his father's footsteps. But perhaps his biggest mistake was letting Alex go first down the airplane's stairs. He had to watch her tip her face up and squint against the sun, wind in her hair, as a voice called, "Welcome to Cupid's Arrow!"

"Kill me now," King must have mumbled, because Alex looked back at him, blinking and wide-eyed.

"That could be arranged, you know?" she whispered, too low to be heard over the sound of the waves and the idling jet. And then she turned away from him, as if blown by the breeze, and everything about her tightened—her shoulders and her tone. It was like a magnet hovering over a pile of metal shavings. Something snapped into place—from the line of her shoulders to the set of her jaw as she slipped on a pair of dark glasses.

She wasn't Alexandra Sterling anymore.

She was Mrs. Donna Dixon.

And she was angry.

"We are so glad you made it. How was your flight?"

King might have forgotten about the other woman, if he'd been a different kind of man. She was somewhere on the soft side of middle-aged, long flowing dress and big flowing hair that was a little too red to be natural. She looked like the kind of woman who would very much like to join a cult if only she could find one with adequate amenities. And maybe that's what she was building here, he had to think, as she eyed their jet and inched closer.

"Welcome to the place where your inner cupids will renew the arrow of love." The woman brought her hands together and bowed as if she'd just recited some ancient and sacred text and not the biggest bit of gibberish that King had ever heard in his life.

It was all he could do not to roll his eyes, but Alex didn't have that problem.

"Hello, I'm Donna. This is my husband"—she made a half-hearted gesture in King's direction—"Dimwit."

"David," King put in, but his dear wife wasn't in the mood to bother with technicalities.

"That's what I said," she muttered just loudly enough to make sure the words would carry.

He held out a hand for the woman. "David Dixon, nice to meet you."

"Charmed." The woman eyed him up and down like maybe she might be better off if David were back on the market. King couldn't help but chuckle when he saw Alex bristle.

"Donna and I are thrilled to be here. Isn't that right, sweetheart?"

"Sweetheart?" She wielded the word like a whip. And then her lips quivered and her eyes went misty. Even her skin changed color.

King was raised among the best spies to ever live. He'd studied at the foot of the masters, dining on tales of clandestine missions and covert operations. It was not at all hyperbolic to say that his grandfather alone changed the trajectory of the world. That was Michael Kingsley's bloodline—his legacy. His fate. But King had never—ever—seen anyone do what Alex did then.

She wasn't pretending to be Donna Dixon from Denver. She *was* Donna Dixon. And she was on the verge of tears.

"That's not what you called me last night."

"Darling." King kept his voice low, turning his body as if that might make the words more private. "We've been over this—"

"You mean while you were under someone else?"

"I have never cheated on you!" King shouldn't have been so offended, but he was. Her hair blew around her in the breeze and the ocean air was dewy on her skin and King felt his heart stop beating. "I haven't looked at another woman since I met you." The words turned to acid on his tongue. "So help me, I'd give anything to be lying."

King looked away and slid on his own dark glasses. Looking at her was like staring at the sun.

"Oh my." The voice brought him back. "Don't we have our work cut out for us?" The stranger slapped her hands together like *This should be fun.* "My name is Flora. I like florals." The woman gestured to her long, flower-covered dress as if they might have missed it. "I will be your personal cupid."

She gave one of those ridiculous bows again while, behind them, the staff started unloading a mountain of luggage from the cargo hold of the plane. The designer suitcases alone were probably worth ten grand, not to mention the clothes and accessories (and gear) contained within them. King only hoped it was enough. Because he had to get into that compound and then off of this island before something killed him, and at the moment, he wasn't sure which was more dangerous—the arms dealer on the other side of the mountain or the woman who was standing right beside him, staring daggers.

"No offense, Flora, but I'm starting to worry this island might not be big enough for the two of us." Alex looked at King like she might slice right through his carotid with her gaze and save herself the hassle of a messy divorce. "Is there, like, a hotel on the other side? A Ritz maybe? I'd even do a Four Seasons? Can I check in there?"

"Oh no!" Flora's serene expression turned to panic. "You must never go to the other side of the island."

"Why?" Alex got a devilish gleam in her eye. "Is it clothing optional? Because that wouldn't be a problem."

King tried not to swallow his tongue.

"No," Flora was saying. "Nothing like that. Just"—she cut a nervous glance between them, eyes pinballing back and forth like she didn't know where to put the lie to make it stick—"zoning issues."

"Zoning?" King asked. "I thought the island was private."

"Oh, it is!" Flora's voice had taken on that too-pretentious-to-be-real tone again. "It's just . . . well, it's more *semiprivate*. We have this side of the island." She pointed from the rugged line of mountains that split the island down the center to the black sand beach and lush green jungle. "Why would we venture over there when we have paradise here? Besides, I doubt you could even reach the other side. The mountain is . . . high." She looked up at it like she couldn't think of any other word. "And there are cliffs and rockslides and, besides, you'll have plenty to keep you busy right here. Now kiss."

At first, King thought he must have misheard her because the words ran together as if they were one thought—one sentence. As if she hadn't just said—

"Kiss!"

"I'm sorry, what?" King demanded, and the woman rolled her eyes as if he were the one being ridiculous.

"It's tradition, here, at Cupid's Arrow"—she did the ridiculous bow again—"that I ask all of my lovers"—she gestured at King—"to begin their time here by kissing their lovelies." She gestured toward Alex. "Everyone kisses when they arrive and then again as they leave and as much as possible in the middle." She gave an exaggerated wink. But, just as quickly, grew serious. "I need to see what we're working with."

What she was working . . .

"Well, *lover* . . ." Alex lingered on the word. She was enjoying herself far too much as she turned to him. "She wants to see what you're . . . working with."

King had been in and out of covers for the past two years but it had never felt so easy. He didn't even have to think about what he was doing. In fact, for the first time in his life, he didn't think at all. He just slipped an arm around her. "You know exactly what I'm working with." And then King just . . . forgot. About everything—the plane and the mountain and the way the Atlantic lapped against black sand and glistened in the sun. Even Flora seemed to fade into the background as Alex went up on her tiptoes and pressed her lips against his.

That was it. Just a brush. Just a whisper. It should have been enough. But it wasn't. And when their lips parted, he felt her fingers in his hair and he slid his hands down her waist, gripping and grabbing and holding on, needing . . . something. More.

More heat. More pressure. More time. More—

Alex pulled away and King let her go, and for a moment there was nothing but the sound of his heart and the lapping of the waves and Flora's breathless whisper.

"Well, I suppose we can work with that."

chapter twenty-three

Present Day
The Island

ALEX

Alex watched the jet stairs descend slowly and waited for a wave of ocean air and déjà vu to overwhelm her senses—either that or plain old-fashioned regret.

But all she felt was a thong that wasn't exactly staying where it was supposed to. "Remind me never to let you go shopping for me again." She scowled up at him, but King was too busy sliding on his dark glasses, slipping on his mask of cool confidence and rich guy calm.

"Oh. Are we pretending I don't know the size and shape of your body . . . darling?" The word was a taunt on his lips. "Is that how we're going to play it?"

They were close. The open door was right there. And there were stairs. People trip on stairs. People fall down stairs and bust their heads open. People—

"David!" The voice flew on the wind. "Donna!"

"Flora." Alex and King spoke at exactly the same time.

She watched him pull on his mask—become David Dixon from Denver right before her eyes.

"Hello, Flora," he called with a wave.

"Now isn't this a sight?" Flora looked them over with a grin. "How are the two most beautiful lovelies I have ever seen?"

Alex was careful on the stairs. Careful on the tarmac. She was careful . . . always. All the time. She'd been careful her whole, entire life, and she was suddenly tired, far too tired to fight when King slipped an arm around her shoulders.

"We're well, Flora. How are you?" he asked the woman who was looking between the two of them and bouncing—like at any moment she was going to vibrate right out of her skin.

"Oh, I'm ecstatic! I literally screamed when I got David's call. I had a feeling that this moon tide would be especially fruitful. I just didn't know that my two favorite lovelies would be back—to allow our healing waters to bless you at this most important time. Donna? Are you excited?"

"Uh . . . yes?"

"I always tell my lovelies, this is the greatest mission of their lives—the ultimate challenge."

"The ultimate . . ."

"I am just so happy that the two of you are back—and for Fertility Week!"

Alex was torn; should she die of mortification now or kill King first? Who was she kidding? She could multitask. But first—

"Oh. No! You see—"

"This is our most special time, when lovers and lovelies unite for the purpose of recreation *and* procreation," Flora went on. Then she lowered her voice. "There are certain . . . advantages . . . to being a private island. No police. No silly indecency ordinances. This week, our island will become a cornucopia of bounty—"

"Oh boy," King muttered.

"You should feel the wind in your hair, the salt water on your skin. The moon on your ripe and fertile bodies."

"Ripe and . . ." Alex muttered.

"Fertile," King blurted. "She said fertile."

"Let the island guide you through this, the most natural thing in the world. Let nature take its course. Of course, respect others, but . . . if no one is around . . . I'm just saying, do you see that big rock over there? Triplets."

"How nice." Was Alex staring daggers? She felt like her eyes might have turned into literal knives.

"Now . . ." Flora clapped her hands together. "I didn't get to ask on the phone, would you like the optional Blessing of the Womb?"

"No!" Alex blurted. "I mean no. Thank you. No."

"We're all good. Womb-wise." King winked at Flora and, damn the man, let his hand drift down to rest on Alex's abdomen. She wanted to push it away—break his thumb. Maybe toss him into the sea, but all she could do was turn and look up at the man who was staring down at her, saying, "She's perfect just the way she is."

"Oh." Flora gave a whole-body shiver, then giggled. "Such a beautiful couple. But I'm not going to lie. When I think of where you started . . ."

chapter twenty-four

Eight Years Ago
The Island

KING

After twenty minutes of walking, King was certain of one thing: Cupid's Arrow was a very stupid name for a very beautiful island. Merritt might have even been right to call it "paradise" but he was never going to tell her that.

They followed Flora down lush, green paths surrounded by wild orchids and singing birds. Even though there were obvious signs of civilization, it was as if the lights and buildings had sprung from the island itself—like the volcano had spit them out a millennium ago and Flora was some ancient goddess whose job it was to keep things dusted.

"It's beautiful." Alex must have read his mind.

"Thank you." Flora turned back and . . . yeah . . . gave the weird bow again.

"Is the whole island like this?" Alex tried. She was subtle when she needed to be and—King hated to admit it—*good.*

"Oh no." Flora sounded concerned. "The other side is much too steep and . . . inhospitable."

"What about hiking?" Alex tried again. "I love hiking and—"

Flora stopped so quickly that King almost collided with her back. "We *do not* go to the other side of the island."

"Of course." King glanced at Alex. "Surely this side is big enough for both of us?"

She wasn't even acting when she scoffed and said, "We'll see."

Something about the look Flora was giving them made King suddenly worry that maybe the Farm hadn't trained them well enough. It was like Flora of the Made-Up Sayings could see right through their covers and into the heart of them. Worse, it was like she saw something the two of them had missed, and King didn't like it—not one bit.

"Come along, lovers!"

King spoke five languages, but he was starting to hate that word more than any other. When Alex gave him a come-hither look over her shoulder and mouthed *lover*, he rolled his eyes and turned back to the mountain terrain and tried to make the most of the situation.

They'd ridden in a Jeep for twenty minutes, up a steep, winding trail, and then they'd walked for twenty more. Alex had done it in heels, and King wanted to strangle Flora for not at least asking if they wanted to change clothes first, but Alex was looking at him like they'd hit some kind of jackpot and won the undercover lottery.

The path was wider here, with wooden blocks stuck in the ground for makeshift steps, but King slipped his hand into Alex's anyway. He could have listed off a dozen reasons—from maintaining their covers to the fact that she would be nothing but a liability if she fell and broke her leg—but as they followed Flora up the final twisting bend, he didn't share a single one. He just kept climbing until they came through a break in the trees, stepping out onto—

The edge of the world.

Or so it looked.

It wasn't the highest peak—or the roughest—but no one could deny the view was like something out of myth as they stood there, looking out over a sea of steep mountains and lush, green foliage. A wispy layer of clouds circled the jagged peaks that stood in the distance, and King thought the whole island must be a study in contrasts: rocky and lush, hard and soft. Terrifying but beautiful.

Kind of like the woman beside him.

"Gasp," Alex whispered. It was a tone of voice he'd never heard her use before, and King couldn't help but turn. He wasn't staring, he told himself. But he also couldn't look away. "What?"

"Nothing. I just . . . Nothing."

"Come, lovers! Come!" Flora was beckoning them along the top of the ridge to a wide, open spot in the trees. A half-dozen couples were already standing there, all of them a little sweaty and nervous, and King wondered how long they'd been up there, waiting.

"We are gathered here to welcome our hearts and our minds into the state of cupidism and tranquility." Flora did the weird and possibly offensive bow again, and King wondered if he should just hurl himself into the volcano. Their intel said it was dormant, but that might give it a kick start. Surely the Agency would cut them some slack if an eruption cut their mission short.

"Now, lovers, as we begin our journey of transformation, I ask you to introduce yourselves and share why the goddess has brought you to our island."

What religion is this? King wanted to shout, but he already knew the answer: it was the church of profit and pretension and Flora was its high priestess.

King glanced at Alex and cursed the short plane ride from the mainland. There's a reason people prep for undercover work for weeks—why the same teams go into the field together time and time again. There's a shorthand that's needed. A level of trust. A—

"I'm Donna." Alex jumped right in. "And we're here because he said he wanted to strangle me with a garden hose!" Alex pointed at King, then burst into tears.

"That's just ridiculous." Ten sets of eyes were glaring at him. "Do you people have any idea how hard it would be to strangle someone with a garden hose? An extension cord, yes. A strand of Christmas lights, obviously."

"And he hasn't touched me in months." Alex was silently sobbing, but all King could do was scowl.

"If you want me to touch you, then all you've got to do is say the word, sweetheart. Any time. Any place."

They were standing way too close and breathing way too hard. He didn't even notice when Flora turned to the next couple in the group. "Tell us about yourselves."

"I'm Jennifer." She was the kind of beautiful that came from being very young and very wealthy. Her hair was perfect, and her makeup was painstakingly applied to look as if she wasn't wearing any makeup at all. But the most obvious thing about her was the look on her face that said that, somehow, she'd ended up in the wrong life—or maybe just on the wrong island. She jerked her head at the young man beside her and said, "And that's my idiot husband, Todd."

They looked like they should be on spring break and not at a resort that charged six figures to save dying marriages.

"Hi. We're—"

"*We're* here on our honeymoon," Jennifer cut Todd off with no small amount of anger and irony.

"It was the most expensive," Todd whispered in the tone of a man who had already had this conversation. "You said 'just book whatever's most expensive.' And this was the most expensive!"

"Do we look like a marriage in trouble, Todd?"

Even the birds went silent—as if they were afraid of chirping *You do now.*

"We want a refund." Jennifer wheeled on Flora.

"I'm afraid—"

"We should stay," Todd said. "We're here. It's beautiful." He flashed her a look that could only be described as puppy dog eyes. "*You're* beautiful."

"Fine." Jennifer crossed her arms over her white dress and looked like she would have thrown a fit if she wasn't afraid it might mess up her makeup.

"Oh. Well then. We're the Johnsons," a woman on the other side of the clearing chimed in. "I'm Felicia. This is my wife, Kimberly. We do something like this every five years, just as a tune-up."

"Like a colonoscopy," her wife put in.

"*Ooh,*" the group said in unison.

"We're both MDs," Felicia added, and everyone smiled as if that made the image make sense.

The other guests took turns, going around the circle, but King, frankly, tuned them out. Half of his brain was paying attention, of course (because half of King's brain was *always* paying attention), but the other half was scanning the trees and the mountains—the distant waterfalls and steep cliffs that seemed to slice the island down the center. From that vantage point, he could just make out the place where the coastline curved and the ocean met a mountain so steep, the trees didn't even try to grow there.

That's where they tried to climb, a part of his brain put in. It was no wonder the other CIA teams had failed.

"We welcome our lovers and invite you to—"

"No, I don't have any gum, Todd," Jennifer whispered loud enough to be heard from the other side of the circle.

"—open your minds and your hearts to this new experience. And each other," Flora droned on. King would occasionally catch bits about goddesses and the elements and maybe a little bit of astrology thrown in for good measure, but he was too busy taking in the cliffs and the trees and the rocky ledges covered with lush, green grass.

And there—in the distance—a fortress. It was the only word that would do the structure justice.

"Is that . . ." Alex murmured.

"Yeah," King whispered. "That's it."

It was on the opposite ridge, just below the clouds, looking like it had grown out of the mountain itself—nothing but stone walls and steep descents. There were towers with views of the water, but as far as King could tell, just one road in and out—a steep, narrow path that zigzagged down the mountain's side.

"I don't like this," Alex whispered under her breath, and for once, King couldn't argue.

On the other side of the circle, Flora was practically vibrating. "This was once a powerful volcano. Full of fire and ice."

"I highly doubt that," someone said before another voice chimed, "Shut up, Todd."

"Hot and cold come together in this place."

For the first time, King thought that Todd might have a point.

"Just as you—our lovers—must come together. And work together. To soar over adversity and pass through the valley of your love."

"Does she actually know the meanings of these words?" King whispered, but Alex shhhhed him. As if *he* were the one being ridiculous.

He was just getting ready to say so when Alex gave him a nudge. "Look." She pointed to the place where the clouds were parting and a helicopter was dropping out of the sky and landing on a pad near the fort.

"Guess that's one way in," King whispered.

"Excellent! Just excellent!" Flora was clapping. "Now, where to begin . . . David? David, why don't you start us off?"

King honestly felt sorry for this David guy until an elbow connected with his ribs and he looked down at Alex, who cocked an eyebrow, and one word landed in his mind: *wife*. Followed quickly by *mine*. And then . . .

David, she mouthed. And he had to shiver because, that's right . . . He was David. And . . .

He'd forgotten.

King hadn't even known it was possible, but—

"You're wasting your time." Alex spun on Flora. "David doesn't share. Anything. Ever." She crossed her arms and stared daggers while King wound his mind back far enough to hear Flora's original question.

Lovers, what did you think when you first saw your lovelies?

"You might as well call on someone else," Alex was saying. "David doesn't—"

"Three things," he said, and Alex went silent. "I thought three things the first time I laid eyes on her. I thought she was the most beautiful woman I'd ever seen. I thought she'd be the death of me. And . . ." It was like the whole world leaned forward, listening. Waiting. Even the birds stopped singing as he said, "And I thought . . . there are worse ways to go."

chapter twenty-five

ALEX

Technically, their room wasn't a room. It was a bungalow. But as Alex took in the small building tucked between the tall trees of the jungle and the black sand of the beach, she couldn't help but think it was actually the most opulent shack she'd ever laid eyes on.

There were dark wood floors and high arching ceilings. Between the rattan fans making lazy circles overhead and the breeze blowing off the ocean, it was no wonder the sheer white curtains kept billowing and dancing in the moonlight. Like ghosts. But that wasn't what Alex was afraid of. Because while the room had a tiny fridge stocked with two bottles of champagne, and there were two bathrooms (one was outdoors) with two fluffy white robes and two sets of slippers—two oversize chairs and two mints on two pillows . . .

There was only one bed.

For a moment, Alex just stood there, looking at it numbly, wishing she could talk to Zoe, because her sister was the only person Alex knew who would actually appreciate the situation. She was also, unfortunately, the last person Alex could ever tell.

They were on different paths now, but maybe they always had been? Like whatever cosmic or genetic fate had split them in two in the womb was still there, standing between them. Alex had thought that being away from her sister would get easier now that it was a matter of national security, but that didn't change the fact that . . .

"There's only one bed."

Alex didn't realize she'd said the words aloud until she heard another voice ask, "What's that?"

"Nothing." It was sloppy, standing there, saying things aloud, forgetting that she wasn't alone, so Alex went to her CIA-issued suitcase and threw it open. There was a screwdriver in her cosmetics case, and Alex got to work, checking inside vents and unscrewing light switch covers and—

"What are you doing?" The man had the nerve to sound bored.

"It's called clearing the room?" she whispered. "Maybe you've heard of it?"

"You don't have to do that." King was hanging up his shirts. All white. All expensive. All a thread here or a dart there from being identical.

"Of course I have to do this. It's protocol, or did you forget that, Mr. Photographic Memory?"

"You don't have to do that because I already did it."

"We just got here!"

Oh, she hated him. Even in this he had to be first.

"I did it with this." He pointed to his wristwatch and held out his arm. He had annoyingly nice arms. Big bones with those ridiculous forearms displayed prominently with his sleeves rolled up. But then he bent down and took off his shoes and that was the thing that threw her. It was so . . . human. For the first time, she realized that a part of her had always wondered if King might actually be a robot.

She looked back at the device on his wrist. Alex was instantly leery. And jealous.

"What's that?"

"Bug detector. Among other things. It finds anything that's wired and blocks anything that's wireless."

"Where did you get it, and why didn't they give me one?"

"I made it." He sounded almost bored.

"You made it?" Did the words come out more mocking than she'd intended? Yes. Did she take them back? Not even a little bit.

But King, the jerkface, just *shrugged*. "I make things."

"You *make things*? What? In your Evil Genius lab?" That time, she really did mean to sound mocking and she wasn't even ashamed of it.

"Everyone needs a hobby." Then he turned back to straighten White Shirt number 10 (this one was linen). "The room is clean,

Alex." There was something in the way he looked back at her, soft and a little indulgent. "I wouldn't take a chance . . ." He trailed off, like there was more to that sentence, but he caught the words and pulled them back. "I wouldn't take a chance." There was a period that time. It wasn't even up for debate. "Go take a shower. Or do your nails—"

"*Do my nails?*"

"Or . . ." There was a shelf of old paperbacks by the wet bar. The literary equivalent of *take a penny, leave a penny*, and he pulled one off the shelf at random and tossed it in her direction. She caught it one-handed. "Read something."

"I've read it." Alex tossed it back. He caught it with his nondominant hand because, even in that, he had to top her.

"No, you haven't." He tucked the book back in its place.

"End of chapter seven," she said flatly. "The heroine shoots the hero in the leg."

For a moment, King just stood there, blinking. Then he started flipping through the pages, searching. Desperate to prove she was lying. When he finally found it, he stopped and looked at her, and Alex didn't even try not to smirk.

"You're not the only one with a good memory, you know?"

He turned back to the shelf and reached for another one, but it was all Alex could do not to roll her eyes. "She pretty much falls in love with him in chapter five because he buys her a foot warmer. Which, by the way, just proves how low the bar is for most men, romantically speaking."

He picked up another paperback, but Alex just crossed her arms and said, "Her Scottish ones are better." King was looking at her like she'd just sprouted a third eye. "What? Everything is better in Scotland. The heroes wear kilts and live in castles." She wiggled her eyebrows just to mock him. "Come on. If you're going to have a fictional man, he might as well have a kilt. And a castle." Alex thought that was an excellent point, but King didn't look convinced. He just stared at the shelf, bewildered.

"Have you read all of these?"

No, she hadn't read them all. In fact, she hadn't read anything fun in a very long time. But that didn't change the fact that—"I used to read romance all the time to my . . ."

And then she stopped. Alex didn't know what was worse, the look in King's eyes or the memory of Zoe lying in a hospital bed, too weak to turn the pages. Alex had done that to her. *It was Alex's fault.*

"Sterling . . ."

"Myself," Alex lied. "When I was bored or alone. You should try it. Reading for fun. It makes one a more *empathetic* person." She stuck her tongue out, then went to the bathroom and closed the door. She turned the shower on full blast and gripped the edge of the sink and tried not to think about why she didn't want to look in the mirror.

"Alex?" There was a gentle knock. "Open up."

"What is it?" She jerked open the door, and there he was, soft eyes full of something that looked a lot like worry.

"What's wrong?"

"Nothing." She went to close the door again, but he blocked it in a way they didn't have to teach at spy school.

"Alex—" he started, but it was already too late. It was already too much.

"Don't call me that."

"There aren't any bugs. We can—"

"You call me Sterling. Or Alexandra when you want to be especially mocking. We're not friends, Kingsley. We are partners. Temporarily. Because Merritt and the Agency and the freaking country need us to be. But we are not . . . I appreciate you stooping to working with me, and I'm sorry I've been forced upon you—*again*. But we are not friends. I would think someone with an eidetic memory could remember that much."

Alex would have given her life savings to know what he was thinking in that moment. Not that she cared. Except she really, really cared. And she hated that most of all.

He backed up three whole inches but didn't let the door close. "Tell me who you read them to."

She didn't know why he cared. She really didn't know why it

mattered. But he was looking at her like *she* mattered. Like she was the only language he couldn't speak—the only code he couldn't crack. She was the photograph his mind couldn't hold on to, and he *needed* to know the answer to this question. Like this small piece of information was the key to her cipher and he needed to find the thing that would finally make her make sense, and Alex couldn't help herself.

She whispered, "My sister."

The air was hot and thick with steam. It filled her lungs. It was getting hard to breathe, but she could see him clearly.

"*Zoe.*" It was like watching a Rube Goldberg machine that had been running for two years suddenly come to its ultimate conclusion. The last piece fell into place in his mind. "Zoe's your sister." It wasn't a question, and King seemed almost giddy with the possibilities. "Is she older? Younger?"

"Younger." That could have been the end of it—*should* have been the end of it. But something made her add, "By seven minutes."

And then Michael Kingsley, Boy Wonder of the CIA, just stood there, totally dumbfounded while the pieces came together in his mind. "You're a twin. You're . . . Are you fraternal?" She shook her head, and he let out a gasp. "Identical?"

"That's most common alternative, yes."

Then he leaned against the doorframe, like his legs couldn't quite support his weight. "Sweet mercy. There are two of you."

For a moment, it almost sounded like a compliment.

"She doesn't know," Alex blurted. "About me. About this . . . She doesn't know what I do, so you can save whatever lecture you were going to give me about—"

"I'm not going to give you a lecture." He looked cool, even in the stuffy room, eyes taking in her face, like he was wondering if maybe she and Zoe had pulled a *Parent Trap*, like maybe she was an entirely different person and he was mad that he'd somehow missed the clues.

But then his expression changed. Something occurred to him,

and Alex honestly didn't know what he was thinking until he whispered, "So I guess you told me yours . . ." He didn't have to explain.

Alex thought about the not-quite-game she and King had been playing for the better part of two long years. "I did. So is this the part where you tell me about Nikolai?"

"No." He couldn't look at her.

"Because it's need-to-know?"

"Because it's way too painful." Then he turned around. He closed the door. And Alex didn't ask a single question.

When she got out of the bathroom twenty minutes later, King was lacing up his hiking boots. "I'm going to go take a look around."

"Is that a good idea?"

"It's our only idea."

Maybe it was all in her head, but it felt like he was trying to not face her.

Suddenly, there was a flash of lightning outside—a boom of thunder. And then the hardest rain that Alex had ever heard slammed down on the roof of the bungalow.

"King! Wait," she called before he reached the door. "If you insist on going out in this, I'll go with you."

"No, Al— Sterling." He half stumbled over the word. "Get some rest. I won't be long."

Lightning flashed again, and Alex didn't want to admit it, but it scared her. She didn't want him out there. Getting hurt or getting lost.

"We'll look in the morning. Come on. Come to bed. If you get caught in a mudslide or fall down a mountain and bust your head, Merritt will blame me. And then she'll kill me. And then we'll both be dead and the CIA will never recover." There was something strange about his face—like he was amused in spite of himself and that amusement made him angry, which just pleased Alex even more. "Fine." She knew better than to force his hand and make him dig in his heels. "Do whatever you want, but I'm going to bed, and you can join me or—"

"I'll sleep on the floor," King said like it wasn't even a debate. Not even a question.

"Fine. If you're committed to the chivalry act. But just so you know, I'd rather share the world's largest bed than be in the field with someone whose body isn't operating at full capacity because they were too stubborn to get a good night's sleep."

She turned off the light and turned onto her side. The bathroom door opened and closed and then the shower turned on. She was almost asleep ten minutes later when she felt the bed dip.

"Just so you know," he whispered, "the chivalry isn't an act."

The worst part was, she already knew it.

chapter twenty-six

Present Day
The Island

ALEX

It was the same bungalow. The same curtains. The same storm brewing outside—lightning on water and a hot, wet wind blowing off the sea. In a way, it felt almost like they'd never left. But in another . . .

Alex looked at the bed and didn't even try not to gape. "Is that supposed to be . . ."

"I think so."

In Alex's defense, she'd never seen the female reproductive tract made out of rose petals before. Hopefully she'd never have to see it again.

King scanned for bugs while Alex took a shower. When she got out, he was already lying on a pallet on the floor. They'd shared the bed eight years ago, but that was then and this was—

"I'll take the floor tomorrow night," she told him, and he nodded, but his face was blank and the night was dark and the silence hung in the air like the rain. "What?"

"Nothing. I was just thinking . . . with any luck we'll be gone by then."

Alex crawled into bed. "Don't be silly. When have we ever been lucky?"

In the darkness, with the blowing breeze and coming storm and animals calling through the night, it felt like an excellent question.

chapter twenty-seven

Eight Years Ago
The Island

ALEX

Alex slept.

It shouldn't have come as a surprise. The bed was big and soft and the sheets felt like satin and butter had a baby. The ocean breeze was still blowing through those gauzy curtains and, outside, the sun was starting to rise, breaking over the horizon in an explosion of color that made the sky look like a swirl of sherbet.

She couldn't remember the last time she'd felt so rested. Like the part of her brain that was always worrying had finally turned off. Rebooted. There were no memory-hogging apps running in the background of her mind, and as she pushed herself upright and stretched, she felt almost . . . afraid. Like feeling good because none of your alarms have been triggered and then realizing that's because the alarms are down.

She wasn't sure what she was aware of first—the faint sounds of singing or the sight of the bathroom door opening in a cloud of steam.

Instantly, Alex reached for the gun under her pillow. She had it trained on the man in the towel before he had a chance to drop it.

"So this is what wakes you up," King said, turning to the closet and pulling a pair of shorts off a hanger. His hair was wet and his chest was bare and Alex forgot to put her gun down. She had the sudden feeling she might just need it because the man on the other side of the room was a stranger.

"Sterling?" King said, loud enough to tell her that maybe he'd been saying it for a while now. "You gonna shoot me or can we get to work?"

"What?" She rubbed her eyes and looked out the window at the rising sun. "What time is it?"

"Mission o'clock. Maybe you've heard of it?"

He was shimmying into those shorts. They were disappearing up beneath the towel. Because . . . right.

Towel.

Chest.

Skin.

So much very warm, very wet skin stretched tight over oh-so-many muscles and . . .

Michael Kingsley was ripped. It shouldn't have been a surprise. She'd seen him fight and run and lift. She'd known him for years, but had she? Because she'd never thought he was an ab guy. Maybe an "I eat a balanced diet because my body is a temple" guy but definitely not a "Someday I might need to go undercover as an underwear model" guy.

"Yo. Sterling."

"Did you just . . ." Alex blinked hard, not quite appreciating the irony that *that* was the thing that woke her. "Did you just say 'yo'?"

"We need to find a way to the other side of the island."

He was sliding on that white linen shirt, rolling up the sleeves and . . . Yeah. What was she thinking again?

And then he was . . . close. And there. He was *just right there*, sitting down and leaning close with something like worry in his eyes as he asked her, "Are you okay?"

She wasn't okay. She'd slept so hard, she'd actually forgotten where she was—she'd actually forgotten *who* she was.

She was someone who hated Michael Kingsley.

"Of course. I just . . ."

She turned to face the windows and the sunrise and the sea.

"I did it, too." Even after she'd processed the words, she didn't really understand them. The voice was very soft and very close, and it sounded like confession feels.

"What?"

He didn't even bother to look guilty. "I slept."

Oh. That. It should have felt comforting, knowing the Great Michael Kingsley had done the same thing. Maybe it was okay to be human. *This time.* So Alex pushed her hair out of her eyes and choked out, "Professional hazard. Won't happen again."

"Of course it will." The bed shifted as he rose. She wanted to wheel on him and shout, but he was already walking away, tossing over his shoulder, "Because, like it or not, you feel safe with me, Sterling. You *are* safe. And, like it or not, I'm safe with you, too."

He was right about one thing.

Alex didn't like it one bit.

Fifteen minutes later, Alex was out of the bathroom and pulling on some shoes and rushing to catch up to the figure who was disappearing down the winding path. "Where are you going?" Alex darted out in front of him.

The sun was up and the air felt warm and sweet. Birds were singing in the trees, and it sounded like a white noise app—because, in Alex's world, even the birds were an illusion, and she didn't know what to make of it, the realization that her fake husband was the only thing on that island she could count on.

"Where do you *think* I'm—"

"Good morning, Cupids!" Flora appeared on the path ahead of them.

"Good morning," King said back.

"Did my lovers sleep well?"

"Like the dead." He didn't take his eyes off Alex.

"I hope you're ready for a cupid-filled day! Did you remember to wear your swimsuits?"

"Yup!" Alex waited for Flora to turn and head for the dining hall, and then she inched closer to King. "Come on. Let's get out of here—"

"You can't come with me." He jerked back so fast, he almost sounded afraid.

"I *have* to go with you," she reminded him.

"No. You have to go"—he waved at Flora's retreating back—"ignite your inner goddess or whatever. And I need to go find a way into that compound."

Alex was aware, faintly, of other couples walking down the path, filing out of bungalows and toward the smells of breakfast.

"No," Alex said simply, and King pinched the bridge of his nose.

"We have to figure out how to get to the other side of the island, remember?" he whispered.

Alex cut her eyes at the other guests disappearing into the main building. "And we're supposed to be here *together*, remember?"

"But we're not supposed to get along. Remember?"

"Oh. How can I forget?"

"Oh, David! Donna!" Flora called. "You don't want to be late. We have a big morning. We're doing trust falls!"

"*Trust falls.*" It was almost adorable how annoyed he sounded. "Please. Please just go with the others. Keep them busy and out of my way—"

"No."

"Why does everything have to be a fight with you?"

"Why does everything have to be your way? If *I* have to do trust falls, then *you* have to do trust falls."

He was already shaking his head. "You don't need me for that."

"I literally do! Who do you think is going to catch me, *David*? No one. No one will catch me when I fall. I literally—"

"Don't act like you're not capable of catching yourself." King looked like he didn't know whether to scream in frustration or hang his head in shame. "Don't act like a part of you doesn't prefer it that way."

Did she prefer it that way? For the first time, Alex honestly wasn't sure of the answer.

She'd slept with him. She'd *slept*. But the biggest twist was: so had he.

"Why do you get to go climb a mountain and I have to do the touchy-feely crap? Is it because I'm a girl?"

"It's because you're better at it than I am!" He hadn't meant to say it. She could tell by the look on his face, but the words were out and he couldn't pull them back so he didn't even try. "You're better, okay? People like you. They trust you. They want to be in your orbit because you have the gravitational pull of the sun. Because *you* are good at *people*, and I'm good at . . ." He pointed toward the dense forest and jagged cliffs and the millions of ways there were to die on that island. "Anything but people."

He was the most entitled, arrogant man she'd ever known, and he was standing there, looking sheepish and embarrassed and guilty.

"Please . . ." He inched forward and lowered his voice. "Please don't make me do this."

Alex was still staring at him. She wanted to say no, but he so clearly wanted her to say yes that she found herself wondering— wavering. Did the great Michael Kingsley III actually need her?

"Very good! Now come along!" Flora was saying as she led the group back down the trail. They were getting closer. It was almost too late.

"I can do it," he whispered. "Buy me some time, and I can find us a way to the other side of the island."

"Now everybody stay together!" Flora called. "Strictly speaking, we aren't supposed to be going there, but—"

It was the only thing that could have made Alex look away from him. "Going where?"

"The other side of the island."

chapter twenty-eight

ALEX

Forty-five minutes later, they were still walking. The sky that had felt so bright when they left was now hidden behind a dense canopy of trees. The ground was rockier, the undergrowth thicker. They were off the beaten path in every sense of the word, and Alex could feel the group getting restless.

"You'd think we could do this a little closer to home," someone grumbled, and someone else agreed, but Alex stayed quiet beside King as they brought up the rear.

They were almost to the base of the mountain that sliced the island in two, and the trees were growing thicker. Everything was so green, it was almost black, and even the birds looked brighter in the stillness.

"Keep an eye out for a good place to climb." King slid an arm around Alex's shoulders and whispered near her ear as they hung back and let the group get a little distance.

"I don't think there *is* a good place to climb." Every now and then the trees would part and they'd look up at cliffs that seemed even steeper, sharper. Deadlier. From that vantage point, it looked like they might as well try to climb the clouds.

They were alone—with the others walking ahead and the sounds of the forest all around them—but Alex wrapped her arm around King's waist, just in case.

"Think we can split off from the group?" he wondered.

"Get lost?" She couldn't keep from smiling.

"We could say we got turned around," he offered.

"We could say we got turned on," she said, and he chuckled—too quickly and too loudly, like he'd surprised even himself. The cocoon of safety she'd felt the night before was still with her in a way that made her wonder if it wasn't just the bed and the bungalow. If maybe it was—

"David!" Flora shouted from the top of a rise. "Donna!" She wasn't that far away and yet it was hard to hear her because there was a sound beneath the words—a low rumble that was turning into a roar, growing louder and louder with every step as they inched up the incline and then looked down . . . and gasped. But Flora just beamed and said, "We're here."

So it turned out "trust falls" were less "clichéd team building activity" and more—

"OMG, Todd, take my picture!" Jennifer was whipping off her (white) cover-up and posing in front of the sapphire pool in her (white) bikini, while looking up at the waterfall that cascaded down from a hundred feet overhead, falling like a curtain, obscuring rocks and cliffs and mossy grass. A foamy mist caught the sunlight and turned the air to rainbows, but all Alex could do was peer as the pool rippled before them, the water clear and deep and gorgeous.

Flora brought her hands together. "Welcome, lovers, to the first day of your Cupid Quest."

"She really needs to pick a theme and stick with it," King grumbled, and Alex didn't even bother to *shhh* him.

"As we ask the goddess—"

"Is it a goddess or Cupid?" King whispered, but Alex had to wonder.

"I think Cupid *is* a god?"

"Then *say* god."

He probably could have lived with the rest of it, but the inconsistency was going to be the death of him. King didn't just like order. He *needed* it, Alex was coming to realize. What she didn't know was why.

"As we encircle our lovers and find our inner—"

"I'm sorry." King's hand shot into the air. He was almost at his breaking point and Alex shouldn't have been enjoying it, but she was. "What—exactly—is the objective here?"

King had been the first to master everything they'd taught at the Farm, but he was going to fail Cupidism 101, and Alex wanted to ask if there would be actual report cards. Maybe diplomas. Or transcripts. She wanted one framed and hanging in the house she didn't own. She wanted to cherish it like the best friend she didn't have. She wanted it to be the pet she'd never bring home. Watching King fail at Couple Camp was her mission now. Her reason for living.

But Flora just looked . . . concerned. And confused. And then she said, "It's probably better to just dive in."

She meant it literally, Alex knew. Why else would they all be wearing bathing suits after hiking to the most beautiful natural pool she'd ever seen? Still, she wasn't quite prepared for the sight of King whipping off his shirt and shoes and then jumping in the water and holding out his arms like he might catch her. Maybe that was why she didn't move.

"Don't tell me you can't swim." He grinned up at her, a challenge in his voice—a dare in his eyes. Then he pushed his wet hair back and droplets slid across his skin and—"Hello. Donna!"

Alex jumped so quickly, she surprised even herself, and when she came up, spitting and gagging, he was grinning in a way that made her want to drown him. "*What?*"

"I didn't say anything." But he wanted to. He wanted to mock her and . . . tease her? Alex wasn't certain. He was still the most condescending man she'd ever known but there was something like fondness in his eyes. Like he was amused. With her. Like she was the only part of this whole thing that didn't make him want to scream.

Flora was pulling large pieces of foam out from behind a boulder and setting them afloat in the water. They were like a cross between extrawide surfboards and yoga mats, and Alex could tell just by looking that King was in denial about where this was going.

"Lovers, choose a mat and join each other in Cupid's sacred embrace."

"I could be climbing . . . something . . . right now," King growled as he held the mat still while Alex wriggled onto it, and then climbed on behind her. The mat dipped. She almost fell in. Together, they were trained in at least eight forms of hand-to-hand combat, but they were going to fail "trust falls" and Alex regretted ever mocking him.

There was no obvious current in the pool, but there was a massive waterfall, so the surface was choppy and unsteady and so were they. Alex and King were young and athletic and agile. They were also two of the most competitive people on the planet. King didn't want to be here—doing this—but he'd rather die than be bad at it, and he wasn't the only one.

"Lovers, bring your lovelies closer. Center yourselves on your mats and within your lover's aura."

"Are you the lover or the lovely? I've been meaning to ask," King whispered.

"Shut up and spread your legs."

"See . . . when you say things like that . . ." he grumbled while she scooted into the V of his thighs.

"No, Donna. Turn, lovely," Flora said, and King cocked an eye as if to say, *Well, I guess you're the lovely*, but Alex was too busy thinking . . . realizing . . .

"Lovers, entwine your bodies. Legs over legs. Arms around shoulders. Cuddle time is couple time. Donna, your legs should be . . ." Alex knew. She knew and so she did it, but that didn't mean she *liked* it. At all. They were wrapped together like a pretzel, mat floating in the water, bouncing with the not-quite-waves. They were seated, at least. But close. Very close. If either of them moved, they might tip, and tipping would mean losing, and they did not lose—*ever*. So Alex and King stayed on that floating mat in that ultimate paradise and tried not to look too much like people who had never been in love.

A voice echoed from across the water. "It's not my fault you never learned how to swim, Todd."

"Do you think we should help . . ."

"Get over here." King pulled her closer. "Are you going to let these people outcuddle us?" His big hand was on the small of her back, his big thighs were underneath her legs.

"Fine." She scooted closer. Practically straddling him now.

"Lovers, breathe in unison with your lovelies. As one chest falls, another rises. Your breath becomes their breath."

"Great," King whispered. "Now you're gonna kill me with carbon dioxide."

"Is that a challenge?" Alex didn't know how, but she got even closer.

"Cuddle time isn't just about touch. It's about contact." Flora was walking around the shore like a very colorful drill sergeant. "Legs gripping. Torsos touching. Gazes locked and arms entwined. Contact isn't touching—it's *joining*. Bodies. Hearts. Minds."

Their mat had floated so close to the waterfall that Alex could barely hear Flora over the roar. She could barely see the others through the mist. She could barely remember the Farm or Cartagena or any of the reasons why it was weird to be on that mat in that place with that man. She wasn't aware of anything but the feel of his chest brushing against hers, the caress of his breath on her skin, so warm she was suddenly covered in goose bumps. They were closer. Their grips were tighter. They were adrift somewhere in paradise, but she didn't see a thing—not the rainbows or the couples or the cliffs.

Condensation pooled on her skin, and when King swiped a finger across her cheek, she felt it in her core.

"Well done, David! Donna!" Flora was saying, but Alex was too busy thinking about how she'd never noticed the little flecks of brown in his eyes. And then those eyes moved—just a flash. Just a flicker—down to her lips, and she could have sworn they both stopped breathing. His hands were warm on her back, pulling her closer. Holding her tighter—

"Sterling . . ." The word was more breath than whisper, and she couldn't even scold him for the slip because they were lost behind a curtain of fog and mist and—

"Watch out!" someone yelled, but it was too late.

They were too close to the waterfall, and a split second later, the water hit the edge of the mat, pushing it under and flipping them both into the water and under the falls. For a moment, there was nothing but a constant, pummeling pressure, like a wave that never crested, pushing Alex down and holding her under. Beating her like a fist. Like a hundred fists. Bubbles floated all around her, but there wasn't one to breathe, and Alex knew there was no coming up from this, no fighting nature or gravity or—

King. She had to get to King, and so Alex swam away from the bubbles, out from under the pressure of the falls and toward the hand that was grabbing, reaching, pulling her to the surface.

"Are you okay?"

"I'm . . ." She couldn't catch her breath. She couldn't even think. "I'm—"

"Sterling!" He shook her.

Alex pushed her hair out of her face and looked at King, who was studying her like he didn't know whether to curse her or kiss her.

"David!" a voice yelled in the distance. They were on the other side of the falls, Alex realized. Trapped between the curtain of the water and the stone of the mountain, alone in a cave—or grotto— that was hidden by the mist. The others were still on the other side, yelling, "Donna! Are you—"

"We're okay!" King shouted, but he never took his eyes off of Alex. It was like they were the only people on earth, wrapped in a cocoon of silence and stone and—

"Sterling . . ." That time, the voice was low and deep. A warning or a prayer. He was just right there—kissing distance apart. And he was drawing closer. And closer. Until—

He stopped. His gaze slid off her, and Alex pulled back. Even in the cool water, her face went red because . . . of course he wasn't going to kiss her. Kissing is for people who don't hate each other. Kissing is for—

"Sterling." That time, he laughed—a *ha* that echoed off the stone and was lost under the roar of the falls as King pointed behind her and Alex turned to see a circle of light in the shadows, bright and shining through the stone on the far side of the cave.

"Is that . . ."

"A tunnel," King whispered.

"Wait." It mattered. She knew it mattered, but her lungs weren't quite working. Her brain wasn't quite working. It took a moment for her to realize—"If the sun is shining through there, then . . ."

"We don't need to go over the mountain," King said.

"We can go under it." Alex didn't know whether to grin or groan because the mission was on, but the moment . . .

The moment was over.

chapter twenty-nine

Present Day
The Island

KING

"You could stay here," King tried, but Alex glared at him because glaring was apparently her favorite form of cardio.

If there was one clear advantage to Fertility Week, it was that the group bonding and therapy sessions were set aside for private reflection and romantic couple time, leaving this couple plenty of time for what they had to do.

"Just an offer." King threw open his suitcase and started digging for the latch to the hidden compartment. "Last time, it was easy enough once we got to the other side."

"Last time, significantly fewer people wanted us dead."

He gave a shrug because that was easier than saying *Suit yourself.* The compartment clicked open to reveal an array of weapons and tools, and King started pulling out his favorites.

"What's that?" Alex actually sounded offended.

"What? This?" He picked up a gun and inserted a clip. "I know it's been a while, Sterling, but these are called weapons."

"Sarcasm doesn't become you, Kingsley."

He couldn't help himself. He laughed. But there was something in the set of Alex's shoulders.

"I thought you were out of the life." Her voice was softer than he liked it. Almost fragile.

"I *was* out." He dug another clip out of the bag. "But I wasn't dead. You didn't honestly expect us to go in there unarmed, did you?"

She gave him a *give me some credit* look, then she went to the wall of the bungalow and unscrewed the air vent and pulled out a duffel bag. "Not exactly." He gave her a look. "What? Like you've never left a go bag before."

He smiled but didn't say a word because there are some things a smart man should never say to Alexandra Sterling. Especially if she is holding a weapon.

The walk was longer than King remembered. Or maybe just heavier.

Eight years before, the jungle had been silent and the moon had been full and the woman beside him had felt like an ally—or at least not a stranger—as they'd inched along the narrow path around the pool that led to the edge of the falls.

"Watch your step," he warned.

"I know."

This time, it felt like maybe she was going to hold his head underwater until the falls beat some sense into him. He felt like maybe he was going to let her.

"Toss me that—"

She threw a bag, and it hit his chest a little too hard, but he didn't say a word; he just slipped through the little gap between the stone and the falling water and then let his eyes adjust to the darkness of the cave.

A moment later, a flashlight flickered to life, and he stood silently, watching as Alex swept the light over the cave floor and the cave walls and then—

"Oh no." The light froze and so did she. "Where's the tunnel?" It took a lot for Alex Sterling to panic. King still wasn't sure he'd ever heard it, but in that moment, she was close. "There was a tunnel?" Her voice ticked higher than usual, the words a little faster. "There used to be a tunnel, right? There was a tunnel right there!"

She pointed to the place where dozens—maybe hundreds—of

stones were cascading out of the cave wall and piling on the floor, and King bit back a curse. "Looks like there was a cave-in."

"Ya think?" she shouted.

"Hey, this isn't my fault," he shot back.

"Yeah, well . . . it *should* be."

"That doesn't even make sense!"

But Alex was already going to the stones and trying to pick them up and toss them aside.

"Alex."

"Maybe I can shift them . . ."

"It's blocked."

Alex spun. *"That's why I'm trying to shift them!"*

He should stop her, King thought.

He should help her.

He should toss her over his shoulder and take her back to the bungalow and not let her leave until they forgot about the last year and about Scotland and about . . . everything. But King couldn't forget—it was a biological impossibility—so he just leaned against the grotto wall and crossed his arms and tried not to sound smug when he told her, "Well, don't forget to lift with your legs."

It was ten years later, but she was still the girl who didn't know when to stop fighting. Which was probably why it hurt so much that she had eventually stopped fighting for him. So King just stood there, watching her sweat and curse and then finally step back and pronounce, "I think the tunnel is blocked."

"You know, I think you're right." He wasn't mocking her. He didn't dare. "Come on." He pushed off from the wall. "We're not getting through tonight, and the mountain will still be here in the morning."

Alex didn't speak. She didn't move. For a moment, there was nothing but the sound of falling water and the sight of the most beautiful woman he'd ever known still staring at that pile of stones as if she might grind them into dust with her bare hands. She'd do it too. Just to show the rocks who was boss. So clearly King wasn't thinking right—too much oxygen and jungle air, too many late nights and near misses—and that's why he held out his hand, and, instantly, felt like a fool. He had a picture-perfect memory, but it was like he'd forgotten the last six years had even happened. He should have known Alex wouldn't make that same mistake.

"Never mind. I'll—" He was already turning back to the gap between the wall and the water when a hand slid into his.

"You're right. Let's regroup in the morning."

Two minutes later, they were on the other side of the falls when, suddenly, Alex stopped moving. Moonlight glistened off the pool, and it felt like a spotlight after the darkness of the cave. The air was sweeter, and the sky was brighter, and it felt like maybe things were changing when she reached for him and whispered, "Take off your clothes."

She was tearing at his shirt and at hers. It was a frantic, crazy thing, and King wanted to ask a hundred questions, but he also didn't want to say a word or break the spell because, a split second later, Alex was diving into the water and King had no choice but to follow.

"Ster—" King started, but Alex was launching herself at him. It was a blur of cold water and hot skin as Alex smothered his mouth with her lips and the words—

"Shut up and kiss me."

King knew what was happening. *Someone was coming*—they had to be. Because this wasn't a kiss—it was *a cover*—a pretense. A ruse.

But the feeling of Alex's wet skin against his was real—the feel of her legs around his waist. They were almost weightless in the water, and King gave in to the feelings he was too tired to deny anymore. King had been lying his whole life, but the lies he told in that moment were to himself.

She was back.

She was there.

She was his.

Her lips parted under his. Tongues seeking, hearts pounding, chests rising and falling and—

"Of course, this is my personal favorite. I tell all our lovers that—Oh my." Flora's flashlight froze as it swept across the pond. King didn't have any doubt what they were seeing.

Alex's arms around his neck, wet hair and flushed skin and two people so tangled up in each other they might drown—they could drown and never even notice because, in a way, they had already gone under.

"Ooh!" Alex turned, pressing her (very naked) chest into King's (very naked) chest. She looked so modest and demure and . . . caught. She looked caught and oh so guilty. It was all he could do not to grin because no one did that better. No one did anything better, and part of King hated that he'd never told her.

Alex glanced back over her shoulder at Flora and the two maintenance guys who seemed to have the good sense to look shocked.

King brought a hand to the back of Alex's head and pressed her tighter against him. These jerks didn't deserve to look at her—leer at her. They didn't—

"Well." Flora let out an awkward giggle. "It seems the falls are . . . occupied."

"Well, you said we should make ourselves at home," King reminded the woman, and he felt Alex sink against him. Like she was suddenly trusting and soft and sweet. Like she felt . . . safe. "Now if you'll excuse us." The look he shot at the maintenance guys was a little harder than it needed to be, but he didn't care. Alex was naked in his arms and no one was going to leer at her. Not even King himself.

"I'll let you two . . ." Flora trailed off as if she couldn't find the words. "I'll see you later."

King listened to their footsteps fade into the chorus of birds and animals and the whistle of the wind in the trees until the only sound was Alex's heart pounding against his.

"I think . . ." he started, but he didn't want to say that it was over, they were safe, she should slip out of his arms and out of the water and away from that moment that felt suspended somewhere out of time.

"I think it's over," she said instead.

And King just stood there, trying to forget that it was true.

They were both silent as they crept back to the bungalow, clothes slightly askew because nothing ever fits right on wet skin. They both needed hot showers and sleep and some kind of Plan B, but at least they weren't talking when they saw Flora sitting on a big, flat rock near the edge of the path, waiting.

"Are we in trouble?" King asked, but she pursed her lips and pushed the words away.

"Don't be silly. I'm not waiting for you." (She was totally waiting for them.) "I'm just an old woman." (She wasn't old.) "Who likes to sit out under the stars sometimes. And think. And remember."

"I'm going to go . . ." Alex gestured to the bungalow and the shower and anywhere away from him. With any luck, she'd be in bed, pretending to sleep by the time he made it back.

"You know . . ." Flora's voice was soft. ". . . when you crawled off that plane eight years ago, I thought I'd never seen two people who needed to be locked in a room naked together more than the two of you. In fact"—she got a mischievous glint in her eye—"I considered it . . ." Flora looked up at King, eyes twinkling in a way that hinted at some deeper understanding that made him wonder if that place might have a little magic after all. "Now I get the feeling that you tried that."

There were no warning bells, but King heard them all the same. Flashing lights and blaring sirens screaming *DANGER, DANGER.*

There are some things spies just don't admit. Especially to themselves. But all King could do was look up at the stars and whisper, "It wasn't enough."

Five minutes later, King was slipping into the outdoor shower and turning it fully cold. He wanted to clean off, wake up. Snap himself back to the reality and the mission because King wanted his life back.

His rules and his protocols and his walls. He didn't need the CIA, and he sure as hell didn't need her.

What King actually needed were answers. Someone was after King and Alex, and neither of them would be safe until he figured out who. And why.

"Just answer me this . . ." When she appeared in the outdoor shower, she didn't even glance at his body—not even a subtle peek—and King tried not to feel so disappointed. "How are you not freaking out right now? Because, if you haven't noticed, we're going to have to find a new way over that mountain."

"We *have* a way over the mountain," he stated simply.

"And there are a few tons of volcanic rock blocking that way, so . . ." Alex trailed off when he smiled. "What?" She sounded almost scared. "What are you—"

"This isn't the only place we've ever broken into, you know?"

At first, she looked confused. Then concerned. Then . . . intrigued. He knew the moment she remembered—

"Michael Kingsley, are you suggesting that we do it like Amalfi?"

"No." King didn't even hesitate, he just inched closer. He was staring right into her eyes when he said, "I'm saying we do it *exactly* like Amalfi."

chapter thirty

Seven Years Ago
Amalfi Coast, Italy

ALEX

Alex didn't see King for a year, so she died her hair a deep, dark red because it was the boldest color she could think of—guaranteed to make her stand out in ways a good spy never would. She told herself she was doing it to spite him, but, the truth was, Zoe had a book deal. Her twin was going to be a published author, with her picture on the back cover of (hopefully) a million novels. She'd be going on tours and doing interviews, and they needed to look as unidentical as possible from that point forward, so Alex experimented with center parts and lip injectors.

She did a stint undercover in Quebec and brushed up on her French, then started perfecting her Russian. But, mostly, she tried to stay busy.

She took up knitting.

She gave up knitting.

She got really good at shoving knitting needles into the necks of sparring dummies.

She reread all of her sister's favorite novels and had dreams about telling some mystery man the plots of every one while she sat on kitchen counters she'd never have and he made food she'd never eat.

She imagined laughing.

But that just made her cry.

And she didn't think about Michael Kingsley every hour.

It was merely every day.

When the letter showed up in her mailbox, Alex didn't bother asking how it had reached her. The Agency knew all her safe houses, but the thin envelope didn't look like it came from Langley. There was no name. No address. No stamp. Just a one-way ticket to Italy and a note that said: *See you soon*.

So by the time Alex found herself standing on a crowded pier, looking out over the Mediterranean's choppy waters, it was almost a relief to turn up the collar of her coat and say, "Hello, Merritt."

A ferry was making its way toward them, churning along, full of tourists and commuters and people in love. Alex found herself uncharacteristically annoyed by the thought of it.

"Hello, darling. Come give an old woman a hug."

For the first time since she'd known her, Margaret Merritt looked her age. Alex didn't like the way Merritt walked up the ramp to the ferry, hunched over in a way that had nothing to do with the chill. Her skin was a little too pale and her eyes had lost that touch of sparkle. Maybe it was a cover. A ploy. Or maybe time catches up with everyone eventually, even people who have lived their whole lives hiding in plain sight.

When they finally made it on board, Merritt looked Alex up and down and told her, "You look tired." She wasn't being rude—that wasn't in Merritt's nature. Things like fatigue simply mattered in their world. People needed to be quick—sharp. *On it*. And Alex hadn't slept well in a year. Since the bungalow and the breeze and the deep breaths on the other side of the bed.

"Thank you for coming." Merritt made room on a bench as the rest of the seats filled up on the ferry.

"Anything for you. You know that."

"I do." She sounded adorably smug and almost like herself. Maybe the old lady look was a cover, after all? Maybe . . . Merritt coughed. "I've been better."

Oh. Oh no.

The ferry was about to pull away from shore. They were drawing up the gangway and the seats were almost full as Alex looked around, a little more obvious than she should have been. Maybe she was getting old too. Or maybe she was just getting sloppy.

"Is he coming?" She toyed with a thread on her sleeve.

Merritt smirked. "He's already here."

They found him on the top deck near the aft of the boat, leaning against the railing and looking over the rocky shore. Houses were nestled among the cliffs like birds that had made their nests there. The roads were steep and narrow, and the beaches were covered with rocks, but there was a reason those cliffs were sprinkled with mansions and the water was dotted with yachts. It was one of the most beautiful playgrounds in the world, but the man at the back of the ferry looked like he'd seen better. He seemed almost bored. And maybe that's why all the women (and a few of the men) on the top deck watched him out of the corner of their eyes. He was the kind of man it would feel amazing to impress.

When Alex stepped toward King, he turned and leaned against the rail, watching as the wind blew her hair—too wild and too red— around her face. "You changed it."

"Let me guess. Too bright? Too bold? Too—"

"I like it." He shifted and looked down at the water. Like he didn't trust himself to look at her. "It suits you."

"Is that an insult?" Alex cocked her head. "Because it didn't quite sound like one, but I might be rusty."

King made a sound that was almost a laugh, and she wanted to ask a million questions. She wasn't prepared to see him smile. "It's good to see you, Sterling."

Did he . . . *mean it*? It actually sounded like he meant it, but Alex might have been wrong. She was probably wrong.

"Are you feeling okay? Head injury? Personality disorder? Ooh! Did they finally perfect face-swapping technology, because if they did . . ." He was laughing. At her. *With* her. Like she was . . . amusing. "Okay, now I'm worried. What's going on with you?" she asked, but he just looked at her like that was one secret he'd never tell.

"Okay, you two, cut it out," Merritt ordered. "We're attracting attention. Act like you like each other."

Alex expected King to blame her hair. Or her clothes. Or maybe just *her* in general, but instead he tugged her close and pressed a quick kiss to her forehead before wrapping her up tight. "Better?" he whispered, but Merritt just stood there, a curious look in her eye.

"Slightly."

People were still looking, but now they stared at Alex, jealous that she got to snuggle up to Michael Kingsley and burrow into the warmth of his wool peacoat and broad chest. She half expected someone to try to throw her overboard.

And then he maneuvered so that she was standing against the rail, pressing against her from behind, arms bracketed around her like it was his job to keep her safe. As if Alex hadn't been keeping herself safe since she was five years old and realized no one else was going to do it because everyone else had to worry about Zoe.

Instantly, Alex bit back the thought. It wasn't fair—to her parents or her sister or, especially, King. She had no right to read anything into that moment. He was just doing his job because covers were survival and survival was the game, so Alex didn't say a thing as he put a hand over hers on the railing, intertwining their fingers, as if the two of them had been tangled together for years. She smiled when she realized it was true.

"Why do I get the feeling you didn't come all this way to play matchmaker?" King almost sounded bored.

This time, it was Merritt's turn to look out over the water and the cliffs like she would have given anything to be a regular person on that ferry, going to or from a regular life. But when she spoke, the words were steel. "Recognize anyone?"

She pulled a photograph from her pocket and King took one glance. "That's him. The buyer in Cartagena."

"It is." Merritt smiled like she was going to give King a gold star. "He's been using those emeralds well. In addition to various large purchases from our friend on the island, he's had his fingers in all kinds of nasty pies."

"Who is he?" Alex asked.

"His name is Viktor Kozlov." Merritt's voice was too low to carry on the wind, but she gave an almost imperceptible glance at the people on the top deck. Families and tourists and couples who, unlike King and Alex, were actually in love.

"So he's Russian," King whispered. He sounded like he didn't know whether to be relieved or disappointed, but Merritt gave a dry laugh, like *Kids today . . . So sweet . . . So naive . . .*

"Of course he's Russian. And he's been a very busy boy. Smarter than average. More ruthless than most. He has a weakness, though."

"He's a man," Alex blurted, and Merritt smirked.

"He is." Merritt seemed a little more like herself when she said, "And as such, he's been in the market for a mistress."

"*No.*"

The word was so sharp—so sudden—that Alex expected to see a flash of lightning. The word was *charged*, and maybe that's why it took her a moment to realize the arms around her were going tight. It was like a switch had flipped and everything about King froze solid. Like he turned to stone.

"Absolutely not." King's arms turned to granite around her, but he kept his gaze on Merritt. "She won't do it."

"Who won't do what?" Alex felt lost and she didn't like it. She was trying to pry free, but he was too big and too strong and too . . . angry?

"Alex is *not* going to go undercover as Viktor Kozlov's plaything." *Wait. What?* "She won't—"

"Maybe I will?" Now she was the one getting angry.

"*You won't.*" His voice was iron. It wasn't a premonition. It was an order, and Alex didn't like what it was doing to her. She was ready to breathe fire, but she was also . . . touched. For the first time in a long time, someone was looking at her like they cared? Wait. *Was* that what caring looked like? Felt like? She had to be mistaken. But before she could ask for clarification, Merritt laughed.

"Of course Alex isn't going to be the mistress." Merritt gave an indifferent shrug with one frail shoulder.

"I'm not?"

"He's already found one. And he bought her a lovely little place to hide away in."

When the ferry went around a bend in the shore, they saw it. Alex followed Merritt's gaze to the stark, steep cliff on the far side of the little inlet—the rocky beach and olive trees. And the most beautiful house that Alex had ever seen.

"Why are we here, Margaret?" King asked because he knew there was more to the story.

"I thought the two of you might like to break into it for me, but if you would rather not—"

"I'll do it."

The arms pulled away, and Alex didn't realize how cold the wind would feel without them.

"May I talk to you?" He was glaring down, hand tugging, like he had to get her away from Merritt before she could spout any more bad ideas.

But bad ideas were Alex's favorite kind sometimes, so she leaned close to Merritt and whispered, "What's our time frame?"

"Now!" King tugged. He wanted to drag her away, but Alex wanted to be difficult, so she stayed right where she was, confident that he wouldn't cause a scene. Because King was genetically opposed to scene-causing. "Sterling. Do you see that?" He pointed to the house that was slipping away as the ferry moved on. "The fortress with the fences and walls and literal cliffs? And . . . is that a guard tower?" He squinted into the distance.

"Oh, come on . . ." She rolled her eyes. "It's not that hard."

"It is incredibly hard."

"We can do this."

"I know we can." He ran a hand over his face. His shirt was open at the collar and his coat was unbuttoned and his hair was just a little longer than it used to be. Maybe it was the sea air, but it was almost wavy. He looked like someone who was a little mysterious and a lot dangerous, and Alex couldn't help herself: she liked it. "She can send a black bag team for this."

"Can you?" she asked, and Merritt had the good taste to look slightly guilty.

"I would rather not." She'd chosen the words with so much care that Alex had to wonder what she wasn't saying.

"Sterling." King's voice was low. And dark. And careful. "This isn't like the island. They don't need us for this."

"Actually, Michael, I do."

They both turned and looked at Merritt. She was old and weak and growing weaker. They would have gone anywhere for her—done anything. Even this. But King just asked, "Why us?"

It was an odd thing, to watch someone shrink in front of your eyes, but that's what Merritt did then. "Because all the people I trust are dead. Because I am an old woman, and I'm alone. Because there's one more thing I need to mark off my to-do list before it's too late." It physically pained her to admit, "Because I'm too old and too weak to do it myself."

Alex was young and strong and in her prime, but she still knew the feeling, and so she said, "I'm in."

chapter thirty-one

KING

The first task was simple, but that didn't mean it was easy.

"Do you have it?" King asked, and he watched Alex try not to roll her eyes.

"Of course I have it. I've had it since the boutique and the jewelry store and the pharmacy. I've had it since you declared 'this will be easy' two hours ago. Spoiler alert: it isn't all that easy."

Which was an understatement. They needed eyes and ears on Kozlov's compound, but the place was a fortress and that was the problem. Luckily, Irina, the new girlfriend, had already moved in. Un-luckily, Kozlov either didn't trust her—or he didn't trust the rest of the world—because Irina had two goons who never left her shadow.

King had already cloned Irina's smartphone and matched the case. All that was left to do was make the switch. It was something he'd been working on for a while—a new piece of software that would sync across her devices and turn every phone, tablet, and computer in the house into a bug or camera as soon as they got within range. It wasn't as good as sending in a black bag team, but it was better than nothing, and they'd take what they could get—at least for now.

King guided Alex to a small table on the other side of the dance floor from where Irina sat. Waves lapped at the rocks beneath them as they sat surrounded by twinkle lights and live music and all the overpriced limoncello a person could hope for. The weather had turned, and it felt more like spring than winter as they sat there. He slipped an arm around her shoulders. People needed to think they were in love.

On the other side of the dance floor, Irina squealed as three mini-Irinas joined her.

"Do you think she's pretty?" Alex asked.

"Yes." Of course she was pretty. Kozlov wouldn't have had an ugly mistress. "Though probably not as pretty as she thinks she is." She was twenty-one and had spent the past two hours taking selfies and filming videos of herself, which King wouldn't have minded, ordinarily, but it's hard to swap a person's phone when it's glued to their hand.

"What aren't you saying?" Alex asked.

"Nothing."

"You never say nothing."

"I say nothing all the time."

Alex shifted in her seat and leaned closer. Twinkle lights reflected off her cheekbones and shone in her eyes. "You want to know what *I* think you're thinking?"

"I *know* what I'm thinking."

"I think you're wondering what Merritt isn't telling us."

That's exactly what King was thinking, but he didn't dare say so. The clock was ticking, so he pushed out of his chair and said, "Come on."

"What?"

"We need to get closer. Dance with me."

"Dance?"

"Yes. The mutual swaying to music."

"Did you just ask me to *mutually sway* with you?"

He didn't say anything else. He just raised one eyebrow, and a moment later her hand was slipping into his and they were moving around the floor, heading toward where Irina sat with her back to the dancing couples, her phone in her hand. *Her phone was always in her hand.*

"Follow my lead," he said, and for once, Alex didn't argue.

"Do you think there's actually something we're waiting on or does Merritt just want an extended holiday on the Mediterranean?"

King hadn't considered that option, but maybe he should have.

"Possibly. But Kozlov is still a bad guy, and we're still in the bad guy business," he whispered near her ear, and when she shivered, he realized the air was still chilly. Summer wasn't quite there yet. "You still have it?"

"No. I threw it in the sea." She didn't roll her eyes, but she could have. The sun was down, and the lights overhead were growing brighter, and, suddenly, Alex looked away, almost guilty. "I'm sorry."

"No. It was a stupid question. I'm sorry I asked it."

"That's not it." She held a little tighter to his shoulder. "I'm sorry she keeps making you work with me."

Was that what she thought?

"I don't . . . I mean . . . You are . . . Who do you usually work with?" he blurted, then studied her out of the corner of his eye. "Is there anyone . . . Tyler, for example . . ."

"I'm better alone. Always have been."

King was better alone. He was cranky and demanding and impossible to please. She was none of those things.

"Sterling—"

"Probably for the best, though, right? I don't want to get anyone killed. A really smart guy told me I was going to, you know. Maybe I don't want to risk it."

"I was wrong."

He expected her to taunt or tease, but when she spoke again, she sounded sad and resigned and not at all like the girl in the *Future Spy* hoodie. "You're never wrong."

He was, though. He was never wrong about the past, but he was often wrong about the future. From the moment he first met her, she'd surprised him. For example, he never would have dreamed she would say—

"Do you ever think about what would happen if we stopped hating each other?"

King pulled back so fast his neck popped. "I don't hate you."

"You just don't respect me."

"Are we really going to fight about why we fight?"

"A girl's got to have hobbies." Alex forced a smile that was so unlike her that he stumbled to a stop on the dance floor. People were staring. They looked like they were about to break up. Or he was about to go down on one knee and pull out a ring. Or something. They weren't far from Irina's table and the guards were going to get suspicious, but all King could do was gape at Alex and say, "We don't have to fight."

"What else can we do?"

"We can do anything!" he snapped, throwing an arm out and pointing to the coast and the sea and the world, big and beautiful and all around them. They spoke ten languages between them. They had so many skills. They could go anywhere. They could do anything. But they were there and they were . . . them. And—

He didn't see the waitress, not until it was way too late. His arm was swinging out again, and this time it caught a tray of drinks, sending the glasses soaring through the air and crashing onto the nearest table, leaving everything doused in glass and booze and smelling like lemons. Irina jumped out of her chair with a screech. Her phone flew out of her hand and skidded ten feet across the dance floor.

As it turned out, the job was easy after all.

chapter thirty-two

KING

It took more than a month of surveillance. They probably could have done it in half the time, but Merritt was being cagey. Or cagier than usual.

She found them a yacht that they kept moored off the coast, and he and Alex spent their days riding up and down the twisting highways on a Vespa, Alex's arms around King's waist. They spent their nights watching the house through a telescope, lying on the big loungers on the top deck, eating pasta and looking at the stars.

"What are they watching tonight?" King plopped an olive in his mouth while Alex stood at the telescope that was currently trained on Viktor Kozlov's living room. Whatever she saw made her sigh, a little jealous. "*Goldfinger*! Ooh, this is a good one. Q gives Bond an Aston Martin with an ejector seat."

"That's not genuine tradecraft."

"Take that back!" Alex gasped, offended, but it was all King could do not to smile.

"I guess we've learned one thing about Kozlov—he's even more obsessed with spy movies than you are. And that's saying something." He pushed the olives away, not trusting himself when they were within reach, and Alex went back to scanning the roofline and the grounds.

"There are six perimeter guards tonight," she said, stepping away from the telescope.

"So they double the watch when the old man's on the premises." King made a mental note and Alex made a real one, logging the observation in her own secret code in a tiny book that she sometimes tucked into her bra. Not that he'd been noticing. Or, well, any more than he noticed everything because that was his birthright and his job and the key to his survival.

"I wonder what they've got in that compound?" King still didn't know what Merritt wasn't telling them. But she definitely wasn't telling them something.

"Besides a very angry Russian and his presumably angrier mistress?" Alex reached for the olives.

"What makes you think Irina's angry?"

"Trust me. I've seen Viktor Kozlov. The woman who signed up for that job hates him. And herself. And . . . OMG—"

"Do people really say 'OMG'?"

"Michael Kingsley, are you . . . laughing?"

"No. I have something in my eye."

"That's for crying. You were." She leaned down and pulled his hands away from his face. "You were smiling. At me. Because I'm delightful. Say it."

"Do we know how many deliveries they get a week?"

"Three. Groceries, flowers, and linens. And don't change the subject—"

"You are . . . amusing." He really didn't want to admit it. "At times."

"I knew it. You adore me. I'm adorable."

The moon was full, and the sky was clear, and they were far enough from shore that it felt like he could make out every star, but all King could do was shake his head and say, "No comment."

Alex must have decided to give up while she was ahead because she dropped onto the lounge beside him. The yacht rocked and swayed, but King could hear the gears turning in her mind. It was like she was gathering her thoughts and her courage, but when she spoke, it wasn't much more than a whisper.

"You know, I'm an excellent climber."

He hated that he could tell when she was serious. He loathed that she was her most serious right then.

"No."

"We know the guards. The rotations. It wouldn't be hard."

"It would be extremely hard."

"I could do it without ropes."

"Absolutely not!"

"Why not?"

"Because it's a death sentence! Those cliffs aren't straight up and down, Sterling. Which would be bad enough. The middle section is almost all overhang and . . . No."

"Fine." She sounded like a teenager who had just been told she couldn't have the keys to her dad's Maserati. "Whatever. As long as I don't get you killed, right?"

He wasn't smiling anymore. "Exactly."

If anyone from the house was scanning the sea and the ships, it was important that they look the part, so that was why he tugged her closer. One of her legs twisted until it was lying over one of his, and through it all, the dark waters of the Mediterranean kept lapping against the hull and the moon kept shining overhead and the silence stretched out around them like the night.

"It wouldn't be the first time, you know?" The words were so low, they were almost swallowed by the sea and King almost didn't hear them. But he did. "I've been almost killing people my whole life. Longer even."

"I'm afraid your math doesn't make sense there, Sterling." He wasn't actually expecting her to laugh. Not like she thought he was funny but like she thought he was . . . sweet. Innocent. Almost naive. As if she knew something he didn't.

"Shows what you know; I almost killed someone in the womb."

"What—"

"Never mind." She tried to get up, but he wasn't about to let her go, so he pivoted, trapping one of her legs under one of his.

"What are you talking about?"

"I know you remember. What I told you—about my sister . . ."

"There are two of you." He still kind of couldn't believe it.

He'd never seen her look away from a challenge, back down from a fight. Alexandra Sterling wasn't someone who looks the other way, period. But that's exactly what she did.

"I'm too much. Isn't that what you said?"

"Sterling—"

"You're right. I was always too much—even before I was born. I took up too much room, and I consumed too much energy, and I drained everything and everyone around me. I almost killed her. I almost killed the person I love most, and I didn't even have opposable thumbs yet." She gave a sad, dry laugh. "Imagine what I can do now that I have knives."

She sounded insane because that was how she wanted to sound. She didn't want anyone to see how raw that wound was—how much it had shaped her and changed her and brought her to that moment and that world.

"Hey—"

"It was her heart. Mostly. It was small and underdeveloped and full of holes like Swiss cheese."

"Sterling—"

"She was just a few days old the first time they cut her open. We were lying in the nursery, me a baby giant and her . . . They had to do it again, of course. And again. And again. My first memory was of a children's hospital in Germany, shouting that the doctors should take my heart instead. I wasn't using it." It was the saddest smile he'd ever seen. "Haven't used it since."

"Sterling."

"Good night, King—"

"Alex."

He wasn't sure if he'd ever said her name before. He didn't stop to think what it meant, the fact that he couldn't remember. "I didn't mean . . ." All those times he'd said she was too much—too bold, too brave, too strong, and too foolish. She'd been told she was too much her whole life, but—"I like your heart just the way it is."

She nodded slightly and started to turn but looked back at him, like she'd almost forgotten—

"She's okay, you know? My sister. She's . . . happy? I think?"

"Are you happy?"

If he lived to be a hundred, he'd never know what made him ask it. What made her stop and look at the lights on the far coast and the dark water—the vast sky full of twinkling stars. And him.

"I am tonight."

Long after she was gone, King just sat there, thinking to himself that, for the first time in a long time, so was he.

chapter thirty-three

ALEX

"Hello, dear."

Alex had honestly forgotten Merritt was down below, which might have been a mark on the "maybe Alex isn't cut out for covert operations" side of the ledger, but Alex didn't show her surprise—which might have been a mark on the other one.

"I don't suppose there's any chance you didn't hear that?"

She looked across the plush room to where Merritt stood, gazing out the windows at the lights that dotted the coastline. The older woman gave her a look that was somewhere between *you wish* and *give me some credit*, but her smile was soft and indulgent. "You're going to be good, dear. But for now, I'm still better."

Merritt walked to a bar cart and poured two glasses of something dark and liquid. She handed one to Alex. "Michael's family—"

"I know. He's a baby duke . . ."

She hadn't really meant to say it, and luckily, Merritt's laugh cut her off. "A what?"

"Nothing." Alex took a sip and sank down onto the sofa. "Just something my sister . . . Nothing."

Merritt walked back to the window and looked out at the water. Her white hair stood in sharp contrast to the black night, and Alex studied her reflection in the glass: she looked like a woman who had seen everything. She'd been to all the places and done all the things, and now her whole life was one long case of déjà vu, but she wasn't even mad about it. Because, this time, she still had a chance to change things.

"He has a photographic memory." The words floated across

the darkened room. "Did he tell you? Michael? His grandfather had one, too." Merritt smiled at a memory. "In 1969 the KGB infiltrated the CIA headquarters in Berlin. Do you know what they got?" She turned and looked at Alex, who was smart enough to stay silent. "Nothing. Just a single piece of paper that said '*Khoroshaya popytka, tovarishchi.*'"

"*Nice try, comrades,*" Alex translated, and Merritt raised her glass in a silent *cheers.*

"He had committed the files to memory—all of them. Every form. Every letter. He carried three decades' worth of secrets around in his mind until the day he died."

"Okay." Alex wasn't entirely sure what the point was, but she was sure that Merritt had one.

"Michael is like him."

"I see." Alex didn't see, though. Not really. It was like asking someone who had lived their whole life underground to describe the sun. "Michael's father is good too." Merritt's face went darker, like an old-fashioned lamp and someone had just turned the oil down. "Or he used to be."

That was it—the point of the story, and Alex stayed quiet and still and let the shadows ask the questions. "You see . . . Michael's father hasn't been in the field for a long time. And he hasn't been . . . himself . . . for even longer."

Merritt caught Alex's gaze in the reflection, but she didn't turn. She didn't have to. She knew Alex well enough to know she'd have to ask—

"What happened?"

"His wife died," Merritt said simply. She sipped her drink and turned from the window. "To this day, I don't know which was harder on Michael—losing his mother or watching his father . . . fade. It didn't just break Michael's heart, Alexandra. It broke him." Merritt gazed into the distance for a long time, but then her expression changed, less sadness, more all-seeing, all-knowing deity. "I know he's hard on you."

Alex just sat there, blinking, trying to understand the sharp turn of the conversation. She'd been the villain of the Michael Kingsley Story for so long that she couldn't quite keep up.

"I won't take unnecessary risks, I promise. I'll—" *Keep him safe. Be careful.* "Find a way to get to Kozlov. I'll do it by myself if I have to."

"Oh, I don't think *he's* the one he's worried about."

Of all the cryptic things that Merritt might have said, that one was the biggest mystery to Alex, but she didn't ask a single question—not until Merritt placed the crystal tumbler on the bar cart, then walked toward the door, and suddenly, Alex had to know—

"Can I do this?" Alex cringed a little, but she couldn't hold the words back, so she didn't even try. "Am I good enough?"

Merritt's smile was a whisper in the shadow, soft and easy to miss. "You will be."

chapter thirty-four

ALEX

It was another week before Merritt found them in the galley kitchen, arguing over the proper way to fry an egg—

"No part of a fried egg should be crispy, Sterling. If it's crispy, you did it . . ."

But King trailed off when Merritt appeared in the doorway, smirking as she said, "It's time."

Of course, by then Alex had already spent several days shopping and planning and watching King do geometry in his head. (Which was honestly kind of sexy, though she would have rather died than say so.)

Finally, the conditions were right and they couldn't put it off any longer. She didn't want to think about how—if it were up to her—she might have put it off for forever.

"Are you sure this is a good idea?" Alex asked as they crouched on the cliffs that looked over Kozlov's compound. The helicopter had left that morning, taking Irina and Kozlov back to Moscow. They weren't due back for another week. The movers and decorators were gone, and the house was finally settled.

This was their window. If they were crazy enough to take it.

But maybe Alex was getting older—or maybe King was just rubbing off on her—because for the first time in a long time she thought that crazy might be overrated.

"Of course it's not a good idea." King's voice was softer than she was used to. "It's *your* idea." There was just enough moonlight that she could see the white of his teeth and know that he was teasing, so she snatched the black nylon rope out of his hands and threw it into a perfect knot.

"I didn't hear you coming up with any better ones."

"You're right." He nodded sagely. "You didn't."

"And the place is empty," Alex said, almost wistful. "For now."

"It is."

"And the faster we get this done, the sooner we can leave each other's company," Alex pointed out, but King stayed silent for a long time. Then he gave a slow, soft nod.

"Of course."

"Never lay eyes on each other again."

The town down the coast did fireworks every Tuesday, so Alex shouldn't have been surprised when she heard a low, subtle *boom* in the distance.

"That's true." He was breathing a little harder than he should have been. This was their window. They needed to take advantage of the distraction and the sky full of color and the noise.

This was their window.

And still . . .

"Sterling . . ."

Alex held out the crossbow, saying, "Do you want to do the honors or should I?"

For a moment, she was sure he hadn't heard her because his eyes never left hers, like the answer was already there, floating back and forth between them.

Then, overhead—*boom*. Light filled the sky, like every star in the heavens had picked that moment to start falling.

King shook his head. "You do it. You're a better shot." *Did he really think that? Did he really . . .* "Sterling," he prompted, and Alex shook off the thought. She aimed the bow and fired, watched as the rope unfurled, whipping through the night.

A moment later, he was tying off their end and checking the tension, saying, "I'll go first."

"But—"

"I'm heavier," King snapped, then recoiled, like he wanted to pull the words back. "If it can hold me, it can hold you. This part . . . I'm not going to argue with you about this part."

And, suddenly, Alex couldn't remember how to argue—how to speak—because he was looking down at her like he would have given anything to shoot that crossbow the other direction, to slide her right back to the boat and out of harm's way.

"Whenever you're ready."

Alex had forgotten about their comms units. And Merritt. And even their mission. She'd almost forgotten her own name when he looked at her and said, "I'll see you on the other side."

And then he was flying, disappearing into the night.

Two minutes later, Alex followed.

chapter thirty-five

Present Day
The Island

KING

King didn't like it. Not the angle or the equipment or the woman who was lying beside him, almost vibrating with glee—and a small amount of skepticism.

"Tell me again why you had a crossbow in your luggage?"

"It's called planning for contingencies," he said, but Alex was Alex. Nothing was ever as obvious—or as easy—as it should have been.

"But"—she made quote marks with her fingers—"*crossbow contingencies*. What are those, exactly?"

"Give it to me. I'll do it." He held a hand out, but she jerked back.

"No. I like it. I've never had a travel crossbow before."

"You still don't have a travel crossbow. *I* have a travel crossbow. And I can take it—"

But Alex was already rising to a knee, taking aim, and firing into the night. The line unfurled, disappearing into the darkness between the peak where they were currently lying and the wall of the compound that was nestled into the cliffs a hundred yards away.

"If this has all been an elaborate ruse to throw me into a volcano, then I honestly have to applaud the commitment," she said as they both peeked over the edge of the cliff.

"That's not a volcano. I don't think."

"Oh, but the fall would kill me." She sounded almost upbeat about it.

"There is that," he said.

The compound hadn't changed that much in the eight years since they'd last seen it. It was still nestled into the cliffs overlooking the sea. Still isolated and angry, with its stone facade and narrow road that zigzagged up the steep incline—the only way in. Or out.

Almost.

He pointed to the helicopter that was sitting on the landing pad that jutted out from the side of the mountain. "Our guy is home this time."

"He is."

"So I guess we should do this . . . now?" King hated the uptick in his voice—the uncertainty in his gut. It had to be this way, he told himself. And he had to do it with her, but he hated that, too, and he didn't stop and let himself think about the fact that he didn't want to work with her and he didn't want to work without her. He didn't want to be there. And he didn't want to be anywhere else.

"King?" Alex was saying. "You got weird."

"I was just thinking . . ."

"I told you, you don't need to redo the math. I checked it. The math is—"

"What if we stopped?"

"What?" Now she sounded confused.

"We've done a lot of bad things to a lot of bad people, Sterling. And now one of them wants us dead. So forgive me if I want to take a minute and imagine a future where we stopped looking for trouble."

"We did that. Then trouble came looking for us, remember?" Of course he remembered. "And they don't want us *dead*," she went on. "Dead would have been over in Vegas. Dead would be done by now."

"You're right."

"Someone wants us *alive*, which is a whole lot scarier."

"I know."

"Someone from our shared and terrible past wants *something*, and I intend to find out what it is from the best lead we have."

King blew out a tired breath. "He's the *only* lead we have."

"Exactly." She looked triumphant. And so beautiful, it hurt. The moon was full and the stars were bright and there was no sound but birdsong and crashing waves and the little voice in the back of King's head, telling him he was out of other options.

"Besides, we were good at being bad. Weren't we?" she asked over her shoulder.

"We were the best," he said.

And then she threw herself over the edge, disappearing into the darkness and the night.

The balcony doors were open, and King hated the sight of them. They felt like a trap. But there was nothing he could do but marvel as Alex slipped across the balcony like a phantom, then breezed through the doors like a ghost.

She was almost weightless, formless. Fearless. She moved like smoke, and she danced like fire, and he almost felt sorry for anyone who got in her way as she slipped across the old stone floors. With the sounds of the waves breaking against the rocks down below, it was almost tranquil except for the sound of . . . shooting?

The lights were off, but the room was full of flashes of color and little *pings* and *bangs* that echoed off the old stone floors. That must have been why the figure in the chair didn't turn—didn't even falter—until he felt Alex's gun against his temple. "Remember us?"

The controller in the man's hand dropped, shattering on the floor. His face turned red and Dr Pepper dribbled down his chin. He looked like he couldn't decide what to do with the bottle because he'd never been held at gunpoint before.

On the screen, there was a bang and a flash of fire, and Alex said, "You're dead."

King turned off the television and switched on the overhead light, but the man in the chair just sat there, staring.

"I don't think he remembers us?" Alex looked up at King. "I've got to say, I'm gonna be disappointed if he doesn't."

The guy had to be at least thirty, so he wasn't a kid, but that was the word that came to mind, maybe because he was drinking Dr Pepper at three a.m. while playing *Call of Duty*. Or maybe it was the softness of his face and his features that made Alex cut King a look that said, *This is the most fearsome arms dealer in the world?*

The man fumbled and put the Dr Pepper on the side table, and then he picked up a bag of something orange. "Cheez puff?"

"No thank you?" Alex didn't sound so sure.

"Okay. I just . . . I wasn't expecting company."

"We dropped by." Alex smirked. "Hope that's okay, Mr. . . . You know . . . I don't think we ever got your name."

"Call me TriBlade." The guy gave a cocky smirk, so King cocked an eyebrow and Alex cocked her gun. "Or Franklin," the guy mumbled. "My real name is Franklin."

They could have asked if it was his first name or his last, but in the end, it didn't matter and they both knew it.

"Okay, Franklin." King crossed his arms and leaned back against a credenza. "Now we're going to ask you some questions and you're going to answer them or else I'm going to let her do that to *you*."

"Do what to me?" the guy asked, so Alex pulled an action figure off a table and hurled it through an open window and out toward the sea.

"That was a collectible."

"And now it flies," King said.

"There's no reason to do anything to me." He threw his hands up. "I'm not a bad guy."

"You're the definition of *bad guy*." Alex sounded annoyed.

"No, I'm not. I'm . . ." He thought of something. "Ask Merritt!"

King felt Alex go still—everything but her grip on the gun—that went tighter.

"Seriously?" Franklin's jaw went slack in disbelief. "Merritt didn't tell you? I'm a broker—a dealer. After the two of you paid me a visit and left me your little . . . gifts."

"I think he means the bugs," Alex whispered.

"Yes. I surmised as much," King told her.

"Merritt reached out, and now she's . . . like . . . one of my best clients."

"So you're an informant?" Some things were starting to make sense to King. But not everything. Not yet.

"I am a businessman." Franklin sounded defensive. "A free agent. A . . . useful person to know when people like you need to talk to people even worse than me." He got out of the chair and walked to a glass-fronted fridge, where he pulled out a fresh Dr Pepper. "Want one?"

"No thanks. I'm good." King felt cold. This wasn't how he thought this was going to go, and if there was one thing King hated, it was surprises.

"How about"—Franklin turned to Alex and added with an exaggerated *wink wink*—"your lovely wife? Say, how are things on the other side of the island? I heard they got a new chef. Flora won't let me order takeout, though."

"Flora—" Alex started, but Franklin's laugh cut her off.

"She's my big sister. You didn't know?" He laughed harder. "Behold"—he held out a hand, gesturing to the island all around them—"our inheritance. I make more money with my side than she does with hers, though." The Dr Pepper opened with a fizz.

"Congratulations."

"Now." Franklin dropped into a leather desk chair and crossed one leg over the other. He looked ready to make a deal. "To what do I owe the pleasure?"

"I think you know." King pointed at the painting that was hanging over the desk. Three daggers formed a triangle. "We just saw that. Tattooed on the arm of a man who tried to kill us in Las Vegas."

"Oh. That's my personal symbol. Three blades, you see. TriBlade. My whole organization kind of . . ." Recognition seemed to dawn. "Oh shit! Javier. Is he okay?"

"He is not," Alex said simply.

"That's too bad and . . ." The man kicked back and eyed King. "*Surprising.* I didn't think you liked the violence."

King hated the violence, but that didn't change the fact that—"It was unavoidable."

Franklin nodded slowly, as if he understood. As if he'd been there himself. As if that was the cost of doing business. "Poor Javier. He was good. Not good enough, though, I guess." He gave a sigh that said, *Oh well*.

"So our question to you is pretty simple." Alex prowled closer. "Why, *exactly*, did you send him to kill us?"

It might have been the shadows or the hour or the sound of the sea, but it seemed to take forever for the man to understand. "I'm sorry . . . *me*? You think *I* want you dead?"

He leaned back and studied King and Alex. "Oh no. I'm what you might call . . . a fan." He pointed between them. "I ship it. Gotta say—kind of exciting to see you two working together again!"

"Then why did *your men* try to kill us?" King was running out of patience.

"Oh, they didn't." Franklin sounded so strong—so earnest—King almost wanted to believe him. "I'm just a broker. I thought you knew. Merritt never told you?" There he was, using her name again like he had any right to say it. Like they were old colleagues—old friends. Like they were all on the same side and everything else was just a technicality. "I'm a matchmaker, so to speak. I put people who have needs"—he held up his right hand—"in touch with people who provide goods." He held up his left and then brought them together. "Or services. It's all very civilized. Murder for hire is hardly my forte."

King could actually see Alex's patience starting to wane. "So who hired you *this time*?"

They should have shut the doors—turned on more lights. They should have done something because King couldn't get a read on that moment or that conversation or that man. Because the guy with cheese-puff fingers was suddenly looking at Michael Kingsley as if he might be a fool, even as he whispered—

"*Nikolai.*"

The word sounded like a shot fired from long range in high wind, like something that had been chasing King for ages and was about to find its mark. But Franklin just sat there, shaking his head like he might be on candid camera—like it might all be a joke. "I thought you knew—"

"Nikolai doesn't exist." King was going to throw him out the window himself.

"Ha. That's . . ." Franklin trailed off. "Wait. *What do you mean?*"

"You just said the tooth fairy tried to kill us," King snapped.

But Franklin was shaking his head, confused. "No. Nikolai is . . . like . . . my *best* client." Franklin scooted forward. Alex cocked her gun. Franklin scooted back. "Look, I don't know—"

"*I do*," King snapped. "Even if Nikolai were real, he'd be dead or in a nursing home by now, so—"

"Merritt isn't in a nursing home." The kid had the audacity to smile.

"I should put you in the ground." King would have done it, too, but Alex was there, pulling him back.

"King, calm down. King . . . Michael."

It was the only word that could make him stop. His name in her voice. So he pointed at the man-child in the chair and snapped, "He's lying."

Franklin gave a hapless shrug. "Have it your way. I just know what I know. Hey, you guys like Mexican food? I'm feeling nacho-y."

"You have one more chance to tell us who hired you," Alex warned, but Franklin just sat there, slowly shaking his head as if maybe Alex and King weren't as good as he'd been led to believe.

"No. Nikolai didn't hire *me*."

King pinched the bridge of his nose. "But you just said—"

The smirk on Franklin's face faded. The vein in his neck pulsed. He was the most serious man in the world when he whispered, "Nikolai hired *everyone*."

The word itself wasn't ominous, but King could feel it, swirling in the air and bouncing off the walls. They'd come to that island for the truth, but this was the kind of answer that only led to five more questions, and—

Franklin was reaching for a drawer.

"Hands!" Alex ordered, and he backed away slowly, raising his hands in the air but glancing down at the desk.

"There's a picture in the top drawer," he said.

King wouldn't have put it past Franklin to booby-trap the place, so he pointed to the drawer and said, "You get it. *Slowly.*"

"Nikolai . . ." Franklin started but trailed off when King made a sound. "Or *whoever is using that name* doesn't want you dead." He reached inside the drawer, then pulled out a photograph and tossed it on the desk in front of them. "Nikolai just wants *that*. And he's hired every free agent in the world to track the two of you down and get it for him." He made it sound so simple—so easy. He looked almost smug when he asked, "Look familiar?"

chapter thirty-six

Seven Years Ago
Amalfi Coast, Italy

ALEX

It probably shouldn't have been so anticlimactic, the way Alex felt as she slipped off her harness and slid into the shadows of the house.

King had already disabled the alarm, and Irina and Kozlov were gone, so there were only two guards to contend with and, at that time of night, they were making their rounds of the perimeter fence. The house was empty. Just Alex and King and the shadows.

"I guess we're alone." Even King sounded mildly disappointed. After so much recon, it felt like there should have been . . . more?

"Does this feel too easy to you?" Alex whispered even though he was right—they were alone—but something in Alex's gut was telling her something was wrong. This wasn't safe. This wasn't good. And the worst part was the look on King's face—the cocked eyebrow and clenched jaw that told her he was feeling it too.

"Don't look a gift horse in the mouth," said the voice in her ear. "Let's just get this done. And take it slowly. Those cameras blur if you move too fast."

Merritt was listening—and watching—from the boat. Her zip-lining days were over, but she was still with them, and it should have made Alex relax, but there was something that had been niggling in the back of her mind for days now. One look at King told her she wasn't the only one.

"And what, exactly, *are* we doing?" King leaned close to Alex, staring in a way that made her want to punch him until she realized he was actually looking at the tiny camera embedded in the frame of her glasses.

"We're searching for something." Merritt had the tone of a woman who was wishing she'd just done it herself.

"Searching for *what*? Exactly?" Even Alex was running out of patience.

"Merritt?" King prompted.

It was hard to say, with the distance and the darkness and the static coming through the line, but Alex could have sworn that Merritt—a woman who had been doing scary stuff for more than half a century—was trembling when she said—

"*Viktor Kozlov's nuclear option.*"

King found Alex's gaze in the darkness. He found it and held on. "Are you being literal right now?"

There were always rumors about missiles that went missing after the fall of the Soviet Union. Someone like Kozlov would have the connections . . . the money . . . the desire to keep a pet nuke. And if he had one . . .

"Merritt!" King snapped, and Alex heard a sigh through the earpiece.

"Is there a warhead in that building? No. Is there something there that, if my suspicions are correct, might lead to one? Absolutely." Merritt's voice sounded like ice, and Alex could have sworn she felt the room freeze over. "Now start looking."

Okay, Alex thought. *Okay. Okay?* "Looking for what?"

"*You're* not looking." Merritt sounded like the legend she was when she said, "I am. Now stop talking and take me through that house. Slowly. Show me everything. Start in the office."

"But—"

"I'll know it when I see it!" Merritt snapped, and Alex had to wonder. . . . It felt sloppy. Ill-conceived. Like the most *un*-Merritt-y of missions.

But all she could do was say, "Okay."

The office was just an office. They found computers and phones and technology of all kinds, but Merritt couldn't have cared less.

The kitchen was professional-grade and pristinely clean, but Merritt wasn't interested in anything—not even the tomato Alex found that was in the shape of a perfect little red heart.

"If we had some kind of clue . . ." King was growing frustrated.

"Just keep looking," Merritt ordered when Alex turned down a long hall and stopped dead in her tracks.

And shouted, "OMG!"

Instantly, she wished she could pull the words back because she sounded young and silly and . . . like Zoe, but Alex couldn't help herself as she looked at the glass cases that lined the long, dim hall.

It reminded her of the displays at the Farm—soft white light shining on shelf after shelf of history.

Lipstick cameras and little tin boxes of toothpowder with hidden compartments. There were vintage shoes with retractable knives in the soles, cuff links that doubled as lockpicks, and a pair of earrings that appeared to be a two-way radio.

But when Alex reached the item in the center of the case, she couldn't help herself: she gasped. Because it was so magnificent, it should have only existed in the movies. Or her dreams.

It was a ring—just a ring. Except it *wasn't* or else it wouldn't have been in Viktor Kozlov's spy gadget museum, and that just made Alex love it more.

The band appeared to be platinum, with intricate swirls that turned into a circle of tiny diamonds with a large red stone in the center.

Alex had never considered herself a jewelry person. In her quest to be as different from Zoe as possible, she'd eschewed most girly things as soon as she learned what boxes the world sorted women into.

Reading romance novels: Zoe.

Watching spy movies: Alex.

Wearing pink: Zoe.

Wearing black: Alex.

Caring about clothes and jewelry: Zoe.

Caring about nothing and no one: Alex.

But as she stood in the subtle glow of the display case, staring down at a ring that was both ornate and simple, old but timeless—there wasn't a doubt in her mind that it was also beautiful but something else.

"I wonder if the gem is actually a cyanide tablet?"

She waited for King to say something like *We have a job to do, Sterling,* but her mind was going now, rolling downhill fast and picking up steam. "Do the diamonds spell out a secret message in Morse code or—*ooh!*—maybe the ruby is a three-dimensional map, and if the light hits it just right—"

"It will show where to dig for the Ark of the Covenant?"

Yes!

"No. I just . . ." But Alex trailed off when she realized King wasn't mocking—wasn't laughing. He was just standing there, smiling, which was odd enough. But the weirdest part was that he was smiling—at her.

"You like that?" He pointed to the ring like it was a key piece of intel—the final step in Operation Make Alex Make Sense, and he wasn't going to quit until he'd cracked it.

Alex looked back down at the ring. It seemed like something made for a different world—a different time. And, not for the first time, Alex wondered what it might have been like to be a different girl.

One who got to pick first. One who didn't have to worry that the world was going to wake up one day and realize that everything—literally everything—was entirely her fault.

There was static in her ear and Merritt's voice had gone silent, so it felt like Alex was alone with the soft light and the stillness and the man who, for once, wasn't staring at her like she didn't belong there. For once, Alex felt like she was exactly where she was supposed to be.

"I love this kind of stuff," Alex admitted guiltily. "I love that something could be more than . . . Never mind."

But he was suddenly closer—warmer. "Go on."

"I love that things can be . . . more."

Alex could be the prettiest girl at MIT *and* the number one student in the college of engineering. She could be Michael Kingsley's nemesis *and* the best person to have his back on this mission. Alex could be Zoe's best friend *and* the reason her sister had almost died.

"A toothbrush isn't just a toothbrush when it's also a hand grenade?" he tried, and Alex could feel her face turning red, but the look King gave her was kind and indulgent and— "Try it on."

Now Alex knew she was hearing things. Maybe she'd been hit on the head and was currently in a medically induced coma. There was no way that Michael Kingsley of the Photographic Memory Kingsleys was telling her, "Go ahead."

"Oh no!" Alex pulled back. It was like she'd been burned.

"Go ahead," he said again, but Alex knew better. It was some kind of trap. He was a snake with an apple, trying to get her kicked out of the garden for good. She couldn't trust him. But there was something in his eyes as he opened the case and pulled out the ring. "My grandfather used to have a whole closet full of things like this. I think they're in the Spy Museum now. But when I was a kid . . ."

There was an insult in there somewhere. He was calling Alex a child, maybe. He was saying she wasn't smart enough or experienced enough—or maybe just jaded enough—to be there.

So Alex pulled on her cover—her shield. She retreated into her mission, and she stopped thinking like a girl who was enamored with a shiny ring and started thinking like a badass spy who needed to be spying, badassily. "We've got to—"

A burst of static filled her ear, and Alex flinched as Merritt's voice screamed, cutting in and out, the words fractured but clear, saying, "*Now!*" and "*Out!*" And then . . . "*Kozlov.*"

Alex looked at King, terror on his face. The comms units in their ears were state-of-the-art; they'd come a long way from the gadgets and gizmos on the shelves in front of them, but nothing was perfect.

"Say again," King asked.

"You have company!" Merritt sounded scared. And if Merritt was scared . . .

Light flashed across the windows. A helicopter was making its descent. Kozlov and Irina must have decided to come home early. Which meant . . .

"Merritt!" Alex snapped. "Tell us what we're looking for so we can get out of here!"

"I don't . . ." The voice sounded small and frail and then, suddenly, harder than stone. "Burn it down."

They didn't hear her correctly. Right? They didn't hear—

"Burn it all down."

King was shaking his head. "Do you seriously want us—"

"To destroy everything in that building, Michael? Yes. That's exactly what I want you to do. If we can't find it . . ." There was a beat, a moment of staticky sadness as King and Alex looked at each other like they were finally on the same side. They had the same questions and the same fears. And the same orders.

"But . . ." Alex started.

"They'll never know you were there. Now go. Burn it to the ground."

So that's exactly what they did.

chapter thirty-seven

Present Day
The Island

KING

King might never fully understand the woman beside him, but he knew exactly what she was thinking as they stared down at the photograph of the small platinum ring with the big red stone in the center.

A hot, humid breeze was blowing through the open French doors, but he could almost hear the distant boom of the fireworks—see the flashes of light in her eyes when she said, "We've *seen* it, sure." Alex sounded annoyed. "But we don't *have* it. We never *had* it."

But Franklin's eyes were crinkling; his lips were quirking. He looked like he was intrigued and inspired and a little infuriated, and King, obviously, knew the feeling—had claimed it and staked it and made it his own—and no one, least of all a guy calling himself *Tri-Blade*, was going to encroach upon King's turf. No one had the right to be more annoyed with Alexandra Sterling than he did.

But Alex was almost blissfully unaware of the effect she was having on the man. For a good spy, Alex was almost always unaware of that. But that didn't change the fact that she was angry.

"That ring was destroyed in a house fire on the Amalfi Coast! *Destroyed*. As in, turned to ash. As in *poof—smoke!* As in . . . We. Do. Not. Have. It. And you can tell your mystery employer that we don't have it. We burned it to a crisp seven years ago, so thanks for playing, but this has all been for nothing."

She was spinning to leave, glorious in her rage and indignation, when Franklin gave a low, cold laugh. "Maybe I'll let you tell Nikolai yourself."

"No." She wheeled on him. "Whatever he hired you to do, it's over because—We. Don't. Have. It."

"Oh, but like I said, he didn't hire *me* to find *it*." This time, the kid looked like he was the one who might laugh. But, just that quickly, his expression turned serious. "He hired *everyone*"—he let the word settle—"to find *you*."

"Well, congratulations. You found us. But we're leaving now, so—"

"Are you?" It was the calm in Franklin's voice that had King worried. "Because, see, here's the thing. . . . You are, after all, very good and—like I said. I'm a fan. So I thought, hey—why should I go looking for them when they're going to come looking for me?" There was movement in the doorway. The unmistakable *click* of a cocking gun. "And here you are."

And then all hell broke loose.

There was a man on the patio, blocking the doors. He was alone, and that was the good news. But he was employed by one of the largest arms dealers in the world and that was the bad.

Instantly, King dove, dragging Alex behind a couch while the man shot the hell out of Franklin's living room. "*Not the TV!*"

A moment later, the firing stopped. The man was reloading? Rethinking his life choices? It didn't matter because King was up and over the couch in a flash. The shooter must not have been expecting it because he actually stood there, watching King rush him head-on, barreling into him and knocking him back across the stone patio. He stumbled, unsteady, and King kicked, sending the shooter staggering and then tumbling backward over a low stone wall.

There was a crash—the sound of breaking tree limbs and possibly body limbs, but that didn't matter because lights were going on around the compound. An alarm was starting to sound.

And they were running out of time.

But Alex was lunging for Franklin. He pulled a gun, but Alex swatted it out of his hand as if he were nothing. They fell to the ground, and Alex straddled his chest, pressing down and staring daggers.

"Where is Nikolai?" She banged his head against the ground. "Who is he?"

"Alex . . ."

There was the sound of distant gunfire and shattering glass. Pieces of stone were flying around the room as bullets slammed into the walls, but Alex had one mission—one goal. "Tell us how to find him!"

"Oh." Franklin gave a bloody grin. "Don't worry. He'll find you."

King could only think of one thing: Alex. He had to get Alex out of there. He had to get her safe. So he reached down and pulled her off Franklin and dragged her toward the door.

"You'll never get off the island." Franklin laughed so hard, he shook. "The road will be blocked in two minutes. You'll never get down."

"That's okay." Alex cut her eyes at King. "We're not going down."

The helicopter was thirty feet away, down a narrow set of stairs cut into the stone on the mountain's side, and if they could reach it . . .

"Do you think he knows who Nikolai is?" Alex asked as they ran.

"I told you. Nikolai isn't—"

"Or *whoever* is using the name," she spat. "Do you think he knows?" She looked up at King, nothing but trust and uncertainty in her eyes, like she didn't believe herself anymore. Like he was the only thing that was real and she trusted him. Needed him.

"It doesn't matter." And it didn't because more shots were ringing out from overhead; they were officially out of time. So King pushed Alex toward the helicopter, then turned and fired back quickly.

"Are you sure you can fly this thing?" he asked, but she gave him a look like she'd never been more insulted in her life.

"Give me two months and a credit card and I could build this thing."

That's my girl.

He didn't say it—*wouldn't* say it. But he thought it. He was going to think it every day for the rest of his life.

They were still firing on them from up above. King heard Alex wince—

"Alex!"

But she was already climbing into the cockpit. A moment later, the blades were starting to turn. And she was shouting, "I'll leave you!" over the roar of the spinning blades. "Don't make me—"

He dove into the cabin just as the helicopter started to rise.

"You okay?"

She kept her gaze on the dark horizon.

"Never better."

King must have lost track of how far they'd gone or how long they'd been in the air. He didn't know if it was five minutes or five hours before Alex spoke again.

"Why on earth would they think we have that ring?" She was honestly asking. Like this was a puzzle on a game show and they'd each win a brand-new car if only they could get the answer right. "King?"

The sun would be up soon. Already, the sky in the east was morphing into a watercolor of pinks and grays and violets. People would be after them again. The helicopter probably wouldn't have enough range to get them much farther than the Portuguese shore. Which was fine. They'd need to ditch it anyway. He'd get them to a safe house. They'd regroup. Rest. Think. They'd—

"Kingsley!" The helicopter was losing altitude and Alex was losing patience. "We blew up Kozlov's house and everything in it. We turned that ring to ash, so what are we going to do?"

The sun broke over the horizon, beams shining through the clouds, but it didn't feel right. Inside of King, everything was dark and gray.

"King?"

"We're going to get the ring."

"Yes. Great plan." Sarcastic Alex he could handle. Sarcastic Alex he was used to. "Except we can't get the ring because of the aforementioned *explosion*."

Her cheeks should have been flushed from adrenaline and rage, but if anything, she was going paler. She seemed almost unsteady—her voice all but quivered when she asked, "Why do they think we have that ring?"

It was like she knew the answer—like she'd known it for the past two hours. Two days. Two years. Like she knew the truth because, deep down, she knew *him*. He closed his eyes and tried to stop the thought in its tracks, shoot it dead.

She knew him.

"Michael—"

"They think we have it . . . because I stole it."

The good news was they didn't crash and the sun was rising. The bad news was that Alex was staring at him, mouth gaping. And her skin was the color of paper. There was sweat on her brow and—

"Alex?" She was shaking her head or maybe just trying to stay awake. He couldn't tell anymore. "Are you okay?"

"Where is it, King? Where is it *right now*?"

But all King could do was look out the window and whisper, "Scotland."

She closed her eyes so tightly, it was like she was trying to weld the lids together, like she didn't want to see anymore, and if she couldn't see, then maybe she wouldn't have to hear either. Like it was all too much—too quickly—or maybe like it wasn't nearly enough.

"Why? Just . . . why?" Her voice broke.

He would have given anything not to tell her, "Because it made you smile."

chapter thirty-eight

Six Years Ago
London

The strange thing, in hindsight, wasn't that King had never been to Merritt's London flat before—it was that he was able to find it at all. Either he was getting better or she was getting worse, and King didn't know whether or not that was better than the other option: that she'd outlived all her demons and there was no one left alive to chase her anymore.

When King spotted the camera in the lobby, he gave a little nod, so it was already too late to turn back by the time he climbed the stairs and stood, fist poised to knock, outside her dark blue door.

The conversation was going to be more embarrassing than scary, but somehow that was worse. He'd been having it off and on with an imaginary Merritt for six months, trying to change his own mind. But some words are like cancer—you have to cut them out to keep them from spreading.

So that was why he was still standing there, fist in the air, when Merritt threw open the door two minutes later.

She wasn't dressed for company. There was no red lipstick, no red nails. She looked lovely and beautiful and sagely wise—still like the woman he knew, but somehow softer. Older. And not for the first time, Michael Kingsley wished he could invent something that would turn back time.

"Yay. You found me." She wasn't being sarcastic. She was almost . . . proud. Like she'd trained him well and he'd passed the test and now maybe she could walk away and know her legacy was intact.

"Tea?" She was already sweeping into the kitchen and taking an electric kettle off its base. Steam rose and turned the windows opaque. They looked like how his whole world felt—a life you could see right through and still have no idea what might be waiting on the other side.

"Well . . . are you going to make me guess?" She wasn't talking about the tea. She knew it. He knew it. So King slid onto a stool and rested his elbows on the kitchen counter.

When he was a scared ten-year-old kid who'd eaten nothing but peanut butter and dry cereal for two weeks because his mother had been on her way to the store when it happened, Merritt was the only grown-up who'd noticed. She'd shown up one day and done the laundry and thrown away the funeral flowers and made his father get out of bed. She'd hired a housekeeper and found him a therapist and told him stories, late into the night, about what his grandfather had said when he saw his grandmother for the first time.

She'd talked about the Cold War and hot summers and a million little things no ten-year-old should ever have clearance to hear. She'd brought the past to life, and that had helped him forget his mother was dead, and so he owed Margaret Merritt. He'd owe her for the rest of his life, and yet . . .

"Why are you here, Michael?" It wasn't a question. It was an order.

"I'm going to do you a favor. And then you're going to do one for me."

She put her tea down. There was no teasing note or playful twinkle in her eyes when she said, "Okay."

King had been practicing what to say for days, but the words never did land right, and he'd learned a long time ago that if you can't do something well, you should, at least, try to do it quickly.

"I'm not going to ask any questions about Amalfi and why we were doing an off-the-books-op with no— Don't deny it, Merritt." He watched her open her mouth to speak—the lies were already gathering behind her eyes because, like any great spy, she believed them. She needed lies like she needed the caffeine in that cup or maybe the air in her lungs. "I know you," King told her. "And I know whatever that was in Amalfi wasn't for anyone *but* you. But I trust you. Hell, I *love* you. So I'm going to take Amalfi with me to my grave, but . . ."

"In exchange," she prompted when the silence lasted a little too long.

"In exchange, I'm going to ask that"—this was the hard part—"you *never do that again.*"

"Okay." She took a sip of tea and hid her smirk. "As you wish. No more off-the-books—"

"No." He was shaking his head and wishing he'd stayed in bed—in Europe. In the womb. "No, you will never make me work with her again."

In Merritt's defense, she didn't ask *work with whom*, but in his defense, she didn't really have to. He'd only had one partner in Amalfi and besides . . .

Besides . . .

His father was still alive, but in so many ways, Merritt was the only family King had left, and he couldn't look at her. He wished he could make her stop looking at him. Keep her from saying—

"You work well together, you know?" He *did* know. "Your talents are very complementary."

"I know."

"I thought you'd put your differences behind you?" Now she sounded curious. "The fighting seemed different this time. Almost . . . playful?"

It was. It is. And that was worse. He couldn't believe she was going to make him say it—spell it out, admit it to himself. He couldn't believe Margaret Merritt—perhaps the world's greatest living spy—didn't know that was worse by a factor of a million.

"Michael?"

"Please." Was that his voice cracking or was it something else, deep inside of him, that wasn't going to mend? King didn't know anymore. Didn't exactly care. In fact, from that point forward he wasn't going to care about anything, he decided. That was the only way he knew not to let this business win, by refusing to play the game. "I'm not going to be my father, Merritt."

He pushed away from the counter and headed toward the door. He'd said all the things he needed to say and a few more he probably shouldn't have, and the best thing to do was get out while he still could.

"Michael?" She stopped him at the door.

"I'm not going to be my father." He kissed her cheek. Her skin was soft and paper thin, and he vowed to remember the feel of it, just in case it was the last time.

She cupped his face. "Consider it done."

chapter thirty-nine

Six Years Ago
Berlin, Germany

ALEX

It had been a year since Amalfi, but Alex wasn't counting the days. She was happy, in her own way. She'd run a nice op out of Sydney and the higher-ups at Langley were happy with what they'd been seeing. Her Russian was good, and her tradecraft was sharp, and she hadn't had to work with Michael Kingsley in ages, so it had been a good year.

She cut her hair short and stopped taking Zoe's phone calls because that was better for everyone. Her sister was healthy—she was fine—so Alex had two missions at that moment: (1) keeping her that way and (2) whatever the Agency told her to do.

That's why she didn't ask a single question when she walked into the old, abandoned warehouse on the outskirts of what used to be East Berlin. She just said, "Hello, Merritt."

The old woman had a twinkle in her eye when she gave Alex a hug, and Alex got the feeling this wasn't just a social call. It never was.

"So where is he?" Alex looked around, waiting for King to materialize out of thin air and announce that her shoes were impractical and her hair wasn't covert enough. Then Alex would have to roll her eyes and ask if the stick up his butt could be used as an actual weapon. It was their thing. She was almost looking forward to it. It was almost as if—

"Hello, stranger."

The words were right, but the voice was wrong. The footsteps on the concrete were wrong. The feeling in her gut was wrong, wrong, wrong, because . . .

It wasn't him. It wasn't him. It wasn't—

"Tyler?" She almost didn't know him, he looked so different. Rougher. Harder. Hotter? *Had Tyler gotten hot?* Alex blinked and tried to make it make sense. He'd lost the softness that filled his face, his too-big, too-trusting grin. This life changed everyone, but she felt a little sad to see that the sweet guy she'd met at the Farm had morphed into this slightly darker version.

She'd seen him a few times over the years. Always in passing. They'd say something like they'd have to work together soon. Or at the very least, they should grab lunch, keep in touch. But spies don't do that. Even she and King . . .

What?

There was no she and King.

"Hey!" Tyler was pulling her into his arms and squeezing her a little. It was that thing that normal people do when they see old friends. Some people called it *hugging*. But she and King didn't hug.

She and King . . .

He wasn't King.

"How are you?" Alex pulled back and squeezed his (larger than she remembered) biceps and tried to sound like women always sound in movies about high school reunions. Like things were amazing! And awesome! And her life was everything she'd ever hoped it would be!

But the CIA didn't train fools, so Tyler the Suddenly Rugged didn't buy it. "You look disappointed."

She rolled her eyes. "Surprised? Yes. Disappointed? Never!" And then Alex hugged him again because it really was good to see him. And not just because he'd put on a little muscle and grown a little scruff and, all in all, looked like the kind of guy she should have wanted. Maybe she *would* want him? Maybe they'd do espionage and also kissing. They could fall in love and their life would become the kind of story that would make her sister swoon. But she could never tell him that because Tyler didn't know about Zoe. *No one* knew about Zoe.

Well, no one except . . .

"How have you been?" Alex asked, and instantly, she wanted to pull the words back, because Tyler's eyes went dark. He practically winced.

"Undercover." He wasn't smiling anymore. "Nine months."

"Wow. Nice!" It wasn't, though; she could tell by looking at him. Suddenly, the muscle and the scruff made sense. He'd been someone else for the better part of the year, and it had changed him. Because sometimes you either change or die. Alex made a mental note. She was going to need it soon.

"Is it?" He huffed out a laugh. "I can't remember." Then he laughed again, a real one this time. "Don't tell King."

His voice was a little too loud to be a whisper. He was teasing her. Maybe. Probably. But Alex couldn't stop herself from pulling back too quickly. The Agency was going to put a letter in her file for Insufficient Covertness. She was going to lose her cred and his respect, but she couldn't stop herself from blurting, "What makes you think I talk to King?"

He had to have noticed the panicked tinge to Alex's voice, but he had the good sense (or good tradecraft) not to show it, and Alex had to wonder if maybe Tyler had been the best spy from their class at the Farm all along—maybe while she and King had been duking it out, Tyler was leaving them both in the dust and they hadn't even noticed. She'd even managed to forget about Merritt until she heard—

"He's here, you know?" It took all of her self-control for Alex not to spin. "His grandfather owned a penthouse in the Schlossberg Building. Michael just moved in."

"Oh." King would hate that Merritt had told her that, but then again, he'd probably never find out. Alex would certainly never be in a position to tell him. "I assure you, the only reason I would care about Michael Kingsley's place of residence is so that I can stay far, far away."

She watched Tyler smile but not quite laugh—little lines around his eyes. A lone dimple in one cheek. He looked like a guy who was growing into a man, and Alex waited for a flip in her stomach—for a tingling in her palms. It should have felt nice, having a partner whose eyes she didn't want to claw out, and she told herself it was a delightful change of pace. Really, she should have insisted upon it long ago.

But she still jumped a little when Tyler slung an arm around her shoulders. "So, you ready to get your hands dirty?" Alex's hands had been plenty dirty. Hadn't they? She wasn't some green recruit, but she'd never worked in deep cover, so maybe Tyler had a point. He dropped his voice. "You ready to work with a real spy?"

He was teasing. Joking. But Alex didn't laugh. She just forced a smile and said, "Who needs Michael Kingsley?"

Tyler chuckled and Merritt huffed, but Alex just stood there, starting to worry, even as she asked, "So what do you have for us?"

Merritt looked uncertain for the first time since Alex had known her. "Possibly nothing," Merritt admitted. "But there has been chatter of late."

"Chatter?" Alex asked, and Tyler ran a hand through his hair.

"Kozlov." *Oh.* Alex felt a chill go down her spine at the name. Viktor Kozlov had only gotten bigger—more dangerous—in the last year. Half the world's intelligence services had task forces dedicated to the man, and . . .

She looked at Tyler. "Is that where you've been . . ." Somehow, she knew. "You were in deep cover? *With Kozlov?*"

Alex wanted to ask him a million questions. She needed to know—

"Yeah." A shadow crossed his face, and suddenly, the changes in Tyler made sense. Of course he'd grown harder, leaner, darker. "Not all of us can do our missions on private islands with gourmet chefs." He laughed again. "Anyway, Kozlov's got a shipment coming in tonight and I want to get eyes on it. I thought you might want to get a little closer to the action, but if not . . ."

"No," Alex blurted. "I'll do it."

"I'm no Michael Kingsley." He was teasing again. Wasn't he?

So Alex grinned. "That's why I'm saying yes."

"Okay, let's do this thing," Tyler said, but Alex had to wonder, *What thing?* But also: *Do how?* She didn't know the mission or the objective, the risks or the plans. She didn't know anything, except . . .

He's not King, the little voice in the back of her mind whispered. And rest of her whispered back, *But isn't that what you wanted?*

Alex followed him into the sunset, trying very hard not to think about the answer.

chapter forty

Present Day
Somewhere in Portugal

ALEX

King hot-wired a car. Ordinarily, Alex would have protested and insisted she do it herself, but she was glad to let him do the dirty work. She was relieved to watch him drive. It was getting harder and harder to keep her eyes open. And her side was feeling stickier and stickier. Soon, the adrenaline would fade and something much, much worse would take its place, but until then . . .

She was aware, faintly, of him talking to her, asking her questions. Maybe complaining. Definitely growling. It was her fault—whatever it was. Except it wasn't and that made it worse, somehow, but she was just too tired to argue.

She closed her eyes.

The world swirled.

She forced them open again because she was afraid that, if she slept, she might dream, and, if she dreamed, she'd hear the words again:

Because it made you smile.

They hurt more than the bullet.

"Alex?"

Was she out? No. Not quite. "What?"

"You sleeping on the job over there?"

Was that a joke? It sounded like one, but King didn't joke and nothing felt funny anymore.

"Alex . . . we're here."

We're where? She thought she said the words, but maybe she didn't, because he was looking at her oddly. It was the middle of the day, and the sun was too bright. She wanted the darkness back. *Darkness good. Bright light bad.*

It almost made her laugh.

"Come on."

He slammed his door. It took all her strength to open hers. "Where are we?"

"Safe house."

"No." Alex shook her head, but the force of it almost tipped her over. "No. The Agency can't find—"

The world tipped on its axis, and Alex had to reach out to steady herself against the door.

"Hey." He was too close. He was going to feel how sticky her shirt was or see how pale her skin was or—

"Just tired."

Somehow she climbed the steps. She watched him open the door. "It's not one of theirs." He sounded almost insulted that she would think otherwise. "It's clean. Or, well . . ." He flipped on a light. "Not in the literal sense."

As soon as she saw the room, she understood. It wasn't much more than a cabin—stone walls and rough-hewn furniture. The whole place was covered in a thick layer of cobwebs and dust, and it wouldn't have surprised her to find out they were the first people who'd set foot in there for fifty years.

"Welcome to the Kingsley family version of the summer house. Grandfather liked his secrets." That had to be the understatement of the century. "He never told the Agency about them."

"Them?"

"He had a whole network of these back in the day. Safe houses. Seaside cottages and mountain cabins. Old train cars and sewers. He even had a penthouse."

Alex went cold. She shivered. "I remember."

"Oh." Then King was the one who went pale. "Right." Alex wanted to laugh, too, but it hurt too much. "You sure you're okay? You look kind of . . ."

"Did he tell you about these when you were a kid? Bounce you on his knee and say, 'In '61 I got a nuclear scientist over the wall in a hot-air balloon? Hid him out in a Portuguese rail car for . . .'" Alex coughed. She caught herself on the back of a chair, too tired to go on.

King was looking at her oddly. "Something like that. You okay?"

"Fine. Bathroom? I'm assuming . . ."

"Yeah. Sure." He pointed to a door. "Through there. I think?"

She closed the door and leaned against a dusty sink. Dust was bad but hot water was good, Alex's tired brain told her as she dug in the cabinet. There were sterile packs of gauze. An unopened bottle of rubbing alcohol. It was going to hurt like hell, but . . .

She pulled her shirt over her head and looked at the hole in her side. The blood wasn't too thick. It had stopped flowing, and the wound was clean and—

The door opened and Alex turned too fast. She watched his eyes go wide and knew it wasn't because of her second-favorite bra. No.

She watched him watch her. She waited for the *I told you so*. For the warning or the scold. It didn't even hurt—much. But it was also the most pain she'd ever been in as he inched forward and opened the package of gauze and said, "I have you."

There was a scar, higher on her side. Old and healed over. It didn't hurt anymore. She barely even felt it in the shower, just a part of her she'd gotten used to.

And yet she could feel the moment when he saw it. When his finger brushed against that patch of rough, imperfect skin, it felt like being licked by a flame.

"I have you." He was holding the gauze to the wound, but it was the scar he was staring at. "I have you."

And Alex couldn't help but whisper, "Again."

chapter forty-one

Six Years Ago
Berlin, Germany

King couldn't sleep anymore, so he didn't even try. He never enjoyed doing things he wasn't good at. Some things got better with practice, of course. But sleeping just got harder, so he sat in the shadows of the penthouse apartment that had once been his grandfather's favorite safe house. He nursed a scotch and looked out the window at a city that felt like it was still drawn in black and white.

It felt haunted. Like at any minute, he'd have to shoot a line from the balcony and fly over the wall. Like the Cold War wasn't over.

Like it was a war he'd never win.

King knew he should get up, go out. Maybe find a woman. But that thought only made him wince. Not because it would be hard—it wouldn't. They'd go back to her place for a while and then he'd come back here, and after he'd probably feel better, sleep better, think better. And it was the last thing in the world he was going to do.

Because no matter who he found or what she looked like . . .

When the sound came, it was a dull, distant thud that King almost didn't notice. If he had been a different kind of man, he might have thought it was a ghost. He was just starting to tell himself it was probably nothing at all when it came again—hard, but fleeting. More pound than rap. And King reached for a weapon as he eased toward the door.

Very few people knew he was in Berlin. Even fewer knew about his grandfather's old penthouse or King's current plans. Maybe it was the ancient pipes, he was telling himself when the pounding came again, softer now. And fading. Disappearing in the distance, getting farther away even as King inched closer to the door.

He didn't check the peephole. He just cursed himself for waiting to put up the cameras as he cocked the gun and threw open the door. And stopped breathing.

Because the figure in the door was leaning against the frame, face pale, hands shaking. Breathing hard and clutching her side like she'd just sprinted a mile at high altitude.

Alexandra Sterling shouldn't have been there. She would never have come there—not to him. Not unless . . .

"Mercy."

And then she fell into his arms.

chapter forty-two

KING

Every family has their legacy. Some are fame or fortune. Some are bad reputations and the universal knowledge that only a fool would lend them money.

The Kingsleys were known for their brains.

Literally. His grandfather's legendary memory. The fact that Michael, somehow, had it too (though Merritt once confessed that his might be even better). But King knew something most people didn't—that the Kingsleys' real legacies were pessimism and preparation.

They saw contingencies a thousand yards off. They ate worst-case scenarios for breakfast. No one could predict the future, but if they tried hard enough, spies named Michael Kingsley were quite good at knowing what was coming, or so he'd always thought.

He'd been wrong, though.

Because never in a million years would he have been ready for her.

"Sterling!" He shook her, just a little. Even though he didn't want to jostle her—hurt her. He just needed her to wake up and tell him he was an asshole. He just needed her . . . "Alex!"

Luckily, three generations of pessimism meant he was at least somewhat prepared, or so he told himself, as he carried her limp body through the empty apartment and laid her on the old settee by the window.

He ripped open her shirt and looked down at the too-red blood against her too-white skin.

She shouldn't be here.

She shouldn't be like this.

She should have had backup and medical help and something and someone so much better than him.

But maybe she *did* have those things? Maybe she'd chosen him anyway?

"No." The word was a whimper, low and thin like paper. "No." She was tossing. Turning. King had to hold her down. "No. Hurts."

She was delirious and maybe dying. That's the only way she'd ever say such a thing to him.

"I know, sweetheart. I know. Shhh. I have you. Hang on."

There were supplies in the closet, and King didn't waste any time. He cordoned off the parts of his brain that were trying to panic and went back to the basics to start at the beginning.

Entry wound.

Exit wound.

And a hell of a lot of blood.

"No." She tried to fight, but she was no stronger than a kitten who hadn't found her claws yet. "No."

"Yes, Alex. Shh. Easy."

He had to get her sewn up. He had to give her something for the pain. He had to think.

He couldn't think.

For the first time in his life, his brain stopped working.

"No! No."

"Shh."

"Please don't cut me open!"

"It's okay. It was a through-and-through. You're—"

"I'm not her. I'm not her. I'm not—" *Was she undercover? Was she targeted?* "I'm not Zoe." She was clawing at his chest. She was going to hurt herself even more. Then she bolted upright, but she didn't feel the pain. There was nothing but guilt on her face when she said, "I'm the one who killed her."

And then she collapsed against the bloodstained velvet as King found a vein and plunged a needle into her arm.

"No."

"It's morphine. Shhh. It's okay."

"No . . ." She tried to turn. "King." He stopped moving. "I need . . ."

"I'm here. What, Alex? What do you need?"

Her eyes opened. She was almost herself when she said, *"You."*

"Alex?" Her eyelids fluttered, and she came, slowly, awake, and King tried to keep the panic out of his voice. But he had to talk to her. It had already been an hour and they were running out of time. He had to know—

Was she clean? Was she followed? Was someone going to come bursting through that door to finish the job?

Dark eyelashes fluttered on pale cheeks, and he wondered if it might already be too late.

"Alex, come on. Wake up and fight me." He was cleaning the wound and had to warn her—"You're gonna hate me for this, but . . ."

The alcohol hit the wound, and she jerked. "Already do."

To King, it sounded like music.

"Hey." He looked into her eyes. How had he never noticed how green they were?

"Love what you've done with the place." Every word hurt, he could tell, but she choked them out anyway because she was still Alexandra Sterling and he wouldn't have wanted her any other way.

But then she coughed and curled in on herself in agony. She was going to need more morphine. But first . . .

"Who did this to you?" King didn't recognize his own voice, it got so dark so quickly.

"Doesn't"—she twisted, as if the settee and not the hole in her side was causing her discomfort—"matter."

"It matters." It did, and he didn't even bother to explain why. "Who, Sterling? Tell me." She looked up at him, gaze a little hazy, from the pain or from the meds. So he used a bloody hand to push her hair back. "Tell me. I need to know."

He *would* know—either then or in the future. He'd find out. And then he'd find them. And then . . .

"Who, Sterling?"

"Russians." She closed her eyes and exhaled the word. "Kozlov."

Kozlov. Of course it was Kozlov.

"Were you jumped? Are you compromised? Listen to me—Sterling. Alex! Stay with me. Is this about Amalfi?"

She winced as she shook her head, but it must have hurt more to speak. "New op."

"Were you followed? Do I need to get you out of here?"

"I don't think so."

King felt his pulse slow down. His adrenaline was fading, and so was hers, which meant the pain was going to get stronger. She'd need another shot soon. But first he had to know—

"What was the op, sweetheart?"

"Tyler. Tyler ran it. It was fine."

It wasn't fine, but King just smiled and smoothed her hair and gave her a little more morphine before he watched her fade, bliss on her face for one split second.

"Michael . . ."

"Sleep, sweetheart. Sleep. You're safe here. I've got you."

He had her.

And he hated that, very soon, he'd have to let her go.

chapter forty-three

KING

King didn't have a lot of time, but this couldn't wait. He needed intel, sure. But, more than that, he needed to hit someone and this was a good place to start.

"King!" Tyler threw open the door. "To what do I owe the—" King's fist connected with his face, and Tyler stumbled back, cursing and bleeding, but King just brought his forearm up to Tyler's jugular, pressing hard and slamming him back into a wall.

For a moment, Tyler just stood there, blood running from his nose and breath coming hard until he smiled and choked out, "—pleasure."

He gave a bloody grin, but King didn't think it was funny.

"What did you do to Alex?" King's voice sounded like how midnight feels, but he kept his gaze locked on Tyler's.

"Alex is . . ." Tyler couldn't breathe. *Good*. "Alex is . . . fine." He tried to push King back. "Let me . . ."

"*What happened to Alex?*"

"I don't know!"

King had the element of surprise and a whole lot of rage, but Tyler was still a trained operative and, in a flash, he freed himself, pushing away from King and staggering across the floor.

There was a lamp on in the living room. The TV showed a soccer game from somewhere in the world, but the flat was dark and bare and basic. It wasn't a safe house, but it wasn't a home, and King wasn't in the mood to be social.

"What the hell happened tonight?" King kept his voice low, his hands steady. His grandfather always said that there are two types of people when things go wrong—the kind for whom the world gets slow and the kind for whom the world gets fast, and King had never been more certain he was the first kind. "What did you do to—"

"I didn't do anything to her!"

"Then why is her blood all over my front door?"

That time, when Tyler stumbled, it was because the words had hit him. "What?" He looked stunned and shocked and . . . guilty. "Is she—"

"She's alive," King ground out. "No thanks to you."

Tyler seemed a little unsteady as he headed for the tiny kitchen and poured himself a drink.

"What happened?" Even King was afraid of how his voice sounded, but Tyler just shook his head.

"Viktor Kozlov happened." Tyler found a dishrag and held it to his bloody lip, but that wasn't the reason King saw red. "He's—"

"I know Kozlov."

"Bullshit!" Tyler shouted. "You've read the reports and seen the data. I spent the last nine months up to my neck in his filth. *I* know Kozlov. I . . ." The fight seemed to go out of Tyler, and he threw the rag into the sink, anger turning to guilt that was coming off him in waves.

"What happened tonight?" King asked.

"He was expecting some kind of shipment, so I set up surveillance to see what it was. Alex was helping me. That was it. Hang out in the shadows and try to get a look at whatever Kozlov was buying. *That was it.* But we couldn't get a good line of sight, so Alex and I split up." He pulled two beers from the old refrigerator, but King didn't dare reach for one because, at that moment, the bottle just looked like a weapon. "I didn't know about Alex . . . I didn't know."

King's mind had been noisy since the day he was born, but right then it was tranquil and calm. He could see *everything*. He could hear *everything*. He knew how this was going to end because there was only one outcome he'd accept.

"Okay. Here's what's going to happen. You're going to give me the names of anyone who might have seen her tonight. You're going to tell me where they are. And then you are never going to contact her again. Do you—"

"That's not up to you, is—"

King slammed a knee into Tyler's groin because he didn't trust his hands not to choke the life out of him. To his credit, Tyler stopped fighting.

"*Do you understand me?*" King asked, slower now. "She doesn't exist. She died tonight—bled out on the street where you left her. Alexandra Sterling is gone, and if you forget that . . . I will do to you what I am going to do to them."

"Oh yeah?" Tyler actually laughed. "What are you going to do to them? You're a computer guy, King. A desk guy . . ." Tyler took a sip of his beer, resigned and a little sad. "A good guy."

But King just shook his head. "Not tonight."

chapter forty-four

ALEX

Alex remembered the dreams. She was five years old and the doctor was getting ready to cut the wrong heart open. He'd been handsome at least, the doctor. Grumpy, but kind, and she'd trusted him even though he thought she was Zoe. Even though he didn't know the ways she was the weak one. Even though he didn't know that she was the twin who really needed saving.

When Alex blinked open her eyes, she didn't recognize the ceiling or the sheets or the pain shooting through her side. Her mouth was dry and her skin itched and—

Morphine. That's how she always felt on—

Alex reached under the pillow but there wasn't a gun, and that was when she knew she was in trouble.

That room and that bed and that pain. It was the kind she wasn't used to. Usually, Alex only hurt on the inside. But now . . .

There was the sound of running water. A light under a door. And Alex knew she should have been terrified because she was in no shape to fight. But, somehow, a part of her knew she wouldn't have to.

The door opened on creaky hinges, swinging on its own because the house was too haunted or too old, and that was when she saw him.

A single light burned over an old-fashioned sink. There was a mirror on the wall and black-and-white tiles on the floor and a shirtless Michael Kingsley running his forearms under the faucet like a surgeon prepping for an operation.

She watched the water turn red as King's arms went back to their right color, and Alex didn't know it was possible to sway while lying down.

"Whose blood is that?"

He turned off the water and grabbed a towel and came toward her, bare feet almost silent in the dark.

"No one. Nothing. Go back to sleep."

But it wasn't nothing. It wasn't no one. And that was why Alex wanted to claw her own skin off.

"Hey. No." King was reaching for her. "Lie back down."

"What happened?" Alex hated how her voice broke, too weak and soft and fractured. She didn't want to let him see her like this, but there wasn't a soul on Earth she'd trade him for, and she didn't understand it. It was like that bed. She couldn't remember how she got there, but that didn't mean she didn't want to settle in.

She pointed to the bloodstained sink. "Is it mine?"

She watched him think about the answer. The lights were out and the sun wasn't up, but she could see him better in the shadows. It was their place in the world, neither light nor dark, day nor night. They were professionally gray, and he might have been the only person in the world who understood, but before she could get the words out, Alex closed her eyes, wishing her life wasn't just some unending conversation of things she couldn't say.

"Who, King?"

"It's not yours." He smoothed her hair away from her forehead, then rested a hand on her face—not like he was feeling for a fever, but like he just wanted to feel *her*, so Alex closed her eyes and leaned against his palm, relishing the coolness of Michael Kingsley until—

"I've got to go." She threw the covers off. "The sun's almost up and—"

"Get back in bed."

"I need to keep moving. Protocol—"

"The hell with protocol. Put your feet on the bed, Sterling."

"I need to call it in. I need—"

"Alex!" King snapped, but it was the sound of her own name that stopped her. She wasn't Sterling anymore—not even Alexandra. "You're clean." His voice was so soft, so close. "You're good."

She glanced at the bathroom again, streaks of red on white, and Alex grew even more afraid of the answer.

"Whose blood is that?"

He couldn't touch her anymore. "It's not yours."

"King . . ." If he could do it . . . "Michael?"

He couldn't face her anymore. "No one is going to come looking for you. It's taken care of. It's done."

He didn't say anything else. He didn't have to. The look on his face—the way his eyes couldn't meet hers—it was all she needed. All that mattered.

He wasn't that guy. He'd always been dangerous and intense and lethal, but he wasn't *that guy*. He was . . .

"Michael." Alex's voice cracked. Her lips quivered. Her whole body was starting to shake and she didn't know if it was fear or shock, she just knew that her teeth were starting to rattle in a way that only happened in cartoons. She couldn't make herself stop shaking. She couldn't make herself stop feeling.

She couldn't make it stop. "King . . ."

"Shhh. Easy. Rest."

She was back in bed then, covers wrapped around her, and she wasn't even sure how it had happened. She just knew Michael Kingsley was leaning over her, brushing a strand of hair out of her eyes.

"I'm too cold." She was still shaking and she didn't even know how to stop.

The sun was almost up and the sky was the color of doves. Little strips of light fell over a room with high ceilings and ornate moldings. The bed was some kind of antique, made for another era. Ethereal and gorgeous, but there wasn't another stick of furniture in the room, so it wasn't a surprise when he said, "That's my only blanket. Stay here." Like she was going anywhere. "I'll turn up the heat."

But Alex had a hold of his arm and she couldn't let go. She didn't know why. She just knew that he was as much a part of her as an IV. He'd have to be ripped out.

There had been lectures at the Farm about first aid and body heat, so she wasn't only thinking about Zoe's favorite novels when she threw back the covers and whispered, "Come to bed."

They had to share because they were both exhausted. It didn't matter that King thought the threat was over, there were always new threats—a whole world full of them. He needed his rest, and she highly doubted there were any other beds.

But she didn't say any of that, because Michael Kingsley was a very good spy. He knew a lie when he heard one. So he slipped between the covers, and, for the first time, Alex stopped shaking.

He tugged until her head rested on his shoulder and his arms held her tight.

"Does it hurt?"

It did, but not in the way he was asking.

"Michael . . ."

"Shh."

"Where's Tyler?"

"On his way back to Langley."

"Oh." She didn't know how she felt—relieved or disappointed? The night was fuzzy. She remembered . . . very little. "It wasn't his fault. We split up."

"He let you out of his sight. It was his fault."

"I'm a professional."

"He went in with no plan, and you got hurt."

"How did you know there was no plan?"

"*Because you got hurt.*"

His body had gone taut with tension. It took all of Alex's strength to admit, "I got made."

"You're clean."

"The shooter—"

"Won't bother you."

"But—"

"I found him," King blurted. "He won't talk."

"But—"

"He *can't* talk, Alex," King said, harder now. "He won't talk. Ever again." She wanted to ask a million questions, but he just squeezed her tighter. "No one is ever going to hurt you again."

When Alex closed her eyes, she felt something soft and wet brush across her forehead, but that was silly. She was imagining things. It must have been the drugs. The blood loss. It must have been anything else because Michael Kingsley didn't give forehead kisses.

But when he said, "Sleep," for the first time in her life, Alex did exactly as she was told.

chapter forty-five

Present Day
Somewhere in Portugal

ALEX

In the end, it was the sound that woke her.

Part of Alex's brain never slept, of course—the part that was always listening and worrying and wondering when her luck was going to run out. But she'd slept on the island eight years ago. And she'd slept in Berlin. And she'd been sleeping for hours, it seemed, because when Alex opened her eyes again, the sky was dark outside the tiny cottage and the only sounds were crashing waves and the deep, steady breathing beside her.

So, it turned out, the common denominator wasn't blood loss (too bad). It was King.

She looked at the other side of the bed and the man who was stretched out with his shirt off and one arm thrown over his eyes like the moonlight was going to blind him.

His hair was so much longer now, and she never thought she'd see him with a beard. She certainly never thought she'd like it. His hair was darker too, like he hadn't seen the sun in ages, and Alex had to marvel at the difference. People can change in a decade, and spies change more than most, but as she studied the man in the moonlight, she could barely remember the boy from the bar with the perfectly pressed shirt and squeaky clean perfection.

"It didn't scar too badly."

She hadn't realized he was awake, but there he was, staring at her across the expanse of white sheets that he must have found tucked away somewhere because they weren't even a little bit dusty.

He turned on his side, hand reaching out carefully—like he was afraid to touch her. But he didn't reach for the bandage and the wound. He reached for the rough patch of skin the size of a nickel.

"I had a good doctor, I guess," she said as his thumb made a slow, gentle sweep over the scar. Back. Forth.

"You could have bled out tonight."

"It was just a graze," she told him. And it was true.

"You could have said, 'Oh, hey, King, remember when we were being shot at? It turns out I got hit.'"

"I got grazed." But when she tried to sit upright, she swooned.

"You got shot," he corrected. Then he tugged her down beside him. He closed his eyes and whispered, "Again."

chapter forty-six

Six Years Ago
Berlin, Germany

ALEX

When Alex woke, the sky was gray again and the sun was going down, sinking low over the rooftops to the west. She should have been mad at herself for sleeping away the day. The Agency was going to be looking for her, asking questions. There were reports to file and briefs to give, but when she threw off the covers, a sharp stab of pain surged through her midriff and her whole body vibrated like a piece of tin that had been hit with a hammer. She could almost hear the *clang*.

"I wouldn't do that if I were you."

King was leaning against the doorframe, arms across his chest. Those long legs crossed at the ankle as if some Hollywood director had told him to stand there until they got the light just right. But it was the look on his face that made Alex go a little woozy: worry and frustration and fear all trying to hide behind a crooked grin.

This was King At Home, and she got the feeling that very few people ever had the luxury of seeing him here, with his bed-mussed hair and long-sleeve tee. Old sweatpants and mismatched socks.

"Morning, Cowboy."

For a split second she wanted to pull the words back because maybe he didn't remember the bar and that first night. Maybe she should have pretended she didn't either. But then a hint of pink tinged his cheeks, so Alex tried to get out of bed.

"If I offer to help, are you going to try to kill me?"

"Maybe."

"Good." He laughed because, evidently, King At Home did that. "That means you're back to normal."

He walked toward the bed and put a hand on her forehead. Alex leaned against the cool, soft weight of it because she couldn't help herself. It felt like the first time someone had touched her in years.

"That's better."

Was he talking about her fever or the way she leaned against him? Alex didn't know. Didn't exactly care.

Then he bent down and pushed a strand of hair out of her eyes. She didn't think. She just blurted—

"I want . . ."

You to kiss me.

You to hold me.

You to tuck me back in and let me sleep for five more years.

"To take a shower."

He rose slowly but smiled as he told her, "Stay here."

A moment later, she heard the sound of water running.

There was a bandage around her waist and a small Band-Aid on her arm. Alex looked around the room, really studying it for the first time. She spotted a bag of saline and an IV drip hanging from the bedframe, a plastic trash bag full of bloody gauze. It looked more like a hospital room than a bedroom, and, for the first time, Alex saw the situation clearly. The pain in her side made so much more sense and so did the look on his face when he walked back to the bed and said, "Come on."

She just wasn't expecting him to swoop her up into his arms.

"I can walk, you know? I've been doing it for a while. I can even do it in heels."

He shouldered the bathroom door open wider, then set her on the marble countertop of the most beautiful bathroom she'd ever seen.

"You were out for three days."

"I . . . Oh." That couldn't be right. He had to be lying. But he wasn't. She could see it in his eyes, because there were two things she knew for a fact about Michael Kingsley: he didn't lie, and he didn't forget.

So she looked around the bathroom instead, at the antique tiles and ornate light fixtures. She didn't know anything about architecture, but she thought it was probably built after the First World War and, miraculously, not destroyed by the second.

The largest clawfoot tub she'd ever seen was half full of sudsy water, and the air was thick with steam.

"Those bandages are watertight, but it's probably best not to soak too long."

Alex knew it was silly, but nothing had ever looked as good as that warm water, so she slid off the counter and tried to walk toward it.

"Easy," he told her, hand on her elbow, his chest at her back.

She was wearing one of his white dress shirts. It hit her at midthigh and the sleeves were rolled up. She must have looked like death warmed over, but that's not how he was looking at her.

"Do you want me to . . ." He made the universal motion for *turn around*, but Alex didn't even have to think about the answer.

"No."

She was far past modesty at that point. He'd already seen her. Dressed her. Cleaned her wounds. He'd saved her.

"Good," he blurted. Alex started undoing buttons, but her hands didn't want to work right. "I mean . . ." He was blushing. "I don't want you to fall. Head injuries are . . ." The fabric parted. "Worse. They . . . bleed. And . . . bad. They're bad. And . . ." Alex was stepping toward the water. "Here."

He held her as she sank slowly in, watched her settle against the rolled lip of the tub like he knew he was supposed to leave but his feet weren't taking orders at the moment.

"Sit up." She didn't even want to argue, and that's how she knew she'd almost died. When she heard the water turn on again, felt the gentle spray from a handheld nozzle, it felt almost sinful, the way the warm water sluiced down the line of her spine.

"Close your eyes," he told her, and then the warm water brushed against her scalp and down her filthy hair. "Lean back against me." She let her head fall back and rest against the palm of his left hand while he gently worked shampoo through the strands with his right, and Alex forgot about nudity and wounds and mortal enemies. She wasn't thinking about Russian bad guys or missions or feelings that were too dangerous for the CIA.

There was just King and the hot water and the feeling of big, strong hands that had no right to be that gentle. The water seeped into her battered bones, and it felt like coming clean in a way she'd never been.

"I'm okay now."

It took a long time for him to whisper, "I'm not."

chapter forty-seven

ALEX

The apartment was, in fact, art deco. Lovingly restored and preserved by King's grandfather and then his father and now by King himself. High ceilings with ornate moldings and glossy hardwood floors. Tall windows with no curtains and rooms with no furniture. It was the apartment of a man who had everything he needed but nothing he wanted, and Alex tried to reconcile that with the man she thought she knew. Not for the first time, she tried to make King make sense.

There was only one closed door, so, of course, once she was clean and dry and steady on her feet, she opened it. She wasn't prepared for what was waiting.

"What's all this?"

It was probably supposed to be a guest room or maybe—in another life—a nursery. But King's version had nothing to do with art deco. Instead, there were long metal tables and walls of monitors. The lights were off but the whole room glowed red and green, like Technology Christmas. It was a maze of devices and wires and whiteboards covered in scrawl.

Some might have wondered if that was what the inside of King's mind looked like, but Alex knew better. King's mind was straight rows and laser-printed labels, alphabetized shelves and color-coded files. King's mind was perfect. This room, though—this was where King could let his mind go free.

She was just starting to tell herself that she shouldn't be there when she saw it—a stone that was small and green and precious. And then, instead of feeling cold in Berlin, she was hot in Cartagena. She was watching Merritt hand King a little bag full of emeralds. She saw him dump them out on his palm and then examine one small stone.

That small stone.

"I dropped one. In the hotel room that first day," a voice said from the door. He'd put on a pair of jeans and a dry shirt, but his socks were still mismatched and that one detail made her want to cry, but she didn't have any idea how to explain it, so she just pointed a finger at him.

"No, you didn't. You palmed it. You *stole* it!" she accused. Or teased. Even she wasn't sure of the difference.

He gave a guilty grin. A little shrug. And then the shy confession of, "I tinker."

The words didn't make any sense—at least not at first. But then she watched the way he scanned the room. It was his domain, but it was like he was seeing it for the first time because he was seeing it through her.

Alex ran a hand over the glossy shelves. "I love what you've done with the place."

"It clears my mind. Working with my hands. Doing things. Building things."

"And this?" She held up the emerald.

"I might have made some improvements."

"Oh." She wanted to mock him but she couldn't quite pull it off.

"Does it play music? Sync to the cloud?"

"It's waterproof now. Better range."

"Very convenient."

"Almost unlimited battery life."

"Excellent." But she couldn't stop herself from smiling. "You stole it."

He smiled down at his feet. "I stole it." He looked like a little boy who was sheepish and guilty but absolutely going to do it again because getting caught would be worth it. "Are you hungry?" Alex hadn't thought about it until then, but she wasn't hungry. She was ravenous. "I made soup. If you don't like it, I can make something else. Or go pick something up," he said as she followed him through the nearly empty rooms.

"You don't have furniture."

"I have a pot. And some flatware. A couple of bowls." It was almost cute, how defensive he sounded.

And then it felt almost normal, the way she settled onto the lone chair at the lone table and watched him move around the old-fashioned kitchen. He heated the soup in his one pot and then poured it into his two bowls, and then they ate in near silence as he leaned against the counter, watching her every move.

She ate two bowls because, of course, Michael Kingsley was an excellent cook. She was just contemplating how wise (or embarrassing) it might be to ask for a third when he said, "You talk in your sleep."

She hadn't been expecting that. Not because she didn't know. She'd spent her whole childhood sleeping on the other side of the room from Zoe, after all. But no one else had ever mentioned it before.

"In German. You speak German. When you sleep."

Oh. "That's probably because I dream in German."

His head shot up in surprise. "You do?" It was like it was the first thing she'd ever said or done that had actually surprised him.

"And French," she added.

"Not English?"

"Sometimes. But mostly . . . it doesn't matter. My head translates so fast, they all sound the same"—she tapped her temple—"in here." King was looking at her oddly, studying her in a way she'd never seen before, as if she'd just become more mysterious, but also, at the same time, suddenly made sense. "What?"

"Nothing," he blurted a little too quickly. "I just thought I was the only one. I didn't know . . ."

And something about that made Alex bristle. "That I was qualified."

"No. That you were like me."

Alex was many, many things, but like King? Never.

She wanted to ask him what he meant—if it was a compliment or an insult, if she should have been offended or enraged. But she couldn't think of the words—not in any language—so, instead, she just said, "My mother was a language teacher. And we lived . . . everywhere. My father's job took us all over. Engineer," she filled in before he could ask. "And everywhere we went, Mom would make us learn the new language, but she also wouldn't let us forget the old one. For a while, she had a rule that we had to speak Latin at the table." Alex had to smile at the memory. She and Zoe had made so many Caesar salad jokes. She smiled down at her empty bowl, and for the first time, she felt not empty. "It wasn't as useful as she thought it would be."

"I'm sure."

"What did I say?" Alex asked, but he tilted his head like he didn't follow. "Last night?"

"Oh." Suddenly, it was like he didn't want to face her. He got her bowl and carried it to the sink.

"King—"

"*Michael*," he said too quickly. "Last night—when you were sleeping. And before. . . . You called me Michael."

"Oh."

It didn't explain the way that he was acting, except for all the ways that, maybe, it did.

"Did you hate that?"

"No." He shook his head and studied her, gaze sharper than the knives and twice as deadly. "Not even a little bit."

chapter forty-eight

Present Day
Somewhere in Portugal

ALEX

So it turned out, once Alex wasn't about to pass out from blood loss, she was able to reevaluate her opinion on the safe house. The walls were covered with fishing nets and rusty hooks. Taxidermied turtles, old hats, and two hundred magazines from the summer of 1968.

"It's . . . something."

"My understanding is that it came fully furnished." King sounded almost amused.

When Alex looked out the window, she saw they were right on the water. She heard crashing waves and squawking seagulls. The house was at the top of a cliff, but a narrow staircase zigzagged its way to the shore. If she looked straight down, she could just make out a rocky beach and a little cove that must have been great for smuggling.

"It was his favorite safe house for seafaring escapades."

"Were there a lot of those?"

"There was every kind of escapade. He did it for a long time."

"Your grandfather?" King looked at her like he didn't understand the question. "Not your father?"

They'd known each other for ten years, and she'd never mentioned his dad. She'd never asked the obvious questions. Maybe because she didn't want to pry or maybe because she didn't want to die, but Alex was out of patience. And they were out of time.

"A long time ago, you said that you'd tell me—"

"I know."

"I don't care how much it hurts, King. It's time. We have to talk about it. You have to tell me."

Honestly, the scary part was that he didn't even try to argue. He just nodded and said, "My grandfather—"

"Was the Berlin station chief in sixty-two . . ." She remembered.

"It was the height of the Cold War. The Soviets and the CIA were in a never-ending chess match, constantly moving pieces on the board. One of those pieces was an operative they called Nikolai. He was their queen. Seemingly everywhere. Doing everything. But the thing you need to know about Nikolai is . . . he doesn't exist."

"But—"

King closed his eyes and cut her off. "He was a legend—a ghost story. *Be good or Nikolai will get you.* Even if he *had* existed—which my grandfather swore he didn't—he'd either be dead or a very old man by now." Alex remembered the way the two guys at the Farm had talked about Nikolai—like he was the Easter Bunny or Santa Claus. But also like he was the only dark spot in the legacy of spies named Michael Kingsley.

"There was always chatter," he went on. "Was he real? A lie made up by the KGB—a boogeyman custom-made to keep the Agency guessing? My grandfather's theory was that he was an amalgamation of a dozen different operatives operating on both sides of the Iron Curtain. And then the Curtain fell, and the Soviet Union crumbled, and the oligarchs rose up in its place. No one should have cared about an old spy who probably never existed. . . . No one *did* care."

"And then . . ." Alex was afraid of whatever came next. But she had to know. In a way, it felt like their story had been building toward this for ten years—longer.

"And then we ran out of milk, and my mother and grandmother decided to go to the store, and our car exploded in the driveway."

Alex could have formed a million theories, but none would have would have come close to that.

For a long time, she just stood there, slack-jawed and stunned.

She couldn't even say she was sorry. There wasn't a word in any of her languages that could make it better, so she didn't say a thing.

"There was a note in the mailbox. *Spokoynoy nochi*."

"Michael . . ."

"*Good night*," he translated—not because Alex didn't know but because those were the words that haunted him. "I was ten years old. We'd just moved to the States. My grandfather had passed away, and my grandmother was living with us. Dad was out of the field, but there wasn't any reason he couldn't work out of Langley. The Agency put us in transitional housing and . . . we were out. *We were getting out.* The Cold War had been over for decades, and we had nothing to do with the Russians, but then . . . Dad decided to write a book. About Nikolai. It was nothing more than ghost stories, or so we thought, but . . . He must have gotten too close to something the Russians wanted to hide. *Or someone*." He stopped and looked at her, piercing and stoic. "It was meant for him—the bomb. It was meant for my father, but it killed his wife and his mother, and the guilt . . . I lost him too." He looked out the window. "It just took him a lot longer to die."

"Michael . . ."

"He loved my mom too much, and it broke him. He became . . . obsessed. The world's foremost authority on someone who doesn't exist. But now . . ."

He looked at her through the shadows, found her gaze, and held on tight.

"Now Nikolai wants us?" she guessed, but he just shook his head.

"Now Nikolai wants that ring."

"And so . . ."

She'd never seen him look so hard—so lethal. "Now we go get it."

Six Years Ago
Berlin, Germany

ALEX

Alex didn't remember falling asleep on the sofa, just a faint, dream-like memory of floating through the air. Of strong arms and the brush of warm lips and an almost silent whisper.

Sleep well, sweetheart.

But it was probably a dream.

The man sitting beside her on the bed, however, was very, very real as Alex came awake too quickly.

She started to bolt upright, but a big hand pressed her down, a gentle reminder not to move and not to fight. That there are some stitches in life you shouldn't tug at. One glance at King's face told her it wouldn't take much to make them both unravel.

"What . . ." Her throat was raw, and the sky was dark, and she didn't know why he was sitting there, fully clothed, instead of lying on the bed beside her.

"What time is it?"

He didn't own a clock. She supposed it was because he didn't need one. She usually didn't either. Her internal alarms were finely tuned and tightly wound, but somehow, in the last few days, the second hand had stopped ticking. Time was never on their side.

"Michael . . . you're scaring me." The old Alex would never have admitted it, but that was before the bullets and the blood and . . . "What is it?"

"I'm out," he said to the shadows, and Alex's sleepy brain couldn't think of anything except—

"Of the closet?"

"No." Was that a chuckle? She couldn't tell. She just knew that the room got suddenly colder when he said, "The Agency."

She'd misheard him. He was speaking a language she didn't know.

"What did you just say?" She propped herself up as much as she could with a gunshot wound, but right then she barely felt it.

"I'm leaving the Agency. The life. I'm done."

"I . . ." Alex couldn't make the words make sense. There were so many thoughts swirling around in her mind, but for some reason the thing that came out was, "I can't believe you're telling me this while I'm half dead and half naked."

She couldn't believe it when he laughed. "You're always one or the other."

He wasn't wrong, but he also wasn't joking.

"King . . . Michael." That was when he looked at her. His finger brushed away a strand of hair and tucked it behind her ear.

"I'm out. I can't do this anymore."

"As of when?"

"Tonight." The word was the kind of black that sucks up all the color—all the light. The full range of the spectrum could disappear inside it and get lost there.

"Is this about Tyler?" She was half afraid to say the name. "What you did?"

"Tyler's fine. Tyler's safe. Tyler isn't . . ." He looked down at her. She felt small in one of his big T-shirts and even bigger bed. "It's about you."

Alex had never heard his voice crack. She'd never seen his hand shake. She'd never seen . . . *him*. Not like this. She watched him draw a long, deep breath and then choke out the words, "I have a photographic memory. Do you know what that means?"

"Of course I know what that means. I'm not a moron, Kingsley."

"Do you know what it—"

"It means you remember," she shot back, but he just sat there in the stillness, as innocent as a little boy and as tired as an old man when he whispered—

"It means *I can't forget*."

It was the same thing, but it was also completely different, and Alex didn't want to think about the burden.

"I remember, Alex. Every bullet. Every knife. Every scab and scar and scratch. I remember all of them. The memories are just right here"—King tapped his temple lightly—"but you're not. And that's okay. As long as I know you're okay. But, someday, Alex . . . Someday you won't be. And then it will kill me." He got to his feet. "Someday it will kill me too."

"Michael—"

"So I'm out." He drew a ragged breath, and suddenly, he looked tired and worn-out, and Alex couldn't help but think about his father— his grandfather. The fact that he'd probably been the only kid at preschool who knew the Moscow Rules by heart. He'd been doing this job since the cradle. Their world was like a carnival ride, and the man in front of her wanted to get off. I want you to come with me."

At least, that's what Alex thought she heard. But Alex was wrong. She had to be. There was no way he was saying, "Come with me, now. Today. We can . . . Come with me."

Alex knew as soon as the laugh burst free that she was going to regret it for the rest of her life. He eased back like she'd hit him. Like she'd *hurt* him.

"Michael, we can't . . . I can't . . . We're spies."

"We don't have to be."

"People don't just stop being . . . us."

"We'd still be us." He brought a hand to the back of her head and cupped her nape, fingers weaving through her hair. "We'd be better. We'd be together. And we'd be free."

"There is no free." How could the man with the perfect memory have forgotten that? King and Alex could never be anything but what they were: people who were trained to be someone else but never really happy?

"What do you think's going to happen? What's your plan? This is you, King." She took a deep breath and closed her eyes. "*Michael.* Do you think you can just buy a fortress somewhere and pull up the drawbridge and live happily ever after?"

"Why not?" The words were so sharp, they might have cut her.

"Where are we supposed to go?"

"We can go anywhere."

"What are we supposed to do?"

"We can do anything! They trained us for this—for exactly this. We can go *anywhere*. We can be *anyone*. They trained us to be ghosts, but right now, all I want to be is happy. All I want . . ." He pulled back. Like he was afraid to touch her. "Is you."

Alex didn't know what was happening, but her gaze was suddenly blurry. Like a windshield in the rain with busted wipers. But it didn't make any sense, because Alex didn't cry. Alex didn't *long*.

The thing that Alex had wanted since she was nine years old, she had. The person she wanted to be, she was. She was already living her Best-Case Scenario, but the way he looked at her said that moment was his Break in Case of Emergency. And the emergency . . . was her.

But . . .

She was shaking her head. She was backing away. It was way too much and way too soon, and Alex cursed the hole in her side because she wanted to turn around and run as fast as she could. But then she realized what this meant: King wouldn't be waiting when she got there . . .

"What is it?" His voice was softer. Closer. "Sweetheart, tell me . . ."

"I'm . . ." She'd been so happy a week ago when she'd gotten the call from Langley and been told about the assignment. It had seemed like such a good thing. But now . . . "I'm going undercover."

"You don't have to go." He actually let out a deep breath, like this wasn't so bad, this could be fixed.

"No. It's important."

"So are you. So are we."

"It's Kozlov."

He froze. He went so still so quickly that she had to wonder if he was even breathing. But she could see his mind working, like clockwork, gears turning. She could actually see his mind change course.

"Okay." He straightened. "One last mission. Together."

"No."

"I'm going with you."

"You can't."

"But—"

"It's not a mission," Alex blurted, and she knew the moment when he realized what that meant, but she said it anyway. "I'm going into deep cover."

But King was shaking his head. "No."

"I have to. Now. Before I'm too well known. They need a female operative—"

"*No.*"

"Someone with experience but who isn't likely to be recognized." It was her saddest smile. "I'm perfect."

The old King—*her* King—would have made some caustic comment about perfection. He would have teased or maybe chided. He wouldn't have looked so terrified, he could scream. But this new King—her new King—looked dry and gray like dust.

"I have to do this." Alex stared down at her hands. She was brave enough to go deep inside one of the most dangerous organizations in the world, but she wasn't brave enough to look at Michael Kingsley. "I know you don't think I'm good enough."

"Are you kidding me?" He pushed away, words like a knife between them, cutting that moment into two separate pieces: before and after. "That's not it, and you know it."

She didn't know it. She didn't even know what *it* was, and he must have seen it in her eyes because he gave a sad smile.

"You're the best, Alexandra Sterling. You were always the best. *We* were the best." He swallowed hard. "Or maybe I'm the only one who felt it."

He wasn't. She'd felt it too. At every step, it had been there, beating beneath her skin like a pulse, but that didn't change the fact that—

"I have to do this, Michael. I have to. . . . This is all I ever wanted to be. Since I was nine years old. It's the only way bad people can do good things, so—"

"Is that what you think?"

She couldn't take it—the softness of his voice. She couldn't look at him. That was how a girl gets burned.

"You are not a bad . . ." He got it, then. She could see it in his eyes because he shifted, softer now. "You didn't kill your sister."

"I know. She's alive."

"Even if she had died, it wouldn't have been because you killed her. You didn't do that."

They were the words Alex had needed to hear her whole life, but no one had ever said them—until then.

"Kozlov . . ." she started because it was either that or become some other person. A girl who cries and cares and loves. But girls like that get hurt.

"I have to stop him, King. I'm in. I'm already in, and I can stop him. I can."

But he was looking at her like he was trying to memorize her face and her voice. Like of all the things he'd never forget, the only one he wanted to hang on to forever was her.

"I get it . . ."

"When I'm done . . . When he's gone—"

"When he's gone, there'll just be another Kozlov." He gave a long, sad sigh. "There's always another Kozlov."

But there was only one of him.

"King—"

Then he leaned close and pressed a kiss against her forehead. "The apartment is yours for as long as you need it, sweetheart." He looked into her eyes. "It's yours."

I'm yours.

He was already in the kitchen and halfway to the door before Alex started thinking clearly enough to follow.

"Wait!"

He reached for something on the counter. Alex recognized the green stone, but now it was set in a beautiful gold cuff, and King didn't say a word. He just picked it up and clamped it around her wrist.

"Your emerald . . ." Her eyes were wet, and her throat burned.

"It's yours now. If you ever need me . . . I don't care where . . . I don't care when . . . If you need me, press the stone, and I'll find you." That time, when he kissed her, his lips lingered on her skin. "I'll always find you."

"Don't." She caught him before he could turn. Maybe it was instinct—or maybe it was fate—but the next thing she knew, she was in his arms and her back was against the wall, legs wrapped around him as their arms tangled together and their lips met and their tongues sparred. It was part kiss, part fight—part surrender. A code that spelled out *this this this*.

It was the scariest moment of either of their bullet-ridden lives, and Alex almost forgot how to breathe.

She forgot her name. Her covers. Her lies. She forgot all the things she'd been trained to remember.

She forgot.

And she wanted to stay right there—right then—forever. Because, in the next moment, she was on her feet again, and he was turning and opening the door.

"Take care, Sterling."

And then she was Sterling again.

And then he was gone.

Two months later, Alex was standing on a windy airstrip outside of London when she met a man with a crooked smile and sad eyes. It was the look of a man with absolutely nothing to lose, and, immediately, she understood him, even when he looked her up and down, studying everything from her new boots to her new hair. Even when his gaze lingered on her new bracelet.

"So you're the one who's going to make my life miserable?" he asked, but there wasn't any heat behind the words.

"Says who?"

The man—Jake Sawyer from MI6—just gave her a long look—a whole conversation in his eyes when he said, "Michael Kingsley."

She didn't hear his name again for a long, long time.

chapter fifty

One Year Ago
Russia

ALEX

Alex wasn't supposed to be there, but she wasn't going to let that stop her.

Not when she'd been undercover for five years.

Not when she'd burrowed her way so deeply into Kozlov's inner circle that she could practically see the rotten core.

Not when she was so very, very close to taking down someone who was so very, very evil.

Alex and Sawyer had a theory and an agenda and a plan that absolutely did not involve her doing a black bag job by herself, so, yeah—

Alex wasn't supposed to be there.

But something was *wrong*, and Alex couldn't trust anyone at the moment—not even herself. So she was silent as the grave as she slipped through the shadows of the Kozlov compound, worrying about what she had to do.

The thing that made Kozlov so dangerous was that he had the ruthlessness of a twenty-first-century villain in the body of an old-school spy. He'd been KGB, and his tradecraft was still sharp, but there were rumors about a database—one single cache of information that included everything from contacts to calendars, inventories to investments. There was a computer somewhere in that compound where the mother lode was stored. And as soon as Alex found it . . .

Well, it sounded too good to be true, which meant it probably was. But Alex had to take the chance.

Rumor had it, there were only two copies. One was a backup housed at a second location, but one was supposedly *here*, and Alex had an idea where to look, so she stayed silent as she slipped through the shadows toward Kozlov's empty office—not skulking because skulking was for amateurs. No, Alex strutted. Alex *belonged*. Half of Kozlov's goons were in love with her and the other half were terrified of her. (With a fair amount of overlap in the middle.) So she didn't act out of place as she picked the lock on the office door and stepped inside.

A few days before, she'd felt a draft coming from the glass-fronted shelves that lined the wall behind Kozlov's desk, and Alex had come to one conclusion: there was a secret room back there. And what better place to keep a secret computer?

So that was why Alex stood there in the middle of the night, staring at the kind of display she'd seen twice in her life: once at the Farm and again in Amalfi.

She looked across the illuminated shelves full of lipstick cameras and tiny transmitters and wondered what Kozlov would do if he ever learned that Alex had been the one who'd turned his most prized possessions into ash. He'd done his best to rebuild the collection, but there was a reason Alex had been avoiding those particular shelves.

They made her think about Amalfi.

And Amalfi made her think about King.

And thinking about King made Alex feel.

And feeling was careless and reckless and far too much like the girl in the airport Ramada, waiting for her chicken fingers and flirting with strangers. Feeling would get Alex killed, and right then she had a reason for living, so she was careful as she took in the tall shelves that seemed embedded in the old stone wall.

She was examining the sides of the cases when she heard the doorknob rattle, so she didn't waste a minute before diving under the desk. She was having trouble breathing when she heard the words—

"Come, Sergei. Close the door."

Kozlov.

He was supposed to be at the Lake Como house with Mistress Number Three, but he wasn't. He was there. Which meant . . .

"Our house is not secure," the old man whispered, and the little hairs on the back of Alex's neck stood straight up. The air flowing through the vent in the floor felt like a sandstorm. She *felt* everything. She *heard* everything. Her heart was a drum so loud, it was going to get her caught.

"Sir, I assure you. The migration is complete." There was no mistaking the deference in Sergei's voice. "The servers are safe. They cannot be breached from the outside. There are only two places on earth where someone can access your data. Here and at the backup, and as you know, the backup is constantly moving. I assure you—"

"That is not my worry."

Kozlov drew a heavy breath. He sounded . . . tired. And old. Computers and data migrations were of no interest to Viktor Kozlov. He was a spy's spy. A man from another time. He was like Merritt, Alex realized. And the thought made her homesick.

"We have a spy in our midst, Sergei. A traitor. *A mole.*" Kozlov sounded furious but also . . . excited? Like he was back on familiar turf—they were getting the band back together and his covert glory days weren't over yet.

"How can you know?"

Alex watched Kozlov's legs move toward the shelves. His voice was full of wonder when he said, "I have collected many things." The old man opened the glass doors and moved his trinkets around like they were action figures or porcelain dolls. "I once had a ring that was used by the greatest spy to ever live. Did I tell you?"

Sergei hummed in a way that sounded like *This again?* but the word he uttered was—"No."

"In the old days, there was one prize that was coveted above all others: *the double agent.*"

Alex hadn't moved in minutes, and yet it felt like she froze—*time* froze. The whole world froze except for Kozlov.

"Things were civilized in those days. There was honor among

spies, and if you could get one to turn and work for you, it was the greatest achievement. Double agents were rare and they were legend. I have long wanted one of my own." He pulled a can of shaving cream off the shelf, unscrewed the false bottom, and pulled out a key. "He has told me the most interesting things."

Alex couldn't feel her hands. She couldn't feel her feet. She couldn't feel anything but terror because there was one thing she knew for certain:

Kozlov didn't just *want* a double agent.

Kozlov *had* one.

"I see," Sergei said slowly. "Shall I bring the girl to you now or—"

"No," Kozlov cut him off. "She could still be useful to us. We must be careful of her, though. She is dangerous."

Then Kozlov slid the key into a tiny gap in the stones beside the case and turned. The case slid open, and the two men disappeared inside, but Alex didn't move. She barely breathed. She just sat there thinking—

You have no idea.

Thirty minutes later, Kozlov's data was on a flash drive, and the flash drive was in Alex's bra, and she was almost to the garage when she heard a voice behind her.

"Alex?" It was darker and lower than when she'd first heard it. But, then again, so was Sawyer. "Hey." He inched toward her, knowing something was wrong because Sawyer was good. He'd always been good.

Except what if he wasn't? What if he was very, very bad, and Alex didn't want to think about the possibility. He'd been her only friend—her only ally—for five years. He was the only person for a thousand miles that she could trust, but—

He has told me the most interesting things.

"What's wrong?" Sawyer glanced behind her, making sure they were alone. There were no cameras in that stretch of hallway. No guards.

No witnesses.

"Hey. You're scaring me," he said, and Alex forced a laugh.

"Not scared. Disappointed."

"But—"

"Kozlov didn't go to the lake house," she said. "He and Sergei are up to something. We're gonna have to do it another time."

"Oh." Sawyer ran a hand through his dark hair. He looked tired and worn—like paper in a very old book, faded and thin, but she could still read him.

"Sorry you got out of bed for nothing."

"That's okay. I don't sleep, remember?"

Alex had trusted Sawyer from the moment he'd first appeared on that tarmac and said King's name into the wind. She'd trusted him, but that was the problem, wasn't it? Because, at that moment, Alex couldn't even trust herself, and suddenly, the gold cuff was a heavy, familiar weight on her wrist—more talisman than bracelet—and she saw Sawyer cut his eyes down at it.

"You ever going to tell me the story behind that?"

"No," she said, but he smiled the smile of a man who already knew, and then he inched away.

"You sure you're okay?"

No, because Kozlov has a mole, and I can't swear that it's not you.

No, because I know what I have to do but there's not a soul I can trust to help me.

No, because I was with someone in the womb, but I've been alone ever since—alone and afraid—and there's a part of me that's still waiting for my chicken fingers to get there, wondering if I'm actually good enough for the guy on the other end of the bar.

No.

No.

No.

"Yeah. Of course." She cocked a hip. "Never better."

Five minutes later, Sawyer was gone, and Alex was adjusting the rearview mirror on Kozlov's favorite car as she sped down the winding drive.

One down, she told herself as, behind her, the compound exploded.

One to go.

chapter fifty-one

Present Day
The North Sea

"I know why they want the ring."

King jolted upright, not entirely surprised to realize he'd been sleeping. The ferry was small and the sea was rough—the bench was hard as a rock—but they'd been traveling for two days, and between the stolen cars and high-speed trains, he'd managed to steal, at most, six hours of rest since they left the Portuguese safe house. It made sense that he would have drifted off eventually. So he wasn't surprised, but that didn't mean he wasn't embarrassed.

"What?" His voice sounded too rough. It almost got lost in the wind.

"The ring. I know why they—or he. Or *she*? I know why Nikolai wants it." Alex had said that she was seasick, but she'd lied. King watched the way she stood at the railing of the little ship that was battling the cold, rough waters. Spray misted around her, turning the air to tiny rainbows in the streaks of sunlight that sliced through the clouds. "When I was undercover, I heard Kozlov talking one time. . . . You know how he was obsessed with spy gadgets?"

King almost smiled. "Like the ones we burned to a crisp seven years ago?"

"Exactly." She huffed out a silent laugh. "Well, one time, I heard him brag that he used to own a ring that belonged to the greatest spy who ever lived. Which, in hindsight, sounds a lot like . . ."

"Nikolai." King stood up to walk to the railing. The ferry rose and fell with the waves, and he tried to keep his gaze on the cold, gray horizon. "And you think Nikolai wants their ring back?"

Alex shrugged, but winced. She tried to hide it, but he knew her too well by that point. He could always tell when she was hurting. "It's time to change your bandages."

"They're fine."

"Okay." King turned and leaned against the rail. He didn't bother to argue with Alexandra Sterling in the same way one shouldn't bother holding back the tide. "No problem. I hear infections are very flattering these days."

"Okay."

"Some spies do their best work with a fever."

"I said okay." She sounded angry, but she looked more *annoyed* with a touch of *happy someone finally cares.*

There were only a handful of people on the ferry, and everyone else had the good sense to stay inside, so they were alone when they settled onto the bench and Alex cautiously raised her shirt up. She'd been right. It really was more of a graze than a gunshot, but it had bled like the dickens and the skin was angry and red.

"It might scar," he warned.

"Darn. I guess my beauty pageant days are behind me."

But all King could do was say, "Ordinarily, I'd think that was a joke, but with you I never know."

He tugged off the old bandage and put on a fresh one, but Alex kept her gaze straight ahead, wind in her hair. She should have been shivering. It was January on the North Sea. The wind was straight from the Pole, and the mist flying off the water felt like sleet, but it was like she didn't feel it. Like she'd spent her whole life teaching herself not to feel anything, and King wanted to go back in time and tell the girl at the airport Ramada that it was okay to feel, it was okay to hurt, it was okay to be too excited and too angry and just generally too much. He hated that he had ever made her feel like not enough.

"Alex . . ."

When she turned to him, she was so close and her skin was so warm as her hand cupped his face. "Did I tell you I like your beard?"

She was looking at his lips, and it was like the last year had been a very bad dream.

"Alex . . ." He inched closer, needing her heat and her weight and . . . her. He needed her, and he'd never stopped and that's what he wanted to tell her—show her. And never let her forget. "Sweetheart . . ."

But the sea chose that moment to dip too quickly. The ferry felt like a roller coaster, and a cold spray blew across the bow, chilling them both to the bone while Alex turned a shade of green that King had never seen before.

"You okay?" Now he was honestly worried. "I thought you liked boats."

"Yeah, well. I didn't have a great time on the last one."

chapter fifty-two

One Year Ago
The Middle of the Mediterranean

ALEX

It was the middle of the night in the middle of the Mediterranean, and a woman just woke up a ton of bad guys.

Alex didn't know whether she was lucky (there were only so many "constantly moving" locations for Kozlov to keep his backups and she'd guessed it on her very first try). Or supremely cursed. (Since when do Russian thugs *not* finish the whole bottle of vodka?)

She'd sprung for the good stuff and you couldn't even taste the tranquilizers, but then the morons had to go and drop the bottle and waste half, so now—instead of taking her good sweet time—Alex was running across the deck of Kozlov's megayacht, Russian curses flying on the air along with the bullets.

So. Many. Bullets.

She was almost to the aft, though. Arms pumping. Wind in her hair. There was no way she was going to make it to her lifeboat in time, but Alex told herself it didn't matter.

Even if she died . . . even if all she managed to do was destroy Kozlov's backup . . . then that would be enough.

The flash drive was already safe. There was only one other person in the world who could access it, and she was far away and blissfully innocent. She was going to stay that way too. Because Alex hadn't talked to her sister in years. With very few exceptions, no one even knew Zoe existed.

And it wouldn't matter anyway because time was almost out.

The clock in her head was ticking down.

Five.

Four.

More shots. More curses.

Three.

Two.

And then Alex leapt into the air, diving deep as the goons fired overhead, bullets piercing the water like falling stars until—

One.

Flames filled the sky, and Alex dove deeper beneath the waves, hiding from the heat and the debris that fell like rain.

She gasped when she finally surfaced, but all she saw were floating pieces of smoldering rubble and smoke so thick, it blocked the stars. The dark waters of the sea lapped against her, and Alex's mind grew foggy from the smoke and the trauma and the knowledge that she was a long, long way from shore.

Maybe someone would see the flames. Maybe someone heard the explosion. Or maybe it was all too late, but that didn't matter.

The flash drive was safe.

The backup was gone.

Even if Alex didn't make it out of this, it wouldn't all be for nothing. People would know that her good heart and her strong body hadn't been wasted. She wasn't just the girl who had almost killed her sister; she was also the woman who had taken down Viktor Kozlov, so a deep sense of peace came over Alex as she floated on the inky black water and watched the smoke swirl across the sky.

She crawled onto a piece of debris and closed her eyes. She was starting to drift—on the waves and in and out of consciousness, when—

"If you need me, press the stone and I'll find you. I'll always find you . . ."

The voice filled her mind as Alex reached for the bracelet and pressed against the emerald. She felt the *click* and watched it start to glow—a green light flashing in the dark. Beating like a pulse, the only thing keeping her alive as the stars grew brighter and the night grew later—

And later—

And later—

Until a low distant hum filled the air, and, suddenly, the moon was too bright—too close—beaming down on Alex like a spotlight as the water got rougher and the sound got louder and—

There was a shadow in the moonlight, falling from the sky and getting closer. And closer.

And closer.

Strong arms wrapped around her. Lips pressed against her skin. And a familiar voice said, "I have you. I have you. I have you."

Alex felt her body start to rise as the arms squeezed tighter.

"You're safe now," the voice said, and for the first time in a long time, it was true.

chapter fifty-three

One Year Ago
Scotland

ALEX

Alex lay in bed for a long time, staring at the man asleep in the chair beside her. His hair was mussed and his clothes were wrinkled, and he couldn't have been further from the dude in the bar at the airport Ramada. In short, Michael Kingsley had never looked worse, but he'd also never looked better, and for a while she just nestled into the soft sheets and warm blankets and watched a soft ray of sunshine streak across a jaw that was rough with stubble.

She must have made a sound, though, because he bolted upright, as if mad at himself that he'd fallen asleep and left her alone and unguarded.

"Did I ever thank you for the bracelet?"

He started to lunge for her but held himself back somehow. Like he didn't want to scare her. Like a part of him thought it might still be a dream.

"Hi," Alex told him.

"Hi." His voice cracked.

There were a million things to say in that moment but only one that mattered. "You came for me."

He put a hand on her forehead like he was feeling for a fever, but he left it there like he couldn't stop touching her quite yet. "Always."

And then he kissed her—soft and then hard. It was the kiss of a man looking for his last breath.

When she tried to sit up, he said, "Easy," then he helped her lean against the pillows. "Where does it hurt?"

"Everywhere? Nowhere?" Alex was honestly guessing. She'd hurt so much and for so long that she didn't remember what the lack of pain actually felt like. *Hurt* was her default state. "How long . . ."

"Two days."

That explained the wrinkles and the stubble and the way her legs felt as if they couldn't quite hold her when she struggled to her feet.

"I have to go," Alex blurted. "I have to . . ." But she trailed off when she realized she had no idea how that sentence was supposed to end. "Do . . . something?"

"Do you?" King was honestly asking. He wasn't arguing or fighting or telling her he knew better. "What do you need to do?"

"I need . . ."

Her hair was crusty and stiff with dried salt water. Her skin was sticky with sweat and soot. She was wearing nothing but a too-big T-shirt she absolutely hadn't put on herself, and it was easy to imagine King, Boy Scout that he was, closing his eyes to strip her out of her wet suit, doing war with himself over what was worse: looking at her body without permission or letting her get sicker and die.

"I need . . . to take a shower?" Alex looked around the room. There were gray stone walls and floors covered with thick rugs, windows framed by heavy curtains. The light fixtures were downright medieval, and yet the whole place felt warm and safe and . . . his. This wasn't some safe house. This was *the* safe house. But it probably wasn't enough.

"I'm not safe. And if I'm here, then you're not safe either."

"Try me."

"I kicked a hornet's nest."

King actually laughed. "Judging by the amount of debris in the Mediterranean, I'd say you blew one up." Alex didn't bother to deny it. "Kozlov?" he guessed.

"I have to go."

"Do you?"

Alex had to think about the answer. The flash drive was safe, and the backup was gone, and there was probably a manhunt of insane proportions going on all over Europe. Kozlov hadn't been in the compound when it exploded, so now he was going to be out for blood. The Agency would have a host of other questions. As soon as the intelligence community realized what Alex had, the whole world would be gunning for her: good guys, bad guys, and literally everyone in between.

She had to get to Langley. She had to turn herself in. She had to . . .

The words came back again, ringing in her ears. *"Double agents were rare and they were legend. I have long wanted one of my own. He has told me the most interesting things."*

Kozlov had a mole, and Alex felt her legs give out. She dropped to the bed and King surged toward her, worry in his eyes that morphed into something far, far different when she looked up at him. And grinned. "Actually, no. I don't have to go . . . anywhere."

She huffed out a laugh because surely that wasn't true? She *always* had to be going somewhere or doing something. Alex had spent her whole life running from her sister and her parents and her past—from a universe that looked at her and wondered if she was even worth it. Alex had been running her whole life, and now that she was actually, literally, on the run, she had to wonder . . .

Where was she supposed to go? What was she supposed to do? Surely she was supposed to be *doing something*, but right then she was too busy watching King deflate. He was what the Macy's Thanksgiving Day Parade probably looked like at five o'clock, hot air seeping out of him. Wilting before her eyes. He'd been bracing for a fight because that was who they were. Or who they used to be.

She tried to read the last five years on his face. He should have looked like a stranger, but instead, he felt like home, which was why Alex knew she shouldn't stay.

"I really *should* go—"

"Back to bed," he said. "I agree. Great idea."

"No. King. It's not safe. You're not safe."

"Let me worry about me. Let me worry about you. In fact, why don't I take charge of all the worrying for the time being?"

"You got out!" She didn't mean to yell, but it felt, somehow, like it was either that or whisper. Like those were her only two options. His hands were on hers and she'd never been more obsessed with his fingers. "You got out, and I'm not going to drag you back in."

"I'm not in. I'm with you. I'm wherever you are."

Her eyes closed of their own volition, like they wanted to keep her treacherous tears in. She wasn't brave enough to let them fall.

"They'll come for me." This time, it was a whisper, but King didn't care as he leaned close and whispered back—

"Let them try." Hands cupped her head, and he leaned down to look into her eyes. "No one's going to look for you here because I got out five years ago and we hate each other. Remember?"

Alex hated how her voice cracked when she asked, "Do we?"

Suddenly, the whole world hinged on the answer to that question.

"You're safe with me. You will always be safe with me." He pulled her close, and she couldn't stop herself from leaning against him. "Let me keep you safe."

"But—"

"No one knows about this place, and even if they did . . ."

He didn't say anything else. He just bent at the knees and lifted her into his arms. It wasn't the first time he'd carried her, but it was the first time in a long time that she'd been awake—that she'd have memories of it. She wanted to press them in the pages of her mind and save them forever. But that just made her sound like Zoe. Then again, maybe there were worse ways to be.

When King pulled back the curtains of the window, Alex wasn't sure what she was seeing. The building was big and made of stone. There was a tall tower in what looked like another wing and a stone wall that seemed to encircle—

"Is that a *moat*?"

"It is." He sounded almost smug as Alex gazed beyond the walls at the vast rolling hills and thousands of empty acres and slowly realized—

"You bought a castle? With a drawbridge?" She couldn't help but laugh.

"I bought a castle." He tucked her hair behind her ear. "With a drawbridge."

A quiet, jaded voice in the back of her mind asked *How?* and *When?* and *With what money?* but the word that came out was, "Why?"

It took him a moment to admit, "An operative I used to work with told me that's what it would take."

"To do what?"

"To be safe from her." *Oh.* "But the thing is . . . I don't want to be."

It was the bravest thing that either one of them had ever said, and Alex didn't want to let him win. But even more than that, she didn't want to let it pass.

Sometimes the bravest thing you can do is just stop fighting, so Alex brought her mouth to his. It wasn't even a kiss, just a brushing of lips. It was just a whisper—just a promise.

And then she pulled back, a little sheepish and scared, but that didn't stop her from saying, "I've wanted to do that since Berlin."

And then his fingers were in her hair and his lips were on the soft skin of her throat. "I've wanted to do this since the island."

She pulled his mouth to hers, and their lips parted as everything became deeper, darker. More. In every way more.

"I've wanted to do that since Cartagena," she breathed as he pressed her against the wall, giving her his weight and all his attention as he lifted her one more time—as rough and as hard as the stone at her back—before growling—

"I've wanted to do that since the Ramada Inn."

And then he carried her back to bed and dropped her on the mattress, but he didn't move for a long time. "You can put it down, sweetheart."

"What?" she whispered while he kissed the corner of her mouth.

"The world." He looked at her like *Isn't it obvious?* "I'm going to carry you for a while. You don't have to do anything but hold on."

chapter fifty-four

KING

"What's in this room?" Alex asked the next morning. She'd been up since dawn, and after, eating her weight in pancakes, she'd set out to see every inch of a castle that, it turned out, had a lot of inches.

"Oh, you don't want to—" King started, but it was too late. The door was already open, and Alex was already throwing back the velvet curtains and shining light on . . . chaos. Or madness. Or—who was King kidding? It was both.

"Yeah. About this room . . ." King had been avoiding the space for months, and it looked so much worse than he remembered. He'd been telling himself since the funeral that he'd clean it out soon. He'd take the newspaper clippings off the pinboards and paint over the writing on the walls and cram all the "evidence" his father had collected through the years into boxes labeled so neatly that no one would ever know that there was nothing but insanity inside.

King told himself he'd been too busy, but the truth was, being inside his father's room was the closest thing to being inside his father's mind, and King knew it was a treasure—a gift. His father was gone, but his thoughts were still there, and King couldn't bring himself to pack them all away just yet.

"King . . ." Alex's eyes were too big, too worried.

"My father got sick. A couple of years ago. He came here to live with me . . . in the end."

"Oh." She looked surprised. "You took care of him?"

King's throat was full of cotton for some reason. It was all he could do to nod.

He walked to the section of the wall that was nothing but anagrams of the word Nikolai—as if maybe the best codebreakers in the world had just missed it.

"I told you about him. Didn't I? That he was . . ." *Obsessed. Insane. That something terrible happened a long time ago, and one of the smartest men on the planet reacted in the only way he knew how: by trying to make the puzzle make sense.* "He thought he was getting close to figuring out who Nikolai was." King pointed to the part of the wall where the photographs lived—pictures of another age in black and white. "But he wasn't." It was all he could do to admit, "*This* is the cancer that killed him."

And then Alex's eyes got wet and King's throat got raw, and when Alex came toward him, it was so slowly, he almost didn't realize it was happening. Like a gravitational pull that kept them in each other's orbit—that wouldn't let him pull away.

Her arms slipped around his waist, and her head rested on his chest, and he wondered if she could hear his heart beat. He wanted to know if she realized how easily she could make it stop.

"I'm glad you got to be with him. And take care of him," she said into the cotton of his shirt.

"I'm glad I get to take care of you." He pressed a kiss to the top of her head. He wasn't expecting her to go stiff, but it was like she'd frozen in the sea and her body had just realized it.

Something was wrong. He'd said something or done something, but King didn't know what and he wanted to cut his own tongue out.

"What? What is it?"

When she pulled away and looked up at him, she didn't look like a badass spy. She looked like a little girl and, suddenly, he got it.

Alex had spent her whole life watching people worry about Zoe, take care of Zoe, nurture and cherish and care for Zoe. Her family hadn't had the bandwidth to worry about a second sister, and so Alex *had* to be okay. Alex had to be strong. Alex took care of Alex. And suddenly, everything about her made sense.

"I'm not the sister people take care of."

He pressed a kiss to her forehead and whispered, "You are now."

chapter fifty-five

ALEX

Alex got sick.

Not the kind of sick that comes with bags of O-negative and tri-age kits. It was the kind of sick that means chicken soup and saltine crackers and watching *The Price Is Right* on the sofa by yourself all afternoon.

It was the kind of sick that comes from finishing your last final before Christmas. The kind of sick that only happens when you let yourself stop running long enough for the world to catch up.

So she slept so long, she dreamed. And then she laughed so hard, she cried.

Her nose turned red and she carried a box of tissues with her wherever she went. King found an old-fashioned hot water bottle and tucked it by her feet, and she made him read her favorite historical romance novel aloud to her every night by the fire. And, through it all, she just kept thinking that it was winter in Scotland and he cared whether or not her feet were warm. Zoe had once said that was what love was.

Zoe was right.

Outside the old stone walls, the wind blew and moaned and smelled like snow, but even in that drafty castle, Alex stayed warm in King's sweatpants and thick wool socks. They ate soup and played Scrabble.

They kissed and they touched and they spent their nights skin to skin, and for the first time in her life Alex was happy.

And she tried every day to forget it wouldn't last.

"I got him."

There was a bathtub in the bedroom. It sat in front of a fireplace that looked large enough to roast a whole hog. The tub was five feet long and four feet deep and it wasn't hard to imagine some highland warrior soaking away the aches and pains of battle. It was a tub made for another age, and Alex was more or less obsessed with it because it was wildly impractical (It was a *bathtub*! In the *bedroom*!) and utterly perfect, and she was up to her neck in bubbles when the words came—

"You haven't asked, but I did it. I got him."

"Kozlov?" King put his book down. He was lying on the bed, little horn-rimmed glasses perched on his nose. She would have mocked him for those years ago, but now they made her insides turn to lava.

Maybe that's why her skin felt so cold when she said, "There's a flash drive."

She couldn't face him when she said it, but that didn't mean she couldn't see.

In the mirror, she watched his face change, everything going alert. Like a Cold War bunker flickering to life after decades of collecting dust and being forgotten. He'd been out of the game for five years, but no one ever stops being a spy, let alone someone named Michael Kingsley.

"So it's true."

He didn't try to deny that he'd been paying attention to the chatter, and Alex didn't try to lie.

"Whatever rumors you've heard . . ." She ran a hand through the soapy water. "Yeah. They're true. The backup was on the yacht."

"And the yacht is at the bottom of the Mediterranean."

Alex gave a shudder and a shrug and a nod all at once. The water was hot, but she was suddenly cold and numb and shivering. When she closed her eyes, she could feel the waves lapping against her, telling her to go to sleep. To just give up. That her mission was over and it would be okay to just let go.

"Kozlov has nothing without it." She balled a washcloth in her fist and squeezed until the warm water trickled through her fingers. "Nothing except a lot of guns and goons and nothing to lose, so . . ."

"He's more dangerous than ever."

Alex nodded and let herself sink lower.

"Alex?" When had he gotten out of bed and crossed the room? She didn't know. She just knew he was there and leaning over the tub, steam on his skin and fire in his eyes. "Where is it? Where's the drive?"

"It's . . ." The words didn't come and she didn't know why. She should have told him. She could have. She *would* have. She was wet and naked in front of him. She'd blown her nose in front of him approximately five thousand times. She'd told him about her sister and her past. Alex had shown King . . . herself. Not her cover or her persona or her lies. He saw *her*, and that made him dangerous. Because she trusted him, but she didn't trust herself.

"It's someplace safe," she told him.

"Tell me where it is and I'll go get it."

"You can't."

He didn't ask her to explain, because King wouldn't waste time with such a silly question. "Then let's go get it together."

Alex curled up in the water and let her cheek rest on his cupped hand. "It's safe where it is. If I go get it, they'll find it, and then they'll find me." She rolled her head back and looked at the flames. It was harder than it should have been to say, "I don't want them to find me."

He took off his clothes, then slipped into the tub behind her, pulled her back against his chest, and held her tight. "Neither do I."

chapter fifty-six

Present Day
Scotland

KING

King never wanted to go back to Scotland. There'd been a time when he'd thought he never would. But, in the end, he'd invested too much money there. Too much time. Too much history. And too much her.

So, eventually, he'd had to come back without Alex. He'd just never planned on coming back *with* her and, at the moment, that was the problem.

"This doesn't look familiar." Alex peered out the car window, looking around at the little dirt road that was barely more than a trail.

"Back door," he said as he pulled the car behind a hedgerow. He turned off the engine but didn't open the door. Instead, he just sat there, hands gripping the steering wheel like a man desperate to keep his life on the road. He couldn't even face her when he said, "You could wait in the car."

"Ha!" She waited a beat, studying him out of the corner of her eye. "That was my ironic laugh."

"I know."

"Because it's not really funny, but it's also *hilarious*."

"I get the picture." He undid his seat belt and secured the emergency brake.

"Because *you* thought *I* would wait . . . *in the car!*" It was the punch line of a joke that wasn't funny anymore, so King got out and slammed the door, but Alex was still looking at him like she didn't know whether she should be horribly offended or terribly amused. Then, suddenly, she grew worried.

She crawled out of the passenger side and studied him over the hood. "When have I ever waited in the car?" It was a test and he was going to fail it.

"Never. Okay? Sorry I—"

"Why on earth would I—"

"Because I asked you to?" He whirled, but all the fight went out of him. She was going to find out eventually, but that didn't mean he was in a hurry to tell her. "Because I'm an idiot—which you know. So come on."

He took off walking cross-country. After thirty minutes, they climbed a rocky hill, and he heard a near-silent wince and risked a glance behind him.

"You okay?"

"I'm fine, and so help me, if you tell me to wait in the car again, I'll . . ." But she trailed off as they crested a ridge and looked down at the castle in the valley below. The sun was setting in the west, painting the sky with color until the stone walls and high towers looked like something from another age.

He'd been an idiot to buy it. It had cost a fortune to remodel, but he just kept hearing her in that damned bungalow on that damned island, talking about Scottish heroes and castles and what a dream man would look like. He'd been a fool to think it could ever be him.

"What are the odds someone is watching this place?" It was one of about five hundred questions King currently had on his mind, but at the moment, it was also the most pressing. "Because you're acting like you think someone found your Fortress of Solitude."

King wanted to tell her she was wrong. That he'd been careful. That no one knew about this place—no one but him and Alex and two dozen tradesmen who all thought his name was Mr. Masterson—but King didn't know what was real anymore, so he sank to the ground and pondered the castle in the distance.

"There are forty-eight blank hours in my mind, Sterling. There are things I've been trying my whole life to forget, but the thing I'd give anything to remember is just out of reach, so yeah . . . I'm going to sit here and wait until I'm sure we're not walking into an ambush."

"*Again*," she added helpfully as she sank down to sit beside him.

Because they didn't know who was after them. They didn't know if this mystery villain was CIA or KGB or something altogether different. They didn't know anything except they had to be careful.

But all King could do was smile and echo, "Again."

It was dark and silent when she whispered, "I spent the last year thinking I'd never come back here."

He didn't say what he was thinking: that he'd spent the last year praying that she would.

chapter fifty-seven

One Year Ago
Scotland

ALEX

Alex had never believed in happy endings, but as the days and nights stretched out, she started to wonder if maybe her sister was right—like maybe they were possible. Like maybe one might be possible . . . for her.

The only person who could have known was Zoe, and suddenly, Alex wanted to hear her sister's voice. She wanted to ask what love felt like. She wanted to know if this was it.

King kept a bunch of cell phones in his workshop. There was a box labeled BURNERS, NEVER USED, so it shouldn't have felt like a risk, the act of picking one up and turning it on and typing in the number that anyone but a trained spy probably would have forgotten by that point.

It was for a service—a number only she and Zoe ever used. During Alex's first few years with the Agency, there had been messages from her sister every day. Then every week. Alex didn't remember the last time she'd gotten one. But, then again, she also couldn't remember the last time she'd left one. So she honestly wasn't expecting to hear the voice on the line, saying, "You have one new message."

"Hi. Uh . . . Is this still the number for Alex?"

Even when Zoe was at her sickest, they'd always had the same general features—they'd always *looked like* twins. But they'd always sounded slightly different. Zoe's voice was brighter, lighter. Zoe sounded like the sun, and Alex closed her eyes and waited for it to warm her.

"I hope so. Anyway . . . it's me."

Alex knew that voice even better than she knew her own. Zoe was constant. Zoe was sure. Zoe was always *Zoe* while Alex had been a million different people. So it didn't make any sense that the voice on the other end of the line felt darker. Worried. Different.

Zoe sounded afraid, and the first thing that went through Alex was a shot of terror. She felt like she'd touched a live wire and she was going to burst into flames because Zoe was sick again. Zoe needed surgery. Zoe needed a transplant. Zoe was dying. Zoe was—

Scared.

"So . . . uh . . . I'm not exactly sure what's going on, but I got a call today from a man you work with," the shaky voice said, and Alex felt her heart ice over.

Kozlov.

But Zoe kept talking, and Alex almost couldn't believe it when she said, "Mr. Collins says you need my help?"

Collins? At first, Alex couldn't even place the name. It took her a moment to remember the slick operative with the sly smile and nice suits—an Ivy league pedigree and good connections. He was the kind of guy King *should* have been. A spoiled suit with more ambition than sense. Alex knew him, but only barely. He wasn't anything to her. He wasn't anything. But somehow, he'd found out about Zoe. *He'd called Zoe.* And . . .

"I'm trying very, very hard not to make a *Pride & Prejudice* joke right now." Zoe sounded like she was going to laugh to keep from crying. "So that should tell you that . . . you're scaring me, Alex. So if you get this, please call me? Please? If not, well . . . I guess I'll see you in Paris."

The line went quiet and Alex's blood went cold.

She was safe and sound in Scotland, but her heart was outside her body—it always had been.

And it was on its way to Paris.

chapter fifty-eight

"I need clothes."

Alex had spent the last few days in King's old sweats and ratty sweaters and she hadn't minded at all until that moment. He wasn't sure what had changed, but something had, and whatever it was, King didn't like it.

"Where are my clothes?" she snapped.

"You mean the wet suit I had to cut you out of because you were in shock? Those clothes?"

She was looking under the bed. "Where are my shoes?"

"Alex?"

"I can't leave without shoes."

"Why are you leaving? Where are you going?" She was still frantically searching and then, just as quickly, she gave up and pulled on a pair of his old sneakers. "Alex, what happened?"

"I need thicker socks." She darted to the dresser and started shoving things around.

"Alex, stop!" It was an order and she froze, but she didn't turn. He tried to soften his voice. He didn't want to scare her. "What happened?"

She was facing the mirror, but she didn't look up. It was like she was afraid to look at him. Like she was afraid to say—"They have my sister."

Everything made sense in that moment, but he couldn't let her panic. He had to pull her back. "Okay. But I need you to tell me, *what happened?*"

"I called Zoe. . . . There's a service we used to use. She left a voicemail and . . . Paris. She's on her way to Paris. Someone told her *I'm* there, and she thinks I need her and . . . I have to get to Paris."

She closed her eyes tight, and he saw what she couldn't say—what she had been hiding for years—that Alex needed Zoe. She always had and she'd never said so—never admitted it—not even to herself. Guilt and fear were waging war inside of her, so King had to think—he had to think for both of them.

"You can't go."

"Of course I'm going! I *have* to go!"

"Why, Alex? Think. Why would someone lure Zoe to Paris *now*? They're trying to flush you out. Because you're right—they're looking for you, and they can't find you. And that's just proof that you're safe here."

"She's my sister!"

"She's *bait*."

It was almost like he'd slapped her, she stumbled back so quickly, looking up at him like he was a stranger—like he was the enemy.

"How dare you—"

"And that's not all she is!"

Alex morphed from angry to afraid. "What do you mean?"

"Why are they doing this, Alex? Really? Because you've been in deep cover for five years, and now you're running for your life. What are the odds that Zoe would be able to get a message to you and flush you out? Think about it. Why else would they . . ." But her face was morphing, changing. Her hand flew to her mouth, holding back a silent gasp. "What did you just realize?"

Alex blinked like a very scary movie was playing behind her eyes. "The bank. They need her to access the bank."

"Bank?" But King's mind was already leaping ahead, doing the math before he even had the numbers. "You put the flash drive in a bank vault." Slowly, Alex nodded. "Switzerland?"

"Zurich."

"Good." He was looking around. Now *he* needed to pack. "You wait here; I'll go to Paris."

"No."

"Alex—"

"They have my sister!"

"They don't have anyone yet. We'll call Langley—"

"Langley has a mole, King." That stopped him in his tracks. She hadn't said a word about it, but she hadn't said much about anything. She was sick and tired and so burned out, he thought she might turn into ash and blow away, so he hadn't pressed her. "I heard Kozlov talking. That's why I ran, but I didn't know who it was and—"

Suddenly, the last few days flashed across King's mind, but this time he saw everything differently.

She wouldn't tell him where the flash drive was. She didn't trust him. She . . .

"You thought it was me."

"No." Her face was red and her eyes were wet. "You're the one person I knew I could trust."

She trusted him. She'd never said she loved him, but somehow that was better, so he pressed a quick kiss to her lips, then pulled back. "Stay here. I'll go—"

"They have my sister!"

"Which is why you have to stay here!"

"But—"

"I'm not going to let them get you too!" He was shouting, but he felt like huffing and puffing and blowing the whole castle down. And he would have if it hadn't been for the look on her face. "I'm going to get your sister, and then we're going together to get that drive." He threw open a dresser drawer. "What bank is it in?"

It was the wrong question at the wrong time—King knew it before the words were even out because, suddenly, Alex was as gray and as hard as the castle's walls.

"Why? So you can take it?"

"So one of us can be smart for once!" He wanted to pull the words back. Swallow them whole. Choke on them if he had to, but he was too mad to see straight, much less function. "Alex—"

"Yeah." She gave a cold, dry laugh. "You got me. I'm still the girl in the *Future Spy* hoodie, and you're still the guy with all the answers."

"Wait."

"You may be the Great Michael Kingsley"—she leaned into his space—"but I'm the one who took down Viktor Kozlov."

"And I'm the guy you called to come save you!" King started to pull his own hair out. "No. I didn't mean . . ."

But Alex was already backing away. She was shaking her head like he was just another in a long line of men who couldn't wait to betray her. She'd been undercover with Kozlov for five years. She'd almost died doing what the whole damn Agency hadn't been able to accomplish—and doing it alone.

Because she *was* alone. And in a way she always had been.

She was halfway down the stairs when he caught up to her. "Where do you think you're going?"

"Where do you think?"

"You *can't go to Paris!*"

"And how are you going to stop me? Tie me up?"

He was already shaking his head, saying, "Don't tempt me."

She huffed out the kind of laugh you only give when nothing is funny. "You're not going to break me, Michael Kingsley."

"That's funny. Because you've been crushing me for years." It must have been the tone that stopped her because she froze halfway to the door. "As long as you have that drive . . . As long as they even *think* you have that drive, you aren't safe. You're not safe anywhere but here. So *stay here*. Please. I'll go get Zoe. I'll bring her here. I'll fix it. Just give me time to fix it."

"Fine. You can come with me—"

"No!" There was a room at the end of the hall that showed what happened when the woman you loved didn't come home. King wasn't going to take the risk—not with Alex. Not when he finally had her. He wasn't going to lose his heart and his mind and his life. Not if he could help it. "I watched you almost die. Twice. I held your limp body in my arms and cleaned your wounds and sewed your skin and willed your heart to keep beating. And I can't . . . I can't do it again."

It would kill them both this time, and so he had to stop her. He had to *stop this*—this terrifying ride that he'd never wanted to take in the first place.

"Twenty-four hours, Alex. Please. Just give me twenty-four hours to put a plan together and—"

But she was already heading for the door. "I'll call you from Paris. You can meet me and—"

"No." He didn't know where the word came from, but, this time, he didn't want to stop it. "If you walk through that door . . . Alex!" She turned and considered him. "If you leave, then don't come back."

So, of course, she never did.

chapter fifty-nine

KING

King was drunk when he picked up the phone, but of course he re-membered the number.

"What?" Sawyer sounded tired and out of breath and so frus-trated, he could scream, and that's how King knew he was right—Sawyer was looking for Alex because Alex was the only person alive who could make someone that angry.

So King sighed. And whispered, "Paris. She's on her way to Paris."

chapter sixty

Present Day
Scotland

King had known for over an hour that the coast was clear, but he'd stayed on the frozen ground at the top of the ridge anyway, lying on his stomach and looking down like some kind of medieval invader, dreading the moment when he'd have to breach the castle walls.

There were a half-dozen security systems monitoring the property's perimeter—both high-tech and old-school—so there wasn't a doubt in his mind they were alone. But he couldn't make himself go down there.

"Well?" Alex was getting impatient. She was smart enough to know that it was time, but that didn't make it any easier because the longer King lay in the dark with Alex, the more he thought about the reason why she'd left.

"Have you talked to her?" King asked softly. The name was like a hand grenade and he was careful as he pulled the pin. "Zoe?"

Beside him, Alex shifted on the ground. "No." She sounded . . . sad? And mildly petulant. And King wanted to know if the rift was because Alex had run away from her sister too. Or was it because Sawyer was smart enough to keep the love of his new life far away from the dangers of his old one? "Have you?"

"No. Well, not exactly. Come on." He started to push up from the ground, but Alex tugged him back down.

"What do you mean, '*not exactly*'?"

Oh no. He really didn't want to be the one to tell her. But now he kind of had to tell her. "Sawyer called me a few months ago. Looking for you."

"Oh."

"He wanted you to be there for . . . the wedding."

"They got married?" Her voice ticked up. There were tears in it. Of course there were. Her sister had gotten married. Without her. And it hurt. It had to hurt.

"Six months ago. In Zurich. It was small. Just big enough to make it official. They tried to find you. They *wanted* to find you . . ."

"Good. Great."

But it wasn't great. King could tell by the tone of Alex's voice and the set of her shoulders as she started pushing to her feet. "At least you didn't have to wear an ugly bridesmaid dress," he tried to tease, but Alex was entirely too quiet and the night was entirely too still. "Hey. It's okay. I'm sure she would have loved for you to have been there. I'm sure . . . They tried to find you."

They weren't the only ones.

It was dark and it was late and they were both tired and sore and hungry. Her side had to be killing her, but that wasn't where the pain was coming from—he could see it in her eyes.

Alexandra Sterling had never done anything halfway in her life, so when she decided to run, she didn't just hide. She ceased to exist. But for the first time, she seemed to realize that the world had kept going on without her. Time passed. Seasons changed. People fell in love and got married and no one sat around waiting for her to come back.

Well, no one but him.

"Come on." She started easing down the embankment.

"You know . . . you can just—"

"So help me, Michael Kingsley, if you say the words 'wait here,' I will strangle you with your own intestines."

"That is disturbingly graphic." He stood and started down the craggy slope. "Been thinking about it for a while, have you?"

But Alex just huffed and drudged along beside him. "I am cold, and I am hungry, and I desperately need a bathroom, so, no, I won't just 'wait here.'"

"Fine."

"We're going to get the ring, and then you're going to feed me. And let me use your tub." So help him, he'd almost forgotten about the tub. "I am going to drink tea and change this bandage and—"

They were over the drawbridge and standing at the door, but King couldn't bring himself to open it. The moon was high and the clouds were gone, and there was nothing but a cold wind and the fog of Alex's breath as she looked up at him. Her hair was blonde again—just like when he'd first met her. Little strands blew across her face and stuck to her lips. He wanted to pull her closer. And he wanted to push her far, far away.

"What? What is it?" she asked. "King—"

"I don't know what's in there," he admitted, but Alex rolled her eyes.

"Pretty sure that's why we've been lying in the dirt for four hours, so—" She pushed open the door before he could stop her.

"Alex!"

But she was already inside. And freezing. He saw the moment when she registered what she was seeing.

Empty bottles and piles of trash. Curtains drawn tight to keep out the sun, and a thick layer of dust over everything. A chair was lying on its side and, instantly, Alex went on high alert. "Okay. So someone *was* here." She turned in a full circle. "Do you think this is where they grabbed you?"

"Alex—"

"They *must* have grabbed you here."

"No. They didn't." He righted the chair and pushed it out of the way.

"But—"

"I left a mess," King blurted. "It's no big deal."

"*You* left a mess? Ha!" She was seriously giving him the side-eye—until she glanced back at the bottles on the kitchen counter, the piles of dirty plates in the sink. It looked like there'd been a party. It smelled like there'd been a wake, and King couldn't face her. The last thing he wanted to do was explain. "King—"

"I told you to wait in the car," he ground out.

"King—"

"Come on. Let's get the ring and get you something to eat, and then we'll get out of here."

"King." Her voice was too soft—too close. "What happened?"

"What do you *think* happened, Sterling? The love of my life walked out—"

"You told me to leave!"

"I did." He nodded and bit his lip—wanted to bite it right in two. "And then you disappeared without a trace. I didn't know if you were alive or dead. Safe on a beach somewhere or locked in a dungeon. I just knew it was my fault. I just knew . . . As mad as I was at you, the only person I hated was myself. Now let's get the ring and get out of here."

He walked to the wall and threw back a hundred-year-old painting to reveal a state-of-the-art safe. Carefully, King spun the dial and threw open the door.

There were files inside and stacks of cash. His grandmother's pearls. The German Luger his grandfather had stolen during the war. King dug through bits and pieces of a half-dozen different lives and covers and realities. But the most important thing about that safe was the thing that it was missing.

"What is it?" He could tell by the tone of Alex's voice that, deep down, she already knew.

"The ring." He turned to her slowly. "It's not here. The ring is gone."

chapter sixty-one

ALEX

It wasn't there.

Alex would have thought King was lying—she would have thought King was wrong. But King was never wrong, so all she could do was stand and gaze into the little black void and say, "Where is it?" Because it didn't make any sense. *Nothing* made sense. "King—"

"It was here."

"Well, clearly it's *not* here."

"That's impossible." He started clawing through the safe, tossing stacks of cash and piles of passports on the floor. "It was here."

She spun and looked around the cluttered room. "Are you sure no one grabbed you here and ransacked the place?"

"No." King braced his hands on the wall like maybe he was going to push it over—tear the castle down stone by stone with his bare hands.

"Because either you took the ring out of the safe or someone took it out for you. So which is it?"

"I . . . I don't remember."

"You remember everything!" she shouted, but King was shaking his head.

"I didn't take it out."

"Where are your cameras?" Alex spat.

"What?"

"Don't tell me this place isn't wired to the nines."

"Not on the inside."

She didn't believe him. "King."

"This is my home, Sterling. Or it was."

"Fine." Alex crossed her arms. "Then show me your exterior cameras. Let's see who came calling while you were gone."

"No one can get into that safe but me—not without blasting it to bits, which clearly didn't happen, so . . ."

"So why would *you* take it out?"

"I wouldn't! I would keep it in there. Just like I've kept it in there since the safe was installed five years ago."

"Either you took it out before you left for Vegas—"

"No. *Never.*" He was shaking his head. "I wouldn't do that."

"Or someone got in here without your knowledge, probably after you left. So what is it, King?"

He looked like there were a thousand things he could have said and not one he dared to utter. So he just turned and said, "Come on, let's go look at the cameras."

Alex thought she knew that castle. She'd spent almost a week roaming the halls and dancing in the kitchen—soaking in the tub. But she'd been half dead and half in love and, surely, between those two things, she had plenty of excuses for being mostly stupid.

So she could almost forgive herself for forgetting about the room at the end of the hall, but as soon as they turned the corner, she remembered.

"Wait."

"What?" King asked, but Alex was already heading toward the door.

"We don't need the ring. *We need Nikolai.*"

"I know."

Now she was getting giddy. "And the world's foremost authority on Nikolai used to work right—"

"Wait!" King said, but it was too late. Alex was already turning the knob and throwing open the door—

To chaos.

It was still his father's room. The walls were still covered with his father's ramblings and research. But it was different now because there was a new layer on top of the old madness—a year's worth of newspaper clippings and photographs. Notes and manic scribbles—

Stay in Europe (somewhere she speaks the language?)

Go somewhere new? Morocco? South America? Australia?

Associates?

Who does she know?

Who does she TRUST?

Alex turned slowly, following the pieces of red string that stretched across a wall of maps, past high-tech monitors, blinking with lines of code.

The room had changed, but it was also exactly the same because his father's work had been slowly papered over with a new search for a new subject.

And, in the middle of it all, there was a new photograph.

Alex remembered the moment when he'd taken it. She was wearing the top to a pair of old pajamas, and she was trying to flip a pancake in the air, but, it turns out, it's easier to kill a man with a shoelace than it is to flip a pancake, and the result was batter all over the ceiling and dripping down onto her hair.

She was staring straight at the camera. And she was laughing. She was happy. She was his.

"You were gone," she heard him whisper. "I had to find you. I know why you left, and I know why you didn't come back, but . . . I had to find you."

Suddenly, it all made sense. The bottles and the broken things. Even the beard. He'd spent the last year looking and worrying and trying not to become his father. "Michael . . ."

"Where were you, Alex? Just tell me. Where were you?"

"You said not to come back." She didn't want to have this conversation—because it wouldn't be a conversation. It would be a fight. No. It would be *the* fight. They'd been avoiding it for days because they didn't have the time and Alex didn't have the bandwidth.

They had to find the ring.

They had to find Nikolai.

They had to figure out why the world was chasing them, because that was the only way they could stop running. Alex needed to stop running, because she'd been running for a year . . .

From him.

"Alex . . ."

"You said to leave, so I left."

"Where were you?" King roared, but then he pulled himself back. "Never mind." He was backing away. He was the one leaving this time and she couldn't find the words to stop him. "I'm going to go find something to eat. Stay. Go. Do whatever you want."

He was embarrassed. He was ashamed. He was—she looked around the room—exactly what he'd been afraid he'd turn into. Alex wanted to hold the ten-year-old boy who had lost his mother to a bomb and his father to a mystery. She wanted to turn back time.

Alex didn't know how long she stood there, staring at the walls covered with King's theories and guesses and leads.

He hadn't even been close.

There was a time when nothing could have made Alex prouder. She'd outsmarted and outrun the Great Michael Kingsley, but all Alex felt was lonely.

She wasn't mad at herself for running, but for the first time, she wondered what life might have been like if she hadn't done it quite so well.

The phone number of the service she and Zoe used was scrawled on a piece of paper and tacked to the center of the wall, which made sense. That number would have been King's best clue for how to reach her.

Maybe it was the sight of the number . . . or being back inside the castle walls . . . or maybe she was just feeling Big Feelings and she didn't like them and didn't understand them, but Alex suddenly needed to talk to an expert.

It had been a year since she'd heard her sister's voice, so Alex picked up the phone and dialed, not really expecting to hear—

"You have seventeen new messages."

They dated back a year and, suddenly, she held her breath and closed her eyes and waited for—

"It's me." Alex felt her heart stop beating—because he'd called her. Of course he'd called her. But it was like listening to a ghost when he said, "I'm sorry, Alex. I'm so, so . . . Come back. Please. Or call me. Just . . . I'll meet you anywhere. I'll do anything. We can go get Zoe together. Just call me, Alex. Please."

There was a beep on the line and a new message from two days later.

"I hope Zoe's okay. I hope you're okay. Because I'm not."

Beep.

"I heard about Italy. About Kozlov. And I know you know you're safe now. I know you know . . . Come back. Please. I'm sorry."

Beep.

"Merritt says she hasn't heard from you, but she swears you're probably fine. It's been six months, Alex. Please tell me you're fine."

Beep.

"I miss you."

Beep.

"I need you."

Beep.

"Come back."

Beep.

"Please."

Beep.

"Come"—the voice slurred; her heart broke—"back."

Beep.

The last message was the most recent, of course. She was expecting that. She just wasn't expecting—

"*Wednesday, January fifteenth,*" the mechanical voice chimed, and Alex felt the world tilt for a moment because—

Wednesday. One of the missing days. Someone had left her a message. Someone had called her. Someone—

"It's King."

Wait. King had called her?

She wanted to yell for him in the other room—stop the recording and hit the speakerphone. It was their best clue in days—their *only* clue. But—

"Look, I know you hate me and that's fine, but I'm not calling for me. Sterling . . . it's Zoe." Her heart fell through the floor and her mind flashed to a million worst-case scenarios: *Her sister was hurt. Her sister was dying. Her sister was—*

"In Vegas," the voice on the phone was saying. "Sawyer's been trying to find you because . . . they're eloping. Or they were. When they got off the plane, Zoe collapsed and . . . it's her heart. And, Sterling, it's bad. I'm trying every number I have for you because I know you might not get this. But if you get this . . . please. You need to go to Vegas. Now."

It was so urgent. So convincing. So . . . real.

It sounded so real, but it wasn't. Alex knew it wasn't, because Zoe and Sawyer were already married—King had told her so himself. Her sister had been married for months, and King knew it. He knew it. But he'd lied.

Suddenly, Alex's heart was racing and her mouth was dry because she finally knew why she'd dropped everything and gone back to the States. She knew what the bait in the trap had been.

And, most of all, she knew who had set it.

"Hey. I found some of those digestive biscuits that are actually cookies." King was standing in the doorway. "If you're still hungry and want that bath, I could . . . What?" He studied her, eyes wide. "What's wrong?"

"When did Sawyer and Zoe get married?" she asked, and he looked at her like maybe she'd hit her head.

"Six months ago." He took a bite of a cookie, then licked a crumb off his lip.

He was coming closer and she was inching back. She'd been going over it in her head, calculating angles and figuring odds, for so long that it didn't make any sense—but it did. It was like she'd known it for days but she'd kept her eyes squeezed tight, totally unable—or just unwilling—to see . . .

She held up the phone. "Then why did you call me last Wednesday and tell me they were eloping to Vegas?"

He looked at the phone. His eyes went wide.

And then she tried to kill him.

chapter sixty-two

KING

"Alex—" King barely had time to duck the punch. She'd been out of the game for a year, but that didn't mean she was out of shape. "Alex, wait!"

Too late. She was already lunging, forcing King to drop and roll, trying to get out of her way because he had to talk to her—he had to make her understand or see reason or . . . something. He had to find out what had caused all this and then he had to stop it.

"What are you doing?" He sprang to his feet and held up both hands, but Alex just prowled closer.

"So that's where you got the money. Tell me, were you always working for Kozlov? Or did you take over after I killed him?"

"What are you talking about?" He was so shocked that he forgot to sidestep when she charged; it was all he could do to redirect her momentum, and in the next moment, they were slamming into a row of shelves, sending six months' worth of work tumbling like dominoes.

King twisted, trying to take the brunt of the fall, but monitors and books were crashing to the floor. Glass was shattering. And Alex looked like she hadn't even noticed.

She just loomed over him. "Tell me everything or I'm going to kill you."

King was stunned and dizzy, and his tongue tasted like blood. "Looks like you're gonna kill me anyway."

"Yeah." She actually smiled. "I probably am."

They both saw it at the same time—the gun that he kept under the table—and in a flash, they were both rolling across the floor, diving for it—and of course she beat him there.

"Alex—"

BOOM! A vase shattered.

She aimed again and King dove. He had to get away. He had to make her see. He had to—

Hide.

He was hiding in his own home from a woman who was eight inches shorter and sixty pounds lighter, but in a way, it was fitting. He'd been hiding from her for six years. For longer.

"What are you talking about?" he called over his shoulder, hunching behind the desk.

"I got your messages."

Oh. Toward the end, King had only called when he'd been drinking. He never thought she'd actually hear those blasted messages, and now he was terrified of what he'd said.

"Alex, I can explain!" he shouted, which was a mistake because—*BOOM!*—a gunshot tore through the wood.

King was caught—between the wall and the woman and the words he couldn't say.

And then he remembered the fireplace. It hadn't worked in ages. He'd considered it a fire hazard for his father and too much trouble for himself. But the old stones and heavy mantel were pretty. They were charming. And, most of all, the cold firebox made a great place to hide a shotgun.

King dove and rolled and came up with it. "Stop!" he shouted when she came around the desk.

She had the pistol trained on him, and he had the shotgun trained on her, and they were both breathing too hard. It wasn't the fight; it was the adrenaline. The fear. The wondering how it had ever come to this and could they ever fix it?

Should they fix it?

King stopped to wonder if maybe he was wrong. Maybe this fight and this moment were predestined—something set in motion at the airport Ramada and always meant to be.

"Alex. Please."

"Why?" Her voice broke, and that broke him. He'd seen her bloody and bruised and clinging to life. He'd seen her angry and giddy and so frustrated, she could scream. But he had never—ever—seen her cry.

"*Why?*" Alex shouted, shaking the gun with the word.

Why did he tell her not to come back?

Why did he keep calling when she'd done exactly what he'd asked?

"Why *what?*"

"Why did you lie about Zoe and trick me into going to Vegas?"

"I . . ." King had a hundred explanations right on the tip of his tongue, but all he could do was shake his head and spit out, "What?"

"Don't deny it."

"I don't . . . Alex, I have no idea what you're talking about."

She cocked the gun. "Tell me where the ring is. Or— Wait. Does the ring even matter? Was that a long con, too?"

"I have no idea what you're talking about!"

"Are you Nikolai?"

It hit him harder than a punch. "No."

"Then tell me where the ring is!"

"You know where I wanted to put that ring? On *your finger*. That's the only place I ever wanted to put it, but that wasn't exactly an option now, was it?"

He watched her recoil, like the words hurt more than the bruises. Like the worst thing a spy could ever do was dare to love out loud. Like that was the thing that was finally going to kill them.

"Come on!" she shouted, shaking the gun. "Let's finish this!"

But King had been battling his feelings for so long that he couldn't even remember what it was like to stop fighting. He couldn't even remember what had ever made him start.

"King!"

He dropped the shotgun and kicked it to the other side of the room.

"Okay." He held his arms out wide. "You want to win? You win. You want me to be the bad guy, I will be. But if you kill me . . . and you're wrong? Then you're dealing with this by yourself, and so help me, Alex, I can't live with that."

"Stop talking." She shook the gun at him again. "Stop . . ."

"Think about it, Alex. Think about us!"

"There is no us."

"There should have been."

"I . . ." A tear rolled down her cheek. "I don't know what to say."

"Then I'll go first." He took a slow step toward her. "I should have gone with you to Paris. I should have watched your back and brought you home. I shouldn't have wasted a year looking for you, and I never should have made you doubt me. I . . ."

"I never should have gotten on the bus."

Is that what she thought? Is that—

"No." King shook his head.

"You were right."

"I was wrong!"

"You told me not to get on the bus, but . . ."

King saw her hand flex. He heard the gun fall. He watched as her walls crumbled and her will dissolved, and then he was flying across the room and pulling her into his arms, kissing her temple and holding her tight.

"I needed you on that bus," he said between heartbeats. "I needed you then. And I've needed you every moment since then. I will need you until the day I die." He held her face in his hands and searched her eyes. "Listen to me. You're the best spy I've ever known, and you're the only thing I've ever wanted." She cinched her eyes tight, but more tears spilled over, sliding warm and wet down her cheek. "I'm grateful every day for your good heart, sweetheart." She gave a silent sob. "You deserved it, and you didn't waste it, and every single person on this planet is better off because of you. Especially me. Do you hear me? Do you—"

Her kiss felt like a promise. Her sigh sounded like a prayer. Then her hands were in his hair and he was pressing her against the wall, feeling her weight and her skin and the warm brush of her breath, and Michael Kingsley forgot all about the broken glass and broken hearts. He forgot everything he'd ever seen and heard. He forgot his own name.

He forgot.

The house was a disaster. The room was ruined and his father's work was shot to hell, but King couldn't bring himself to care because Alex was beside him, drawing patterns on his chest.

They were lying on a blanket of debris—scattered clothes spread across broken glass and splintered wood, black-and-white photos covering the floor like fallen leaves.

It was over. But it was also far from finished, so as badly as King hated to ruin the moment, he couldn't let it go. Not until she knew—

"Security consulting. That's where the money came from. I do security consulting and tech development for people who pay well. Government contracts. Casinos." She made a noise. He felt her stir. But he had to say the rest of it before it was too late. "I didn't try to lure you to Vegas." He rubbed a hand over his face, and—not for the first time—cursed the blank spots that lingered at the corners of his mind. "At least, I don't think I did." He ran his hands through his hair. He hated this. "I don't remember. I don't."

"I believe you."

She did. He could feel it in the way her body relaxed against him as they lay on the floor, surrounded by what was left of two obsessions. The moon was like a spotlight, beaming through the window, and it was like they were the only people in Scotland—in the world.

"Oh, King . . ." Alex thumbed through the index cards that were scattered across the floor. "Did you really think I was working on a cruise ship as a singing waitress?"

"I will admit, it was not one of my stronger theories."

"What about"—she squinted to make out his handwriting—"Alaskan dog sledder?"

"Like you couldn't win the Iditarod."

"Oh, I could totally win the Iditarod, but . . ." Alex trailed off as she reached for one of the old photographs and held it up to the light. "What's this?"

King twisted to get a better look. "That would be the first Michael Kingsley and his blushing bride." King barely recognized his grandparents in the picture. His grandmother looked so young. His grandfather looked so happy. But there was a third woman in the photo, standing in the background and looking so very, very pleased with herself.

"King . . ." Alex's voice changed. She wasn't teasing anymore when she asked, "Who knew you had that ring?" The night was suddenly too quiet—too still. "You told someone, didn't you? Who?"

Her hand trembled. The photo shook—rippling across the decades—and, eidetic memory or not, King knew he'd remember that sight for the rest of his life, even as he closed his eyes and whispered, "The same woman who's wearing the ring in that picture."

chapter sixty-three

Three Months Ago
London

KING

The light flickered on, but King didn't even squint against the glare. If anything, he welcomed the discomfort. Like a sharp pinch, it was just enough pain to prove he wasn't dreaming.

"I don't remember giving you a key."

She hadn't even glanced in his direction, but Merritt didn't have to. She was part magic and part myth, so of course she knew who was lurking in the shadows of her London flat. She'd probably known he was coming before he did, but she didn't say a word as she took off her coat and walked to the kitchen and filled the kettle for tea.

"You need better locks." It came out more petulant than he'd intended, but he hadn't gotten anything else right lately. Why should that be any different? "I picked up your mail." He pointed to the pile on the counter.

"I see that. So considerate."

She started flipping through the letters and bills but paused when she got to the envelope from Paris, ripped it open, and pulled out two tickets. "Oh good."

"I didn't know you were a ballet lover."

"I go every year."

Merritt secured the tickets to her fridge with a magnet. It was too ordinary a gesture for a woman who had lived such an extraordinary life, and King didn't know how to reconcile those two things in his mind, so he just said, "I thought we were supposed to avoid predictable patterns of behavior."

But Merritt merely smirked. "That's for people who don't have box seats."

The kettle screamed, and a moment later, she was sliding a cup of tea across the counter. "I'd offer you something stronger, but I think you've had enough. Unless the goal was to cross over from *inebriated* to *totally pickled*?"

"I can't find her." King looked out the window. A light rain was falling outside, cold and streaking down the glass. It reminded him of hotel bars and chicken fingers and women who have the good sense to stay far away from him. "It's been nine months, and I've looked everywhere. I've asked everyone. She's *gone*."

"She's in the wind," Merritt said because Merritt still thought there was a difference.

There wasn't. *"She's gone."*

"Michael—"

He was off the stool and prowling toward her, stronger now. The hole in his chest was like a cup of black coffee, sobering him up and making his blood sing. "Where is she?"

"Michael—"

"If anyone knows where she is, it's you."

"I don't know."

"Tell me where she is!" He'd never shouted at Merritt before. He swore he never would again, but King wasn't in control then. The fear and regret were winning. "Where is she?" His voice was softer, but it was the look in Merritt's eyes that almost broke him.

Kind and pitying and more mother than mentor—more woman than spy. "Alex is supremely gifted in many ways, but her greatest talent might be her ability to hold a grudge."

"I just wanted her to wait. I just wanted her safe. I just wanted . . . *Where is she?*"

He wasn't crying—that would have been a relief. Right then he was a boiler that was malfunctioning, pressure building on the inside with no way out. It was going to make him explode.

"Where is she?" He looked back at the windows and watched the raindrops race each other down the panes and through the fog.

"Oh my dear boy, you really loved her, didn't you?"

And those were the words that broke him.

"I even . . ." He sank into a chair and looked out at the rain and the night and the streets that wouldn't lead to Alex Sterling. "I even got her a ring."

chapter sixty-four

Present Day
Scotland

ALEX

Alex felt the rise and fall of King's chest, but her own lungs had stopped working before he'd even finished the story.

"No." She pushed up and looked down at him. "No. You're wrong."

"That was the first—and last—time I ever said those words out loud, Alex. It was the only time. Merritt knew." Fingers combed through her hair and made her scalp tingle.

"Okay." She settled back against him, too bone-tired and weary to worry anymore. "Off the top of my head, I can think of five bad ideas. What about you?"

"That depends." He blew out a tired breath. "Do you know where you can get a switchblade? Or a garter belt?"

chapter sixty-five

Two Days Later
Paris, France

KING

King had made a mistake. A bad one. He never should have suggested Paris, and he never should have let Alex pick out the dress. And when she turned and pulled her hair over her shoulder and said, "A little help?" he never should have pressed his lips to the back of her neck before he reached for the zipper.

He should have thrown her over his shoulder like a caveman and started implementing Plan B because he could read her mind and he didn't at all like what she was thinking—

"So it turns out . . ."

"Don't say it."

"That spies *do* go on missions that require tuxedos and ball gowns!"

He knew it. He just knew it. She was never going to let him live it down, and King grimaced, knowing it was already too late. "This is a highly unusual situation."

"So, in other words, I was *right*—"

"That remains to be—"

"And *you* were *wrong*."

"I don't think we can really go with"—he made quote marks around the word with his fingers—"*wrong*. It's more like the exception that proves the rule."

But an hour later, as he watched her walk down the sidewalk, long leg peeking out from the very long slit in the very expensive dress, King had to think that maybe James Bond had been onto something after all.

King felt powerful and suave and a little like his whole life had been building to that moment—and that woman. But when she stopped on the sidewalk, he could see the tension in her eyes. Her hand was a little too tight in the crook of his elbow.

"You sure about this?" He pressed her up against a lamppost and away from the flow of people who filled the sidewalk. The streetlights were getting brighter, and the sky was getting darker, and it felt like the easiest thing in the world to tell her, "We can still run. Disappear. Hide?"

He wasn't ready for the look on her face when she turned to him—the feeling in his soul when she squeezed his tuxedo lapels tight and whispered, "I'm through loving you in secret."

Then they both turned and looked at the opera house. A minute later, they disappeared like smoke on the wind.

chapter sixty-six

ALEX

The Garnier Opera House might have been one of the most ornate buildings in the world, but the most impressive thing about the private box wasn't its view of the stage and the world-class ballerinas. No, it was the white-haired woman who sat near the back and didn't even bother to turn when King and Alex slipped inside.

"The seats are better near the rail," King whispered as he slid into the empty chair beside her.

Merritt—being Merritt—didn't seem surprised by the voice. "Too exposed. But you know that already. Don't you, Mi . . ." She trailed off at the sight of the gun.

"We don't want to cause a scene," King said slowly.

She gave him a chastising look. "Of course not."

The lights were down and the music was loud and the other occupants of the box appeared to be approximately one hundred and twenty years old. No one had even glanced in their direction, and they were sheltered, there at the back of the box, but King gestured with the gun anyway, wordlessly telling Merritt it was time to take this outside.

The promenade was empty, and they didn't pass a soul as they headed toward the Grand Stairs. King stood in the shadows of one of the massive pillars and studied Merritt, who looked out over the towering space with an appraising eye. "Impressive, isn't it?" She glanced up at the gilded walls and mosaic-covered ceiling that towered overhead. "But a little gaudy for my taste."

Any other day, Alex would have agreed, but at the moment, all she could do was look at the woman she used to idolize and ask, "What's so important about that ring?"

"I don't know what you're—"

"Stop lying." King sounded more tired than angry—like a child who's been given five different answers about how Santa fits down the chimney and *would someone just tell him the truth already*. He was old enough to take it. But Alex wondered if it was true. She'd known Merritt for ten years—loved her for ten years—but King had known her since the cradle. As far as she could tell, Merritt was the only kind of family he had left. This wasn't a mission. It was personal, and Alex could see the strain of it. She wanted him to be able to put it down.

"Come on, Merritt." Alex scoffed. "I called *you*, and ten minutes later people were shooting at us in Vegas."

"People have been shooting at you for longer than that. It's hardly my fault."

"What's so important about that ring, and why do you need it?" Alex asked again. She never expected Merritt's icy calm to shatter.

"I don't need it! I never needed it. I never even *wanted* it, and if you'd done as you were told in Amalfi, none of this would be happening."

"*What* wouldn't be happening?" Alex did the talking because she had more patience than King at that moment—which was scary. But Merritt's laugh . . . that was terrifying.

"You two are such . . . children. You are children playing at being spies. You don't know what it was like. You don't know what's at stake. You don't—"

"Then explain it to us!" Alex snapped. "This is your chance to explain. You owe us an explanation."

The Grand Stairs of the Paris Opera House felt small all of a sudden, full of three people, one gun, and a universe of secrets and lies. Somewhere, the music was building and swelling, but Alex could barely hear it over the pounding of her blood. Ten years' worth of instinct and experience were telling her they'd been there too long. They were too exposed. This was wrong and bad and . . .

Merritt's gaze flickered away—lightning quick—as a flash of something filled her eyes. "It's not too late to come in from the cold." Her voice was louder, calmer. She was the woman from the Farm again. Gun or no gun, she was the one calling the shots. "Turn yourselves into the Agency and stop running." It was like someone had flipped a switch.

No. It was like someone *was watching*.

"King . . ." Alex started, but he was too deep—too focused. Too angry.

"You owe us the courtesy of the truth," King snapped.

"Maybe." Merritt straightened her spine. "But what I'm *giving* you is the courtesy of a head start."

"King!" A voice echoed off the marble, and Alex turned to see Tyler standing down below, in the place where the wide staircase split and branched before climbing to the second floor. He wasn't more than thirty feet away, but it was like looking at him across an ocean—across a decade.

"Hello, Tyler." King was still mad about Berlin.

"Are you coming in?" The question sounded innocent enough, but Tyler's hand was unbuttoning his tuxedo jacket. He was reaching for his gun.

"Not today," King called back, and Merritt sighed.

"Do yourselves a favor, my darlings." Merritt's gaze was granite as she whispered, "*Run*."

And then all hell broke loose.

The music that had been growing and swelling in the distance turned into a crescendo, rising then cresting before turning into a thundering roar of applause. Tyler spun, surprised by the sound, and King grabbed Alex's hand and took off.

They weren't running from Tyler or Merritt. They weren't even fleeing the guards who seemed to appear out of nowhere, blocking their way and sending them hurtling down another corridor.

No, it was like they were running from destiny, something set into motion decades ago in another country by other people. A lifetime of secrets and lies that spilled over the years and across continents. This was who they were. This was what they did. And there was no one on earth Alex would rather do it with than the man who was currently holding her hand and running—

"Stop!" The opera house was a maze, and somehow, Tyler was up ahead of them. He stood there, breathing hard and face flushed, like he was the one who was running for his life. Like he was the one who was almost out of options. "It doesn't have to be this way."

"Oh yeah?" King shifted until Alex was behind him.

"Just come in, King. Alex." Tyler shook his head in a silent plea that could only be translated as *Don't make me do this.* "Just—"

The noise of the opera house changed then—a *click click click* that reverberated down the halls as the auditorium doors swung open and ushers locked them into place. In the next instant, the applause died and the crowd swelled, pouring into the corridors, flooding the space with tuxedos and ball gowns and laughing, talking people.

"Kingsley!" Tyler shouted, but the crowd was too loud.

The corridor was too full.

And Alex and King were already gone, floating out onto the dark streets of Paris with the tide.

chapter sixty-seven

KING

"Starting to rethink my stance on ball gowns and covert operations." Alex stopped, teetering on her high heels long enough to give her gown a rip. The slit in her skirt soared higher, but she didn't even stop to care. They just ran faster.

"This way." King steered her down another street. This one was narrow and darker, lined with tiny cafés and candlelit tables, so he draped an arm around her shoulders and they slowed their pace— just another lovesick couple out for a stroll as they tried to blend in. But blending wasn't good enough. They needed to disappear.

The street must have been popular with tourists, because a band played "La Vie en rose" in the distance, and King felt her lean against his shoulder and sigh. "I guess we finally made it to Paris."

He pulled her into a shadowy alcove and framed her face with his hands. "Should have been here with you a year ago." He brushed a kiss across the corner of her mouth. "Should have followed you. Should have . . ."

There were sirens in the distance—lights and the sounds of shouting men—and Alex tensed. Her gaze flew over his shoulder, watchful. Worried. "They shouldn't have been able to throw up this kind of net this quickly."

"Merritt knew we were coming."

She pulled back and studied him, something like heartbreak in her eyes. "Merritt knows *us*."

For the first time in a long time, he wanted to tell Alex she was wrong, but she wasn't. Merritt knew them better than they knew themselves—it was why she'd spent the last ten years forcing the two of them onto yachts and into hotel rooms and car trunks. She'd been playing this game since before they were born, and for the first time, King wondered if she'd still be playing it after he was dead.

King wasn't going to let that happen, though. They were almost to the bridge. And if they could get there . . .

A police car zoomed down the street, blue light spinning in the night, so King pressed Alex into the shadows and waited for the car to pass before he said, "Come on."

"Michael—"

But King had her hand in his and was already leading her away. Even when the band stopped playing. Even when the tires screeched and the sirens wailed.

"Michael!" Alex was looking over her shoulder because she knew what it meant.

They were running out of time.

"Come on!" She tried to pull him faster. She tried to make him run. "They're looking for us, or do I need to draw you a map?"

But King knew exactly where they were when he pulled her to a stop and pressed her against the railing of the bridge. The Seine was rushing below them. The City of Light was shining all around. Paris was alive and so were they—for the moment.

"Come—"

"Wait." He was too big and too stubborn for her to pull. "They're looking for *us*."

"I know! That's why—"

"*Us*, Sterling. Alex." Something about the way she turned to him . . . something about it broke him, because the love of his life was no fool. She was already shaking her head.

"No."

"We should split up."

"No."

"We have a better chance apart. They're looking for a couple. If we split up . . ."

King knew the odds and the theories. He'd memorized the protocol in the cradle, and he would take the truth to his grave because, like it or not, Michael Kingsley and Alexandra Sterling were very good spies. They just made each other stupid sometimes. And it had to end. Now.

"No!"

"Listen to me." King cradled her face in his hands. "Maybe I was wrong—"

"You're never wrong." He watched her try to pull the words back. "I mean, you are, but only when you disagree with me. Which makes you wrong right now!"

"Alex!" He had to make her listen. He had to make her see. So he said, "*Mercy.*"

"No." A tear slipped down her cheek. "Michael—"

"Maybe you were always better off on your own."

"No." She was tugging and pulling—still an unstoppable force to his immovable object.

"I wanted to give you forever." He brushed away a strand of hair that had blown across her cheek.

"You have," she told him. "You will. We will."

But the sirens just got louder, and he tried to force out a smile, because Michael Kingsley knew many things, but in that moment, there was only one that mattered.

"No, sweetheart."

"But—"

"I can't give you forever." He pulled her into his arms and kissed her hard. "But I can buy you five minutes."

Then he picked her up and dropped her over the side of the bridge.

chapter sixty-eight

King watched Alex land on top of a boat that was passing beneath the bridge, but he didn't wait to watch her disappear down the Seine. He could hear her shouting—cursing. Shooting?

Shots were ringing out, echoing over the water and off the bridge, and that's how he knew they were out of time.

King had to lead them away from Alex and the boat, so he started running, praying that he wasn't making the biggest mistake of his life. But that wasn't possible. He'd already made it. A year ago—the day he let her walk out of the castle without him. It was almost fitting that the only way to keep her safe was to send her back out into Paris on her own.

"Stop!" someone shouted, and he found a new burst of speed as he left the bridge and raced down the streets that were becoming bright with swirling lights. Tourists shouted. Sirens blared. And King knew that he just had to buy her a little more time because as long as Alex had time, she had a chance.

But he could hear the sirens coming closer. Paris was a net that was getting tighter and tighter—like a noose. So he darted down an alley, running until—

The alley dead-ended, and King let out a curse that was a little too loud for comfort as he spun and started back the other way, but a shadow filled the mouth of the alley, silhouetted against the light.

"Come on, Michael!" someone shouted. Except it wasn't just *someone*. King knew that voice. King hated that voice. "I know you're in there."

And he was trapped.

Sort of. There was a building to his left. The door was old and half off its hinges. Abandoned. And King was too tired to be stealthy, so he just knocked it down, barged into the big, empty space, and looked around.

Moonlight fell through sheets of plastic. There were stacks of wood and piles of debris. The whole place smelled like sawdust, and King had spent enough time in a recently renovated castle to recognize a historic building under construction when he saw one.

He was just starting to ponder all the ways you can kill a man with construction tools. . . . Alex would have liked that game. He was starting to miss her—miss *them*—when he heard—

"It's over, King."

Footsteps on sawdust. A shadow on plastic sheeting.

"Maybe I'm just getting started?" King shouted back.

But Tyler's voice was as dark and low as the night when he said, "Where's the ring?"

King skirted around a pile of two-by-fours. "What ring? I don't know what you're talking about." King was lying, and Tyler knew it, but sometimes you just have to play the game.

"I'm not leaving here without that ring, Michael."

"Well, I'm not going to tell you where it is—for so many reasons."

"Enlighten me."

"Well, for starters, I don't *know* where it is."

Tyler laughed. "Nice try."

"It's true. Whatever those goons gave us in Vegas . . . it didn't just knock us out. We lost forty-eight hours or so—"

"You're lying."

"All the time," King said because, frankly, King was in the mood to be sarcastic. It was like Alex was still with him after all. "The other reason I'm not going to tell you is . . . I just don't like you very much."

Tyler cocked his gun. "You're going to tell me where it is, and then—"

"Why?" King cut him off. "Merritt wanted that ring burned seven years ago. Why does she want it back now?"

King was inching through the shadows. There was a heavy wrench not far away. If he could reach it . . . If not, there was always the gun in his hand. He was just starting to wonder if he could actually shoot someone he'd known since childhood when Tyler laughed again and, this time, it was different. Something in the sound made King freeze where he stood.

"Oh, I'm sure she *did* want it destroyed," Tyler said, and King's blood turned to ice.

"But not now?" King knew. He knew before he even asked, "Or not *her*."

"Come on." There were footsteps. The sound of plastic being pushed aside. "I thought you were smarter than that. The Great Michael Kingsley." Another laugh, colder and darker somehow. "I thought you knew everything."

And then King *did* know. He'd suspected, sure. But there wasn't any doubt. Not anymore. "Merritt doesn't need it. *You* just want it."

"Very good. A-plus, Mikey my boy. Grandpa would have been so proud. And Daddy too. If Daddy were with-it enough to even know, of course. How is he? Still crazy? Oh. That's right. *He died*."

King wasn't going to take the bait. He wasn't going to get emotional and careless and sloppy. Or dead. King intended to be dead least of all, but that didn't change the fact that his nails were digging into his palms and they were going to draw blood. But that was okay too. He welcomed the pain. It kept him centered there, rooted in that moment and that mission.

"Why do you need Viktor Kozlov's nuclear option, Tyler?"

Tyler laughed again. "Very good. I knew you'd get there eventually. You might as well come out, Michael. You can tell me where the ring is, and then I can shoot you in the head."

That time, it was King's turn to laugh. It must have been the wrong thing to do—or the right one—because when Tyler spoke again, his voice was different. Sharper. The tone of a child who didn't want to be treated like a little kid anymore.

"I can make you talk."

"Torture?" King laughed harder. "There is nothing you could do to me that would hurt more than losing her. *Nothing.*"

It wasn't a lie. It wasn't even an exaggeration, and suddenly, something inside of King broke free. He hadn't just lost forty-eight hours—he'd lost a year. It was like he'd been sleepwalking and staggering along until he woke up in that shack outside of Vegas. Like he'd been half dead and it had taken Alex's voice in the darkness to bring him back to life. Like—

A ringing sound pierced the air, and King watched from the shadows as Tyler checked his watch. Then preened.

"I know there's nothing I can do to you, King." Tyler was pulling a phone from his pocket, keying in the code and answering the call. "But when I think about all I can do to *her* . . ."

A gruff voice on the other end of the line was saying, "We have her. It's done." But King already knew—even before Tyler turned the phone toward the shadows. King didn't have to see the screen to know what he was seeing. He could already hear the video—the screaming.

"Let me go!" Blonde hair blew in the wind as a big man dragged her through the streets. "I'm going to kill you. I'm going to eat your intestines on crackers. I'm . . ."

Certain. King was finally certain.

"That guy's not with the Agency, is he?"

It was so clear then. It should have been clear all along, but King had been too tired and frustrated and blinded by love to notice.

"No. Let's just say he's an . . . associate of mine from my . . . other . . . endeavors."

"Because you're Nikolai."

"Don't be silly. Nikolai is a ghost story." He gave a low, dry chuckle in the dark. "But ghosts can come in handy, can't they?"

"Why create your own reputation when you can just steal someone else's?" King guessed.

"Power hates a vacuum, Kingsley. Don't tell me a smart guy like you doesn't know that? Someone was always going to take over where Collins and Kozlov left off. It might as well be me."

"Were you the *Collins* or the *Kozlov* of this enterprise?" *The CIA mole or the world-class thug?*

"Oh, don't kid yourself." Tyler's expression turned to granite. "I was both."

King stepped out of the shadows. "If you hurt her . . ."

"I don't want to hurt her!" Tyler shouted. And then he laughed. "I want to hurt *you*. The Great Michael Kingsley. How many months did *you* spend in deep cover, huh? How deep did *you* go? Because I went deep, Mike. I went so deep that I don't think I ever came out. Until the day I realized, I didn't even want to."

"You can turn yourself in, Tyler. Get help."

"I don't need help! I did my part for the cause, and now the cause is going to do its part for me. You think you're so great. So special. But what did you ever do? Hell, what did your father do? And your grandfather? They were desk jockeys. Bureaucrats. They . . ." Tyler trailed off as he thought, then, in a flash, decided— "You're right." Tyler raised his gun and pointed it at King's heart. "I don't need you anymore. I have her."

"You will never have her. You'll never even know her."

"I already have her! I already know her! I . . . What? Why are you smiling?"

King couldn't help himself. It was too perfect—too right. And King almost felt sorry for the man.

"What?" Tyler shouted again.

"If you really knew Alex . . ." There was a crunch behind Tyler, a footstep and a breath. "*You'd know she has a twin.*"

At first, Tyler seemed confused when he turned—when he saw her. Because, in that split second, there were *two* Alexes—one who was still on his phone, shouting, "I'm going to choke you with your own kneecaps!" and one who was smirking, almost flirty when—

"Here." King tossed the wrench through the air and she caught it.

And then Alex knocked Tyler out cold.

She wasn't even breathing hard, and she didn't have a hair out of place as she stood there, wrench in her hands, staring down at Tyler's unmoving form. "Was that good enough to clear our names?"

"That was enough," said the woman in the long, dark coat and the short, white hair who stepped out of the shadows.

"You took your time," King complained.

"You can't rush perfection, Michael. Things had to be airtight; you knew that," Merritt said just as the screaming stopped coming out of the phone that was lying on the ground next to Tyler's out-stretched hand.

King leaned down and picked it up just as the goon on the screen pulled his mask off. Sawyer's hair was a mess when he leaned close to the camera and said, "We good?"

"We're good," Alex said, but she kept her gaze on King's—even as the woman on the screen shouted—

"Oh my gosh! I'm so good at decoying!"

chapter sixty-nine

Twenty-Four Hours Ago
Switzerland

ALEX

Alex had thought the cabin would be larger? Or maybe smaller? Nicer? Or maybe more rustic? Honestly, Alex didn't know what to expect from the place she'd spent the last year trying to locate. She just knew that nothing was how it had been in her mind—not the place or her reason for being there and certainly not the man beside her.

"Are you sure about this?" King was still holding her hand.

"I should go in first."

"But—"

Alex smirked up at him. "What would you do if Jake Sawyer showed up on your drawbridge and said he needed me to go away with him?"

"Good point." King gave her a gentle nudge toward the door. "Go forth. Conquer. I'll wait right . . ." He tugged her back and placed a kiss on her lips like he still couldn't quite believe he was allowed to do that. "Good luck."

Then Alex sauntered toward the door.

Her sister was laughing when Alex slipped inside—that was the first thing she noticed. The voice still sounded like Zoe—but freer. Lighter. Happier. She sounded like someone whose heart wasn't broken anymore.

Sawyer, on the other hand, had the look of a man for whom *everything* had changed, so Alex tried to keep her movements slow, her voice even as she said, "Get off my little sister."

Instantly, Sawyer pressed Zoe into the couch cushions and shielded her with his body while he pulled a gun from somewhere and pointed it in Alex's direction.

At first, it was like he was looking at a ghost. But then shock gave way to wariness, and he sounded like the operative she used to know when he said, "Hey, stranger. Why don't you put that gun down?"

Alex hadn't even realized she was holding one, but she'd heard her sister cry out and . . . yeah. Old habits. Old dogs. Something about new tricks or fresh leaves, but Alex couldn't turn over anything. Not until this was finally finished.

So she just smirked and asked, "Why don't you?" Sawyer cocked an eyebrow like he didn't want to hurt her—and he *really* didn't want to hurt her in front of Zoe—but if he had to . . .

Alex looked at her sister. "Hey, Zo." She slipped the gun back into her pocket. "Had to make sure he wasn't killing you."

"Nope. Very much . . . uh . . . alive." Zoe was looking back and forth between Alex and Sawyer like she didn't know if she should initiate a group hug or find shelter. But she was leaning toward hug?

"So . . ." Sawyer started slowly. "Where've you been?" *So many places.* "Who've you killed?" *So many people.*

Zoe tried to get off the sofa, but Sawyer pushed her back down, keeping his body in between them like Alex was a danger to her sister. Alex wanted to snap that she would never, ever hurt Zoe—but the truth was simple: she already had.

"Alex?" She could hear her sister talking, sense her moving closer. Alex didn't just feel the weight of all that had happened—she felt the ache of all that she had missed. Her sister had grown up and fallen in love and gotten married. She'd built a life on that mountain and with that man. Zoe was so, so happy, and Alex was so, so jealous. Sawyer used to say that people like them don't get happy endings, but he was living proof that he was wrong. And if it could happen for Sawyer and Zoe, then . . .

"Long story short, I'm in an enemies-to-lovers situation. And I think I'm gonna need your help."

It seemed to take forever for Zoe to shout, "*I knew it!*"

"Enemies to . . ." Sawyer shook his head. "What?"

"*Enemies to lovers!*" the sisters said in stereo.

"Sweet mercy, there really are two of them," a voice said from the door, and Sawyer whirled, but King already had his hands up. "Hi, Jake."

"Kingsley." Sawyer's voice was even, but his finger was still on the trigger and it wasn't going anywhere yet. "To what do we owe the honor?" Which was "spy" for *You have two minutes to tell me why you're here before I blow your head off.*

Zoe looked between Alex and King, eyes wide and practically mouthing the word *lover.* Then she turned her attention to Alex and grew serious. "What kind of situation are we talking about? Undercovering? Coverting? Because, I don't want to brag, but I am *really* good at coverting."

But King was still standing there, slack-jawed, as he looked between Alex and Zoe. "I mean, I knew you had a twin. I knew it, but seeing it . . ."

"I'm in!" Zoe was saying. "Whatever you need, I'm—"

"Hold on." Sawyer was still holding Zoe back, but he kept his eyes locked on King because he was the biggest threat at the moment, and Sawyer was no fool. "If you think I'm going to let you put my wife in danger—"

"Gasp." Alex couldn't hold the word back as she looked at her sister. "He called you his wife."

Zoe gave a cocky grin. "Hot, right?"

"Can someone please tell me what kind of coverting the love of my life is going to be expected to do?" Sawyer shouted, but all eyes turned to King.

"It's a long story, but the short version is pretty simple: I can't be in two places at one time . . ."

Alex couldn't help but smile as she watched her sister get it. "But I can."

Present Day
Paris, France

ALEX

Alex watched the team from Interpol as they hauled Tyler away and tried to remind herself that she was supposed to be feeling . . . something. Pity or anger or even regret. Part of her knew she should have been mourning the sweeter-than-average guy who had been nice to her ten years before, but, more than anything, she was proud that, deep down, she'd always known that she'd be better off as Michael Kingsley's enemy than as that guy's friend.

"So that's it?" Zoe sidled up to them. Sawyer stood not far away, still in his commando black while Zoe was still dressed exactly like Alex. With hair exactly like Alex's. But the look on her face was entirely, one hundred percent Zoe, and Alex wondered what it would feel like to be more like her sister.

Because Zoe was the strong one. Zoe was the brave one. Zoe was the one who had grabbed life with both hands and taken control. Zoe had said that love and happiness were just as important as strength and success, just as essential and endangered. And now Zoe had peace. Zoe had joy.

Zoe had Sawyer.

"He's dreamy, right?" Zoe cut her eyes at Sawyer. "Go ahead. You can say it. I know you want to say it."

"Is he . . . Is it . . ." Alex didn't even know what she was trying to ask, but Zoe did. Because Zoe knew who Alex was beneath the covers and the lies.

"Is it as great as it's supposed to be?" her sister guessed. "It's better." She sounded almost defiant as she looked at Alex—as if, for once, Alex was the one who needed to be stronger. She'd always thought that settling down meant *settling*. It was right there in the name! But the look on Zoe's face as she watched Sawyer do something as basic as talk on the phone was a kind of bliss that Alex hadn't even known was possible. "He's not my epilogue, you know. He's *my novel*."

And for the first time, Alex had to wonder if maybe happy endings weren't just possible—if maybe they were possible for someone *like her*.

"So, amnesia, huh?" There was something like pity in her sister's eyes. Pity and understanding and . . . intrigue. Like after a decade in covert operations, Alex's life had finally gotten interesting. "Do you remember *anything*?"

"I remember you. And Mom and Dad. And how to build an independent suspension system from scratch." Zoe laughed, and Alex had to think about it. "I always knew who I was."

"That's good." Zoe looked pensive, then a little sad, and then resigned. "Not knowing who you are sucks. But sometimes . . ." Her gaze drifted to Sawyer, and it was like she had turned to watch the sun. Light fell over her face and her features softened. "Sometimes you have to forget who you are to figure out who you want to be, you know?"

Alex did know. She'd been making and remaking herself for so long—over and over again—since before she'd ever heard of the Farm or Michael Kingsley. Alex had spent her whole life trying to be stronger and faster and better. But maybe all she ever needed to be was herself?

"Okay." Zoe slapped her hands together. "Now what's our plan to find this ring?"

King looked like he was going to choke as he walked in their direction. "*Our* plan?"

"Oh, we're a team. Two Sterlings are way better than one."

Alex wasn't sure if she agreed, but she definitely couldn't argue, because she was still trying to reconcile the sight of her sister and King in the same place at the same time. Her worlds were colliding, so she wasn't necessarily thinking clearly.

King glanced around, looking nervous. Almost guilty as he dropped his voice and said, "You should go with them." Was he talking to Alex? He wasn't, was he? He couldn't be, because they were in this together. This was their problem. Their mission. Their life.

"King—"

"I need to track down Merritt." He ran a hand through his hair. "Notice how she's conveniently disappeared? Again. You should go to the hotel or—"

"Or what?" Alex snapped. "We still don't know where the ring is. Or why Tyler and Kozlov wanted it. Or how they got the jump on us in Vegas. Or, heck, *why* we were in Vegas."

Someone cleared a throat, and they turned to see Sawyer sidling closer. He was off the phone but still looking down at the screen, finger moving and swiping until he found what he was looking for and froze. Alex had been undercover with the man for five years, but she couldn't even start to read his face when he said, "According to MI6—"

"Ooh, did you talk to the Duke of Hottington?" Zoe asked.

"Who?" King looked at Sawyer, who gave a nod as if to say, *I'll explain later.*

"They just raided Tyler's London flat, and they found a bunch of audio recordings on a laptop." Sawyer looked at Alex. "Including one he created using a sampling of King's voice, telling you that Zoe was in the hospital in Vegas."

Alex felt almost sick as she turned and looked at King. "He deepfaked you. That's how he got me there." She would have felt silly if it hadn't been so simple. "But how did he lure you to Vegas?"

King was staring oddly into the distance, like a fog was lifting. Like it was a dream he'd only just remembered. His eyes went from hazy and unfocused to laser sharp as he found Alex's gaze and said, "You."

And then Zoe whispered, "Gasp."

chapter seventy-one

Two Days Before They Woke Up in Vegas
Scotland

KING

"Did you really get her a ring?"

When an old acquaintance calls out of the blue in the middle of the night, a normal person is either terrified or ecstatic, but when you're both spies, there's a whole range of other emotions, and King didn't know which one he was feeling as he rubbed his eyes and glanced at the clock by the bed. Three a.m. So either Tyler didn't know what time zone King was in or he didn't care. Or both. King was vehemently hoping it was both.

"Who is this?"

"You know exactly who this is. Now answer the question."

King didn't want to answer the question, but he wanted to give Tyler a speck of intel even less. Six years as a private citizen should have made King less cautious, but it hadn't, so he tried to shake the sleep out of his voice and the scotch out of his system. "Not that it's not lovely hearing from you, Tyler, but this isn't a good—"

"Did you really get Alexandra Sterling a ring?" Tyler asked again, harder this time. "Come on. Admit it."

"No."

"I heard you, Kingsley."

King pushed upright and felt the cold air of the room hit his bare chest. The fire must have gone out. He knew he'd built one—yesterday? Last week? King couldn't remember and it didn't matter. He was glad for the cold air. It was like being thrown into a freezing lake, and, when he surfaced, his head was clearer than it had been in months.

"You heard *what*? *When*?"

Tyler laughed. "She really did do a number on you, didn't she?"

"I'm hanging up now—"

"I was at Merritt's. That night. In the hall, getting ready to knock when I heard the two of you talking. But I need to know. . . . Are you that serious about Alex? Like . . . *ring* serious?"

"What difference does it make? She's gone." King hadn't been willing to admit it—not for the first few months. But he'd been looking for a year, and she wasn't just in the wind. There is no wind in outer space, and that's how it felt. Alex hadn't just left the life, she'd left the planet, and the longer she was gone, the bigger the black hole inside of King seemed to grow.

"You're good, Kingsley," Tyler said. "Always were. But you shouldn't have left the Agency."

"Goodbye, Tyler." King was halfway to hanging up the phone when he heard—

"If you'd stayed, you'd have the best resources money can buy. If you'd stayed, you'd know Alex had a whole host of aliases the Agency didn't know about."

Now King was insulted. "We all have aliases the Agency doesn't know about."

"I know. But if you were with the Agency, you might have the resources to figure out that one of hers just bought a plane ticket to Vegas."

"That doesn't make any sense. Alex hates Vegas."

"Hey. I'm just telling you that one of Alex Sterling's known aliases is getting on a plane. What you do with that information is up to you."

It might be nothing. It was probably nothing. The last two dozen leads had been two dozen nothings, but King wasn't just grasping at straws. He was grasping at lifelines and there was no way he could stop.

"Why are you telling me this, Tyler?"

The question was a good one, but the silence was almost answer enough. For a moment, King thought that maybe Tyler had already hung up—walked away. It seemed to take a lifetime for him to say, "Remember when we were kids? You moved in down the street, and my parents freaked out. The Kingsleys were going to be our neighbors. It was like living next door to the pope."

"So—"

"So she's the only person I've ever seen go toe-to-toe with you. We've known each other since we were nine years old, and she's the only person I've ever met who might have a chance to make you happy. I was there the day the bomb went off, man. I was *there*." Tyler was serious again. No teasing. No mocking. No fire or fury or fear. If anything, he was almost pitying when he said, "You deserve the chance to be happy."

King wasn't so certain.

"It doesn't matter. She's gone."

"And I told you where she's going to be, so get off your ass and do something about it. Tell her how you feel. Make a grand gesture. It's Vegas, man."

"So?"

Tyler laughed. "People get married in Vegas." There was a long pause, and the laughter died, and nothing was funny anymore when he asked, "You *do* still have the ring, don't you?"

King drew a deep breath and ran a hand through his hair. He had an aching head and a year's worth of false leads and battered dreams, but the only thing that mattered was—

"Yeah. I still have the ring."

"So put it in your pocket and get your ass on a plane."

chapter seventy-two

Present Day
Las Vegas, Nevada

ALEX

This time, Alex didn't ask how he got the jet. She just crawled on board and then fell asleep, only to wake three hours later, twisted up with King like a pretzel, her sister standing over them, taking pictures and saying, "They are *sooooo* cute."

"Not a word I usually associate with Michael Kingsley," Sawyer mumbled.

Alex had every intention of smashing the phone into a million pieces, but then King made a noise and pulled her tighter, and that was the last thing she remembered until she felt the jet touch down in Vegas.

She also didn't ask where the car came from. It was just waiting for them on the tarmac—a BMW 5 Series. She wanted to ask if he was going to make her ride in the trunk for old times' sake, but King was already sliding on a pair of sunglasses and slipping behind the wheel, and Alex knew better than to tease him.

He was the guy from the shack again: dark beard, dark eyes— tired and battered and the most dangerous thing she'd ever seen. She couldn't even bring herself to smile when Zoe fanned herself and mouthed *hot*.

They were quiet on the way to the hotel, the questions floating all around them and pinging off the glass. All of them thinking the exact same things:

King had (more than likely) brought the ring to Vegas.

He had (more than likely) taken it to his suite at the hotel.

The last time they'd seen the suite, there had been a giant hole in the window and two bodies on the floor.

King's Vegas safe house was the epitome of *blown*. Alex was certain that, at some point, Merritt would have sent a team, and the team would have cleaned up the bodies and the blood, but the suite had been, otherwise, unguarded for days. Anyone from housekeeping to MI6 could have torn the place apart by that point. There was no telling what they'd find when they got there.

"If they'd found it . . ." Alex put a hand on King's leg.

"Tyler wouldn't have still been looking for it," he filled in as they zoomed up to the hotel and climbed out, tossing the keys to a valet.

No one said the rest of it: that Tyler might not have been the only one who was looking.

When they finally made it to the hall outside the penthouse, King stopped with his hand on the door. He glanced at Zoe. "I don't suppose you would just—"

"He's going to tell me to wait here, isn't he?" Zoe asked her sister.

"No. He's not. Because King is too smart for that, isn't he?" Alex asked pointedly. Sawyer scowled, but Alex just reached for the door and pushed it open. She didn't know what they were going to find. She didn't know where they were going to look or how long it was going to take. She just knew—

"It's about time."

That voice.

The four of them jolted to a stop, and, for a moment, all they could do was gawk at the woman with the white hair and knowing eyes and bottle of champagne. *Pop.* The cork went flying, but still, nobody moved.

"I took the liberty." Merritt poured a glass, then took a sip. "Excellent." Then she removed the silver dome from a tray of fruit and treated herself to three ripe grapes. "Hope you don't mind I took the liberty, Michael." She settled onto the long couch. "When I placed the order, the concierge offered to send that up as well." There was a small velvet box in the center of the table. It was ring-sized and ring-like and just the sight of it brought to mind bended knees and white veils and really excellent cake.

"The jeweler did a lovely job resetting the loose stone." Merritt reached for a tray of croissants and peeled off one fluffy strip. She seemed so casual. So cool. A touch smug, because it hadn't been a contest, but she'd won all the same.

"Jeweler?" King said, then he seemed to process the rest of it. It was strange, watching Michael Kingsley's mind work slowly. "Wait. How did you know about the stone?"

"Oh." Merritt made a sound that could almost be described as a giggle. She sounded light and free and twenty years younger. "Because I'm the one who broke it. Banged it against a banister. Clumsy of me." She took a sip of champagne.

King and Alex had seen the photograph. They knew that ring had once graced Merritt's finger, but there was still so much they didn't know.

"It was at a jeweler's?" King sounded amazed. "All this time . . . Did they . . ."

"Figure out that *this*"—Merritt reached for the box—"is a Soviet-era camera containing film that could compromise one of the most closely guarded secrets of the Cold War?" Merritt pulled out a ring that was even more beautiful than Alex remembered. Then she raised an eyebrow, as if silently daring them to guess, but the words from Amalfi were already ringing in Alex's ears.

"*Viktor Kozlov's nuclear option,*" she whispered.

"It was indeed." Merritt looked down on the little piece of platinum like it was an old friend she thought she'd never see again. The rest of them looked at it like it was a monster.

"It's a camera?" Sawyer asked. "Is the film still in there?"

Merritt nodded. "It is."

"Could it still be developed—after all this time?" King asked, but Merritt had to cock her head, uncertain.

"Possibly. If done carefully."

"Do we even want to know what's on it?" Alex asked, because she knew better than to pull at a string that might make your life unravel.

Spies should have been the most curious people in the world, but they weren't. Because they knew better. Secrets aren't just about keeping things shielded—they're about keeping people safe, and so Alex waited for Merritt to slip the ring into her pocket—for her to declare that it was *need-to-know* and no one in that room had any need at all. In fact, at that moment, Zoe was as much a spy as any of them. Sawyer, Alex, and King had all left the life.

There was absolutely no reason for Merritt to look at King and say, "Guess."

"Missile sites!" Zoe blurted, because Zoe couldn't help herself. "Launch codes! Double agents!"

"Very good, Zoe." Merritt turned to her, and a slow, approving smile spread across her face. "It's nice to finally meet you, by the way. I'm a big fan of your books."

And then Zoe blushed and leaned against Sawyer's side, but Merritt was already turning back to King.

"Everyone knows that the Cold War was the golden age of tradecraft. It's no secret that the KGB's main priority was infiltrating US intelligence organizations. What very few people know is that they did it. In fact, one of the KGB's best agents got so close to the CIA's station chief in Berlin that she married him."

"No." King was shaking his head.

"Your grandmother was a spy, Michael. She was a phenomenal operative. And she was Russian."

"That's a lie."

Merritt laughed. "It is very much the truth. If you don't believe me, we can get this developed." She held up the ring. "It was hers, you know. She loaned it to me on a few occasions."

"How do you know?" King demanded, but Merritt simply smiled.

"Because she told me—when she turned."

"She was a double agent?" Alex had never heard King's voice shake.

Merritt was too cold—too still. Like this was a conversation she'd rehearsed in her head a million times—lines in a play that had been running for too long and she wanted to go on autopilot, hit her marks, and wait for the curtain when she said—

"She was Nikolai."

King looked like he wanted to hurl a chair through a window. He wanted to roll up in a ball on the floor. He wanted to scream, and he wanted to cry, and he looked like it might split him down the middle, he was so torn between the two ends of the spectrum.

"Is it . . ." His voice cracked.

"It's why they killed her." Merritt's voice was flat and even. "The Russians."

"So the note in the mailbox . . ."

She looked into the distance, like that was a question she'd asked herself a million times. "That was them saying goodbye."

A heavy weight settled over the room. Merritt walked to the windows as if she could see all the way across the desert . . . across the ocean . . . across time. "She loved your grandfather, so she turned, Michael. She never gave Moscow a thing. In fact, she fed them a number of well-placed lies through the years. But I knew her picture would be on the ring. I knew it could come back to haunt her someday if it ever got into the hands of the wrong people."

"Someone like Viktor Kozlov?" Alex guessed.

Merritt gave an approving grin. "Kozlov didn't know what the ring was, precisely, but he knew it belonged to her. He knew he could use it to hurt her husband. And her son . . ." Merritt studied King. "*And grandson.* Kozlov wanted a double agent so badly, he could taste it. He would have used that information to blackmail your father, Michael. He was going to use it to blackmail you, and *so I sent you to burn it.*" Her voice was louder, stronger, when she snapped, "Why didn't you burn it?"

"You're right." King was shaking his head. He looked tired and confused and resigned to some fate they couldn't even name yet. "I wish I'd never laid eyes on the thing."

Alex had never seen him look so furious—not at Merritt or Alex.

But at himself. He looked like he could turn the ring to ashes with a glance. But that didn't matter because Merritt was already triggering a tiny clasp and pulling out an even tinier roll of film that was so old and fragile it dissolved the moment she dropped it in the glass of bubbly.

For a moment, they all just stood there, watching Viktor Kozlov's nuclear option melt away.

"So, wait . . . that's it?" Zoe asked. "It's over?"

"Yeah." King studied Alex for a long time, a look on his face she couldn't quite read. "I guess it is." And then he turned around and walked away, and Alex stayed perfectly still for a long time, wondering what had just happened.

chapter seventy-three

ALEX

King was gone. Alex paced the hotel suite, watching day turn to not-quite-night as the sun dipped and the lights of the Strip came alive in neon glory.

"Where is he?" She turned to Sawyer.

"Walking it off."

"Alex . . ." Zoe started, but trailed off when she saw her sister's face as Alex headed for the door.

"I'm going to go find him."

"Alex, wait!" Zoe looked nervous. Then sheepish. Then guilty.

"What?"

"Just . . ." Zoe glanced nervously at Sawyer, something silent passing between them. "Good luck."

Alex was aware, faintly, of the irony. King had spent a whole year looking for her, but now he was the one who was missing. It had been hours. Merritt was gone. It was over.

It was over.

And all Alex could think as she pushed out of the elevators was *What if it is?*

Alex knew what it was like to have the world ripped out from underneath you. To run away and hide because you were still looking for yourself. King had just found out that his whole life had been a lie and . . .

She didn't want to think about the rest of it, but the truth was, Zoe was right. It was over. They had the ring and the villain and the answers they'd been so desperate to find. No one wanted them dead anymore. They wouldn't have to run or hide. Alex had gone from being the only person King could trust to just another woman in Vegas, tired and a little bit desperate.

And she was feeling more desperate by the moment.

What if he was on his way to the airport? Already on a jet? He could be halfway around the world before she even really knew to start looking, but . . . No. Alex wasn't going to panic. She was a trained spy. She could find one infuriating man in a city full of surveillance cameras. She'd tear the whole town down if she had to. She'd—

"Alex?"

Or she could wait for him to find her.

He looked the same but everything was different. They were standing between two banks of elevators, going up and down. Kind of like the feeling in Alex's stomach.

"It's not over," she blurted as soon as she got her wits about her. Except her wits weren't really about her. Hence the blurting. "It's not. For me."

"Listen, Sterling . . ."

"No! You listen. I . . . Please." People were coming and going, in and out of elevators, a steady stream of *ding ding ding*s that formed a kind of bubble made of sound and motion and indifference.

King and Alex were ten years and a million miles from the airport Ramada, but there they were, standing by a different elevator in a different hotel, and Alex could only hope for a different ending.

"You're braver than I am, Michael Kingsley. Okay? You win. You were braver than me in Berlin, and you were braver than me in Scotland. You said it first, and you said it best, and I ran . . . I ran and then I was too stubborn and too proud to come back even though I wanted to. I wanted to every single day, and I know that ring upstairs ruined a lot of people's lives. I know you wish you'd burned it, but I'm glad you didn't. Because without it, I never would have woken up handcuffed to you." Her nose was running, and her eyes were blurry—her throat burned—but she couldn't possibly be crying. The words were like fire on her tongue. "I woke up handcuffed to you, and that's what set me free."

"What are you saying, Sterling?"

Ding. Ding. Ding.

There was only one thought, one answer, one word.

"Mercy."

And then his arms were around her and the world got very still and very warm. She forgot about old spies and older secrets—twin sisters and cursed rings. The only thing that mattered was him. And them. And this.

They might have kissed forever if someone hadn't shouted, "Mr. Kingsley?" A man in a blazer ran up to them, a tiny bag in his hands. "It's ready for you, sir." He handed King the bag, and Alex just stood there, staring.

"What . . . What's that?"

Then King looked sheepish, maybe for the first time in his life. He ran a hand through his hair and looked down at the glossy floor. She imagined it was what he must have looked like as a little boy, guilty but excited, trying to be cool but failing.

"Tyler was right about one thing; sometimes you have to make the big gesture, so . . ." He held up the little blue bag. "I got a new ring. I was going to ask you if you wanted it . . . I was going to ask you—"

"No."

He looked like she'd punched him. "Oh." He stumbled back, unsteady and uncertain. "I see."

Except he didn't see, she could tell by the look on his face, so she inched closer and pitched her voice lower beneath the *ding ding ding*s and the sound of their hearts.

"I want the ring you stole for me. I want the one that your grandmother used to wear and Merritt used to borrow. I love you and I want . . . you. If you want me. I mean . . ."

"Sterling." He slipped an arm around her waist and pulled her tight. "Mercy."

Christmas, One Year Later
Scotland

KING

"I still say it doesn't count if they're not wearing kilts!" Zoe shouted in the direction of the kitchen.

King didn't roll his eyes, and he was proud of that fact. It might have been because he genuinely adored Zoe. Or because he genuinely feared Sawyer. But that didn't mean that he was putting on a kilt for the occasion.

"You wanted a tree, we got a tree. You wanted a fire, we built a fire." King glared at his sister-in-law, which felt a lot like glaring at his wife. He was getting good at it.

"You're in Scotland in winter, and I got you a foot warmer," Sawyer pointed out. "So kilt or no kilt, this classifies as a Zoe-approved Christmas."

"Does it?" Zoe tilted her head and squinted her eyes. "Does it, really?"

"Really!" Sawyer snapped, then headed to the bathroom to wash the tree sap off his fingers.

The days were short that time of year, and six p.m. felt like the middle of the night. King was ready for bed. Of course, those days, he was always ready for bed, but that probably had more to do with the woman who was underneath the covers beside him.

"Are you sure Sawyer's dad and Merritt will be okay coming up from London together?" Zoe asked, and King bit back a grin.

"Will *they* be okay? Yes. Can I guarantee that they won't take down a terror cell for fun on the train? Not even a little bit."

"I think they should hook up." Zoe was picking the cashews out of a bowl of Chex Mix. Where she'd even found Chex Mix on that side of the Atlantic, King didn't know. He'd learned never to question his sister-in-law's ways. But when he gave her a questioning glance, she widened her eyes and said, "What? They're both awesome. I ship it."

"New rule," King said. "You can never use the words *ship* or *hook* in my presence again. Especially when talking about my elderly mentor—who is at least twenty years older than Sawyer's father."

"What?" Zoe looked aghast. "Age gap is hot. Merritt is hot. Sawyer's dad is hot. Hot people should—"

"Do not say it."

Zoe zipped her lips and threw away the key but looked like she instantly regretted it, so she unzipped her lips and ate more cashews.

"What's for dinner? I'm starving," Zoe asked.

"Chicken fingers." Alex cut her eyes at King, and he tried not to grin.

"Yum." Zoe hummed. "That sounds good. I haven't had—"

A crashing sound cut her off, echoing off the stone walls and bouncing all around the castle. Instantly, King and Alex were on alert, old instincts kicking in. None of the perimeter alarms had sounded, so King wasn't panicking. Yet. But there were three former spies in that house, and between them, they'd made more than a few enemies. King lived in fear of the day that one of them would come calling.

He pointed at Alex. "Take Zoe to the safe room. I'll—"

"What is this?"

They all turned to see Sawyer standing on the threshold of the room, something in his hands. Judging by the way the little plastic stick was wrapped up in toilet paper, Sawyer knew exactly what it was, so that wasn't really what he was asking.

No. Sawyer's question probably had more to do with the two

little pink lines that were as plain as day, and King couldn't bring himself to look away because—

Two.

Pink.

Lines.

King was an expert on many things—languages and linear algebra and the best places to buy a passport in what used to be East Berlin—but at that moment, his mind was blank. And gibberish. He was nothing but blank gibberish, with nothing but two little pink lines rattling around in his head like a pinball.

He felt like how Sawyer looked—confused and afraid and . . . excited?

They both turned to the sisters.

"Well?" Sawyer shouted. "Who . . . When . . . Who . . ."

But Zoe and Alex were looking at each other like this was their favorite story ever. They were both smiling when Zoe said, "Guess."

acknowledgments

Writing this book has been a labor of love, and I could not have done it without so many people. I'm extremely grateful to the amazing Tessa Woodward for her guidance and patience—and to the team at Avon and HarperCollins, including Madelyn Blaney, Julie Paulauski, DJ DeSmyter, and Michelle Lecumberry. Thank you so much for all you do!

Thank you to Kristin Nelson and everyone at the Nelson Literary Agency, as well as Kassie Evashevski, Ali Lefkowitz, and Jenny Meyer, for all your support through the years.

I am blessed to have a wonderful family and incredible friends, even when they say things like "You say this every time" and "You'll finish this book! You always do!" and "None of them have killed you yet" and, of course, "No. You can't just give the money back." Thank you. I think.

And last, but certainly not least, to the incredible booksellers and librarians who have supported me for so long—none of this would be possible without you.

about the author

ALLY CARTER writes books about people who fall in love (while try-ing to stay alive). After more than a decade of writing beloved YA titles like *I'd Tell You I Love You, But Then I'd Have to Kill You* and *Heist Society*, she launched onto the adult scene with *The Blonde Identity* and *The Most Wonderful Crime of the Year*. A longtime lover of the holiday rom-com, Ally is also the writer of the Netflix original movie *A Castle for Christmas*.